The Mystery in the Margins

L.L. Gray

Heroic Rose Publishing

Contents

*To those who prefer their mysteries cozy,
their detectives charming,
and their bookshelves never quite big enough.*

Welcome home.

Your FREE novella is waiting

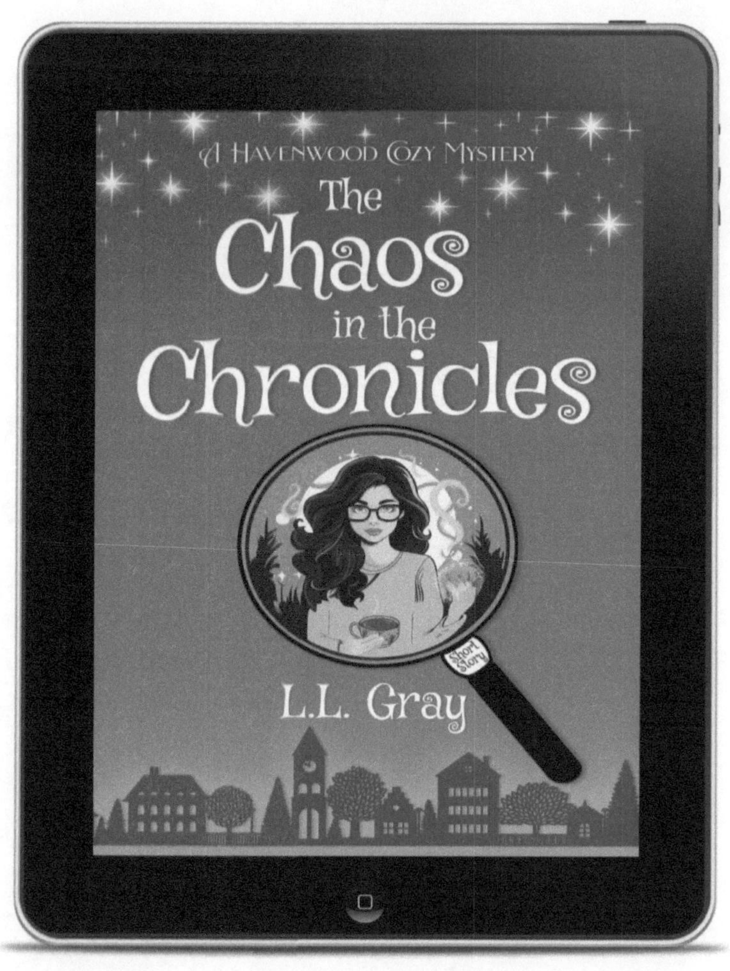

Want a free book?

Of course you do, what madness could possess someone to **<u>not</u>** want free books?
There's no catch - you do sign-up for my mailing list but you can unsubscribe at any time.
There's also no spam.
Ever.
Sign up here to get your free book!

https://www.subscribepage.io/havenwood

Spellbound Welcome

HAVE YOU EVER STOOD on the precipice of an adventure, your toes dangling over the edge, just one powerful gust of wind away from crashing towards a wholly unexpected fate? That's how I felt as the taxi drove through the Connecticut forest laden with brilliant leaves of oranges and yellows that heralded the start of my newest adventure. I was lucky. In just a few more weeks, the gorgeous autumnal display would succumb to the oncoming winter. It was all I could do not to press my nose to the car window and gawk openly like I had when I was a child.

But I wasn't a child anymore. I was Harper Sullivan, daughter of Edward and Trisha Sullivan, recent college graduate, and, even more recently, a business owner. An unexpected business owner. I took a deep breath, calming the storm of emotions rising within me at the mere thought of everything that would accompany this new twist of fate. Instead, I turned my attention back out the window, choosing to be swept away by the breathtaking countryside rather than my memories.

As the taxi broke through the last of the trees, an idyllic little town glimmered in the early afternoon light, looking like it had just appeared as if by magic. Which was à propos, I supposed. The memories I'd been holding at bay suddenly washed over me in a flood. It had been years since I visited Havenwood, but it didn't seem like anything had changed.

I'd spent a magical summer here when I was twelve and then a few long weekends here and there since. When my great-grandmother, Granny Bea, invited me to come help in her bookshop, my parents decided I was old enough to be less of a nuisance and more of a help to the matriarch of the family. Granny Bea, for all that she was my great-grandmother, was never one to be left behind when adventure's clarion call echoed through the forest surrounding Havenwood and reverberated around her bookshop. We tramped all over the woods together, and I listened to her stories about this plant or that berry. When it rained, which it did often that magical summer, Granny and I would snuggle into the cozy apartment above her shop. She built the best blanket forts and let me stay up as late as I wanted so long as I was reading. At first, I thought I was just sneaking it past her. That is until I caught her putting batteries into my flashlight. After that, we had an unspoken agreement. I could read anything and everything I found in her shop anytime I wanted and neither one of us would breathe a word of the sleepless nights to my parents.

Oh, and it wasn't hyperbole when I said it was a magical summer, because it was also the summer I found out I was a witch.

Now, most people probably would've led with that tidbit. But those are the people who wake up one morning to an owl at the foot of their bed, phenomenal cosmic powers, and a preordained path to either become the chosen one or the supervillain, both of which have catastrophic ripple effects on anyone unfortunate enough to be close to them.

And then there are the rest of us.

People like me who lived our everyday lives with just a little extra flair. Take my great-grandmother, for example. She could spot a rare book from a mile away. Or at least, that's how it seemed to my twelve-year-old self. She also seemed to know exactly what book someone *needed*, which was sometimes entirely different from what they *wanted*. Would her gifts be a match for the truly evil forces of the world? Probably not. Unless the evil forces of the world could be vanquished with a stern look and a severe shushing. But with all that, mundane magic is still *magic*.

There are many mundane magical beings out there. I met a load of them when I was visiting Granny. Havenwood was, well, a haven for precisely these types of people. A lady down the street made the best Camembert imaginable. It was make-you-groan delicious and even better when she baked it, adding an assortment of creative toppings that shouldn't work together but just did. However, could she make a half-decent Brie? Not for all the lobster rolls in New England. The mechanic in town was a dwarf who had no desire to adventure with hobbits or wizards in order to reclaim a fortune in gold from a dragon, but you give him a junker of an engine, and he'd give you back something that would make car fanatics green with envy. Nearly every local had some sort of gift that was considered a figment of the imagination by the normal humans of the world. If only they really knew who lived among them...

Havenwood was founded by the Silverthorne family nearly two centuries ago. They were powerful mages that had no desire to wreak havoc or fight epic battles. Clarence Silverthorne and a handful of mundane magical beings sought refuge from the constant fighting and power struggles that seemed to consume the rest of the supernatural world. He'd been the one who initially developed the charms and spells around the town, which made human tourists more susceptible to accepting the fantastic as part of everyday life. Is that *really* a centaur or just an extremely competent horseman? Surely that was just a large dog running through the woods, not a werewolf! Did a local witch actually run the bookshop, or did she just play the part as a gimmick to drum up sales?

Over the years, Havenwood embraced its supernatural origins by creating festivals and events to draw in the tourists who welcomed a little extra magic in their lives. Every August, Havenwood hosted a Renaissance Faire in the large meadow to the east of town. It was so popular that they'd extended the length of the run, lasting well into September. I'd even heard they'd branched out into LARPing events in recent years. Seasonal festivals were a big draw as well, the Harvest Festival culminating in Halloween being a particular favorite. Now that I thought of it, the Harvest Festival was likely happening soon, what with Halloween being only a little over a month away.

The locals wholeheartedly embraced Halloween, often walking around in costume or just as themselves, with no magic obscuring their appearances. Aunty Agatha loved leaning into her witchy persona and often walked around town wearing a black hat and carrying a broomstick on a normal Tuesday, just because. No, she wasn't really my aunt, but she was Granny Bea's best friend, and Granny always said, "Friends are the family we choose." From that summer and forever after, she was Aunty Agatha to me. Just like Granny, she was a witch, but the only magical ability she ever demonstrated when I was around was brewing tea. At twelve, I thought pouring hot water over bits of dried leaves and flowers was some sort of alchemy only adults could enjoy. Agatha proved me wrong. Anything she gave me in a mug was delicious. Her baking, on the other hand? A completely different story. Granny used to chuckle when I'd purposefully turn our ramble in the woods towards Agatha's house, but she didn't truly mind. They'd sit and chat over steaming mugs while I'd take mine out to the small garden as long as it wasn't raining and curl up in the big wicker chair with a book.

As for me? Well, I couldn't brew extraordinary tea or tell someone what book they needed in their lives just by looking at them. I rarely talked about what I could do with my magic. Most witches didn't discuss their gifts outside of their families or covens. It wasn't exactly taboo but was seen as gauche to discuss your magic out in public. Besides, my gifts tended towards metal. No, not in the Magneto, human-magnet and wearer-of-ridiculous-hats sense. Not even in the military sense, although my dad probably would've made me run laps if I even tried it on the base where he was stationed. With me around, the small metal-related annoyances of life vanished, but I couldn't do anything massive, like moving a car or making a statue, even if I had had a semblance of an artistic bone in my body. Which I didn't. I could manipulate small things, and that was about it. If you got a dent in your car, I could pop it out with a touch. Forgot your keys? Two minutes with a bit of coaxing from me and almost any lock would open wide. That was the main reason I didn't discuss my magic openly. I didn't want to be accused of involvement with things going missing or breaking and entering.

Now, I know what most people with a morally gray compass would do with a gift like mine. So why was I here in the middle of nowhere Connecticut instead of, say, robbing banks all over the world? One word.

Dad.

Sergeant Major Edward Sullivan was a no-nonsense career Army man. He lived and breathed the Army. He's the type of guy who got up every day at four in the morning to do his five-mile run, always made his bed before he left the house, never left a dirty dish in the sink, and absolutely wouldn't tolerate his only daughter falling short of his standards.

If he heard even a whisper of my littlest toe barely approaching the line between right and wrong, *whooee*! The creative punishments that man could dream up! Once, he caught me reading the online synopsis of a book for a report I'd procrastinated on too long. Not only did I have to re-do all my work, *after* I read the entire book, but I also had to read what he considered the top ten greatest feats of literature known to humankind and write reports on them to turn into him. Then he made me edit my mistakes and create an oral defense for my written opinions on each book. I was nine.

He always said books were their own kind of magic and should be respected. He'd learned the power of words from Granny Bea. She would read him bedtime stories when he was a child, weaving stories of exciting adventures in far-off lands. I think that was part of the reason he joined the military. To explore all those distant lands and have his own adventures. And now, after too many years, the family was coming full circle with my return to the place where Granny put down her deepest roots.

My thoughts jerked out of the past and back to the present as the cab slowed, turning off Fairy Ring Road and onto Arcadia Avenue. This time, I did press my nose against the window, craning my neck to get my first glimpse of the brightly painted sign above the shop door. Sullivan's Spellbooks. My great-grandmother's legacy. And now, mine as well. Granny's shop was in a prime location in the quaint, touristy town. Just off the primary thoroughfare, which was called Enchanted Lane instead of Main Street because, well, Havenwood. But the shop was still close enough to the center of town to get plenty of foot traffic.

I squinted out the window as the cab slowed to a crawl. Orange and white barriers stood sentinel outside the bookshop. Aggressively yellow police tape barred the entrance and kept out the handful of gawking tourists gathered on the sidewalk. Nervous butterflies sprang to life in the pit of my stomach. What was going on?

The cab driver glanced in the rear-view mirror. "I don't know if I can get past this, miss."

"That's okay," I said. "You can just drop me off here." I collected my bags, paid the driver, and hurried down the sidewalk with a rumble of suitcase wheels. As I approached, I overheard a conversation between two ladies I'd never seen before.

"... police are in the bookshop?"

"I overheard a local say someone broke in."

"Why would someone want to break into such a cute little bookstore? It looks like it belongs in a fairytale, not as part of a police investigation."

I couldn't fault the woman for her estimation of the shop. It was a quaint, two-story building with cream-colored walls and dark wooden support beams. Flowerpots and window planters filled with brilliant blooms decorated the exterior; enough to cause the casual observer to mistake the bookstore for a florist. Granny's shop looked like it belonged in a fifteenth century English village rather than sandwiched between a coffee shop and a... wait? Was that a tattoo parlor? In *Havenwood*? What happened to Nelly's Needlework Emporium? Police in Sullivan's Spellbooks and a tattoo parlor next door? The excitement of impending adventure faded as the gentle breeze of fate turned into a gale storm, blowing me off-course and decidedly in the direction of misadventure.

I shivered, and it wasn't just from the cool fall nip in the air. What had I gotten myself into?

Stolen Legacy

I glanced around, feeling helpless and awkward standing on the sidewalk, clutching my bags, and staring at the police tape keeping me out of my shop. A flash of white in the window caught my eye. Long ears wiggled and then a cute bunny face with a pink nose and bright eyes popped up over the sill, scanning the crowd with a gaze too astute for a normal rabbit. Our eyes met and my jaw dropped.

"Luna?" I gasped.

The rabbit's whiskers twitched twice, and then the creature hopped out of the window. No, it couldn't have been Luna. Could it? She'd been Granny's familiar when I was a child. Well, a witch's familiar might be stretching it, but a "friend who happened to be a talking rabbit" didn't exactly roll off the tongue.

"Psst!" a voice hissed at me from near the sidewalk. "Fluff and fur balls! Harper? Harper Sullivan, is that you?"

I looked down to see an annoyed-looking white rabbit staring up at me. If the folded front paws and tapping back foot didn't give a hint as to her magical nature, the whole talking thing was a big clue that this was, in fact, Luna.

"It took you long enough. I've been waiting *ages* for you to arrive."

"Luna?" I asked in surprise, dropping my bags and crouching down to her level. "Is that really you?"

"Cabbage catastrophe! Keep your voice down! Of course, it's me. How many other talking rabbits do you know?" snapped Luna.

"Well, this *is* Havenwood."

"Your hair needs brushing."

"What?"

"Oh, I thought we were stating the obvious. Now, come along." Luna turned and started hopping down the sidewalk away from the shop.

"Wait! Where are we going?" I asked, grabbing my bags and hurrying after her as quickly as I could through the small crowd pressing up against the barriers.

"To see the Sheriff Jackson, of course. You're the owner of Spellbooks now and responsible for seeing this miscreant brought to justice!"

"There's a miscreant?" I asked, but she'd already headed back towards the shop. I followed her, shooting remorseful looks and whispered apologies to the people I nudged out of the way. I ducked under the police tape as Luna hopped through the front door to the shop. When I stood upright, I came face to face with a werewolf.

Sheriff Jackson was a gruff man with a tanned, craggy face, constantly furrowed eyebrows, and a large mustache curling up from a heavy five o'clock shadow, although it wasn't even eleven in the morning. He wore a blue button-down shirt that was open at the neck, a subtly patterned vest in black and silver, and an old-fashioned hat. He looked like he was in his mid-forties but was probably much older, given the longevity of lycanthropes. In fact, he didn't seem to have aged a day in the last decade. I squeaked in surprise and almost tripped over my bags as I back-pedaled away from the sheriff. If my father hadn't put me on the straight and narrow early on, a single encounter with Sheriff Jackson would've done the trick.

"Sheriff Jackson?" I asked in surprise.

He tipped his hat to me, but his expression didn't soften. "Sorry, miss. This is a closed scene. If you're looking for a book, I'd suggest heading over to the Dusty Tome. Oswald Puddleton will look after you. Just tell him I sent you." He made as if to turn away. Luna appeared behind the sheriff and twitched an ear towards the interior of the shop meaningfully.

Right. Focus. My shop. My responsibility. I stuck out my hand. "It's good to see you again, sheriff," I said with as much adult fake-it-'til-you-make-it bravado as I could muster. "I'm Harper. Harper Sullivan."

Sheriff Jackson took my hand and shook it thoughtfully. "Harper? Oh yes, you're Beatrice's granddaughter. I heard you were arriving today. My condolences. She was a mighty fine lady, and we're going to miss her around here."

"Great-granddaughter, actually. And thank you. I'm sorry it's taken a while for me to get here, but Granny Bea never trusted technology overly much. I received a letter from her lawyer about coming to settle her estate. It must be in here somewhere," I said, digging into my oversized purse that might as well have been an additional suitcase.

Sheriff Jackson looked over my head and narrowed his eyes at the gathering crowd. He frowned under his impressive mustache before stepping back to allow me to enter the shop. "Best come in where we can discuss matters in private," he said.

"Hurry along, Harper. Hop to it," Luna said softly from inside.

I chuckled under my breath, grabbed my bags and tugged them inside the magical bookshop of my childhood. Except it wasn't so magical now. The expected scent of ink and paper lingered, but also carried the faintest hint of dust and the stale air smell of a long-unused room. It looked like a mini tornado had blown through the place. Books were strewn everywhere. Ripped pages settled like snow on the shelves, the counters, and on the cozy reading chairs. My jaw dropped. Granny Bea would be devastated to see her beloved shop in this state of chaos. I knew I was. Even the statues and figurines on the shelves looked like the state of my granny's cluttered, but usually tidy, shop mortified them.

"Oh, no! What happened?" I asked, dropping to my knees and instinctively starting to straighten up a box set of Nancy Drew novels.

"Don't!" Sheriff Jackson said, throwing out a hand. I froze. "This is a crime scene, Miss Sullivan. Please don't touch anything."

My mouth went dry. "Crime scene?" I managed weakly.

"Crime scene," Sheriff Jackson affirmed grimly. "Luna called it in about twenty minutes ago."

"Would've been sooner if those buttons on the phone weren't so small. Cottontail calamity, what I wouldn't give to have thumbs," Luna grumbled.

Sheriff Jackson ignored her and tipped his head towards the west side of the shop. "Follow me," he said gruffly.

I picked my way through the disarray, trying my best not to disturb anything. Although I doubted anyone would've noticed in the mess. Sheriff Jackson led the way towards the glass case where Granny kept valuable or moderately magical texts on display, but locked away until she made a lucrative deal with a collector. The lock was still securely fastened, but the glass was shattered, shards scattered across the hardwood floor. I sucked in a breath. All of Granny's most valuable books were gone.

"What...what happened?" I asked.

Sheriff Jackson put his hands on his hips and considered the mess. "My best guess is the thief or thieves broke in through the garden door leading into the sunroom. Smashed that rock through the window and let themselves in." He crouched and pointed to a fist-sized stone that had rolled under the heavy display case. "Then they shattered the display case and helped themselves. Luna tells me the books inside were valuable. They tossed the rest of the shop, most likely looking for any other rare books. First editions, signed copies, you know the kind. In and out before anyone heard or saw a thing."

I spun to look at Luna. "Even you? You heard nothing?"

Luna thumped her back foot repeatedly in agitation. "I wasn't here," she finally muttered.

"Weren't here? You always stayed in Granny's apartment upstairs. If you weren't here, where were you?" I demanded.

Luna did a fair impression of a turtle, her head almost disappearing into the soft fur around her shoulders. Her voice was so quiet that I almost missed it. "I spent the night in the hutch."

"The *hutch*? But you *hate* the hutch. You always told me it was undignified. What made you sleep out there?"

"Who."

"What?" I asked.

"No, not what, who," Luna corrected.

"I don't know!" I exclaimed.

"Third base," Sheriff Jackson murmured under his breath.

I looked at him in surprise. "What's that?"

"No, What's on second," he said with a small smile curling up one side of his mustache.

"Who's on second?" Luna demanded.

"Who's on first," Sheriff Jackson replied instantly with a little chuckle. Luna and I looked at each other in confusion and then back at the sheriff. He frowned. "Haven't you ever heard of Abbott and Costello? Best joke ever written?"

"Abby and who?" I asked.

"I'll forego the obvious, low-hanging joke because it would go over your head," he said. "Young people these days."

Luna cleared her throat. "As I was saying, I slept in the hutch because of Mr. Wigglesworth."

"Who?" I asked. "Is he the lawyer that's handling Granny's estate? Did he tell you that you weren't allowed in the shop? Because if he did, I'm going to have a word with him right now."

Luna's nose twitched rapidly. "No, it wasn't Nathaniel Ravenscroft. Mr. Wigglesworth is a...cat."

"A cat? Granny had a *cat*?" I asked, trying to hide my smile. Luna didn't strike me as the type to share easily, especially with a cat.

"Yes. An oaf of a creature. He was always shedding and bringing back dead birds and dropping them on the doorstep like some kind of threatening junk mail. I ask you, who would want a dead bird for a gift? Moronic feline."

"Where is he now?"

"Hopefully on his way to another state," Luna muttered.

I put my hands on my hips. "Luna, did you do something to this cat?"

"No! I would never!" Luna said, her eyes going wide. I shot her a skeptical look, and she deflated a little. "At least, not after that thing with the onions and the rooster. But it was a one-time incident driven by pure desperation! After that, I made a promise to Bea. Which I've never broken, by the way."

"I still can't believe you let a cat scare you out of the shop."

Luna's fur stood on end. "He's just always...there. Staring. It's unnerving."

"So, you ran away to the hutch?" I asked.

Luna sniffed loudly. "I *chose* to sleep in the hutch. More restful, don't you know?"

Sheriff Jackson cleared his throat and flicked open a notebook, jotting down a reminder as he spoke. "I'll follow up on the whereabouts of the missing cat. However, Luna says she heard nothing all evening, but the hutch is at the far end of the garden, so I suppose it's conceivable. Did Beatrice have any security cameras in the shop?"

"She hated technology," I said.

Luna spoke at the same time. "She had Gideon."

I slammed the heel of my hand against my forehead. "Oh, of course! Gideon!"

Sheriff Jackson looked confused. "Gideon? Is that some sort of new-fangled surveillance system or something?"

"Hardly," Luna said with a snort. "Gideon is the gargoyle. He and Beatrice struck a deal years ago. He watches the shop from sundown when the stone curse lifts until sunup when he becomes a statue once more. Spellbooks gets a night guard, and Gideon gets a safe place to shelter during the day. Win-win for everyone."

"Where is he now?" Sheriff Jackson asked. I looked up at the door, realizing I hadn't seen the small stone statue in his alcove when I'd arrived.

Luna pointed with her ear towards the floor. "He's down there," she said.

Gideon lay half buried in a pile of books, his stone wings outstretched, and a vicious snarl frozen on his chiseled face, revealing the gargoyle's pointed incisors. I stooped to brush away the books and stand him upright, but a heavy hand landed on my shoulder. I froze.

"Apologies, Miss Sullivan, but until I get one of my deputies out here to take photos of the crime scene, please refrain from touching anything." The sheriff's tone was firm, yet kind. I stood up and tucked my hands in the pockets of my jeans, cheeks warming at the second reminder.

"Speaking of, where are your deputies?" Luna asked, looking out the window.

"We're short-staffed at the moment. Bill is on duty, but you know he isn't exactly cut out for this kind of work," Sheriff Jackson said, waving an arm at the bookshop. "Johanna just finished her shift and couldn't come out anyway if she wanted to. Too much sun out for a vampire today without the proper protection. The new guy, Reggie, is on leave. His wife had a baby a few days ago. However, I told Bill to bring the equipment for me while I secured the crime scene. I'm sure he'll call it in to the techs too."

I raised my hand. "Why isn't Bill cut out for this?"

Luna answered before the sheriff could. "Bill's a centaur. It makes coming into a shop a tricky question of logistics, especially with the unenlightened watching," she said, tipping her head towards the small crowd still gawking outside the shop.

"Ah, here he is now," Sheriff Jackson said, striding outside as a handsome man wearing a police uniform rode up on a horse.

I blinked and looked again. No, that wasn't right. He wasn't riding the horse; he was *part* of the horse. I'd forgotten how it took a while to acclimatize to the glamour charms the Silverthorne mages used around town, even for someone with paranormal abilities. To a normal human tourist, Bill probably looked like a mounted cop. The illusion spell had even confused me for a moment, and I was a witch. However, now that I focused on him with my full attention, the illusion popped like a soap bubble. Bill wore a tailored blue police jacket with gleaming buttons and badge. From the waist up, he was all human, but his four legs were definitely equine.

Bill unslung a bag from his shoulder and held it out to his boss. Sheriff Jackson nodded his thanks, and the two men exchanged a few quick and quiet words before shaking hands. Bill turned and trotted back down the street while the sheriff returned to the front door, carrying a heavy armful of equipment. He set his load down just inside the door and then looked over at Luna and me.

"Bill said Reggie and some of our regular techs are coming in. Good thing it's not the weekend yet, or we'd really be hard up for help. We'll try to hurry, but it's probably best if you give us some space to do our jobs. We'll let you know if our search turns anything up."

"Thanks, Sheriff. I appreciate that," I said.

"To be on the safe side, I think you should stay somewhere else. At least until we get the damage in the sunroom fixed and perhaps install a proper security system," Sheriff Jackson suggested.

My shoulders slumped. I felt deflated and defeated. My first day back in Havenwood was supposed to be somewhat of a bittersweet homecoming. I'd planned on settling into the apartment above the shop, reminiscing about Granny Bea, probably crying a bit, knowing me, and then maybe heading out to see Aunty Agatha for a chat about old times. A break-in and a robbery weren't in the plan. This wasn't supposed to happen. Not in Havenwood and definitely not in Sullivan's Spellbooks.

Luna spoke up. "I'll take her over to the DeLuca's place and get her settled in there until you're satisfied with your investigation, Sheriff."

"Sounds good. If you don't mind, I'll take your contact info and be in touch soon, Miss Sullivan," the sheriff said.

"Sure." I gave him my phone number.

He jotted it down on a notepad. He paused, his pen hovering over the paper as he looked up at me. "And can I assume you're a witch like your great-grandmother?" he asked.

I froze. My magic wasn't something I advertised. Most of the people I associated with didn't know the paranormal world existed outside of Harry Potter World. Those that did would never be so forward as to pry openly. Magic was a very personal thing, something you only shared with family. For example. My dad could mend small objects with a touch and Mom had what was known as a soothing aura. Her presence naturally calmed those around her, easing worries and soothing troubled thoughts. They were small gifts and ones we kept within the family, just like my abilities with metal. However, to ask outright without the person volunteering the information was considered not just rude, but also insensitive. Sheriff Jackson must've read the confused consternation on my face. "Apologies, miss. I know it's not the done thing to ask so openly, but as you're new in town...well, I like to know if there's any dangerous people moving to the area," the sheriff said.

"Oh, well. Yes. That makes sense, I suppose. To answer your question, yes, I am a witch, but my gifts lean toward minor elemental manipulation at best."

"Can you start a fire? Cause an earthquake? Call up a storm?" The sheriff rattled off the questions in rapid fire, letting me know this wasn't the first time he'd asked them.

"No. None of the above," I said honestly.

"Then I think we're done here." He flipped the notebook closed and shook my hand firmly in a way that was a clear dismissal.

"Thank you, Sheriff," I murmured.

Luna hopped over and settled herself into my oversized bag like we'd been traveling companions for years. I hefted the bag, which was considerably heavier now, and grabbed the handle of my wheeled case. Carefully, I navigated through the few people remaining outside the barricade and started down the street.

"Where are we going?" I asked Luna when I was sure loitering tourists wouldn't overhear us.

"You remember Antonio and Honey DeLuca? They own the Enchanted Oasis Bed and Breakfast. The white house with the blue shutters over on Dragonfly Lane. You ran around with their daughter that summer you spent here. What was her name again? Ella? No, that wasn't it. Belle?"

"Bella," I said, memories rushing back to me of a girl just a couple months older than me with the brightest smile and the quickest wit. We'd played together all summer long and promised to be weekly pen pals until we died. Like most promises made by twelve-year-olds, my best intentions far exceeded my dedication to the commitment.

"Yes, that's right. Bella. She's helping Honey and Antonio out with the bed-and-breakfast these days. Hopefully, they'll have a room for us until we sort this whole thing with the shop out."

I glanced at her. "Us?" I asked.

Luna sniffed loudly, her whiskers twitching. "Naturally. You can hardly expect me to stay in the hutch with a thief breaking into places willy-nilly. What if he comes back?"

"To do what?" I asked with a smile. "Steal all the carrots?"

Luna wrinkled her nose in irritation. "Hoppy horrors, I hope not! Although that might be a blessing in disguise. Too much sugar in carrots for an old girl like me."

I chuckled softly and shook my head. Despite the circumstances, I was glad to see Luna, even if she was grumbling. "You'll always have a place with me, Luna. Even after this mess gets cleaned up."

Luna's ear flicked back and forth. "Kind of you to say, Harper. Very kind indeed," she said finally, a slight hitch in her words.

I blinked in surprise. Was that why she'd been in such a mood? What did she think I was going to do? Throw her out on her long, furry ears? The shop was as much her home as it had been Granny's. As I hoped it would be mine.

I stopped in the middle of the sidewalk and swung the bag in front of me so I could look her in the eye. "Luna, you will always have a place at Spellbooks for as long as you want it. I promise." I stuck out my hand, palm up.

Luna looked from me to my open hand and then back again. She blew out a breath, and I swear I could almost see a weight dropping off her tiny shoulders. She placed her front paw in my hand, and I shook it solemnly.

"Thank you, Harper," she whispered, with as much sincerity as I'd ever heard come from the rabbit. She swiped a paw across her eyes. "Oh, for the love of radish marmalade, look at me! I'm turning into a such a whimpering whisker face in my old age."

I smiled at her. "Now that it's settled, let's go find this bed-and-breakfast. I could really do with some food that didn't come out of a plastic wrapper."

Luna brushed another paw across her cheek. I gave her the courtesy of assuming she was adjusting her whiskers and not wiping unexpected ocular precipitation. "Very well then, this way." She pointed down the street once more.

I grinned to myself as I resituated my bags once more, intent on hurrying towards the promised sustenance. I hadn't been lying. I could really do with something that wasn't sugar and caffeine masquerading as food. However, when I looked up, something caught my eye. Across the street, someone stood in the shadowed alleyway between two shops. Whoever it was wore a dark trench coat and a fedora, which seemed an unusual fashion combination, even for this town.

As soon as the person caught me staring, he took two steps back into the alley, disappearing from view. All I was left with was a glimpse of a sandy beard and a creeping sensation curling up my spine. I hurried down the street, looking down the alley as I passed. It was empty.

Was the man in the fedora watching me? If so, why? And more importantly, what did he want?

Sweet Reunions

Enchanted Oasis Bed and Breakfast was a charming establishment nestled in the heart of Havenwood. The B&B boasted a welcoming atmosphere that was magical for both human and paranormal guests alike. The two-story home-turned-guesthouse was a charming fusion of delightful woodworking, gorgeous landscaping, and small-town charisma. As we walked down the flower-lined path to the large front porch, the exquisite smell of freshly baked bread wafted out of the screen door. I sniffed appreciatively at the air. Honey must be baking again. I had wonderful memories of enjoying her epicurean delights when I was a child.

Luna hopped out of my bag and straight up onto the porch, calling out, "Antonio? Honey? Anyone home?"

"Coming, coming!" A man's voice sounded from deep within the house. A moment later, a man wearing a flour-dusted apron that said, "Kissing the chef is always a treat, because it's my wife, and she makes every dish sweet!" As soon as he saw Luna, a huge smile broke out across his tanned face.

"Luna! What a wonderful surprise!" he exclaimed with a hint of an Italian accent, softened by a long time away from the land of pasta and pizza. He turned and called into the house. "Honey, Luna's here!" Antonio dropped to a knee and held out his arms for a hug. "It's been much too long! How are you?"

Luna hopped over and gave him the rabbit version of a friendly embrace which had noticeably more ears involved than the hugs to which I was accustomed. "Good to see you too, Antonio. You remember Harper Sullivan, Beatrice's great-granddaughter?" She twitched an ear in my direction.

Antonio DeLuca rose to his feet, a warm smile on his face. He was one of the humans who'd quietly accepted the existence of the supernatural in the world and permanently relocated to Havenwood. From what I knew of the Silverthorne's spells around Havenwood, they subtly amplified personal perception. If you, as a reasonable and functioning adult, *knew* fairy tales belonged in books and not on the streets of a small town in Connecticut, then the spells helped maintain your worldview. However, if you were like Antonio, a human who had met and married a paranormal, thus accepting the existence of the supernatural as part of his worldview, the spells apparently had little to no effect. I didn't understand all the ins and outs of the Silverthornes' spell craft. From the gossip I'd overheard as a child, the enchantments were elegant, sophisticated, and powerful. I should probably brush up on my working knowledge of the town and its magical protections, especially now that I was moving here permanently. I filed that tidbit away for later reflection, turning my attention back to Antonio.

He looked very much how I remembered him. Laughing brown eyes, a huge mustache over a smiling mouth, calloused hands from his love of woodworking, and a protruding belly from his wife's love of baking. Maybe the laugh lines around his eyes were deeper or there was more silver at his temples, but the good nature of the man washed over me, welcoming me back to Havenwood with all the exuberance I remembered from when I was a child.

"Little Harper Sullivan? Is that really you? Surely not! Before me stands a beautiful young lady, not the scrawny thing that ran around with my Bella!"

"Hello Mr. DeLuca," I said with a smile, an unintentional and yet not unwelcome reflection of his warm greeting.

He grasped my hand and patted it gently. "Antonio, please. You have our deepest condolences. We loved your nonna. She was such a good friend and a kind soul. One of the first to welcome us to town and always happy to lend a hand to a neighbor in need."

"Who is it, Antonio?" a woman's voice called from inside the house, cutting off my response. It was a good thing because I found my throat suddenly choked with tears.

"It's Beatrice's great-granddaughter, Harper, back from her grand adventures overseas," Antonio said as his wife approached.

Honey DeLuca appeared behind her husband, her radiant smile matching his. She was petite, shorter than her husband by at least half a foot, although that was because of her being a brownie more than anything else. Her sparkling caramel eyes and her cinnamon-colored hair complimented her honey-colored complexion. Okay, I'll admit. My impression of her may have been swayed by both the smell of freshly baked treats and the knowledge that Honey was an exceptional baker who took great joy in sharing her gifts. Despite the many differences between them, including their size and magical abilities, Honey and Antonio DeLuca were the epitome of marriage goals and what I secretly hoped I would find in a partner someday. Not that my parents weren't happily married, but it took a special kind of couple who could live and work in tandem every single day and wake up the next morning to do it all over again, even more madly in love.

"Harper? How good to see you again!" Honey said, wrapping her arms around me as if it hadn't been years since we last saw each other. "We were so sorry to hear about your grandmama. Such a dear lady. She always treated us like we were family, especially our Bella. Little gifts on her birthday every year and such a kind heart, don't you know? Oh, do come in dear! Why are we out here on the porch when I have fresh cinnamon rolls just out of the oven?"

"That's very kind of you, Mrs. DeLuca," I said.

"Oh, you must call me Honey. Please, I insist. Bella will be so happy to see you! I do hope you'll stay awhile."

Luna spoke up. "That's actually why we're here. We were hoping you have a room available for a few nights."

"Oh dear, has something happened at Spellbooks?" Honey asked, her expressive eyes darkening in concern.

"Yes, but it's not something I'd like to discuss on the porch if it's all the same to you," Luna said.

"Of course, of course," Honey replied. She wrung her hands together. "The only problem is that we don't have a room available with the Renaissance Faire on at the moment."

"Harper could bunk in with Bella for a day or two. I'm sure she wouldn't mind," Antonio offered.

Honey bit her lip. "We'd better ask her first, but yes. I think that would work nicely."

"I don't want to put you or Bella out," I said, hesitantly.

Antonio threw an arm around my shoulders and squeezed. "Don't be so silly. You're practically family. Let me talk to Bella and we'll sort the whole thing out."

"In the meantime, Antonio, will you please take Harper's things and put them behind the reception desk so she doesn't have to lug them around while I sort out some refreshments?"

"Yes, amore," Antonio said. He winked at me. "Don't worry now. We'll look after you until whatever is going on at the bookshop is put right."

I smiled as a weight I hadn't realized I'd been carrying fell from my shoulders. "Thank you so much, Mr.—" Antonio held up a finger and arched an eyebrow at me. "—I mean, Antonio."

"There, that's better now, isn't it? I'll be along shortly. Save at least two of those cinnamon rolls for me, my love!"

"I'll save you one. You know what the doctor said about your cholesterol," Honey said as Antonio gathered up my bags. She waved at me to follow her. "Come along now. You look like you could use a cup of something hot and some food. Cinnamon rolls, of course, but maybe something a touch more filling?" Honey bustled off down the hall, leaving us to trail behind in her wake.

Luna hopped along after her, but I took my time examining the charming bed-and-breakfast to see how it compared to the impressions of my youth. The Enchanted Oasis was indeed an oasis. The interior of the building was adorned with whimsical touches, featuring intricate woodwork such as carved giggling fairies in the corner and smiling gnomes holding up the banister at the base of the staircase. I gasped in surprise when I realized that someone, undoubtedly Antonio, had fashioned each stair into a bookshelf, welcoming the guests with literary surprises every step of the way. He must've done it sometime in the years I'd been away because I didn't remember the beautiful addition. Pictures of mythical creatures and fantastical landscapes were tastefully displayed amid vases of fresh flowers and fairy lights twinkled in discrete settings among the carved woodwork, giving the whole place a magical feel where it seemed like dreams and reality intertwined.

"Harper? Are you coming?" Luna asked from a doorway leading deeper into the house.

I shut my mouth with a snap, not realizing it had fallen open. "Yes. Sorry," I said, hurrying after her.

By the time we reached the kitchen, Honey had huge steaming cinnamon rolls liberally spread with what looked like fluffy cream cheese frosting set out on plates with a delicate blue floral pattern. "Now then," said our hostess. "Do you want coffee or tea?"

"Whatever has the most caffeine," I said instantly.

Honey smiled in sympathy as she headed towards the coffee maker. "Long flight?" she asked.

I nodded. "Dad is stationed in Germany at the moment, so it feels like dinner time to me," I said as my stomach growled noisily. I grinned sheepishly, pressing a hand to my midsection. "I would've been here sooner, but we only got the letter from her lawyer a few days ago."

Honey nodded in sympathy. "Beatrice was always a fan of handwritten notes. I don't think she ever quite embraced technology fully."

Luna crinkled her nose at me. "Speaking of, once you are settled here, you really should go see Beatrice's lawyer about her estate before he closes for the weekend. When I spoke to him, he mentioned it was a delicate situation that he could only discuss with you once you arrived."

"Oh, well, then I suppose I'd better go over there immediately. I have a meeting with him later, but—"

"You've only just arrived!" Honey interjected. "Have a bite to eat, and you'll feel better. Ten more minutes won't make much of a difference to the lawyer, but it will to your stomach. Besides, we have so much to catch up on."

"I suppose you're right," I said, secretly grateful to have a reason to stay and catch my breath, not to mention a chance to sample Honey's cinnamon rolls.

"Of course I am," Honey said, passing me a cup of dark, wonderful ambrosia otherwise known as coffee. "Here's your awake water. Do you take it with milk?"

I hid a smile at her terminology. "Yes, please."

Honey bustled off to the refrigerator and returned a moment later with a small pot of milk and a plate of greens for Luna to nibble on. Antonio walked back into the cozy kitchen just as Honey settled at the table and wrapped her hands around her coffee mug.

"Now then, tell us everything," Honey said.

Nearly twenty minutes later, Luna had filled Honey and Antonio in on the robbery along with her time in the "dreadful hutch" while I'd filled my stomach with strong coffee and gooey cinnamon rolls. Honey really knew her way around a kitchen, which shouldn't have surprised me, given that she was a brownie, but it had been a long time since I'd tasted anything so delicious. Between living with my parents wherever Dad was stationed overseas and taking trips with them whenever we could travel, my culinary choices hadn't been slim, per se. Just nothing quite like this. The pastry was tender and sweet, the cinnamon filling perfectly spiced, and the creamy frosting had just the right amount of tang. It was perfection in a mouthful.

"You poor dears!" Honey exclaimed as Luna wrapped up her tale. "What a nasty shock!"

"And for it to happen on your first day back, too," Antonio said with a sorrowful shake of his head.

I perked up at his words. It was odd that the shop had been broken into now when it had been left empty ever since Granny Bea passed. "I wonder if that's a coincidence," I mused.

"If what's a coincidence, dear?" Honey asked.

"It's just that it's awfully convenient, isn't it? The shop getting robbed the night before I landed. A day or two later and I might have been there."

"To see that awful thief destroy Beatrice's home and business? Why would you want to witness that?" Luna said with a shudder.

"Not witness it. Stop it." At the shocked expressions around the table, I walked back my bravado. "Or at least call the police sooner. Who knew I was coming in today?" I directed my question to Luna.

She sniffed. "When I saw your letter in the mail, I got that pleasant young man, Finnegan, from next door to open it for me yesterday. Naturally, I shared the good news of your arrival with a few close friends."

"Meaning half the town," Honey said with a knowing smile.

Luna's nose twitched. "I was excited. I couldn't bear to see Spellbooks in the hands of anyone but a Sullivan."

A swell of sadness rose within me at the thought of why the shop was changing hands. I thought I'd done all my grieving when we'd first received notice of Granny's passing. And then again on the plane. And most recently, when I'd landed in Connecticut. The wave of sorrow subsided, leaving an aching emptiness in its wake. Instead of focusing on the grief, I tried to redirect my thoughts to the matter before me. "Speaking of, do you know why Granny Bea left the shop to me instead of Dad? The note from her lawyer was a little vague."

Luna shook her head. "No, but you should go see Mr. Ravenscroft today, especially considering the robbery. He'll undoubtedly want to meet you, read the will, and start the handover process."

I glanced at the kitchen clock. "When I told him I was flying in, he arranged a meeting. I'm supposed to go to his office in about an hour, but I don't want to miss him if he's shut for the weekend so I might head over a little early," I said.

"Are you sure you're up to it?" Honey asked, her sparkling eyes dark with concern. "I'm sure Nathaniel would understand if you wanted to reschedule what with the robbery on top of your flight."

I bit my lip. A nap sounded good. I didn't sleep well on planes, and it had been a long day of travel. Despite the jolt of sugar and caffeine, I was physically and emotionally drained.

"I don't really want to reschedule, but a quick nap sounds divine," I said. "Do I have time?"

Antonio checked the clock. "Nathaniel is quite punctual and won't shut the office early, especially if he knows you're coming. You probably have about forty minutes before you need to leave here. Nathaniel's office is only about a ten-minute walk away."

I covered a yawn with the back of my hand. "You've convinced me. Nap first, then the lawyer."

Honey nodded as she swept up my dishes. "Good choice. Antonio, she can use the Fairy Glen room. The guests aren't due in until later tonight, so we'll have plenty of time to change the bedding. Meanwhile, Luna and I have a proper catch up. Now, the girl needs her rest. Don't talk her ear off," she said with mock severity, waggling a finger at her husband.

"Yes, amore." Antonio leaned over and gave his wife a peck on the cheek.

I followed Antonio out of the room, weariness dragging heavily on my eyelids now that the promise of a nap in a proper bed was imminent. I didn't remember much about the guest rooms from my visits as a child. Bella and I spent most of our time outside or biking around town in pursuit of make-believe monsters to vanquish. I wasn't so tired that I didn't "ooh" and "ahh" appreciatively over the beautifully decorated room with its embroidered duvet of soft lavender pastels and matching decor. What really caught my eye about the room was the view. The windows looked out on a section of the yard which was decorated to look like a little fairy village, complete with tiny, colorful houses and a water wheel leisurely spinning in a slow-moving trickle of a lazy river. Only when I pulled my head back into the room did I see the garden reflected in the room's decor. The pictures on the wall showed fairies frolicking between the very houses I'd just seen in the little garden. Fairy statues played hide and seek behind bottles of complimentary lotions on the nightstand. Even the bedspread looked like an abstract map of the fairy glen done in various shades of lilac.

"Antonio, this is beautiful," I said, sincerity in every syllable.

"We try," he replied, pride ringing in his voice. "But there'll be time for all that later. Enjoy your nap." He smiled as he gently shut the door.

I think I managed to get both shoes off before I collapsed onto the downy softness of the bed and sleep took me, but only time would tell.

Revelations and Riddles

I RUBBED THE GRIT from my eyes as the alarm on my phone chimed merrily. I groaned and slapped my cheeks gently in an effort to chase away the grogginess from my nap. It might have been pleasant sleeping among the fairies at the Enchanted Oasis, but it hadn't been nearly long enough. After a quick farewell to the DeLucas, I followed Honey's directions to the office. Luckily, as promised, the lawyer was located just a short walk away. An uncontrollable yawn blinded me for a moment as I rounded the corner onto Starlight Street and obscured my first look at the lawyer's office.

The red brick building looked simultaneously professional, welcoming, and serious, which was no small feat for a creation of stone and glass. A sign posted on the heavy wooden door told me that this was, in fact, the business of Nathaniel D. Ravenscroft, Attorney. I looked at the letter I'd received anyway, to confirm the name and location. Okay, perhaps it was also to give myself a chance to regain composure.

When I'd received Granny's final letter along with the lawyer's note, I hadn't really read either completely. Grief and regret overwhelmed me. The grief continued to hit in small, unexpected waves since then, mostly whenever I saw something that reminded me of her. The regret slowly morphed into a kernel of guilt. Perhaps I should've spent more time with her, visited more often. Dad, in his gruff yet loving way, pointed out that the logistics of being stationed overseas made it difficult to visit, which was only compounded when I started university. Between online courses, traveling to Scotland where I did most of my in-person university work, and visiting my parents, I hadn't made it back to the States often in recent years. Sure, I tried to call Granny's landline or even email, but one week would stretch to two and then entire months went by without any contact. I'd spoken to her briefly about a week before she passed, but even then, I was rushing off to do something that seemed terribly important at the time and didn't make the time for a long chat. Now, of course, I wished I would've.

Mom tried to assuage my guilt by using her words and her soothing aura when we received the news of Granny's passing, saying Granny would've understood. After all, she'd raised her two children and watched them grow up and move away. I understood the logic of it all, but the emotions hit differently. I wasn't a twelve-year-old kid anymore, and we were the last surviving relatives she had. I wondered what it must have been like for her to only see us when my school schedule and Dad's leave aligned, which was rare.

Resolutely, I pushed my complex roil of emotions to the side. Those were for me to deal with in private. Now, I had to be the adult who was about to inherit Granny Bea's estate and do her proud, even if I still felt like a child wearing her mother's heels and playing pretend. I took a deep breath and pushed inside the lawyer's office. Fake it 'til you make it, right? I put on my most professional smile and marched in with every ounce of bravado I could muster. All of which was profoundly wasted on an empty room.

A pristinely organized desk sat in the corner of a tastefully furnished waiting room. Four comfortable-looking chairs dotted the perimeter of the room, separated by low tables with precisely arranged magazines topping each. Potted plants made the waiting area appear homey, but something felt off. I couldn't quite put my finger on what it was until the door behind me swung open. The spill of sunlight across the thick carpet made the electric light in the room seem even more artificial. With all the windows I'd seen outside, why wasn't there any natural light in the office?

I didn't have long to ponder the question as a middle-aged woman in a pink cardigan and pearls hurried past me. "I'm so sorry. I do hope I haven't kept you waiting long," she said, carefully balancing a large pink box emblazoned with a stylized picture of a fairy and the words "Pixie Pastries" on the side. She eased the box onto her desk before turning to face me with a wide smile. Her eyes were full of sharp intelligence and her softly styled waves had streaks of gray. She dusted her hands free of invisible dirt. "There. That's better. I'm Mrs. Jenkins, secretary to Mr. Ravenscroft. I'm afraid he has a rather important appointment at the moment, but if you don't mind waiting, I'm sure I can squeeze you in afterwards."

I dug into my bag and pulled out the letter on the expensive card stock I'd received from Nathaniel Ravenscroft informing me of my Granny's passing and requesting my presence for the reading of her will regarding my inheritance of her estate. I double-checked the date and time before handing it over to Mrs. Jenkins. "I am here to see Mr. Ravenscroft, and I think I might be his appointment. My name is Harper Sullivan. I'm here about my great-grandmother, Beatrice Sullivan."

Mrs. Jenkins examined the letter carefully. "Oh. I see. I thought you'd be...well, never mind. Please have a seat. I'll let him know you have arrived." She shot a quick look towards the front door and then moved to the opposite side of the room and the wooden door presumably leading into the law firm's inner sanctum. She tapped gently on the door before slipping inside. Curious, I craned my neck, trying to glimpse Granny's lawyer. A glimpse was all I got before Mrs. Jenkins closed the door behind her, but it was enough to see two men smiling and toasting each other with what looked to be expensive crystal glasses holding amber liquid. At least someone appeared to be having a good day. I wondered if Mr. Ravenscroft knew about the break-in at the shop yet or if I'd have to tell him.

Mrs. Jenkins stuck her head out of the office a moment later and looked around the room carefully before swinging the door wide. "Mr. Ravenscroft is ready for you, Miss Sullivan."

"Thank you so much," I said, moving past her into the lawyer's office. The room was everything I would have expected from a lawyer in Havenwood. Small, but not too cramped. A heavy desk framed by full bookcases commanded one side of the room. On the other was a small couch and two armchairs gathered around a wooden coffee table carved with swirls that might have been a gnome's face here or a fairy wing there or could've just been abstract art. I smiled, recognizing Antonio's work. The lanky man by the desk cleared his throat and extended a hand to me with a warm smile. He wore a tailored suit with a subtle purple vest and matching tie and pocket square. His skin was pale, but that might have been due in part to the artificial lighting in the room and the contrast to his almost black hair and eyes.

"Pleasure to meet you. I'm Nathaniel Ravenscroft, and you must be Miss Sullivan," he said, gripping my hand.

His palm felt cool and almost papery under my fingertips. Perhaps he just needed to use more moisturizer. I smiled back and shook it firmly. "Harper, please. It's nice to meet you."

"A pleasure. And you must call me Nathaniel. I'm glad to see you arrived on schedule. The flight was pleasant, I trust?"

"Well, I made it here in one piece," I said dryly, thinking of the long haul in the cramped cabin.

"Wonderful! Glad to hear it. We've all been anxiously awaiting your arrival." Nathaniel turned and gestured to the man behind him. "Please, allow me to introduce Thaddeus Blackwell." The man pushed off the desk where he'd been leaning and gave me a perfunctory nod. He wore his white shirt open at the collar and cuffed at the elbows over dark jeans. His hair was too long to be tidy and not long enough to be a stylistic statement. Dark stubble covered his cheeks and chin and his calculating eyes narrowed despite Nathaniel's friendly introduction. Unable to meet his brooding gaze, my own eyes dropped to the desk where two empty crystal tumblers sat. Who was Thaddeus Blackwell to Nathaniel Ravenscroft? An employee? If so, why the drink? If not, what was he still doing here during my appointment time?

Nathaniel retrieved a manila folder from his desk just as Mrs. Jenkins bustled out of the room and shut the door behind her, leaving the open pink box and cardboard cups positioned as artfully as possible in the middle of the table. "Shall we sit? I find it's much more pleasant to have these discussions when one is comfortable," Nathaniel said, seating himself in one armchair and folding his hands over the folder in his lap. Thaddeus brushed past me to claim the other chair, leaving me confused and with the couch as my only seating option.

Nathaniel cleared his throat and gestured towards the table. "Please help yourselves. I'm told Pixie Pastries makes the best sweets in town, and I also asked Mrs. Jenkins for a selection of coffees in case you are in need of a pick-me-up. I believe we have black coffee, breakfast tea, hot chocolate, and, ah yes, here's the cappuccino."

"Black for me, thanks," Thaddeus said, grabbing the cup with the tick in the Americano box on the side and completely ignoring the pastries.

Although the hot chocolate was tempting, it felt somewhat childish to be sipping on something that usually came with marshmallows in front of my great-grandmother's lawyer. After shooting a longing glance at the sugary drink, I opted for the more adult cappuccino.

Nathaniel tapped the folder in his lap, forgoing selecting a drink of his own. "Thank you both for coming today. As you know, your great-grandmother was a staple of our community here in Havenwood for a very long time. Why, she even welcomed me when I moved my law firm here over fifty years ago."

I blinked at the revelation. Although I knew many supernatural beings who were gifted with a long life lived in Havenwood, Granny Bea included, Nathaniel looked like he was just shy of forty. How could he have moved here fifty years ago with an already established law firm?

The lawyer must've read the surprise on my face. He chuckled. "I see Beatrice never told you about me. I am a vampire." He held up a hand as my mouth dropped open at the open admission. "Not to worry. I've been a 'vegetarian' vampire for several decades now. I prefer my sustenance served chilled and in a bag, as opposed to warm and straight from the source. However, I hope you won't go advertising this to the tourists. When they find out, they seem to think strands of garlic and sharpened stakes are necessary when making my acquaintance. I can assure you that I much prefer a hearty handshake." He smiled reassuringly at me, completely ignoring Thaddeus, so I assumed this news wasn't a revelation to the other man. Suddenly several things made sense, such as the lack of natural light in the office, and Nathaniel passing on the pastries and coffee. I wondered how he came into the office at all during the day, but that was perhaps a mystery for another day. Slowly, I nodded and forced myself to smile back, but it took a concentrated effort of will. Nathaniel Ravenscroft was the first vampire I'd ever met. At least, the first one I was aware of meeting. This *was* Havenwood, after all. Perhaps I'd met another vampire during an earlier visit and hadn't realized.

The lawyer opened his folder, scanning the information within. "Your great-grandmother was quite clear on her wishes regarding dividing her estate," Nathaniel said, steering the conversation to the business at hand.

I couldn't keep quiet any longer. "I'm sorry. What do you mean 'dividing?'" I asked.

Nathaniel looked surprised. "Why splitting it between her two great-grandchildren, of course. You and Thaddeus."

My eyes shot wide, and I swiveled to look at the scruffy man at the opposite end of the table. He wiggled the fingers of one hand at me, obviously not sharing my shock at the lawyer's announcement. "Nice to meet you, cuz," he said with a smirk.

I turned back to Nathaniel. "There must be some mistake," I said, my mouth running away with me before my brain fully grasped that I had a cousin. One I'd never even heard of before.

"It was a surprise to me too, when Nathaniel here told me about you yesterday," Thaddeus said.

I looked between them. My brain couldn't catch up with the words pouring out around me. The lawyer shook his head, his demeanor calm and face impassive. "There is no mistake, I assure you. Beatrice had two children, Harold and Lucille. Harold married and had one son, your father Edward, who then married and had you, Harper. Lucille, your great aunt, bore two children. Through a series of rather unfortunate twists of fate, Thaddeus is the only remaining heir to Lucille's line, which makes you second cousins and Beatrice's heirs. Hence the reason you are both here today."

He paused, allowing me to readjust my worldview. I stared first at him and then swung my shocked gaze to Thaddeus, who just smirked at me like this was all old news to him. I'd just assumed that I was Granny Bea's only heir. She'd never mentioned Thaddeus to me, nor had my father. However, if her lawyer was confident, then who was I to argue? I quickly ran through the brief letter I'd received from him, requesting my presence in my mind. Nothing in it explicitly said I was the only heir. Just that they needed me in Havenwood to settle Granny's estate. I'd incorrectly assumed the rest. A blush burned my cheeks. At least I hadn't made a total fool of myself by admitting my assumptions out loud. I took a deep breath and nodded for Nathaniel to continue.

He returned the gesture crisply. "Very well. Now, as far as her assets are concerned, Beatrice was incredibly clear on the matter. An equal percentage will be transferred to each of you as her youngest surviving relatives. When she discussed the matter with me, she wanted to provide you with enough to be comfortable, not complacent."

"That doesn't sound like Granny Bea," Thaddeus observed. I stiffened at his casual use of *my* nickname for my great-grandmother.

"I may have softened the verbiage somewhat," Nathaniel said with a knowing smile. "Most of her finances are to be split between several charities. I have the list and the figures here," he said, passing over a thin envelope to each of us. "As soon as we settle probate, the funds will be transferred to whichever bank account you prefer."

"Great," Thaddeus said, tapping the envelope on the arm of the chair. "But this seems like something that could've been done over the phone instead of pulling me away from work."

"What about the shop?" I asked softly.

Nathaniel withdrew three matching envelopes that were obviously of a much better quality than the thin, legal one I clutched. He passed one to Thaddeus, another to me, and kept one for himself. Mine was emblazoned with my name, written in Granny Bea's distinctive, scrawling penmanship. "That is why you are here. Her instructions were explicit. We open and read these together. On three?"

Thaddeus nodded his acceptance and Nathaniel performed the countdown, each word falling like the solemn toll of a bell, announcing the demise of my dreams.

"One, two, three."

Numbly, I tore open the letter as instructed and drank in every word of my great-grandmother's last message.

Dear Harper,

First and most importantly, I love you so much, darling girl. I am so sorry that we didn't get to spend more time together, but I treasured every minute I had with you. I have always wanted the best for you and for Thaddeus, which is why I wish to do my part to ease your way now that my journey is coming to an end. I know that each of your parents are well-established and have no need, nor likely any desire, to run my little shop here in Havenwood. As my only two great-grandchildren, I thought one of you might be more inclined to introduce Sullivan's Spellbooks to a new generation of readers. I debated long and hard about how best to divide my estate. The obvious choice was to sell the shop and divide the money. However, that shop is as much part of my family as both of you, and I am loath to emulate the wise king Solomon and threaten to divide my baby.

I'd like to think that my many years on this earth have bought me enough wisdom to avoid such a distasteful fate for Spellbooks. Instead, I propose a challenge of sorts. In one week, Mr. Ravenscroft will arrange a meeting at the shop where each of you will present a plan for the shop and how it would function under your management. Nathaniel knows my wishes on the matter and my own feelings regarding Spellbooks. The person with the plan most closely aligned with my own will be named my heir. Now, why are you still sitting around here? You have work to do! As Luna would say, hop to it!

All my love,
Granny Bea

PS Give Luna a cuddle for me. She'll probably be feeling out of sorts.
PPS Don't let her convince you to get rid of Mr. Wigglesworth.

Tears blurred my vision, making it difficult to read. Images of Granny in the shop danced before my mind's eye and a lump grew and grew in my throat. I fought to keep from sobbing in the middle of the office as another wave of grief and regret swept over me. Granny was gone, and now I might lose Spellbooks, too?

"Is this for real?" I finally blurted out past the lump in my throat, scanning the letter again to make sure I'd understood her intent.

Thaddeus didn't look nearly as surprised as I felt. "That Gran is making us compete for the shop? Yep, you read that right."

Nathaniel looked calm and unruffled by the unexpected turn of events. "I believe this is Beatrice's way of ensuring her legacy lives on. Through her bookshop and through one of you. Now, I believe I have keys around here somewhere for you both." He crossed to his desk, rummaging through the drawers as he spoke. "You may, of course, peruse the books or accounts, but the shop is not open for business until we decide ownership in a week's time."

"That's going to be hard," I muttered, thinking of the robbery.

"Pardon?" Nathaniel asked, looking up sharply.

I spoke up. "You haven't heard? Someone broke into Sullivan's Spellbooks last night and stole the rare books Granny kept locked up behind the counter." Nathaniel looked concerned, but Thaddeus' face darkened with anger. I looked back and forth between the two men. Well, the man and the vampire. Was Thaddeus just a man? I didn't know if he had inherited some sort of power through Granny Bea's line. Sometimes, it skipped a generation, but mostly the gifts that I knew of in our family were small, like my affinity for metal.

"Great! Just great!" Thaddeus spat out sarcastically as he stood and started pacing angrily. "I haven't even been to the shop yet. I take the day off work for basically nothing! The money is going to charity, and the most expensive books have been stolen."

"Now, we don't know that yet," Nathaniel said, placatingly. "Let me talk to Sheriff Jackson and see what's going on."

"What's going on is that this inheritance is next to nothing!" Thaddeus snapped. "You know what? Give me the keys and let me get back to work. At least this day won't be a total waste."

Silently, Nathaniel passed a key chain to Thaddeus, who snatched it out of his hand. "Total disaster. That's what this is," he grumbled as he wheeled on a heel. He pitched his empty cup towards a garbage can before slamming the office door shut behind him. The cup teetered on the edge of the can and then fell to the floor. I stared at it and then at the closed door, not quite believing a grown man could throw such a temper tantrum. If he'd been raised under my dad's roof, Thaddeus would've been running obstacle courses followed by innumerable sets of push-ups for a month for that type of behavior and Dad wouldn't have cared he was a grown man. Silently, I picked up the discarded cup and placed it in the can.

"Thank you," murmured Nathaniel distractedly. He handed me my set of keys. I carefully tucked them in my bag, along with the note from Granny Bea.

"What happens now?" I asked.

Nathaniel ushered me towards the door. "Now, I need to liaise with the police and offer what assistance I can. You, on the other hand, need to follow your great-grandmother's instructions and try to draft a plan for the shop to the best of your abilities."

Was it my imagination, or did the lawyer's final words sound decidedly doubtful of my capacity to plan a future for Spellbooks successfully? I opened my mouth to say something, either to defend myself or put his mind at ease. I wasn't sure which. However, when I looked back over my shoulder, the two crystal tumblers on the desk caught my eye. A snapshot image of Thaddeus and Nathaniel toasting blinked up in my mind.

I shut my mouth as the implications hit home. Neither had appeared particularly surprised at the news of a competition for the shop. Was that because of my heightened emotions at reading Granny Bea's last note to me or because it *wasn't* news to either of them? Was the reason Nathaniel doubted me because he'd already made some kind of deal for the shop with Thaddeus? If so, what kind of chance did I stand?

Of Purpose, Puddles, and Petruchio

FEELING DOWNHEARTED, I MINDLESSLY sipped from my lukewarm cappuccino as I plodded through the town, not really taking in any of the sights, sounds, or smells from the quirky shops I'd found so enchanting as a child. Thaddeus was nowhere to be seen. Even if he had been, I don't know what I would've said to him.

I've never had a cousin before. Let's get some pie and talk. Was pie even the appropriate "get to know a long-lost cousin" food?

Want to reminisce about Granny Bea and share stories of what we remember? Thaddeus definitely didn't seem like the type to swap memories. Grumble and glare, sure, but tell sweet stories of Granny? Not right now. Perhaps not ever.

Did you make a deal with Nathaniel Ravenscroft to win the competition before it even began? Yeah, that would go over about as well as a stone troll on a rope bridge. It wasn't like either of them would admit it if it were true.

Why was I so upset at the possibility? It wasn't as if I'd ever owned Sullivan's Spellbooks in the first place, just misinterpreted a vaguely worded letter from Granny's lawyer. I didn't really care about the money either. As far as I was concerned, Granny could do whatever she liked on that front. No, the reason I was so dejected was because, in my heart, I'd already inherited the shop. I'd made plans, had dreams, and happily fantasized about living in Havenwood above Spellbooks.

Most of all, I'd been looking forward to putting down roots. To having a place to call my own. After being an army brat for most of my life, settling in one place had a certain appeal. Staying here in Havenwood, where I didn't have to hide my magic, and I could feel closer to the roots of my family tree while I established my first long-term home, was...exciting.

I know, I know. When you're my age, you're supposed to want to go see the world, travel to exotic locales, try new flavors, see new things. But what happened when that was the norm? I'd grown up with that life. Traveling here, there, and everywhere. Not that there was anything wrong with that. I just wanted the other side. Inheriting Granny's bookshop in Havenwood seemed like the stars aligned to grant me my wish. My fairytale had its perfect ending. Well, until about ten minutes ago.

Now what was I supposed to do?

Almost like I heard Granny's voice on the wind, the answer echoed in my head.

So, things didn't go the way you planned? Welcome to life. Pull yourself up, sugar pea. Dust yourself off. Take the next step. Don't worry about what's coming a mile down the road. Just put one foot in front of the other and do the next right thing.

I straightened my shoulders and headed back towards Spellbooks to see what I could do to either help with the investigation or to tidy up. Either way, I might find inspiration for such a brilliant plan that whatever schemes Thaddeus had made wouldn't stand a chance. I tossed the coffee cup in the trash and, with a spring in my step, turned onto Arcadia Avenue.

The corner of the building blocked my view. Distracted by my new-found resolve, I wasn't as cautious as I should've been. I crashed into a couple walking the opposite way, sending their packages and bags flying all over the sidewalk.

"Oh, I'm so sorry!" I exclaimed. "I wasn't watching where I was going, and, well, let me help you with that," I said as I scooped up fallen items, many of which were books.

"You should really be more careful," the prim woman with the pinched face said as I handed a stack of books back to her. She shoved them into a paper bag without looking at them.

"Indeed. Crashing into people all willy-nilly! Why it's quite a harrowing experience, in the middle of one's afternoon, now isn't it?" her companion said in a nasal voice. His mustache quivered with indignation. He placed his hands on his hips and sticking out his chest, which had the unintended effect of also causing his prodigious belly to strain the buttons of his waistcoat. I noticed one hand was wrapped in a thick white bandage. He glared down at me as I stood, which was impressive in its own right, given that I must've been at least four inches taller.

"I am sorry," I said, passing over the last of the books. "Do you like to read? You have a lot of books here."

"Do we like to read!" snorted the woman. Her hair was pulled back so tightly that it made her look permanently surprised, which was disconcerting when combined with the glower she leveled my way.

"I should say we don't have time to read," the man interjected. "Too busy doing business, you know. I'm a very important man about town." He puffed himself up, shoving his glasses a little higher on his bulbous nose with the hand wrapped in bandages.

"Oh, are you? My apologies. I just arrived today and—"

Suddenly, the pudgy little man in front of me was all smiles. "Well, you're in luck! We have everything a tourist could want to plan a visit to Havenwood. Maps, local attractions, books on all sorts."

"Well, I'm not really—"

"Interested in the touristy stuff? Just want a good murder mystery to read while you curl up in bed? Can't say I blame you. How about a spy thriller? A romance? Whatever your fancy, the Dusty Tome has it all," the man said with an expansive wave towards the shop he and his companion had obviously just left. Books were crammed into every nook and cranny. Garish advertisements for sales and discounts peppered the window, making it hard to focus on anything without getting an eye ache.

"Oh, do you work here?" I asked.

"Work here?" The woman shrilled a piercing laugh. "You *must* be new to Havenwood. This is Mr. Oswald Puddleton, proud owner of the Dusty Tome." Mr. Puddleton struck a pose as she introduced him. "And I am his wife, Hortense," she finished in a rush.

"What a coincidence," I said. "You know Sullivan's Spellbooks?"

"That little old shop?" Mr. Puddleton sniffed disdainfully.

"Did you see all the police tape around it?" Mrs. Puddleton whispered with the air of an accomplished gossip. "That can't be a good thing."

"Maybe they're finally closing it down. Good riddance, I say!" Mr. Puddleton said with an emphatic nod.

Mrs. Puddleton patted her husband's arm. "Who knows what's going to happen to it now that poor Beatrice has passed? Such a shame. The new owners will have their work cut out for them. Whatever they do, it just can't compare to the Tome, can it, dear?"

"Quite right, quite right indeed!" Mr. Puddleton exclaimed. They both looked at me expectantly. I opened my mouth and then froze, not knowing how to respond without causing either offense or embarrassment. We stood there awkwardly, looking at each other for one breath. Then two.

Finally, Mrs. Puddleton gestured to me, speaking loudly and slowly with much accompanying hand flapping like English speakers often do to anyone who has the audacity to speak another language. "And what is your name?"

That shocked me back to myself. I pasted on a brilliant smile and stuck out my hand. "I'm Harper. Harper *Sullivan*. It looks like we'll be neighbors. I'll be sure to take you up on your offer. I'm never one to pass up a good book." Both of the Puddletons' faces drained of color. I firmly shook their limp hands, keeping my friendly smile in place. "It's so nice to meet you both, but I really must get Spellbooks ready for its big re-opening. I'll leave you to your afternoon and so sorry again for that minor mishap." I waved at them as I sidestepped and left them standing in the middle of the sidewalk with matching stunned expressions on their faces.

If Granny had been there, she'd have been cackling. She was never one to let someone else push her around, but she always advocated kindness. Sure, she wasn't above using Shakespeare's interpretation of killing one with kindness, but if that were the case, I would be Petruchio and the Puddletons, the quarrelsome Kate. I just didn't have it in me to tame the shrewish neighbors at the moment. Not when I already had police in the shop, a theft to solve, and a mysterious cousin trying to steal my inheritance. That was more than enough for my Friday, thank you very much.

Legends and Ledgers

I MARCHED DOWN THE street, my head held high and feeling my usual enthusiasm start to return. I came to Havenwood to uphold Granny's legacy and build my own in the process. No amount of thieves or grumpy cousins or obnoxious neighbors were going to stop me. Not now. Not ever.

The police tape, on the other hand? That might do it.

I slowed as I approached the shop, having forgotten that it had only been a couple of hours. They probably still considered the shop to be a crime scene. How long did it take the police to turn over a crime scene, anyway? That wasn't a question I'd expected needing an answer for today.

A familiar set of long white ears twitched in the window as I approached. Luna's entire head popped up above the sill. She waved a paw at me to come inside and then disappeared. A moment later, the front door swung open, and a young man in a police uniform stuck his head out of the door.

"Are you Harper Sullivan by chance?" he asked.

"I am. How can I help you Officer...?"

"Reggie." He held up the tape, gesturing for me to slip underneath. "Well, technically, it's Reginald Horatio Percival Harrington III, but everyone around here just calls me Reggie. Officer Reggie, if you are feeling formal." He smiled as he shut the door behind me. He had one of those grins that made him look both boyish and almost irrationally glad to be alive. I couldn't help smiling back at him.

"Oh, you're the one who just had a baby, right?" I asked as I placed him from my conversation with the sheriff. "Congratulations!"

"Thanks. A baby boy. We're calling him Patrick because no one needs a Reginald Horatio Percival Harrington IV."

"That is an awful lot of names to put on the shoulders of a newborn," I said with a laugh.

"Tell me about it," Officer Reggie sighed.

"Shouldn't you be with your wife and the new arrival?" I asked.

"I'll head back over soon, but the boss called about this theft, and we're a little shorthanded at the moment."

"I see."

"Actually, that's why I called you in when Luna said you were outside. We've finished photographing and fingerprinting the place, but Sheriff Jackson wants a record or catalogue of the missing books before he relinquishes the scene. The problem is, as Luna here tells me, Mrs. Sullivan didn't get on well with computers."

I laughed. "That's like saying the Titanic had a minor disagreement with an iceberg."

Reggie chuckled. "I take your point. She liked to conduct business the old-fashioned way."

I pointed a finger at him. "That's my Granny."

"The thing is, Luna mentioned that Mrs. Sullivan kept a ledger of her inventory with prices and descriptions and so on. Do you know where it is?"

I glanced over at the rabbit. "Well, Luna would probably know best, but I remember seeing it on her desk in her office upstairs. But that was years ago, when I was a child."

"That's usually where she kept it, even until the end. I imagine it's still there now," Luna chimed in.

Officer Reggie rubbed a hand on the back of his neck. "From what I was told, there isn't any evidence of the thief going upstairs into your gran's apartment, and I feel mighty uncomfortable poking around up there without permission. However, that ledger might give us some valuable information about the missing books," he said hopefully.

"And I'd help him out, but the office door is locked, and I don't have the keys. Or thumbs," Luna said, waving her paws at me. "It makes opening doors or carrying things annoyingly difficult."

"Well, if Luna thinks it's okay, and it will help the investigation, I'll run upstairs and grab it for you," I offered. "Granny's lawyer just gave me the keys to the shop."

"You'd be doing us a favor if you let us take a look. Don't worry, we'll have it back to you as soon as we make some copies for reference," Officer Reggie said with another of his charming, boyish smiles.

"Anything I can do to help," I said. "Give me two minutes."

I hurried up the stairs behind the front desk. As soon as I reached the second floor, the familiar smell of roses, sunshine, and old paper hit me. It smelled like Granny. It smelled like home. Part of me wanted to turn right and reacquaint myself with the cozy little apartment. The one I'd been reminiscing about. The one I'd been dreaming about making my own.

Instead, I turned left towards Granny's office and tried the knob. Locked, just like Luna said. I dug into my bag for the keys Nathaniel had given me and pulled them out. There was a slight hiccup. These were the shop keys. One for the front door, one for the back, but no keys for the living area upstairs. I bit my lip and looked around in case Officer Reggie had decided to follow me upstairs. Thankfully, he hadn't. For anyone else, this would be a problem, but not for me. I replaced the keys and rolled my shoulders back. I took a deep breath, centering myself, and then placed my hand on the doorknob. Closing my eyes, I focused on my magic. In a flash, the metal under my fingertips appeared in my mind's eye. It was like having a 3D image in front of me, but one I could manipulate. Slowly, I pushed each pin into the correct position, holding the rest in place with my magic. Even though this was a relatively simple lock, it still took me a minute. I hadn't opened a lock this way in a while. Finally, I gave the handle a little jiggle, and it turned under my hand. I smiled triumphantly and slipped inside.

Granny's desk was mostly tidy. The worn green ledger book I remembered from my childhood sat on one side of the desk next to a cup full of pens and a stack of books balanced precariously on the other. A small chalkboard nearly obscured by a colorful barrage of post-it notes hung on what seemed like the only space on the wall not covered in shelves. I ignored the bookshelves, filing cabinet, and other miscellaneous office clutter for the moment. There'd be time for all that later. If I actually ended up inheriting Spellbooks that is. I grabbed the ledger and was just about to take it downstairs when I paused.

Officer Reggie said there might be a valuable clue inside. At the very least, there should be a list of the stolen books. The very rare, *expensive* stolen books. A thought suddenly popped into my mind. If Nathaniel and Thaddeus had somehow colluded to give ownership of Spellbooks to my cousin, I wasn't about to go down without a fight. Not only would I come up with the best plan for running Sullivan's Spellbooks, but I'd also solve this case! How could Nathaniel reasonably hand the shop over to Thaddeus if I was the one who found and returned all the books?

Before I could change my mind, I flipped through the pages with my phone at the ready. I found one section labeled "Rare Books". This must be it! Quickly, I snapped photos of every page in the section. Luckily, there weren't too many, but I was sweating by the time I was done. Would Officer Reggie ask why I'd taken so long?

I snatched up the ledger and hurried to the door, shutting it carefully behind me. A thought occurred to me, and I took an extra minute to lock the door with my magic. If a thief broke in here once, it could happen again. I wasn't about to make the next robbery even easier.

Downstairs, I handed the ledger over to Reggie. "Here you go."

"Thanks for that," he said with a relieved smile. "If I can return the favor, all you have to do is shout."

I bit my lip, staring at the mess in the shop with my new investigative eyes. Maybe there was a clue here I could turn to my advantage? Something under the tossed piles of books caught my attention. "Sheriff Jackson didn't take Gideon with him? I thought he'd want to question him, especially given that Granny didn't have security cameras."

"Gideon?" Reggie asked, looking around. "Oh, you mean the gargoyle? No. Not a good idea. Gargoyles can be testy if they wake up somewhere unexpected."

"Testy? Radish ruckus, try downright destructive," Luna muttered.

Reggie shrugged but didn't contradict her. "Regardless, the sheriff plans on coming down just before sunset, so he'll be here when the gargoyle wakes up and he can question the little guy. Maybe he saw something that will point us towards the thief."

I considered his words. "Don't you think it's a better idea to have someone around who Gideon knows? I mean, it would be a shame for Gideon to misinterpret the sheriff's unexplained presence as being tied to the robbery and attack him."

Reggie rubbed his chin. "Hadn't thought of that, but you're right. I mean, the sheriff can take care of himself, but if there's no need...I don't suppose you're available tonight, are you?" he asked hopefully.

"I'd be happy to come back in," I said, glad my gambit had worked. Now, I'd get to hear Gideon's version of events firsthand. I was feeling like a detective already, and I'd only been on the case for a minute.

A relieved smile broke over Reggie's face, making my lips curve upward in response. "I'm sure he'll be glad to hear it. Let me just call him so he knows to expect you." Reggie pulled out his phone and stepped out the front door for some privacy. A moment later, he stuck his head back inside. "Remember, don't touch anything. Still an active crime scene, you know."

I held up both my hands in mock surrender. "Of course. Whatever you say." Reggie nodded and shut the door.

Luna sniffed. "That boy could learn a thing or two about the chain of evidence."

I chuckled. "And how many crimes have happened here in Havenwood?"

"Point taken," Luna admitted grudgingly. Her ears swiveled towards me. "How did the meeting with the lawyer go?"

"Not exactly how I expected," I admitted. As quickly as I could, I filled her in on Thaddeus, the competition Granny had created for the shop, and my suspicions about Thaddeus and Nathaniel Ravenscroft planning something.

"I don't care if he was Beatrice's family. I never liked that boy," Luna grumbled when I finished.

"Wait, you know Thaddeus?"

"Not well," Luna said. "He only visited a few times in the past three or four years. Just after his mother passed away, if memory serves. But he always seemed fixated on money. Enough was never enough, if you catch my meaning."

I nodded slowly. "Yeah, I know the type."

"Do you think he'll come around the shop?" Luna asked.

I shrugged. "Maybe? Nathaniel gave us both a set of keys, so it's a possibility."

"Then I think I'll stay here rather than the B&B. Someone has to watch the shop until Gideon wakes up," Luna said firmly.

"I thought you hated the hutch."

"I'll stay in the *shop*. Without that mangy excuse for a feline, it might even be a pleasant experience once more."

"I don't think that's a good idea," I said.

"Fluff and fur balls! Do you think I'm too old or too fat to outrun either a thief or your cousin?"

I held up my hands in protest. "I may be young, but even I know better than to answer that question. You do what you think is best, Luna."

The rabbit sniffed. "There may be hope for you yet."

Reggie stuck his head back in the door and shot me a thumbs up. "Sheriff says he'll meet you here around six. Does that work for you?"

"Sounds like a plan," I said. A thought occurred to me. "Hey, would it be okay if I looked at the back where the thief broke in? I promise not to touch anything."

Reggie nodded. "Be careful, though. There's a fair amount of broken glass. I wouldn't want to see you get hurt."

"Thanks for the warning. I'll look around and then let myself out. I think I need to grab an early dinner before I meet with the sheriff."

"If you're looking for something easy and fast, the Dragon's Den has good food. It's a little touristy, but the chef is legit, and the portions are huge," Reggie said, his boyish smile back in place.

"Thanks. I'll check it out."

"Great. And what should I do about... Hey! Where'd Luna go?" Reggie said, looking around for the rabbit. She must've taken the opportunity to slip away and hide.

I shrugged and kept my expression innocent. "Rabbits. Can't take 'em anywhere these days, am I right?"

Reggie chuckled and started looking for the disappearing rabbit as I moved towards the back of the shop. The only positive thing I could see was that the thief seemed to have only tossed books around near the front. The back of the shop looked pristine. That is, until I reached the sunroom Granny had converted into a reading room for her patrons. The door leading out to the yard was ajar. It had a smashed windowpane and glass covered the floor.

Hushed, angry voices drifted through the open door. That was odd. No one should be back there. I tiptoed towards the door, craning my neck to get a glimpse of who was outside the shop.

The Neighbor in the Oak

THADDEUS AND A YOUNG woman in a green dress that was much too light for the autumn nip in the air stood close together in the middle of the yard under a huge old oak tree. He gripped her upper arm and shook a finger in her face as he whispered aggressively at her. The young woman cringed away from him, looking close to tears.

Conscious of my newly self-appointed detective status and not wanting to leave fingerprints, I used my forearm to open the door and barged through without a second thought. There was no way that Granny would've stood for this behavior in her backyard, and I wouldn't either.

"What's going on out here? What are you doing?" I demanded loudly.

Thaddeus glowered at me and then released his hold on the young woman, who immediately backed away from him, rubbing at the spot where he'd held her. "None of your business," he said, his voice full of soft menace.

I wasn't about to back down from a bully, even if we were distantly related. "It is my business if it's happening at Spellbooks."

"It's not even your shop," Thaddeus said, taking a step towards me. The woman behind him whimpered softly and retreated another pace.

That little sound got my back up. I folded my arms over my chest and stared him down, channeling my best impression of Master Sergeant Edward Sullivan. "Not yet. Give me a week."

"Yeah, we'll see about that," Thaddeus snorted, walking by me towards the shop and deliberately jostling me with his shoulder.

I huffed in surprise at the juvenile behavior. "You can't go in there," I called after him.

He didn't stop walking, just spoke over his shoulder. "And why not? It's just as much my right to look around as it is yours. Besides, I haven't been here recently. Maybe the old place is completely changed. I doubt it, but it's my right to be here if I want to be."

"I think the police would disagree. You remember the break-in? Someone stole all the rare books?"

"I won't touch anything. I'm just going to look around."

"I don't think Officer Reggie will approve," I called.

Thaddeus just rolled his eyes. "We'll see about that," he said as he moved to the door, pulled it open wider, and hurried inside.

A little sniffle sounded from behind me. I turned to see the young woman curled in around her arm, trying and failing to hold back tears.

"Oh no, did he hurt you? I can—"

"No!" she interrupted me, throwing out a hand. "No, I'm okay. He...just surprised me with some bad news."

I moved slowly so as not to startle her and sat on the wooden bench that curved around the base of the oak tree. "Anything I can help with?" I asked, gently patting the bench next to me.

The young woman sank down on the bench with a mournful sigh. "Can you get rid of him?" she asked wistfully. A little hiccupping sob escaped her.

"Believe me, I'm doing my best," I murmured.

This close to her, I could see that her skin held a subtle tinge of the same leaf green as her dress. Her long hair was a deep walnut brown and had bits of twigs and leaves stuck in it. I wondered if she'd been climbing the tree before Thaddeus had accosted her. "He doesn't seem to make friends easily, that's for sure, but he isn't Beatrice Sullivan's only heir. I'm Harper Sullivan. Perhaps there's something I can do to help?"

The girl's eyes widened, and her hand flew to her mouth. "Oh, Beatrice mentioned you! She always said what a lovely child you were. She wasn't sure you'd ever come back to Havenwood. Not to stay, that is."

"You knew Granny Bea?" I asked, trying to wrack my memory to place this strange, somewhat wild woman in my memories and drawing an utter blank. "Who are you?"

"Oh, I'm sorry. How rude of me. I'm Thistle. Your grandmother let me live here."

I blinked in surprise. Granny's place was small, and she'd never shown an interest in any kind of romantic partner. Then there was the age difference. This woman couldn't be that much older than me, but Granny was...well, witches usually lived longer than a normal human, but it still wasn't polite to ask a lady her age. Let's just say she'd seen several presidents come and go, but how many was a mystery that not even I knew.

"I hadn't realized Granny, um, lived with someone," I said carefully.

Thistle chuckled through her tears. "No, I didn't live *with* your grandmother. I live here. In this oak. I'm a tree nymph."

My brain stuttered. Cognitively, I knew fantasy creatures populated Havenwood, but I'd never met a tree nymph during any of my visits. "Umm, it's nice to meet you," I said, offering my hand to shake.

Thistle ignored my hand and wrapped her arms around me in a giant hug that was over almost as soon as it had begun. "Nice to meet you, too. I'm glad at least one of Beatrice's heirs shares her kind nature." She sat back, a gentle smile on her beautiful face.

I brushed a hand through my hair, both pleased at the comparison and saddened about the reminder of Granny's passing. Perhaps I should've been used to it by now, but I just wasn't. To hide my feelings, I gestured at the tree. "I've never met a tree nymph before. How does it work? Living in a tree, I mean."

"Much like living in any other house, I expect," Thistle said. She swung her bare feet as she looked around the yard. "I do my work and then come home to my little island of tranquility."

"And what do you do for work?" I asked curiously.

Thistle gestured at the beautifully landscaped yard that was really more like a garden. "I take care of all this for Beatrice. I used to live in the woods, but the other nymphs weren't very nice. They were always playing tricks on me. So, I moved into the big city."

"Havenwood?" I asked, bemused.

"Yes," Thistle said earnestly. "When I first arrived, I lived in the cute little birch tree in the park's corner on Lorelai Lane, but people kept carving their names in my trunk or breaking off my branches. Do you know how disconcerting it is when you wake up at three in the morning to someone climbing your home?"

"I can only imagine," I said, sympathetically.

"Well, your grandmother was walking in the park one evening and saw me telling some rude young couple that my home was not the place to proclaim their summer love for each other. She stepped in and offered me her solitary oak in return for turning her yard into a garden, a reading sanctuary, as she put it. It sounded perfect. I moved in the next day and have been here ever since."

"That's a lovely story. So, this garden is as much your home as the bookshop was hers," I said, impulsively reaching across and grabbing her hand. "I do hope you'll stay."

Thistle sniffled and wiped her eyes. "That's not what the nasty man said. He told me I have to go. He plans to knock down the walls and expand the shop, right into my garden! My home will be destroyed, and I'll be forced to go back out into the forest." She waved a hand beyond Granny's garden, over the fence and towards the thick cluster of trees covered with brilliant foliage. A flash of light and a flicker of movement caught my eye. I squinted towards one of the nearest trees. A dark figure wearing a hat held a pair of binoculars in front of his face, and he trained them right on us. As soon as he saw me looking, he ducked behind the tree.

Disconcerted, I patted Thistle's hand. "That's not going to happen," I said, keeping my eyes on the forest, searching for any other signs of movement.

"Of course it is! Even the animals know! The birds haven't come back today, not with all the hullabaloo at the shop going on. People in and out all the time, scaring them off. I don't blame them if they never come back." Thistle let out a little moan and dropped her head into her hands.

A sudden thought occurred to me. I was supposed to be on the lookout for clues. Maybe Thistle saw something last night. "Thistle, I don't suppose you heard something last night? Saw someone breaking in? Possibly someone lurking around? You know, scoping the place out?" I asked, my eyes flicked back to the woods. Whoever was out there had vanished. Was

I being paranoid? Was the guy just some innocent bird watcher or was his motive more sinister?

She shook her head. "I was fast asleep all night, but that werewolf of a sheriff woke me up this morning, what with his tromping around. I'm not surprised the birds are all gone. I wouldn't be able to relax either when there's a werewolf on the prowl."

"I don't think Sheriff Jackson's exactly on the prowl," I demurred.

"You tell that to my birds. And now that horrible man is going to take over the shop, the garden is going to be destroyed, and we'll all have to move!" Her voice rose at the end in a mournful wail.

I patted her hand again. "Nothing is decided yet. I'm sure everything will turn out alright in the end."

"Do you really think so?" Thistle asked through a watery little smile.

"I know so," I said with more confidence than I felt.

A loud bang sounded, jerking both of our attention around to the shop. Thaddeus hammered his open hand on the broken door repeatedly, venting his frustration. Thistle squealed in terror. Right before my eyes, she leaned her shoulders against the tree and, quick as a thought, vanished inside. Officer Reggie stepped into the sunroom, his boyish smile gone and a stern expression on his face. Thaddeus paused mid-swing and then dropped his arm to his side and stormed off around the side of the shop.

"Everything okay out here?" Officer Reggie asked, sticking his head outside, looking uncharacteristically serious.

I nodded. "All good, thank you," I said, waving my hand lamely. How was I going to explain why I was sitting under a tree talking to myself?

"Good. I don't like the looks of that fella. I caught him moving some books around inside and had to tell him to beat it. I didn't think he'd take it so literally though," Reggie said, tipping his head to the door.

Apparently, the officer didn't need an explanation for my mildly bizarre behavior in the face of Thaddeus'. "Why was he moving things around? I thought it was still an active crime scene."

Officer Reggie scratched his head. "It is, and I told him as much when I caught him in there the first time. 'Don't go touching things', that's what I said. But did he listen? No siree." Reggie scowled at where Thaddeus had disappeared. "I might have to call the Sheriff and get him to bring an extra lock for the place."

"Well, I can promise I won't move anything unless I'm given the all clear," I said, drawing an x over my heart.

A genial smile crossed Reggie's face, chasing away the thunderclouds that had settled in the wake of Thaddeus' departure. "And your cooperation is much appreciated. Speaking of, I'd better get going. Oh! Don't forget about the Dragon's Den, now, you hear? Best enjoyed on an empty stomach," Reggie said, patting his own.

"Got it. I'll grab a bite there and then come back to meet the sheriff."

Officer Reggie gave me a thumbs up and then ducked back inside the shop, carefully locking the back door as he went. With the glass gone, I wasn't sure it would've stopped anyone with half a mind to enter. However, given Thaddeus' behavior, it was probably the principle of the matter.

I sighed and looked at my phone. There were just under two hours before my meeting with the sheriff and the clock was already ticking down towards Nathaniel Ravenscroft's decision on who would inherit the shop. I needed to come up with a plan to beat Thaddeus. Which meant adjusting my goal from "become a detective in an afternoon" to something that could actually win my great-grandmother's shop. A dull ache throbbed at the base of my skull. I should probably get some more sleep, but I needed to fill the gnawing pit in the center of my belly with something other than coffee and sugar. Because I was a girl who had her priorities straight, I pulled up the map app on my phone and typed in "Dragon's Den." Food first. Create a foolproof master plan second. Third, interrogate a gargoyle. Fourth, sleep. Was this a typical day in Havenwood, or was I just special?

Dragon Delicacies

HAVENWOOD WASN'T A VAST town, but it was still almost a twenty-minute walk from the shop to the Dragon's Den. I was ravenous by the time I reached the restaurant. The outside was a little kitschy for my taste. Someone carved the stone façade to be reminiscent of dragon scales. A grand arched entrance flanked by tall, matching dragon statues welcomed guests inside.

"Officer Reggie, what have you gotten me into?" I asked under my breath. The dragon statues suddenly tipped their heads back and let loose coordinated bursts of flame into the air. I yelped and jumped, my heart thundering. The door swung wide, and a smiling couple exited, walking past the statues without being turned into charred kebabs. They looked at me strangely as they walked towards their car. I gave them a weak little smile and hurried into the restaurant.

Whoever decorated this place definitely stayed on theme. Dragon skull chandeliers hung from the ceiling, casting a warm, ambient light over diners despite the toothy grins. Murals adorned the walls, depicting breathtaking fantasy landscapes, epic battles, and majestic creatures. Rustic wooden tables for large parties and cozy booths for smaller ones were scattered throughout the space, each with its own carved dragon motif. A bar dominated the center of the room. Across from it and covering almost an entire wall was a giant hearth full of dancing, heatless flames that somehow shifted between all the colors of the rainbow.

A cheerful hostess greeted me. "Table for one?" she asked, her blonde ponytail bobbing as she looked around at the dining area. It was too early for a dinner rush but was still surprisingly full.

I pointed at the bar. "Is it okay if I just sit at the bar? I don't want to take up a table if you're busy."

The hostess shrugged and smiled. "Whatever you like, hun."

"Thanks," I murmured and headed towards a tall, red leather stool. As soon as I slid myself up onto the seat, a bartender with an infectious smile plopped a coaster in front of me.

"I haven't seen you around here before," she said. "Passing through or moving in?"

"I'm not sure yet," I said honestly.

"Ah, to be young again," the bartender said, her smile widening. She held a hand across the bar. "If you decide to stay, I'm Aria. If you're just passing through, then I'm that outstanding bartender with a wicked sense of humor and impeccable mixology prowess."

I chuckled. "I'm Harper, and I would think of something witty to say if I wasn't so hungry."

Aria nodded knowingly. "I don't mind waiting for a comeback, but you should never have to wait too long for food when you're hungry. We've got a couple of good specials today. The Dragon's Breath Burger is huge. Flame-grilled beef topped with spicy jalapenos, smoky bacon, melted pepper jack cheese, and our chef's secret fiery dragon sauce on a toasted brioche bun served with a massive side of fries. If you're not a carnivore, then I'd recommend the Fairy Delight Salad. Greens, sweet berries, candied pecans, and crumbled feta cheese drizzled with a honey-lavender dressing that is out of this world." She pressed her fingertips to her lips and blew a chef's kiss into the air.

"They both sound good," I said. My stomach rumbled loudly. Embarrassed, I pressed a hand to it in a silent appeal for it to behave. It didn't and gurgled again, louder this time.

Aria winked at me. "It sounds like its burger time, am I right?"

"The burger would be great," I admitted. "But could you put some extra bacon on it?"

"A girl after my own heart," Aria replied, shooting me a thumbs up. "What do you want to drink?"

"What've you got back there? Other than what I hope is incredible fire insurance?"

"Oh, that?" Aria said, pointing at the glowing hearth. "Depending on who's asking, it's either superb lighting by a guy who used to do Broadway shows or magic. I'll let you decide which." She winked at me. I wondered if that was her way of testing out the waters with me or a little tongue-in-cheek banter for those in the know about Havenwood's secret. Aria slid a drink menu over the bar to me. "While you have a look at that, I'll put your order in. Otherwise, you might wither away to nothing before my eyes."

"Thanks," I said with a chuckle. The menu was comprehensive and creative. There were drinks on there like the Wyvern's Elixir, Pixie's Potion, and Dragon's Blood Punch. Reading through the menu sparked an idea.

Aria returned a moment later. "Find anything you like?" she asked.

"I think I'll just have some water for now, but do you have some paper and a pen I could borrow?"

She quirked an eyebrow. "Need to make a list of all the necessary dragon-hunting supplies? Because I can tell you the burger comes cooked." She cupped a hand around her mouth and stage whispered. "It's also beef, not dragon meat. I promise. We'd never do that to an endangered species." Another enigmatic smile accompanied her words. I wondered if she enjoyed poking her toe over the line and hinting at the truth of Havenwood. She seemed to.

I laughed. "No but reading through your menu gave me an idea. With this jetlag, I don't want to forget it."

"Nice to meet a fellow messy thinker. Let me get that for you." Aria disappeared into the back and returned a moment later with the pen and paper.

As she passed it over to me, I noticed an intricate Celtic tattoo on her wrist. "That's a beautiful tattoo," I said, accepting the writing materials.

"Thanks. The guy who did it has a little shop over on Arcadia Avenue. It's called Wildwood Ink if you want to check it out. Nice guy, but a better artist."

"Is it next to Sullivan's Spellbooks by any chance?" I asked.

Aria's eyes went wide, and she nodded. "It is. Have you been by to see Finn?"

"No, but my great-grandmother owned Spellbooks. Beatrice Sullivan?"

Aria nodded. "I met her a time or two around town. She was a nice lady. Always willing to help out and lend a hand. I heard what happened. Such a shame. I'm sorry for your loss."

"Thanks. I think she was ready, though. Lived a full life, you know?"

"That's all any of us can hope for." Aria tapped the bar. "Let me get that water for you."

I grabbed the pen and started scribbling a list as soon as she walked away. When Thistle told me Thaddeus planned to expand the shop and destroy the garden in the process, something felt so off about it. Wrong. But not in the "it's a poor plan" kind of way. In fact, it was probably an excellent plan from a business point of view. But it wasn't the *right* one for Spellbooks.

What the shop needed was something like what the Dragon's Den served up, and I don't mean the burgers. The restaurant walked the line between mundane and magical with the ease of a tightrope artist. I needed to do the same with Spellbooks by creating an atmosphere of magical allure that would draw in tourists and locals alike.

My pen flew across the page as I did a brain dump onto the paper, writing down every idea I could. Good, bad, ridiculous, improbable, it didn't matter. It all went on the paper. By the time my food arrived, my paper was already full of every notion I could think of for Spellbooks.

Aria hadn't been lying. The burger was enormous and delicious. I set my paper to the side and gave the burger my full attention, enjoying every bite until all that remained were traces of the delicious sauce on my fingertips which I licked clean before wiping them on a napkin. As I munched my way through the fries, I pulled out my phone to examine the photos I'd taken of Granny Bea's ledger. Each entry included the title, author, publisher, and edition. She'd also included a short, physical description such as a worn cover or stained title page. The final two columns showed the evaluation of price and the price at which it was sold. I let out a low whistle. Granny Bea had made some lucrative deals in her time.

I picked out the entries where the last column was empty. Presumably, these were the books that had been stolen. There were nine books not marked as sold, and I jotted down the titles on the back of my brainstorming sheet. It surprised me when I recognized a couple of titles. Apparently, Granny Bea owned a second edition of *Alice's Adventures in Wonderland* and a third edition of *The Hobbit.* My mouth dropped open when I finally deciphered her notes and realized it was a signed copy. Had Granny Bea met J.R.R. Tolkien? I wondered how that meeting would've gone. I imagined her giving him a piece of her mind about some plot point or another and grinned. I was curious and quickly googled the approximate worth of those two books. They weren't as ludicrously expensive as a signed first edition, which I discovered could range into the millions, but each was worth at least a couple of thousand. Nothing to sneeze at, but would someone really break into a shop and risk jail time for that amount of money? The obvious answer was yes, but something felt off.

I extended my internet search to the other unsold books and turned up exactly zilch, although, given the titles, I wasn't exactly surprised. They all appeared to be magical at first glance. From my experience, magical beings rarely defaulted to technology. If you wanted to buy an ancient grimoire for example, you didn't search Amazon or eBay. You went to the local book dealer who knew a guy who knew a guy, and, eventually, you tracked down the item. Speaking of grimoires, Granny Bea had a couple listed as unsold in her ledger. There was also an alchemical opus on transmutations, a meteorological compendium, a book on astral divination, something called the *Enigma Codex,* and an entry labeled "Serpent's Scroll." I wondered if that was a title or a description. People didn't exactly walk around carrying scrolls these days and, if it was a scroll, wouldn't it be fragile? I knew the Egyptians were famous for their scrolls, but Granny Bea couldn't possibly own a three-thousand-year-old scroll. Could she? No, it had to be something else.

As my internet search reached a dead end, I drew a line under the list of books and paused, my pen hovering above the page. It was all good to gather information about *what* was missing, but I was just as interested in *who* was behind the theft. No, I was more interested in that. Perhaps I should've started with a list of suspects first. My borrowed pen hovered above the paper. Who did I really think was behind this?

Nathaniel Ravenscroft was her lawyer and would likely have a good idea of her assets. But he also had keys to the shop, so why break in? I jotted his name down anyway and then drew an arrow, linking him to the next name. Thaddeus. Other than acting like a jerk, I had no real reason to suspect him, but there had definitely been something going on between the two of them back at the lawyer's office. I tapped the pen against my chin and then scribbled down two more names. Oswald and Hortense Puddleton. As owners of a competing bookshop, they would know the value of rare books. Not only that, but stealing them might also cripple Granny's business, giving them a two-for-one deal.

My pen hovered above the paper as my list of obvious suspects dried up. Who else could be responsible? I thought back to my meeting with the Puddletons. Was it possible Oswald cut himself on the shattered glass in the shop? If not him, then maybe someone else? I added 'anyone with a cut' to my list. And what about the cat? It was still missing. Could the thief have taken the bookshop cat in addition to the books? No, that was silly. Wasn't it?

I reached back towards my plate for another salty potato wedge, only to realize I'd somehow finished the entire pile of fries. At least my stomach was no longer growling.

Aria walked over and I flipped my list of suspects over, a blush creeping up my cheeks. I didn't want her to think I was accusing anyone. "You look like you won," she said as she swept my plate away.

"What?"

"Your list," Aria tipped her head at the paper. "Any dastardly plans?"

"Dastardly? Me?" I said, my face burning.

Aria craned her neck, reading from the page. "A mad hatter's tea party? That sounds fun. Are you a party planner or something?"

"Oh, this? Not really. Just some ideas I have. Nothing dastardly, I promise," I said in a rush.

"Well, that's good to know. I always like to know in advance if I've inadvertently aided in a crime, but it looks like I dodged the bullet today. Come back sometime. I'd like to know how it goes," she said.

I slid off the stool. "I definitely will. And thank the chef for me. That burger was the best I've had in years."

"He'll be happy to hear it. You have a good night now, you hear? And if your messy thinking ends up making millions, I wouldn't mind a shout out in the movie, book, or whatever it is you're working on."

I chuckled. "You got it."

Whispers of Wizardary

The walk back to Spellbooks was slower than the one to the Dragon's Den. I blamed the burger, but, in reality, it was just me. My mind was whirling with possibilities for the shop. I turned them over in my mind, examining each from all angles and sorting them into different categories. There was a "nope, that's crazy" section, an "improbable, but fun" one, and "oh yeah, *definitely*" pile. Whatever was in that burger's secret sauce must've been magic, because my mind felt like it was working at hyper speed.

I was surprised when I looked up and saw I was on Arcadia Avenue, just outside the Dusty Tome. Mr. Puddleton frowned at me through the glass door, his giant mustache quivering with the ferocity of his scowl. I smiled cheerfully and gave him a little wave. Not even the grumpy competition could bring me down right now, not when all the good ideas were flowing like a river that had just burst through a dam. He flipped the sign in the window to read 'closed', then winced as his gauze bandage caught on the wire hook, half pulling it off the palm of his hand.

I frowned, slowing my pace. The bandage looked relatively new, given its color and lack of staining. However, Mr. Puddleton didn't look like the type of man who engaged in physical labor if he could help it. So how had he hurt himself? Perhaps breaking through the window of Spellbooks? He was the competition, after all. I stopped, staring at him contemplatively through the window as he fought to release his bandage. When he noticed me staring, he scowled, but his inattention to his task caused the cuff of his shirtsleeve to catch on the hook as well, nearly pulling the sign off the door.

My mind whirled as I left him there, fighting with the consequences of his passive-aggressive sign flipping. Mr. Puddleton might have a motive, but did he have the opportunity to break in? What about the means? I shook my head, mentally chastising myself. I'd always loved reading a good mystery book, but never imagined finding myself in the position to solve a case on my own without an all-knowing author pulling the strings behind the scenes. Right now, everyone who was in town could be the culprit. I'd have to narrow down the pool by looking at hard facts. Evidence. And while a bandaged hand was definitely suspicious, given the circumstances, it didn't necessarily mean Mr. Puddleton was guilty of breaking into Spellbooks. However, something about the surly bookshop owner niggled at me. Was it just the bandage or had my subconscious identified something my overly tired brain hadn't realized yet? I looked up in surprise to find the sun was setting fast. I tried to put Mr. Puddleton from my mind as I increased my speed. I needed to get back to the shop, so I didn't miss a word Gideon said.

Sheriff Jackson stood outside the bookshop, glancing between his watch and the sun as I rushed up. "There you are. Good. Just in time."

"Hello Sheriff. I hope I haven't kept you waiting."

"No, your timing is perfect, but I wish I had better news to report. We haven't caught a break yet, but we're working on it," Sheriff Jackson said, holding the door wide for me.

I stepped into the cool, dry interior of the shop, the smells of ink and paper welcoming me in with the same nostalgic warmth I felt when I smelled my mother's chocolate chip cookies. "What do you mean?" I asked.

The sheriff followed me into the shop and flipped on the lights. "Well, we took all the photos and sent the fingerprints off to the lab. We're lucky because we have a local one. It usually handles the excess load from the bigger cities, but I asked Silas to put a rush on these. We should have them back in a day. Two at the most."

"Isn't that rather fast?" My mother enjoyed a variety of crime dramas, and even though they turned around those results within each forty-minute episode, I knew that wasn't how the real world worked.

Sheriff Jackson nodded. "It is, but Silas is a sylph. He's an air elemental spirit, or rather, his mother was. He's...a little odd. Doesn't like the big city and all the pollution. But he's incredibly efficient and thorough."

"Well, if you think things are going in the right direction, that's a good thing. What do we do now?" I asked, gesturing to the mess in the shop.

"Wait for the gargoyle to wake up. I don't want anything disturbed until we've heard his account of what happened."

A rustling of papers caught my attention, and I looked down to see the small statue of the gargoyle flexing his wings underneath the discarded books.

"Ah, here we are then. Why don't you stand here so he can see you first?" The sheriff waved me into position. "Remember, try to keep him calm."

"Got it," I said.

Gideon spluttered and shoved the pages off him. "Where are you, you lily-livered, bed-wetting, son of a goat herder? Hamsters! Elderberries! The whole lot! You're all of those and more besides! Why I oughta—" The gargoyle fought free of his literary prison and popped up into the air, flapping his leathery wings and spinning in a circle in search of the missing thief.

I held up my hands, raising my voice to be heard over the noise. "Gideon. Gideon! It's me! Harper. You remember? Harper Sullivan? Beatrice's great-granddaughter."

He spun to face me, a scowl crinkling his features for a moment, before recognition dawned. "Harper?" he asked, squinting at me. "You're taller than I remember."

"It's been a few years," I admitted. Gideon looked the same as I remembered him. About the size of a medium dog, he was a mottled granite gray from the tops of his pointy bat-like ears to the tips of his sharpened talons. Tiny scales covered every inch of his body except for his squashed nose and slitted eyes. It looked like stoney fur from a distance, but each scale was sharp enough to leave a nasty cut if Gideon wasn't careful. I couldn't help but grin as I recalled the time Granny couldn't find a knife and was late for the Fourth of July picnic. In desperation to beat Aunty Agatha in some bizarre bet, she used Gideon to chop vegetables for her salad, only to discover that gargoyle scales will go right through the carrots and the cutting board and the counter. Needless to say, Aunty Agatha beat Granny for the first time that year. Speaking of Aunty Agatha, I made a mental note to go visit her soon.

A grating noise sounded, drawing my attention back to the matter at hand. Gideon yawned, tiny fangs protruding up from his lower lip. His leathery-looking wings, which had been solid stone only moments before, fluttered as he settled himself on the front counter facing me.

"Harper," Gideon said like he was tasting the name in his mouth.

"Yes, and Sheriff Jackson is here as well." I pointed over the gargoyle's shoulder at the officer of the law. The gargoyle spun to look before refocusing on me. "We wanted to talk to you about what happened here last night."

"What happened?" Gideon asked.

"That's what we're asking you," I replied.

"No, that's what I'm asking *you*, because I don't know."

I furrowed my brow. "What do you mean?"

Gideon raised a wing and let it drop in what I took to be a gargoyle shrug. "I mean, it was a normal night. Well, as normal as this town gets, anyway. I rotated from my post outside to the one inside, just the way Beatrice always liked. That is, before she..." The little creature trailed off, snuffling softly. He hid his head under one wing, using the other to wipe his face.

"I know," I said, patting him carefully on the shoulder, so I didn't get cut on his scales. "I miss her, too."

"She made a special door for me in the shop. Rotates and everything so I could spend the day inside if I wanted. I can't tell you how awful it is to wake up to find a bird made its nest in your mouth. Again. Spitting feathers all day, I tell you!"

"Granny Bea was a special lady. We all miss her terribly, but this is why it's so important we figure out what happened last night."

"What happened?" Gideon asked.

"Not this again," Sheriff Jackson groaned. He pushed off the wall where he'd been leaning and jerked a thumb towards the shattered display case. "Someone broke in last night and made off with the most valuable books in the shop. Did you see anything?"

"Nope, not a thing," Gideon said, shaking his head emphatically.

Sheriff Jackson blew out a breath, making his thick mustache dance in the gust of air. "Well, I guess we couldn't expect to get that lucky," he muttered.

"But I heard something," Gideon added as if he hadn't been interrupted.

I leaned forward. "What do you mean?"

Gideon cupped a taloned hand around an ear. "I *heard* something. Gargoyles have great hearing. It was just before sunrise. I was outside, watching the last of the stars disappear, when I heard breaking glass. I thought Luna or Mr. Wigglesworth had knocked something over, but I went inside to check, anyway. Mr. Wigglesworth was curled up in the window right there," Gideon said, pointing towards the front window. "He was fast asleep, so I patrolled the rest of the shop. That's when I found the broken window and the back door ajar. I thought someone had broken in, but I couldn't see anyone. Another crash sounded from inside, so I flew back in here. No one was around besides Mr. Wigglesworth. He had his back up and was hissing at the rare book display like someone stole his milk. Just as I turned, the first rays of the sun hit me, and I felt the change coming. My wings started to turn and, as I crashed to the floor, I knocked into someone. I know it was a someone because they grunted and cursed at me, but no one was there. The last thing I remember is the sound of the back door closing. Then the change took me. Next thing I know, I wake up, and you two are here."

"Interesting," Sheriff Jackson said. "It sounds like the thief knew of Beatrice's security system, aka Gideon here, but perhaps miscalculated the timing to make a clean getaway."

"Or something spooked him into entering before Gideon turned to stone this morning," I said.

"Perhaps," the sheriff mused. "Gideon, you said you crashed into the thief. Did your scales cut him?"

Gideon shrugged. "Maybe?"

"Is it okay with you if I look?" the sheriff asked.

Gideon spread his arms and wings wide. "Sure."

He took a small flashlight out of his pocket. "Where did you knock into this invisible thief?"

Gideon pointed towards his back. I peered over the sheriff's shoulder as he ran the light slowly across the gargoyle's scales.

"There!" Sheriff Jackson exclaimed, pointing at a dark, rusty brown tip of a couple of scales. "That could be blood."

"Maybe," I said doubtfully.

"Only one way to know, and that's to get it tested. Gideon, I'm afraid you'll have to come with me so we can do this properly down at the station."

"But who will watch the shop while I'm gone?" Gideon said anxiously.

"We'll lock it up tight, and I'll send Johanna over to check on it when she does her rounds. It'll be okay. We'll take a sample and then get you back here as soon as possible."

Gideon looked at me imploringly, but I gave him a firm nod. "You'd better go with the sheriff. This could be our best chance to identify the culprit."

"Fine," Gideon grumped.

The sheriff opened the door and waited for both Gideon and me to exit before turning off the lights. He shut and locked the front door behind us.

"Can you find your way, Miss Sullivan?" he asked courteously.

I nodded. "I'm staying at the Enchanted Oasis. It's a short walk. I'll be fine."

"Very well then. Gideon, you're with me." The sheriff turned and marched towards his cruiser parked in front of the shop. Gideon shot me one last look before flying after the sheriff. They drove off, leaving me simultaneously better informed than I had been an hour ago, but also more confused.

"Psst!"

I looked around for the voice.

"Down here," Luna said, sticking her head out between two of the potted plants in front of the shop.

"Luna! How long have you been there?" I asked.

"Long enough to hear everything Gideon told you. Fluff and fur balls! Something doesn't add up about his story."

"For you too?" I asked. "What's bugging you?"

"Who tossed the shop? According to Gideon, the thief broke in, smashed the display case, and left after running into our flying security system, but shut the door behind him."

"Or her," I added.

"Or her," Luna conceded. "My question is: who tossed the shop? There's no time for it in Gideon's timeline."

"Maybe the thief came back."

"Maybe, but a little unlikely, don't you think?" Luna said doubtfully.

"What has me stumped is how the thief carried that many books out the door in such a short time. According to Granny's ledger, there should've been nine in the case. How big were they?"

"Different sizes, but some looked fairly heavy," Luna said.

"How does a thief carry all those books out of the shop while running away from a gargoyle and still close the door behind them?" I asked.

"Maybe the thief ran outside, waited for the change to take Gideon, and then went about the robbery as planned."

"Plausible, I guess. But then why toss the shop? It's not like Gideon was going to wake up soon. The thief wouldn't need to rush. Why throw things everywhere?"

"His mama didn't teach him manners?" Luna asked.

"Well, he was committing larceny, so, yeah, I'm gonna guess etiquette isn't high on his list of virtues. But even with all those gaps, I still have one question."

"What's that?"

"Where's Mr. Wigglesworth? If he was in the shop at the time of the robbery and Gideon heard the door close, where'd he go? Did the person who was feeding him take him?"

Luna twitched an ear. "Agatha fed him, but she'd set up one of those automatic cat feeder things. You know, the kind that you can set and forget? She'd come on the weekends to top it up. But she took a road trip to Vermont two days ago. Something about a maple syrup festival, I think. I don't know when she's coming back."

"So, who was going to feed the cat? And more to the point, where is he?"

Luna thumped one back paw repeatedly against the ground. "To be honest, that's one mystery I don't mind *not* solving. The furry menace can stay lost for all I care."

After a quick discussion, Luna insisted on staying at the shop until Gideon could return, and I didn't have the energy to argue with her after my long day. During the entire walk back to the bed-and-breakfast, questions pounded through my head in time with my footsteps. Why couldn't Gideon see the thief? Why leave and come back? Why toss the shop? And, above all, what did the missing cat have to do with it all?

I still didn't have the answers as I tumbled into the sofa bed in Bella's room. She was out with friends, but Honey confirmed she'd said I was welcome to crash in her room as long as I needed. Honestly, I probably could've fallen asleep standing up if a bed hadn't been available, but I was thankful one was. Sleep wouldn't give me the answers I wanted, but it was a nice consolation prize after my long day.

Schemes and Scones

I WOKE UP TO sunlight and sweet birdsong spilling through the lace curtains of Bella's bedroom, which was both lovely and disorienting. It took me a moment of listening for reveille played over loudspeakers before I remembered I wasn't back on the base with Mom and Dad. I blinked the sleep from my eyes and indulged in a languorous stretch before greeting the first morning of my new life in Havenwood. Where birds sang outside my window, and someone was baking fresh pastries nearby.

I sat bolt upright in bed. Honey. I was at the Enchanted Oasis, and Honey was making breakfast! This was no time to be lazing about in bed, not with her pastries on a plate instead of in my stomach. I rushed to get ready, almost forgetting to brush my hair in the process because the smell was that intoxicating. The burger from the night before was but a distant memory, virtually eclipsed entirely by the scent of Honey's baking.

I pulled on a fresh pair of jeans and a striped sweater, hurriedly running a brush through my thick, wavy hair before I dashed downstairs. Antonio and Honey converted the large dining room into a gorgeous breakfast buffet. Early morning sunlight filtered through delicate lace curtains, casting a gentle glow on the soft pastels and whimsical décor artfully selected to create a peaceful way to greet the morning. A handful of tables dressed in crisp white linen were scattered through the long room, each topped with small centerpieces of fresh wildflowers. Honey had obviously been up early, preparing for when her guests stirred from their beds.

The only people in the dining room this early were a couple that looked as if they could've been newlyweds. They were sipping coffee together in a corner, appearing as if nothing could disturb their bliss. The aroma of freshly brewed coffee lured me to the beautifully carved wooden sideboard, showcasing not only a carafe of the rich, dark brew but also several aromatic teas and delectable breakfast treats. Delicate porcelain platters held freshly baked pastries, still warm from the oven. A colorful fruit display, artfully arranged, added a vibrant touch of color. Glass jars filled with granola, nuts, and dried fruit sat next to bowls of chilled, creamy yogurt, offering a satisfying start to the day.

I poured myself a cup of coffee and added a generous splash of fresh cream as a morning treat. Honey stuck her head into the breakfast room just as I settled at a table with my coffee and a heaping plate of fruit to justify my double helping of cranberry and white chocolate scones.

"Oh! You're up early. I hope you slept well. That sofa bed is comfier than it looks, isn't it?" Honey said cheerfully as she entered the room. She waved at the couple as they drifted out, leaving us alone with the fabulous breakfast.

"I don't think I've had a better night's sleep since...well, ever," I said honestly. "I didn't see Bella though. I hope I didn't displace her."

Honey waved a hand. "No, she stayed at her friend's house to give you some space to recover from your long flight. Jetlag isn't pleasant at the best of times and on top of the news you got about the bookshop?" Honey *tsked* and shook her head.

"It wasn't exactly how I planned to spend my first day back in Havenwood," I admitted.

"Well, today is a new day," Honey said, perching on the edge of the chair across from me. "What are your plans? Something fun I hope."

"Honestly, I'd like to be in the shop, doing some work towards reopening Spellbooks, but the whole police investigation thing means it's not an option."

"I said 'fun'. Spending all day in a dusty old bookshop doesn't sound like fun," Honey admonished.

"Depends on who you ask," I said, smiling over my coffee cup.

"Well, if you're determined to make today all about books, you could head over to the library. One of the local book clubs holds their meetings there every week about eleven." She checked her watch. "Which gives you plenty of time to have your breakfast and a leisurely stroll into town."

"Maybe," I said, drawing out the word. After the eventful day yesterday, I needed to dedicate some time to develop my plan for Spellbooks in order to beat Thaddeus. Perhaps I'd even drop by the police station to see how the investigation was progressing.

"It'd be a good way to re-familiarize yourself with the town. Meet some locals. Get into the book scene here," Honey cajoled.

"I suppose you're right," I said.

"Mama, I hope you aren't pestering anyone," a bright, female voice said. I turned to see a young woman that looked like a softer version of Antonio, but with Honey's caramel eyes, enter the breakfast room. There were hints in her face of a child I'd played with years ago.

"Bella?" I asked.

"Harper! Mama and Papa said you came back for a visit. It's so good to see you again," Bella said, closing the distance between us. She opened her arms like it had been just a few days instead of a few years since we'd seen each other. I hugged her back, feeling the warmth of reunion I'd been expecting since I arrived in Havenwood but hadn't quite manifested until this moment.

Bella pulled back to arm's length, still holding my hands in hers. "I'm so glad you're here! It's been an age! Did you sleep okay?"

"Just fine, thanks. I appreciate you letting me crash in your room."

"Anytime! It's so good to see you. How long are you staying?"

I wavered a hand back and forth. "I'm not exactly sure. I'd planned to move into Spellbooks as soon as I got here, but with everything that's going on, I don't think that will be an option for at least a week." I didn't want to bring down the morning's mood, but a cynical little voice in my head whispered that I might never be able to move into Spellbooks.

Harper squeezed my hands excitedly. "Oh good! That means you can stay here with me. It'll be like when we were kids and constantly sneaking off to have sleepovers."

"No, I couldn't take advantage of your hospitality like that," I protested.

"You wouldn't be. In fact, I *insist* you stay. There. Is that better?" she asked.

I grinned and nodded. "Well, when you put it like that, it would be rude to say no."

"It would, wouldn't it? It's a good thing you're not, then." She winked at me and dropped my hands. "Look, I'd love to catch up properly, but mornings are crazy here. Are you free this afternoon?" she asked eagerly.

I nodded. "At the moment, I don't have any plans. Your mother suggested a book club at the library a little later, but that's about it."

"Perfect! Then I'm laying claim to your afternoon. There is a Renaissance Faire in town this week. You remember the kind? Everyone dresses up in costumes and pretends it's the sixteenth century. There're shops, plays, food, and even a joust. I've been meaning to go again, and today's the last day. Well, they technically run until tomorrow afternoon, but today would be better for me. Are you interested?"

"Sounds fun," I said. Bella's enthusiasm was infectious. "But I don't have anything to wear. I left all my sixteenth century dresses back on the base with Mom and Dad."

Bella put her hands on her hips, and a disapproving frown furrowed her tanned face. "How very dare you!" She laughed, breaking the illusion. "Don't worry. I'm sure we've got something around here. But you could wear what you have on now and everyone would just assume you're a tourist."

"Well, count me in," I said.

"Great," Bella said, pulling me in for another hug. "I'm off around two. See you then?"

"Okay," I said as she bounced out of the room.

"Oh, good morning, Papa," Bella said at the door, stopping to give her father a squeeze before dancing off to do her morning work.

"Buon giorno, amorina," Antonio said, smiling fondly after his daughter. "Good morning to you, too, amore mia." He leaned down to give his wife a kiss on the cheek. "And hello to you as well, Harper."

"Good morning, Antonio. I love what you and Honey have done around here," I said, gesturing to the breakfast spread.

"Ah, that deliciousness is all thanks to my lovely wife. Although Bella is turning into quite the little baker in her own right."

"But the decorations are all Antonio's," Honey said. "See that sideboard with all the carved woodland creatures? He just finished that last month. One of his best pieces yet."

Antonio puffed up with pride at his wife's words. "Just a little something to keep the hands busy, but it turned out decently well, I suppose."

"Decent? Antonio, it's gorgeous!" I didn't even need to play up my admiration. It truly was a stunning piece of craftsmanship. Something niggled at the back of my head, but I debated asking for a favor of the talented woodcrafter.

"You've got a look about you," Antonio observed. "What's on your mind?"

I sighed. "I don't want to put you out, but I was wondering if you'd be willing to make a birdhouse for me. Well, not for me, exactly. For a friend."

"Made a friend already, have you? One that you want to give a gift to?" Antonio gave me a suggestive wink.

I shook my head and waved my hands in front of my body, stopping that train of thought before it left the station. "Nothing like that. Granny let a tree nymph move into the oak behind the shop. Do you know her? Thistle? Anyway, given recent events, she's worried that the birds will move on to quieter locales. She seems shy and a little on edge. I'd like to give her something to reassure her she still has a place at Spellbooks if she wants it."

"That's very thoughtful of you," Honey said.

"It wouldn't have to be anything fancy," I said, already doubting myself. I didn't want to put the DeLucas out, especially as they were already being so generous.

Antonio stroked his chin. "I could use a shorter project, and I already have some ideas I think your friend will like."

"Thank you so much, Antonio. That's very kind of you," I said.

A wide smile broke over his face. "Any friend of yours is a friend of ours. Consider it done."

"Speaking of considering things done, how are those dishes going?" Honey asked, with a twinkle in her eye.

Antonio groaned but caught up his wife's hand, performing a courtly bow over it before kissing the back. "Consider those done as well, amore." He gave me a wave as he headed for the kitchen.

Honey stood. "I'd better check. You know, to see he actually makes it there and doesn't get distracted along the way. Have a lovely day and definitely check out the book club. I think you'd enjoy it."

"I'll think about it, but right now, I'm enjoying this coffee and your scones. Seriously, what is your secret?"

Honey leaned over and wiggled her fingers over my plate. A soft shower of glitter fell from her fingertips, disappearing as soon as it touched the white chocolate and cranberry treats masquerading as breakfast. "Magic," she whispered, and then winked at me.

I scooped up the warm scone and popped a bite into my mouth. It melted into buttery, sweet crumbles that nearly made me moan. Someone else might have discounted Honey's actions as the flair of a committed owner of a supposedly enchanted B&B, but I knew better. Magic scones baked by a brownie didn't happen every day. However, if I ended up staying in Havenwood, maybe they could become a regular occurrence.

Suddenly, I had extra motivation to beat my cousin. One, win the shop. Two, the whole pride thing. Three, magical scones. If that wasn't a trifecta worth fighting for, I didn't know what was.

Pirates in the Library

I'D ANTICIPATED LINGERING OVER my coffee, but either the caffeine, the sugar rush from the scones, or the magic Honey infused into her baking made me almost bounce in my seat, ready to get on with the day. Needing to burn off some of the excess energy, I followed Honey's advice and decided to explore the town before dropping by the book club. The walk would do me good after the generous helping of scones, and if the book club turned out to be a bust, at least I'd have a quiet place to contemplate my next step towards securing Spellbooks.

It was a pleasant morning, but there was still the bite of crisp autumn in the wind. I dashed up to my room to grab a jacket and my favorite green scarf before setting off for the library. The brisk walk warmed me up as my mind wandered. Did the sheriff confirm it was blood on Gideon's scales? Were there any other clues that he'd discovered since last night? How could I ask him any of that without seeming to pry? Had Luna uncovered anything else in her overnight vigil at the shop? I should probably swing by after this and check on her. And where was Mr. Wigglesworth? I felt an uncanny sense of protection for a feline I'd never met, but he was Granny's. I wasn't about to let some creature she'd taken in get lost or hurt. Besides, even though it was still warm enough, winter was coming soon, and New England winters could be bitterly cold.

I was so distracted by my wandering thoughts that I hadn't realized I'd walked straight past the library until I was almost a block beyond it. I turned, hurrying back the way I'd come, but by the time I slipped into the lobby, it was ten past eleven.

A woman with hair so blonde it was nearly white looked up from behind the desk. Her eyes were a heavenly blue and her skin was so pale she seemed to almost glow from within. A stack of books was piled by her elbow as she scanned them one at a time. The computer next to her dinged and chirruped happily with each returned book. A sign at the front of the desk said, "Librarian on duty: Martha Morningstar".

The librarian, presumably Martha, stopped her work and smiled as I approached and asked in a soft, musical voice. "How can I assist you today?"

I pushed my disheveled hair out of my eyes, feeling even more rumpled next to the pristinely coiffed librarian. "I'm looking for the book club. I was told they meet here at eleven?"

Martha pointed down a hall. "They're in the reading room, but I think they've already started. Have you read this week's book?"

A rush of heat flooded my cheeks, and I shifted from foot to foot. "Not exactly. I just arrived in town. My great-grandmother owned Sullivan's Spellbooks. I was hoping to meet some of the book lovers in town."

"Oh, you're Beatrice's granddaughter. Harper, right? She talked about you often. It's lovely to meet you. My name is Martha." The librarian's greeting was so sincere that all my nerves about being considered an unwanted intruder simply evaporated.

"Nice to meet you, Martha. You knew my Granny?"

Martha's laugh was a tinkling delight. "Knew her? She was a staple here. A pillar of the community. She'd come down every Sunday morning and read stories to the children while tired parents got to enjoy a cup of coffee without having a toddler tug on them. Why, her version of *The Gruffalo* was a sight to behold!" Martha shifted her eyes to both sides before waving me closer and cupping a hand around the side of her mouth. "Between you and me, I think the parents enjoyed Beatrice's antics as much as the children," she whispered.

A little warm spark lit within my heart at Martha's story. Maybe I could carry on Granny's legacy, not just in the shop, but also in the community. It was something to consider.

Martha rose gracefully to her feet. "Now, let me show you the way. Best not to get lost on your first day."

"Thank you," I said gratefully.

Martha led me down a hall, turning left at the third open doorway. The cozy little room was filled with a handful of people settled into comfortable chairs and chatting excitedly. A folding table sat in the corner, topped with a pitcher of water and one of those chunky coffee pots where you pressed the button on top and steaming brew sputtered out the spout. Somehow, it always seemed stronger coming out than when it had been put in, although there was no logical reason for it.

"I hadn't realized this week's reading was so thrilling," Martha said as she entered the noisy room.

One woman turned at the librarian's words. She was an older lady, silver hair curled to brush her sharp cheekbones just under horn-rimmed glasses, emphasizing her wide, intelligent eyes. A rather eccentric purple hat decorated with violet and indigo flowers perched at a jaunty angle on her curls while a heavily embroidered scarlet scarf draped over her shoulders. Chunky jewelry in turquoise, azure, and lime green accented her unusual style. "Oh, we haven't even begun to discuss that yet. Why would we talk about a figment of an author's imagination when we have a genuine mystery happening right here in this very town?"

"What do you mean, Charmaine?" Martha asked.

"Haven't you heard about the break-in at Sullivan's Spellbooks? Beatrice would turn over in her grave if she knew what was going on in her shop." The elderly lady placed two fingers by her temple and swayed slightly in her seat. "I predict she might even grace us with a visit before this is all sorted out."

An uproar met her words, not only around the book club but also within me. A mixture of shock and yearning tightened my chest at the thought of reuniting with Granny via a seance. Was such a thing even possible? If it was, Havenwood would be the place, that's for sure.

I wasn't sure what to make of it all when Martha leaned over and whispered in my ear. "Don't be concerned. Her powers are not meant for connections with spirits. That's Madame Charmaine Fontaine, by the way. She fancies herself in touch with the spirits and reads fortunes, whether or not you want it." The librarian's smile was gentle as she looked at the eccentric older lady.

"Is she any good at it?" I whispered back, only half-joking. You never knew who or what you might encounter in Havenwood.

Martha pursed her lips as she tried to hold back a grin and gave a discreet shake of her head. "Yes, and no. She's right once for every dozen predictions, like clockwork. You just never know where yours lands because she makes them all the time." Martha cleared her throat and moved closer to the small circle, interrupting the friendly gossip. "I'd like to introduce Harper Sullivan, Beatrice's great-granddaughter. She's new in town and looking for kindred literary spirits. I told her she'd be welcome here."

"Of course you are," Madame Fontaine said in a proprietary tone. "Do come and sit next to me, won't you? I'd love to hear everything about you. And Spellbooks of course. Have you heard anything?" she asked, leaning forward with the air of an unrepentant gossip.

A familiar nasal voice cut through the noise. "Wait just a moment. How can she participate in a discussion about a book she hasn't read yet?" I looked over to see Mr. Puddleton glaring at me, the fingers of one hand drumming an aggravated rhythm on his rotund belly. The other hand twitched in agitation within the thick bandages.

Madame Fontaine whipped her head around. "Oh, do hush up, won't you, Oswald? How often do we have our very own mystery here in Havenwood? I dare say that if we put our heads together, we might just solve this thing before we finish our meeting today." She spun back to me, patting my knee as I sat in the empty chair next to her. "Now, tell us everything. No detail is too small. One never knows where the next clue might come from, does one?"

Martha cleared her throat. "One might consider introductions before interrogations, Charmaine," she said gently.

Madame Fontaine blinked owlishly through her thick glasses at the librarian and then back at me. "Oh yes. I suppose we could do that. I am Madame Charmaine Fontaine, fortune teller extraordinaire." She bowed extravagantly from her seated position before gesturing to the woman sitting next to her with curly, dark hair and deep-set dimples. "This is Stella. She owns Blossom and Bloom Florists. She barely tolerates the superb mysteries I select, but we love her anyway."

Stella shrugged, not looking the least bit upset. "I prefer a good romance."

Madame Fontaine waved at the man sitting next to her. "And this is Jeremy Rowan, our local botanist-slash-genius. What is it you're researching again?"

The gangly man next to Stella stammered and stuttered, but eventually managed to get out, "I-I-I'm exploring the effects of c-c-climate change on native plant species and b-b-biodiversity in the region. It really is quite f-f-fascinating. When seasonal patterns—"

"Yes, yes," Madame Fontaine said, waving her hand. "That. What he said." Jeremy blushed, and I noticed Stella shoot him an encouraging smile. Maybe there was something blooming between the florist and the botanist besides the native plant species. Madame Fontaine continued without pause. "And next to him is Margaret Jenkins. Don't let her pearls and heels fool you. She's as much a mystery lover as I am and has a keen mind for anticipating even the cleverest of plot twists."

I nodded at her. "Nice to see you again, Mrs. Jenkins."

Mrs. Jenkins sat primly in her chair, her legs crossed at the ankle and hands folded over a leather-bound journal in her lap. She returned the gesture. "And you."

"Next to her, we have our mad mage, Hank," Madame Fontaine said, pointing at the elderly man with a long white beard and a wild cloud of hair poofing up in all directions.

He cupped a hand around his ear and half-shouted. "Eh?"

Madame Fontaine grimaced. "Don't pay him any mind. It's all an act to get attention."

"I don't know what you're talking about," Hank said, giving the coffee cup in his hand his full focus.

Madame Fontaine ignored him and gestured to the last members of the circle, who glowered at me in tandem. "And here is Hortense and Oswald Puddleton, who are our own local literary connoisseurs since Beatrice passed away, rest her soul. They own the Dusty Tome over on Arcadia. Oh! I suppose that means you'll be seeing quite a lot of each other. You are moving into Spellbooks, aren't you?" The elderly lady directed the question at me.

"It's all up in the air at the moment," I said.

"Because of the theft?" Madame Fontaine pressed. "Tell us everything." She cupped her chin in her hands and rested her elbows on her knee expectantly.

Martha cleared her throat and gestured towards the coffee table. "Before we settle in, why don't you all make sure you have a fresh drink? Charmaine, a word?" The librarian arched an eyebrow and tipped her head to the side of the room, indicating she'd like it to be somewhat of a private discussion. Madame Fontaine narrowed her eyes but followed the librarian without protest.

Not knowing what else to do, I headed towards the table to pour myself a cup of coffee I had no intention of drinking. A sharp, nasal whisper drew my attention a moment later.

"Just what do you think you're doing here?" Oswald Puddleton demanded.

"Getting coffee?" I said, holding up my paper cup as proof.

"Not here. *Here.*" He waved his bandaged hand at the room. "These are my future clients. Go find your own somewhere else!"

"Oswald, dear, you really shouldn't wave your hand around so. You might start bleeding again," Hortense said, coming up next to him.

Not wanting to cause a scene, I poured on the charm even though it felt like a bit of a waste to use it on the Puddletons. "Oh, I'm so sorry to hear you were hurt. What happened?" I asked.

"Cut it on some glass," Mr. Puddleton said brusquely.

"Oswald!" Madame Fontaine called commandingly from across the room. "Come over here a moment, will you?"

"The grandame beckons," he muttered under his breath to his wife. She snorted a little laugh into her hand as he turned with a smarmy smile pasted on under his mustache. "Yes Charmaine? How can I be of assistance?"

I decided to take the opportunity to press Hortense for more information. "Such a shame about Mr. Puddleton's hand. How did he hurt himself again?"

"Wouldn't you like to know?" Hortense said with a sniff.

I bit the inside of my cheek to keep from rising to the childish retort. "Well, yes. It's why I asked," I said, keeping my tone mild.

"Hortense!" Oswald called from across the room. She sneered at me and then flounced over to her husband.

My mind was churning. Oswald Puddleton had not only cut himself on glass but had done so recently? And Hortense was unwilling to discuss the matter? Was it just a coincidence? The unpleasant owner of the bookshop in competition to Spellbooks injured around the same time someone broke a windowpane in the shop? Any good detective in the stories disavowed the existence of coincidences, but this wasn't a story. It was my life and coincidences did happen. Didn't they? In my heart, I didn't believe a word of the rationalizations my mind was conjuring up. I decided to try to figure out more about Oswald Puddleton and his recent injury as soon as I could.

Madame Fontaine, Hortense, and Oswald were engaged in a heated, whispered conversation while Stella and Jeremy murmured quietly to each other, all gentle smiles and soft looks. I had no intention of interrupting either group. Instead, I pulled up a chair and sat next to Mrs. Jenkins, who was flipping through the leather-bound book in her lap. Hank stood up just as I sat down, muttering something about sugar and making his way towards the coffee table.

"Is that the book of the week?" I asked, sipping from my paper cup. I grimaced. The coffee was bitter and over brewed. Nothing like the exceptional cup I'd enjoyed with my scones at the Oasis. I didn't blame Hank for trying to mask the flavor any way he could.

"Pardon?" Mrs. Jenkins looked surprised at my interruption. She looked at the book in question and then back at me with a small shake of her head. "Oh no. This is my reading journal. I was just going over my notes on the murder mystery Charmaine picked out for the club this week."

"That's an impressive journal," I said. "It looks like an antique."

"Many people think so, but it's a replica. Hank spotted it right away. We're both more than a little enamored with the subject." Mrs. Jenkins shut the book, tipping it to give me a clear view of the cover.

"What's it a replica of?"

Mrs. Jenkins' eyes sparkled. "This is a reproduction of the journal of Captain Benedict Starling. Have you heard of him?"

I shook my head. "Will you tell me more, please?" I asked, sincerely interested in anything that kept me away from the Puddletons.

Mrs. Jenkins grew more animated as she warmed to her topic. "Benedict Starling was a merchant captain who regularly sailed the Eastern seaboard, often stopping here in Connecticut. Like most captains of his time, he kept journals of his travels, sales, weather, and so on."

"And the weather patterns on the Eastern seaboard intrigue you?" I asked, not seeing the connection.

"No, I'm fascinated by pirates and their lost treasure."

"I'm sorry, what now?" I asked, forgetting entirely about the Puddletons.

Mrs. Jenkins nodded and ran a hand over the cover of her journal. "During the same time that Benedict Starling sailed the Atlantic, another more nefarious captain, nicknamed Blackfin, engaged in daring acts of piracy. According to legend, he amassed a substantial fortune of stolen goods, but he couldn't keep all of his ill-gotten gains aboard his vessel, so he hid the treasure somewhere along the coast of New England. Possibly even near Havenwood. It was a lot more secluded back then."

"And you think there's a clue to the missing treasure's location in Benedict's original journals?" I asked.

Mrs. Jenkins smiled eagerly, apparently thrilled to have an engaged audience. "Yes! Not only that, but I also think that Blackfin and Benedict were one and the same. Based on the analysis of other captains' journals at the time, Captain Starling's accounts don't always match the weather occurrences for the dates written. Also, he would've had to mix his own ink every day, resulting in slight variations in color. However, when experts examined his journals, they found several weeks' worth of entries with precisely the same shade of ink, which would have been a virtual impossibility."

"Unless he was writing several entries at once," I said.

"Precisely. But if he was both merchant and pirate, Benedict would've kept a separate journal to his legitimate business one. This other journal would account for the lag times in his legitimate journals and would have detailed his illicit cargo."

"And you're hoping that it might lead to the location of the treasure?" I asked.

Mrs. Jenkins tapped on her journal excitedly. "In this modern day, there are so few genuine mysteries left out there. Whatever happened to Blackfin's treasure is one of them. Solving it would be a thrill like no other." She seemed to realize what she'd just said and shook herself. A mask of proper propriety fell over her features, hiding the flare of excitement. "I'm sorry. You must think me terribly flighty to be caught up in a romanticized tale of pirates and lost treasure." She gave a self-deprecating little laugh.

I reached out instinctively and gripped her hand on top of the replica journal. "Not at all. In fact, I think it's a fascinating tale and one that deserves to be told by someone who is passionate about it. We might never know what actually happened to the pirate treasure, but didn't someone much wiser than me once say that knowledge is worth more than gold? I think *you* should tell Benedict's story. Even if you don't find the answers you want, it's important to share his story. Don't you think?"

The smile that Mrs. Jenkins gave me started off tentatively, like she was afraid I'd retract my statements by saying it was all a joke or some such nonsense. However, I'd meant every word. After a moment, her smile bloomed fully. "Why, I wouldn't know where to start. How could I possibly write this all down? What would be the best way to share it? Online? A blog maybe? Or a book?" The questions tumbled out of Mrs. Jenkins in a flood.

I grinned, glad to see excitement washing away the self-deprecation. "If you like, once Spellbooks opens again, I'll check our records and see if we have anything that might help you either with your research or figuring out how to share Benedict's story with the world."

"Oh, would you? That would be ever so kind," Mrs. Jenkins said earnestly, grasping my hand tightly.

"It would be my pleasure," I said.

Madame Fontaine called everyone's attention as Martha slipped out of the room. The elderly lady led a lively discussion about the murder mystery I hadn't read, engaging all the regular members of the group with deft skill. I was happy to be a silent spectator and left to my own thoughts. Pirate stories, while exciting, weren't the real treasure. Not to me. I'd just discovered another way that I could use Spellbooks to engage with the community. In addition to my brainstorming from the night before, I mentally added writer's workshops, creative writing, and publishing options to my list. I felt buoyant and exhilarated about the possibilities opening before me, and not even the Puddletons' occasional glares could bring me down.

Puzzling Predictions

At the end of the book club, Madame Fontaine loudly declared I would be welcome back any time. Stella, Jeremy, Hank, and Mrs. Jenkins all applauded while the Puddletons grimaced sourly. Apart from them, I'd enjoyed the spirited discussion even if I hadn't paid a great deal of attention to it. I graciously accepted and was actually looking forward to reading the short fantasy novella Madame Fontaine handed me that had been selected for the next meeting.

"It helps some members if I keep the weekly reading condensed," she said, flicking her eyes towards where Hortense sat scrolling through her phone while Oswald chatted loudly with Jeremy. "If you are interested in a lengthier read, I also run a monthly club, but that one focuses exclusively on mysteries."

I held up the thin book with a picture of a young woman in leather fighting gear in front of a shimmering green background. "I've got enough mystery in my life at the moment. Besides, this looks good."

Madame Fontaine nodded. "I like her work. She's a young, indie author, but it's easy reading. Her plots are fast-paced, and the characters are flawed but interesting."

"I can't wait to give it a try," I said, honestly.

Madame Fontaine suddenly gripped my arm, her pupils expanding until her iris was just a thin line of color around the edge. She spoke in a low, husky voice. *"To the chosen kin, hold true and strong, for when blood's bond falters, trust goes wrong. In shadows deep, help shall appear as unexpected aid hovers unseen, but near."*

My mouth hung open in surprise as Madame Fontaine blinked, her eyes and voice returning to normal. "I'm sorry. I don't know what came over me." She said with a little laugh, brushing an errant strand of hair into place and patting it to make sure it behaved. "I hope you come back next week. Now, if you'll excuse me, I really must talk to Jeremy." She hurried away without another word, leaving me gaping after her. I shook my head, finally shutting my mouth. I knew the citizens of this town could be on the quirky side, but playing up a penchant for predictions was taking it to a whole new level.

Deciding to put the strange encounter behind me for the time being, I waved farewell to Mrs. Jenkins as I slipped out of the reading room, but she didn't see me because she was fully engrossed in furiously scribbling in her faux pirate journal. I smiled to myself, hoping she was working on her passion project about Captain Benedict 'Blackfin' Starling. I didn't know which I was more curious to see: the ultimate story she came up with or her journey along the way.

Martha waved me over from behind the counter as I headed towards the door. She slid a flyer across the desk to me. "I thought this might be of interest, given you are the new owner of Spellbooks."

Rather than explain the complicated scenarios surrounding the inheritance, I accepted the flyer with a murmured thanks. The bright colors and old-fashioned font advertised the same Renaissance Faire Bella told me about. Amid the more popular attractions of jousting, turkey legs, and the crowning of a Faire queen, was a list of shops featured this year.

Martha tapped the flyer. "I thought of you when I saw this."

Buried in the middle of the list was a single line. Blackwell Books: Rare and Exotic Tales to Entice and Entertain. My heart skipped a beat. A rare book seller was in town? Another coincidence or a clue? If he or she wasn't afraid of stepping over the line of the law, it would be a tempting situation. A bookshop, known for its rare books, was closed because of the recent death of the owner. The inheritance not yet sorted among the heirs and one last day of the Faire. If the vendor wasn't a local, he or she could disappear with the haul before the police had even gotten the results back from their lab. Suddenly, going to the Faire with Bella became much more urgent than just catching up with an old childhood friend.

"Thanks for this," I said, tucking the flyer into my bag with the book club novella. "I'll have to check it out."

"Anytime. I hope we see you again around here," Martha said with a charming smile.

I glanced at my phone as I left. There was time before I had to meet Bella, so I headed back to the shop quickly to check on Luna.

A familiar set of white ears poked up over the sill of the front window of Spellbooks as I walked up. A minute later, Luna hopped around the corner of the shop. I crouched down to talk to her.

"Someday, you're going to have to tell me how you do that, or I'm going to think you're a magical bunny."

Luna sniffed. "Fluff and fur balls, I hate the term *bunny*. It's so puerile. Use it again at your peril."

I held up my hands in immediate surrender, maintaining a serious expression. "Noted."

"Also, I *am* magical, or haven't you noticed the whole talking thing? But I still have problems with doors, which is why your granny installed a rabbit door near the back of the shop for me."

I perked up. She'd mentioned that before, but I didn't remember such a thing. "Is that like a cat door? Could that be how Mr. Wigglesworth got out?"

Luna glared at me. "I'll pretend you didn't just ask me that."

"I'm...sorry? I don't know what—"

Luna waved a paw, cutting me off. "Come here, I'll show you." She hopped around the corner and down the tiny alley alongside the shop. I followed, confused. She paused in front of a locked side door that I remembered Granny used for unloading deliveries. Luna tipped her head towards the tiny pet door at the bottom of the thick wood. "Do you really think that ridiculous cat could fit through here?"

I shrugged. "I don't know. I've never seen him," I said honestly.

Luna huffed out a breath. "Well, take my word for it. That beast never met a morsel he didn't devour and has the girth to show for it. He was only good for vacuuming up the scraps, hogging all the best lounging spots in the shop, and occasionally purring at a customer. When he wasn't snoring in a window, that is. Besides, your granny worked with Agatha to create the runes so only I could enter or exit this way." Luna pointed with a paw at minute dark scratches on the frame of the tiny door that I'd first assumed to be normal wear and tear. When I crouched down and looked closer, I could see the marks were deliberately carved into the wood and painted black.

"I didn't come out here to talk to you about that obnoxious walking fur rug," Luna said, pulling my attention away from the tiny door. "Sheriff Jackson stopped by late last night to return Gideon. Apparently, the substance on his scales was blood."

"He injured the thief?" I asked, instantly thinking of Oswald Puddleton and his bandaged hand. Maybe it hadn't been cut on glass at all, but on a gargoyle's sharp scales. Besides, the sheriff hadn't mentioned anything about blood evidence in the shards of glass around the door. I reminded myself that he didn't owe me a play-by-play of his investigation. I added it to my mental list of questions to ask him about. I also needed to ask him and possibly also Nathaniel Ravenscroft when we could get someone in to repair the broken window and clean up the shop.

"Looks that way," Luna said, bringing my attention back. "Gargoyle scales are sharp and there was blood on several of them. Looks like Gideon scraped up the thief with enough scales to cause some noticeable damage, even if he couldn't see the sneaky fluffernutter."

I snorted into my fist to hold back a laugh. Luna's eyes flashed at me, and I fought for composure. "So, we're looking for a...fluffernutter...with some sort of injuries." Again, my mind flashed to Mr. Puddleton. "But if Gideon could hurt them, why couldn't he see them?" I asked.

Luna sat back on her haunches. "My best guess is magic. But even in Havenwood, I don't know of anyone who could manage an invisibility spell. Maybe a mage on par with the Silverthorne family, but what motive would Vivienne or her children have? They basically own the entire town. If Vivienne wanted Beatrice's book collection, she'd just buy them. Probably with an obscene amount of money."

"If it wasn't an invisibility spell, how did the thief get in and out without being seen?"

"Figure that out, and you'll probably find the rapscallion responsible for this mess. Now, I have to return to guarding the shop until Gideon wakes up again," Luna said. She hopped through the door without another word, and I had an image pop into my head of her wearing a tiny helmet and carrying a spear while marching back and forth in front of the door of the shop. She was formidable enough that she probably didn't need the spear. She could eviscerate the thief, should he return, with her sharp tongue and bizarre vocabulary.

Fluffernutter, indeed.

Confounding Costumes

I looked at the costume choices Bella spread out on the floor of her room dubiously. "I have so many questions," I said.

"You live here long enough and having a costume wardrobe just makes sense. Otherwise, you're constantly scrambling to find something for this festival or that town event," Bella said as she surveyed the choices from beside me.

"No, I get that. I can think of several town events Granny Bea mentioned where you could wear those types of dresses," I replied pointing at the handful of vaguely Renaissance-ish dresses on the floor ranging from peasant to royalty and even one in the pile that whispered to me of fairy-in-the-glen. "It's the Star Trek uniforms that are confusing me."

"I thought it'd be fun. You know, act like we're on a mission and all the alien creatures are obsessed with the sixteenth century. Is that too weird?" Bella asked, looking at the officer's uniforms doubtfully.

"No, oddly enough, that part makes complete sense. What's confusing me is *why* you have them in the first place."

Bella grabbed a red shirt up and twirled it around like she was waltzing with it. "It's just they're terribly comfortable, and I think everyone in the future will be wearing them."

I rolled my eyes. "Very clever. But I think I'm going to go the traditional route." I selected a blue overdress that went well with a creamy off the shoulder blouse.

"If you must be boring about it," Bella said, selecting a red dress with subtle gold embroidery that complimented the warm tones of her hair and skin perfectly.

"Boring? In this town?"

"Well, it's all relative anyway, isn't it?" Bella swirled the gown around in a little jig before stepping into her small walk-in closet to give me a little privacy to change while she did the same.

I slipped out of my jeans and t-shirt and pulled on the borrowed dress. I was lucky that we were close to the same size, but it didn't hurt that the outfit had some give to the fabric. Bella called around the door. "Are you decent?"

"All good," I said.

She swung the door wide, revealing her own ensemble and a full-length mirror on the back. "Let's have a good look at you. Spin," she commanded, twirling a finger imperiously. I did so, the skirt opening with a satisfying flare. "You look great. And that color on you!" She blew a chef's kiss into the air.

"It's nothing compared to yours," I replied honestly. Bella looked radiant, but also somehow regal and mysterious in her costume.

"What do you think? Will I win Faire Queen today?" Bella asked, grabbing a fan from the box of accessories on the end of her bed and struck a pose.

"Definitely," I laughed. We smiled at each other across the room, and I couldn't help myself. "Why are you being so nice to me?" I blurted out.

"What do you mean?" Bella asked, sweeping up the unchosen costumes from the floor.

"I mean, we spent one summer together when we were kids. It was a wonderful summer, but we haven't really seen each other in years. Don't misunderstand me. I'm very grateful. For the room, for the costume, for the company, but just...why?"

Bella grabbed some hangers and started putting the costumes away neatly. I grabbed a pile and got to work myself. Her room was cozy, with soft pastel walls that complemented the vintage floral and lace curtains. An antique wooden desk adorned with framed photos was tucked in the corner, and a scattering of potted plants decorated the small bookshelf. Beautiful wood carvings, probably crafted by Antonio, peeked out from behind the pots, added an enchanting touch to the room. With the sofa, Bella's bed, and both our stuff, it was crowded, but not uncomfortably so. As long as we put the costumes away.

Bella cleared her throat, drawing my attention back to her. "Havenwood is a strange place when you live here. I mean, there are some people here who are literally centuries old. Not many of them have kids, you know? Which means there aren't many people my age in Havenwood, especially not ones who actually stay here. And then there's the whole mixed blood thing and all the issues that come with that."

"Wait, what issues?" I asked. I'd never heard of this before, but then again, I'd never lived in a paranormal community for a great deal of time.

"It's the same prejudice you find anywhere there's an 'other'," Bella said with a shrug. "It's different when the tourists come through or even when a human couple settles down here. No one seems to mind that. However, if a human and a non-human get together? It's a whole thing." She waved her arms dramatically.

I frowned. "That seems backward for a town that literally put 'haven' in its name."

Bella tucked the full hangers back into her closet. "I didn't notice it when I was little, but I see the snubs now that I'm older. Mama will be invited somewhere, but Papa's name is mysteriously left off the list. Despite his skill with woodworking, Papa is never asked to help with setting up the town events because he can't work as fast as those who have magical talents. It isn't just the adults, you know. Kids pick up on the way their parents behave. When I was teenager, the kids with powers would go out into the woods to show off, but I was never invited." She held out her empty hands. "Not much for me to show off except for a marginally acceptable ability not to burn things in the kitchen. Don't get me wrong, I can cook. Just not as well as Mama. They never wanted a half-breed baker girl around when they were casting spells out there."

I scooped up the box of accessories. "I didn't realize."

"Why would you? You're a witch, but you didn't grow up here. You never felt the stares or heard the whispers. That's why I came back after university, you know."

"Really?" I asked, passing her the box which she tucked away in the closet.

"Yeah, I wanted to make a difference. To help create a more inclusive environment for younger members of the community. To give them a reason to want to stay in Havenwood as opposed to going off to the city. To show people it doesn't have to be an 'us or them' situation."

"That's awesome. Really awesome of you," I said honestly.

Bella shrugged again. "Yeah, well. You know what they say. If you want to make a difference, start at home."

"Well, I think it's a great idea. If there is anything I can do to help, let me know."

"I think having more open-minded young people in town is a good thing. Once you get Spellbooks open and running again, maybe we could do some events there to help build the community feel for the younger crowd."

"I'd love to. If I ever actually inherit Spellbooks," I said, my mouth running away with me as my thoughts took a decidedly dark turn.

Bella frowned sympathetically and wrapped an arm around my shoulders. "Hey, I'm sorry. This afternoon is supposed to be fun. Turkey legs and jousting instead of old prejudices, book thieves, and mysterious cousins." I looked at her in surprise. She quirked a smile. "Mama told me most of it. I thought this would be a pleasant distraction. I didn't mean to get all serious on you. For the rest of the afternoon, I swear I will only talk about how handsome the local blacksmith is or how much one should pay for a crown." She mimed locking her lips and throwing away the key.

I laughed. "Let's start with the turkey leg, if you don't mind. Then we can think about blacksmiths and crowns."

Bella curtseyed deeply. "Your wish is my command, milady." She hurried through the hair and makeup preparations to complete our looks, chattering happily about the small things around the town or the B&B. I tried to listen but found it difficult as my attention kept returning to her earlier comments. I wondered what I could do to help support Bella in her efforts to make this town a little more welcoming for everyone.

Fair-y Friends

As we walked down to the town's main square, the crowd of similarly costumed people noticeably grew. Bella timed the afternoon perfectly. We arrived at the local bus stop just in time to catch the shuttle to the fairgrounds and avoid the crazy parking. As we drove past the last houses on the edge of town and started down the gentle slope to the meadow, my breath caught in my throat. Below me, in what I remembered being a giant grassy field, there was an entire wooden village complete with individualized shops decorated in vibrant colors, a small jousting arena, an archery range, an area for themed rides, and even a small castle with flags displaying a variety of standards snapping in the breeze. It was an impressive sight to behold.

I leaned over and whispered to Bella. "You said the Renaissance Faire ran for what? A month?"

Bella shrugged. "These days, it's closer to two. It's become a very popular town event."

I pointed down at the Faire. "But those buildings look like they've been there for *years*, not months, and I don't remember anything like this here before. How'd they manage it?"

Bella leaned closer with a twinkle in her eyes. "Magic," she whispered, waving jazz hands mysteriously around her face.

I rolled my eyes. "No, seriously."

Bella chuckled and linked her arm through mine, drawing me into the flow of the crowd exiting the shuttle. "I *am* being serious. You remember the Silverthorne family? The mages who basically own all of Havenwood? They handle the charms that allow tourists to shrug off anything magical as part of the allure of our quaint little town, but they also run all the big town events like this one. The weekend before something like the Renaissance Faire starts, big, corrugated construction walls go up all around the site. The Silverthornes and town workers, aka all those with useful magic, come on down and voilà! We have a Faire ground that looks like it's been here years instead of days. After the Faire ends, they'll break it down and set up for the next event or festival or whatever."

"And this happens regularly?" I asked, looking around in awe.

"Sure. At least once a month. It's how they keep the tourists rolling in. Right now, we have the Renaissance Faire then the Harvest Festival and Halloween. The next month is a LARPing something or other followed by a Dungeons and Dragons themed event, which leads right up to Thanksgiving. Then there's the Yuletide season, or as most normal people outside of Havenwood call it, Christmas. If you think this is a lot, you're going to be blown away in December."

"And these are all town events? On this scale?" I asked, incredulously.

Bella shrugged. "More or less."

"But...how? Just...how?" My brain stuttered to a stop, trying to calculate the working hours, equipment, and resources needed to construct the edifices I saw in front of me. And to do this type of event back-to-back throughout the year?

Bella dug into her purse for her phone and showed the screen to the people checking for tickets who waved us through. "It's amazing what can happen when you have a powerful mage family running the place and a population of mostly magical creatures. Papa even offered to help frequently, despite him being human. He's great with woodwork and all, but like I said, he can't keep up with the magical pace the Silverthornes need for this kind of turnaround. He does what he can to contribute, though."

The surrounding crowd thinned as the tourists drifted off to explore the sixteenth-century wonderland. Off to our left was a bustling marketplace adorned with vibrant banners hung between colorful stalls. The enticing aroma of freshly baked pastries, spiced cider, and roasting meat filled the air. A musician playing a lute stood under an awning, a small crowd gathered around her, the music and her sweet voice luring in even more tourists from our shuttle. Across the dirt road, a trio of acrobats performed stunts of physical prowess and flexibility on a small stage. One woman popped a balloon her male compatriot held between his knees and his over-dramatic look of relief elicited roars of laughter from the crowd.

Bella wove through the crowds, waving at Havenwood locals or pointing out her favorite parts as we walked. The fairgrounds were a teeming array of "magical" beings, including spell-casters performing minor illusions, gentle fairies with delicate fluttering wings, or gnomes bustling through the crowd, hawking their wares. I wasn't sure if it was the Silverthorne's charms or tourists' willing disbelief, but the visitors seemed quite content to accept the sights before them. Perhaps they thought the magic users were simply street magicians using a clever sleight of hand, or the fairies were some sort of hologram or animatronic creations. I didn't know. But the atmosphere of the Faire was one of merriment and joviality.

"What do you want to do first?" Bella asked, peering at the large board where a flyer with the event times for the day was prominently displayed. "You could test your aim on the archery range? Or we could go brew potions. I think they mean perfumes, but it's much more fun to think of them as potions. The joust isn't starting for another couple of hours, but there is a wizard duel on the main stage in forty minutes. Ooh, they have a falconry display this year." She ran her finger down the list, tapping it triumphantly. "Yes! My favorite guy is back!"

"What guy?" I asked.

Bella pointed a finger at the flyer. "Tom the Taunter. He sits in a giant version of the stocks all day and mocks people. For a dollar, you can buy a couple of tomatoes and try to hit him. Most people miss, which makes him taunt them all the more. It's hilarious!"

"You have a strange definition of fun," I said with a laugh.

Bella tapped the flyer again. "Oh, never mind, he's on break right now, anyway. We'll catch him later. So, what sounds good?"

The smell of something spicy drifted through the air and my stomach growled. It had been a long time since breakfast. "Honestly, I could do with some food. What's good around here?"

Bella bobbed her head as she examined the board. "The Goblin's Griddle always does great food. Their troll-sized pretzels are bigger than my head, and they serve them with their specialty chimera-breath mustard that is just out of this world. Mystic Meats is one of my favorites because they grill everything fresh. Their dragon steaks are good, but the unicorn kebobs are something special."

"They grill a unicorn?" I blurted out in disbelief.

Bella chuckled. "I'm pretty sure it's beef, but they put it on a horn-shaped skewer. The nice thing is you can take the kebabs to go and walk while you eat."

"Sold," I said instantly.

"Great," Bella said, pointing off towards the left at the irresistible aromas that were making my stomach do flips. "And after the kebabs, we can head over to Pixie Pastries. Their flavors are incredible. Moonberry, starlight vanilla, ambrosial nectar," Bella gave a little moan of pleasure. "Whoever runs their tasting committee must have the best job on the entire planet."

"That good?" I said, bemused.

"Let's just say that even Mama gets jealous of them sometimes. Oh, and they have this specialty they only make during events like this. It's called the Havenwood Honeycake." She looked around conspiratorially and dropped her voice to a whisper. "It's layered with enchanted caramel and topped with a sprinkle of edible fairy dust. They claim it leaves a trail of whimsy dancing on your tongue."

"What does whimsy taste like?" I asked with a chuckle.

"Only one way to find out," Bella said, grabbing my arm.

Kebabs in hand, we drifted through the stalls of vendors selling all manner of things. There was an apothecary claiming to sell mystical remedies and potions. In the Wizard's Workshop, kids decorated their own wands or mixed specialty scents for enchanted candles. Another stall displayed fantastical artwork depicting mystical landscapes and mythical creatures. The Siren's Song was full of a variety of musical instruments and intricately carved enchanted music boxes twirled by themselves without need of winding.

I pointed at the stall as a wooden ballerina sprouted wings and flew around the miniature forest on her music box before settling amongst the trees once more with a dainty pirouette. "That's incredible! How many of these are actually enchanted?" I asked.

Bella glanced at the shop. "Oh, Azura runs this place. She has a shop up in town as well, but these won't actually have any magic in them. I'm pretty sure these are run on clockwork."

"Is it common for the local shop owners to run stalls?" I asked.

Bella wavered her hand back and forth. "I'd guess maybe about a third of them do. Mama and Papa tried it once, but it's a lot of work, and with the B&B?" She shrugged. "There's only so many hours in the day. But now that I'm back from school full-time, we might be able to swing something next year."

"So, who else is a local here?" I asked, spinning around slowly to look at the bustling marketplace.

"Well, Azura obviously, and the folks up at Pixie Pastries usually have a satellite shop at town events. Let's see. Oh, Fizzit is here this year. He's that goblin over there and specializes in quirky little gifts. Statues of centaurs, gaming figurines, glass baubles, that sort of thing. Remy's costume shop always is a favorite. And we saw Penny as we came in. She was playing the lute, remember? She's the town troubadour."

"Wait. Havenwood has a troubadour?"

Bella looked at me with wide eyes. "Of course. Doesn't every town?" She held the innocent doe-eyed look for a moment longer before breaking into giggles. "Yes, Havenwood has an official troubadour. It sounds better than 'wandering musician' and the Silverthornes think it gives the town a certain ambiance."

"Are there many people that the Silverthornes employ?"

Bella held up a finger. "Not the Silverthornes, the *town*. Although since they own most of it, I suppose it amounts to the same thing. Now let's see, who else is here?" She looked around the fairgrounds, searching for familiar faces.

I looked around, too, but more to drink in the sights. Who was I going to recognize here? A flicker of movement snagged at the corner of my eye, and I casually turned my head, thinking it was another acrobat, or maybe even a juggler. A flash of a man wearing a dark trench coat and fedora wove through the crowd, looking distinctly out of place among the colorful costumes. I frowned. I'd seen someone dressed similarly before. Was it the curse of a small town, constantly seeing the same people? Or was there something else going on here?

I tugged on Bella's sleeve and pointed to where the man in the fedora drifted through the crowd. "Did you see—"

"Wildwood Ink?!" Bella exclaimed. "I didn't know Finn was here."

I perked up, having heard the name before. "Wildwood Ink? The tattoo parlor next to Spellbooks?"

"Yeah, Finnegan moved to town about a few years ago. I remember because Mama invited him to Papa's fiftieth along with half the neighborhood. Have you met him yet?"

"No, but–" I started, craning my neck to find the man in the fedora again, but he had vanished.

"Well, let's remedy that then, shall we?" Bella said, grabbing my hand and marching me over towards the small stall where a man with tousled, wavy red hair and a charming smile knelt in front of a little girl, holding her hand while her mother fluttered behind them.

"Is it going to hurt?" the child asked, poking her tongue through a gap made by a missing tooth and looking nervous.

"Oh no, honey," her mother gushed from behind her. "It's just a little sticker."

The man kneeling before the child ignored the mother and shook his head somberly. "Fairies only become fairy-friends with girls who are brave and true. I'll be right here to hold your hand, but you have to decide if you're going to be brave enough to take care of this fairy for me today. Do you think you can do that?"

The girl poked her tongue through the gap in her teeth once more and then nodded seriously. The man nodded back, placing his other hand on top of hers. "Good girl. Did you know that fairy-friends are some of the rarest people in the world? A true fairy-friend must always be kind to everyone around her and she must always defend those in need. Are you a true fairy-friend?" he asked seriously.

She bit her lower lip, considering his words, and then nodded. "I think I am," she murmured in a small voice.

"Well, let's see, shall we?" The man removed his hand and a colorful fairy smiled up from the back of the little girl's hand. I saw a flash of white paper in the palm of his hand before he quickly tucked it behind his back.

"Mommy, look! I'm a real fairy-friend!" the little girl squealed, waving her hand at her mother.

"I can see that, honey," the mother said, examining her daughter's newest companion in all seriousness. She shot a look over the girl's head and mouthed a thank you to the red-headed man. He dipped his head back, a gentle smile on his lips.

The little girl twirled in a circle and then threw her arms around the man's neck. "Thank you, thank you, *thank you!*"

He grinned and patted her back. "You're very welcome. And don't forget what I told you about fairy-friends."

The girl unwrapped her arms and nodded seriously. "I won't. I promise." She turned to her mother, dragging her away while giving a lecture on the true nature of fairy-friends, as if her mom hadn't been standing there the whole time. The man smiled after them and pushed to his feet, turning to face us.

"And what can I do for you? I'm afraid I'm all out of the temporary fairy tattoos, but I've got some nice unicorns," he said, folding his arms across his chest. I couldn't help but notice the beautiful, curling Celtic knotwork that ran up from his wrist and disappeared under the sleeve of his shirt, which seemed to emphasize rather than hide the muscles in his chest and arms. A green stone set in a silver amulet with similar knotwork patterns dangled from a leather cord around his neck. The well-tended scruff on his cheeks gave him a ruggedly handsome rather than unkempt look, but it was his smile which reached all the way to his sparkling green eyes as he turned his attention fully on me that warmed me straight down to my toes.

"Hey Finn, no tattoos for us today, real or otherwise. I just wanted to introduce you to the newest resident of Havenwood, Harper Sullivan. Harper, this is Finnegan Oakheart," Bella said.

Finnegan extended his hand. "Finn, please."

"Harper," I said, even though Bella had just told him my name. I blushed, thrown off my game by the sparkle in his eyes and the slowly curving smile. He pressed my hand, the warmth in his grip seeming to light a blaze within me, but he let go all too soon.

"Sullivan? Any relation to Beatrice Sullivan by chance?" Finn asked.

I nodded, tucking my hand into the folds of my skirt. "She was my great-grandmother."

His expression softened. "My deepest condolences. I was so sorry to hear about her passing. We weren't neighbors for very long, but she was always so welcoming to this new kid on the block," he said, pointing a thumb at his chest. "She was a genuine treasure to the community and will be missed."

A lump formed in my throat, partially at the memory of Granny Bea and partially at the fact that this stranger had known her more in her final few years than I had. Before I could speak, Finn snapped his fingers and pointed at me. "Does this mean that you're going to be my new neighbor?"

I bit my lip and lifted my shoulder. "It's complicated right now, but I'd really like to." I blushed as Finn's grin widened slightly and hurried to say, "Take over Spellbooks, that is. But it's up in the air at the moment."

"I'm sure you've heard about the theft?" Bella interrupted. "Someone broke in and stole the rare books Mrs. Sullivan kept on display behind the desk."

Finn nodded. "I was the one who called the police. Beatrice's cat showed up at my place before I'd even opened the shop. He's a nice guy, but kind of a lump. Won't move for anything that isn't edible, and he's never come to visit before. When he came over, I tried to return him. That's when I saw the broken door." He turned his piercing green gaze back to me. "Is there anything I can do?"

"Oh! So that's where the cat went. That's one mystery solved. Now, if you know where book thieves hang out, we could wrap up the most intriguing mystery the Havenwood book club has encountered today," I quipped, finally finding my wits again. However, a little voice piped up at the back of my head. Was Granny's neighbor being a little too friendly? Besides, Luna said *she* had called the police. I supposed it was possible they'd both called, but wouldn't reporting the crime lessen suspicion if Finn had been involved? Was he hiding something? Or was I the problem, suspecting everyone who had even the most tenuous links to the theft? Either way, I mentally added him to my list of suspects.

Finn chuckled, his charming smile lighting his face in a way that made me want to remove him from said list instantly. "Not really my kind of folks, but I'll let you know if I hear anything."

"Well, other than that, I need to find someone to repair the broken pane. Oh, and figure out a way to take Mr. Wigglesworth off your hands. But I don't know where I'd even keep him. I'm staying at the Enchanted Oasis B&B, and I'm not sure they take pets," I said, looking over at Bella, feeling the weight of responsibility press down on my shoulders.

She shook her head. "We don't, unfortunately. Mama is horribly allergic to cats."

Finn spoke up. "Well, if you're in a tough spot, I don't mind looking after him for a couple of days. We're getting to know each other, and it's kind of nice to not be alone in the shop between customers."

"I don't want him to be a bother," I said uncertainly.

Finn waved a hand breezily. "Honestly, not a problem. I picked up some kibble for him yesterday. He wasn't a fan at first, but it's food, and he's, well, him. And as for the door, I know a guy. Is it okay if I call him for you?"

I nodded, a sense of relief washing over me and dampening the burgeoning suspicion. "That would be great!" A thought occurred, and I backtracked. "Except the shop is still part of the police investigation into the theft. I don't know if I'm even allowed to fix the door if it might disturb a clue or something." Then there was the whole issue of the inheritance dispute, but I really didn't want to get into that right now. Not to mention I still wasn't sure I could trust Finnegan Oakheart. I needed to stay on my guard and not get distracted by a friendly smile and the boy-next-door charm, although he had both in abundance.

Finn nodded sympathetically. "How about this? I'll give my guy a call and let him know what the situation is. When you get the all-clear from the police, let me know, and he'll be over in a flash. In the meantime, I'll keep an extra eye on Spellbooks for you. Once I return from creating fairy-friends," he said, gesturing at the stall.

"That's so kind of you, but I don't want to put you out."

Finn waved away my protests. "This is what this town is all about. Community coming together, people supporting each other. It's why I settled down here in the first place."

Bella chimed in. "That's what Mama and Papa always say makes Havenwood so special. The community."

"I'm getting that impression," I said.

"Well, community, and the honeycakes," Bella said, tossing her empty kebab stick in a nearby trash can. "I don't want to miss my chance to get one today. Finn, we're heading over to Pixie's. Can we grab a honeycake for you?"

"Better not," he said, patting his flat stomach. "I've already had more than my share since the Faire opened, and we want to give the tourists a reason to come back, right?"

"Good thinking," Bella said with a grin. "But my rational processing goes out the window when I'm hungry, and I'm hungry for honeycakes. C'mon Harper, let's go get some before they disappear."

"Enjoy," Finn called with a wave as Bella dragged me away.

I waved back, thinking about how much I would enjoy getting to know my new neighbor if I won Granny Bea's contest for Spellbooks and he proved not to be involved in the theft.

I mean, the neighbor*hood*. Everyone. Not just Finn.

But maybe especially Finn.

Snooping and Secrets

I LICKED THE LAST sticky smear of caramel from my fingertips as Bella brushed the honeycake crumbs from her dress.

"That was worth the wait in line," I said.

"Right? I already want another one, but I don't think I have room," Bella groaned, flopping back onto the shady patch of grass we'd commandeered under a maple tree dripping with leaves ranging from burnt umber to brilliant goldenrod.

"Me too," I said, leaning back and letting the late afternoon sun beams dance over my cheeks.

"After I recover from my food coma, what do you want to do?" Bella asked without opening her eyes.

I saw my opportunity and took it. "Martha Morningstar showed me a flyer at the library with a list of shops here at the Faire. Among them was a vendor selling rare and exotic books." I dug my phone out of the hidden pocket in my dress, not caring if it was an anachronistic accessory at a Renaissance Faire. I flicked open my photo gallery and pulled up the pictures I'd taken of Granny's list of rare books in the ledger. "Maybe the owner has heard about someone trying to sell the stolen books or could point me toward a collector or something."

"Seems like a long shot, but I'm game," Bella said, rolling onto her side and gesturing for the phone.

I passed it over. "A long shot is all I've got." I quickly explained what I'd witnessed in the lawyer's office, my suspicions that my cousin was playing dirty, and my plan to help the police solve the theft as a way to prove myself worthy of inheriting the shop.

Bella blew out a breath. "Suddenly, my overly full stomach doesn't seem like such a problem. But are you sure you want to meddle with police business? Sheriff Jackson isn't the kind of man who appreciates anyone messing with law and order in this town, however well-intentioned. Besides, Papa always says he's really good at his job. Maybe you should just leave this to the police and focus on developing a plan for the shop?"

"Maybe," I half-heartedly agreed without really meaning it. "But it's just a few questions, and we're here, anyway. Five minutes. In and out, I promise." I made an 'x' over my heart.

"Fine, lead the way," Bella said, pushing up to her feet and handing the phone back.

I tucked it in my pocket as I led the way to one of the noticeboards where maps of the fairgrounds were posted and ran my finger down the list until I found the bookshop. "Looks like it's just over...yeah, there it is. Next to the guy selling the swords." I grabbed Bella's hand, and she groaned as I dragged her through the milling tourists towards the bookshop.

From the outside, the book vendor's stall looked similar to the rest of the Faire. The exterior was adorned with a weathered wooden façade. If Bella hadn't told me they had built it recently, I would've assumed it had been here for at least a decade. Possibly two. A sign written in elegant calligraphy hung above the open front section of the store, allowing for fairgoers to peruse the rather impressive collection. Shelves near the front displayed ancient-looking maps and worn books which looked to hold stories of forgotten legends or enigmatic wisdom. There were also tables displaying colorful books of fantasy lore, enchanting tales, and retellings of ancient myths for the more modern reader. A thin, balding man in period costume stood behind the counter, chatting with the tourists while he rang up their purchases. Another man in a similar but more elaborate costume drifted through the store, amiably engaging browsers. I hissed as the man turned, showing me the side of his face under a feathered hat. A face that I recognize. Without a second thought, I pulled Bella off the street and into the nearest store.

"What? Whoa. What gives? I thought we were going to look at books," Bella protested as I crouched behind a display of colorful perfume bottles.

"We were until I saw who runs the shop," I whispered, craning my neck to confirm what I'd just seen. "I don't know why I didn't put it together sooner."

"Put what together? What are you talking about? And why are we hiding in a perfume shop?" Bella asked.

"*Blackwell* Books? Thaddeus Blackwell?"

Bella shrugged. "Okay, so you know the owner?"

I waved my hands in negation. "I don't just know him. We're related. Thaddeus Blackwell is my cousin. The one whom I'm competing against for Spellbooks."

"Oh," Bella breathed, her eyes wide.

"And isn't it just a little *too* convenient? He's a rare book vendor? Granny Bea's books go missing? Coincidence? I think not," I scoffed. "I'm going to go over there and give him a piece of my mind."

Bella grabbed my arm, holding me back. "You can't do that."

"Why not?"

"Because you have no proof that he had anything to do with the theft."

I frowned. "I'm supposed to believe what? That he just happens to be in town when the books go missing?"

"But he would've been here for the past two weeks, along with most of the other vendors," Bella said.

"And how many of those vendors own rare bookshops?" I asked.

"I see your point, but you still don't have any proof to march over there and accuse him of anything."

I bit the inside of my cheek. "You're right. If I do that, it might tip him off, and I may never find the books."

"Not what I meant—"

"Besides, if he had something to do with the disappearance of the books, he won't tell me anything. Which is why I'm not going. You are."

Bella's mouth dropped open, and she blinked in surprise at me. "You really think he's going to tell me something?"

I shook my head. "Not a chance."

"Then what am I going to do?"

"Be the distraction, of course, while I sneak in the back and have a look around."

Bella folded her arms over her chest. "And how are you going to do that?"

"Shops typically have a back area, don't they? One where employees can take a break? Or where they store extra stock? Maybe Thaddeus is storing more than just stock back there."

"Wouldn't he have to be a special kind of stupid to keep stolen goods in his store?" Bella asked.

"Well, I only met him for a few minutes, but one can hope," I said with more bravado than I felt.

"And how are you going to get in? Or out, for that matter?"

"Leave it to me. Five minutes. That's all I'm asking."

"Where have I heard that before? Oh, I remember. It was that day when we were twelve and you promised me you could climb Farmer Owen's fence to get to his mulberry tree. I had to sit there and listen to him tell stories about his cows for an hour before you showed up."

"That was then. This is now."

Bella dropped her feigned indignation at the infamous mulberry story, looking more uncomfortable with my hastily cobbled together plan by the minute. "I don't know, Harper. This seems like a terrible idea."

"Please, Bella? This isn't just about the books. It's my great-granny's legacy. I don't want her bookshop to fall to Thaddeus. I want it. I want to run it, to have somewhere to call home, to have something to grow and develop that just might become my legacy, too." As soon as the words spilled out of my mouth, I knew they were not only true, but I'd wanted this with a yearning ache deep in my soul for quite some time. It wasn't until I finally said it out loud that I realized just how badly I wanted this life, the shop, and everything.

Bella stared at me and then sighed in acquiescence. "Okay. Five minutes. Don't get caught."

I wrapped my arms around her. "Thank you!"

"Yeah, yeah. You owe me one," Bella grumbled as she started across the street.

I used the crowd to hide my approach and slipped around the corner of the shop just as Bella engaged Thaddeus in conversation. I grinned. She played the enthusiastic, chipper distraction part well. The small dirt road behind the shop was nearly deserted, except for a pair of men a few shops down having a quick cigarette break. My heart started to race. I hadn't expected witnesses, but I couldn't wait for them to leave. Not with Bella keeping Thaddeus' attention on her. This might be my only chance to snoop around. I forced a smile and jerked my chin in a greeting at them like I belonged here. One raised a hand in return and the other nodded back at me before they reabsorbed themselves in their conversation.

Conscious of the men's presence, I made a show of digging into my pocket for a key I didn't have before putting my hand on the doorknob. This lock was much simpler than the one on Granny's office door, but I was out of practice. I closed my eyes, focusing on the tumblers in my mind. The lock might be simple, but the pins were stubborn and hard to move. Maybe it was because of being outside and there was dirt and dust clogging the mechanism, or maybe it was just newer, making the pins more difficult. Either way–

"Hey! Are you okay?" One man called out.

My concentration wobbled, and I almost lost my magical grip on the tumblers. I kept my eyes closed and raised the pitch of my voice. It was a poor disguise, but it was the best I could manage at the moment. "I'm fine." I prayed Bella's distraction was a good one or there was every chance Thaddeus might hear the commotion back here and decide to come check it out himself.

"You could just go around front and get Thaddeus. He—"

The last tumbler clicked into place. I made a show of jiggling the knob before swinging the door wide. "All good. The lock was just a little sticky, that's all. Thanks!" I waved cheerily and slipped inside, closing the door softly behind me. I leaned my back against the door and blew out a breath. That had been too close for comfort. If I was going to make this lock-picking thing a habit, I'd have to get faster.

As my heart rate returned to a more reasonable pace, I looked around the back room of the shop. Perhaps 'room' was too generous of a word. It was more of a narrow hallway, with shelves full of books lining the walls and cardboard boxes stacked on the floor where the shelves hadn't been up to the demand. A small desk lamp glowed on a table at the far end of the hall, providing just enough illumination for me to navigate the space without banging my shins. I heard voices drifting through the thin wooden wall. I thought I could pick out Bella's cheerful chatter, but then a male voice sounded much closer.

"That'll be fifteen dollars. Would you like to pay cash or with ye old credit card?" A softer, female voice answered him, but I couldn't make out her words.

I picked my way through the narrow space to the desk, not sure of what I was looking for or what I hoped to find. On the one hand, I didn't like the idea of my cousin robbing my great-grandmother's shop. However, if I came across a pile of stolen books stacked neatly in the back room of Thaddeus' shop, it might solve a lot of my problems. The books would be returned, and Nathaniel would *have* to declare me the winner of Granny Bea's competition for Spellbooks. There was no way she'd ever condone theft, especially not of her precious books.

The workspace next to the door leading into the shop was really a plastic card table with a lamp, a few papers, and a laptop showing a swirling screensaver. Nothing fancy and definitely no rare books. I pressed the space bar on the laptop and a lock screen popped up, requesting a password. I frowned at the device. My magic wouldn't do me any good against a password-protected computer, and I didn't have the time or knowledge to guess Thaddeus' password. Reluctantly, I turned my attention to the papers, shuffling through them as quickly as possible. Mostly, they looked like inventory sheets and delivery statements. Nothing of particular interest caught my eye. Either Thaddeus had hidden his involvement in the disappearance of the books, or he had nothing to do with it. I realized I didn't know which one I wanted it to be more, which made me feel like a terrible person. Surely, I should be happy that I hadn't discovered evidence my long-lost cousin was a thief, right? I sighed and stacked the papers back into the closest semblance of the disorganized chaos in which I'd found them.

A booming laugh on the other side of the wall startled me and I jumped, scattering papers all over the floor. It sounded so close to my head that I wondered if someone had opened the door without me realizing it. Except there had been no spill of light pouring into the dim storage space. Just a tourist then. A very loud tourist. I crouched, gathering up the papers I'd dropped, when something caught my eye. A single page of yellow legal paper had fallen behind the desk and was trapped between the metal leg and the wall. I scrunched under the desk, stretching to grab the paper. I hadn't seen it in my brief search, so it must've dropped down here earlier.

I carefully wiggled it free, pulling it out and bringing it into the light from the desk lamp. A series of titles written in terrible penmanship greeted my eyes. I sighed. Probably just notes on restocking or what was selling well. I started to tuck the list back under the desk when a title caught my eye.

"Transmutations and transformations," I murmured to myself as I deciphered the almost illegible writing. "Why does that sound so familiar?" I ran my finger down the list, picking out a few more that seemed to tickle at the back of my brain. The final two titles made me catch my breath. *Alice's Adventures in Wonderland* and *The Hobbit*. It couldn't be. Could it? I pulled out my phone and thumbed open my gallery. My photos of Granny Bea's ledger popped up. My eyes flicked back and forth, confirming that the list of rare books from the shop matched the list I'd just found underneath Thaddeus' desk.

"...talk in the back," a male voice drifted clearly through the wall.

"But I still need help!" A female voice this time. I recognized it as Bella's. She sounded on the verge of panic. Quickly, I pulled up my camera and snapped a picture of the list. I could match the titles later in more detail later, but for now, I had to get out of here.

"My assistant can provide the aid you seek, milady. Here, Jake. Can you help her? I need to take this meeting."

I scrambled, tossing the list back under the desk and hastily arranging the papers I'd knocked off on the plastic tabletop. A key scraped in the lock separating the shop from the storage room. My heart rate skyrocketed, and I dashed back down the congested hallway as fast as I could navigate the tangle of boxes. The lock clicked open in the familiar sound of metal sliding against metal. There wasn't enough time. I wasn't going to make it out the door without being spotted. Plan B then. Hide and hope that Thaddeus didn't need to restock the store.

I skidded to a stop and crouched behind a haphazardly stacked pile of cardboard boxes, praying the shadows they cast were enough to conceal me from sight. A moment later, the door leading to the shop swung open, illuminating the storeroom with a slice of natural light. I shrank back against the wall and held my breath. Two different sets of footsteps, one long and heavy and the other quick and lighter. I guessed the first belonged to Thaddeus based on his size, but who was with him? The door shut, cutting off the light from the shop.

"You're interrupting me at my place of business. Again," Thaddeus growled in a low voice.

"Then you should answer your phone," a man's distinctive nasal voice responded with a faint hint of a whine. My eyes flew wide, and I pressed a hand over my mouth to suppress a gasp. What was Oswald Puddleton doing here?

"I told you; everything is in order. You'll get what you want, and so will I," Thaddeus said.

"I want this business concluded tonight. You have my price and the list. I have the books, so let's make the trade," Mr. Puddleton demanded.

"Not possible. Tonight is the last night of the Faire. I need to be here. What about tomorrow, after I close?" Thaddeus suggested.

Mr. Puddleton harrumphed. "Tomorrow is the town meeting. I cannot miss it. I am a very important member of this community, I'll have you know."

"Fine. After the meeting. Your shop. And make sure you have everything. I'd hate to see this deal go south because something was missing."

Mr. Puddleton spluttered. "Of course, it will be in order! Just who do you think I am?"

Thaddeus' voice was low, but it sent shivers chasing down my spine. "See that it is. I want those books."

"Fine. No need to be insufferable," Mr. Puddleton muttered.

"And stop bothering me at work. I've got quotas to meet."

"As do I!" Mr. Puddleton's nasal whine grated on my nerves.

"I'll see you tomorrow night and then we'll both be happy. Eight o'clock at your shop." The door swung open once more, light flooding the hall. Instinctively, I pressed my back against the wall. One set of footsteps retreated, the door swung shut, and the storage area was once more lit only by the dim glow of the desk lamp.

Thaddeus grunted and shuffled the papers on the desk. He grumbled under his breath. "How annoying can one man be? Couldn't just be patient? He—" Thaddeus cut off mid-sentence, something drawing his attention. "That's strange," he murmured, sounding confused.

What was strange? Had I left some papers under the desk or something else to betray my presence? My breaths came more quickly through my fingers. Heavy footsteps started down the hall. He was going to find me. How could I possibly explain why I was hiding in his backroom? My mind went blank, and all I could hear was the pounding of my heart and the steady thud of footsteps growing ever closer.

Suddenly, the door to the shop swung open. "Boss? There's a lady here who's asking about a book."

"So? You work in a bookshop. Help her," Thaddeus over articulated the words in his frustration at being interrupted.

"Umm, I would, but I haven't ever heard of it. Something about a guy named Blackshark or something? It's about pirates and long-lost treasure. I told her if anyone knew anything about an old book like that, it'd be you." Pride filled the assistant's voice.

"Fine. I'm coming." A pause followed by retreating footsteps sounded in the cramped space. The door swung shut, and I heard Thaddeus' low voice rumble from the other side of the wall. Slowly, I blew out a breath. That had been too close.

Not knowing how much time I had, I rushed to the opposite door leading behind the shop and opened it a crack. After peeking through to check the coast was clear, I slipped outside and softly shut the door behind me. No one was lingering behind the shops, but someone might come out for another smoke break. I had no intention of being caught back here. Swiftly, I hurried to the corner and snuck a look into the bustling flow of tourists wandering past the shop front. Bella loitered near the front of the store, trying to look inconspicuous and not doing a great job. Not that I was one to criticize at the moment.

"Psst!" I hissed.

Her head came up and a look of relief washed over her face. I tipped my chin towards the road. She nodded, and we merged with the milling tourists, losing ourselves in the crowd as quickly as we could. I glanced over my shoulder to check to see if anyone from Blackwell Books had noticed anything. Neither Oswald, Thaddeus, nor his store helper were visible. I grabbed Bella's hand and pulled her into a secluded spot near the edge of the fair.

"I'm sorry," Bella blurted out. "I couldn't keep him there any longer. As soon as Mr. Puddleton walked in, your cousin completely ditched me."

I patted her hand. "Don't worry. I'm pretty sure they didn't know I was there."

"What did you find?"

I pulled out my phone and showed her the picture of the list from under the desk. "See here? I thought some of these titles sounded familiar, but it took me a second to remember where I'd seen them before."

"Where?" Bella asked.

I flicked to the next picture. "Here. In Granny Bea's ledger. From just a quick glance, these are the same titles as the missing rare books."

"So?" Bella looked confused.

"So, I overheard them talking. I think Oswald Puddleton stole the books and is trying to sell them. He said he gave Thaddeus a list and has the books. He's the thief! We've got him!" I crowed, holding up the phone triumphantly.

"Are you sure?"

I held up my hand. "He had a bandage covering a cut on his hand, which he claims he got from a piece of glass, but I think it might have been from Gideon's scales. Besides, how else do you think that list got on Thaddeus' desk?"

"So, you think Mr. Puddleton stole the books and is trying to sell them back to one of the heirs set to inherit the shop, anyway? Why would Thaddeus buy them? Why not just report it to the police?" Bella sounded unconvinced.

"Maybe Mr. Puddleton doesn't know that Thaddeus is an heir," I reasoned. "Maybe he's the answer to Mr. Puddleton's prayers. A rare book seller in town for the Renaissance Faire and likely to be leaving soon? Seems like a pretty perfect arrangement, if you ask me."

Bella folded her arms over her chest. "I'm not buying it. Mr. Puddleton might not know Thaddeus is an heir, but Thaddeus does. Again, calling the police would be simpler, wouldn't it?"

I bit my lip as my stomach dropped. "Maybe. But maybe he's trying to play hero and recover the books." I knew I was grasping at straws, but it was the only thing I could think of.

"Just like you?" Bella asked with a small smile.

I nodded grimly. "But if he does, it virtually destroys any chance I have of getting Spellbooks. Why would the lawyer choose me, someone with zero experience running a bookstore over Thaddeus, the restorer of stolen property and rare book connoisseur?"

Bella's smile faded. "I see your point. But could it be the other way around? Thaddeus stole the books and is trying to sell them to Mr. Puddleton?"

A frown creased my forehead as I tried to remember the exact conversation. Finally, I shook my head. "It didn't sound that way to me."

"Okay, can you tell me everything you remember? Every word, every phrase?" Bella asked.

"I'll try," I said, grasping at her idea like it was a lifeline. As quickly as I could, I recounted the conversation in as much detail as possible.

At the end of my recitation, Bella weighed the new information carefully. Eventually, she sighed. "I don't know, Harper. If there hadn't been a book theft in town, I'd say that was a completely innocent conversation. Two booksellers agreeing to a sale. That's all."

"It can't be that simple," I protested. "Those are the two best suspects. Thaddeus, the evil cousin trying to take the shop for himself, or the jealous rival from down the street. One of them had to do it!"

"If this were the plot of some mystery story, wouldn't those both be a little too obvious? What do they call them?" she asked, snapping her fingers as if that would help her memory. "Oh yeah. A red herring."

I weighed her words and then shook my head. "But this isn't a novel. This is my real life. Usually, the most obvious suspect did it, right?"

"I don't know. I'm just trying to think of all the possibilities. And you have to admit, a legitimate book sale *is* an option," Bella pointed out.

I chewed on my lower lip. "But why would they meet here and go into the back office for a private conversation?"

"Maybe it was quieter?" Bella ventured.

"Or maybe they wanted to make sure no one saw them plotting together," I said stubbornly.

Bella looked me up and down in an overly dramatic fashion. "What was in those kebabs? I think they made you into a crazier version of Sherlock Holmes."

I shook my head stubbornly. "Whatever is happening between those two is going down tomorrow night at eight o'clock in the Dusty Tome."

"Great. Even if you are right and one of them stole the books, it's not like they're going to invite you to their meeting." She dropped her voice to imitate Thaddeus' deep rumble. "Puddleton, I know we're doing this naughty stealing thing, but you know who we should invite? Harper."

Her voice rose to a nasal whine with an indefinable brogue. "Fantastic idea Thad, me boy! I'll call her right now."

"When did Mr. Puddleton develop an accent?" I asked with a chuckle.

Bella put her hands on her hips. "Hey, we're critiquing your plan, not my impressions. Seriously though, what's your strategy?"

I grinned. "The plan is to crash their little meeting and catch them red-handed with Granny's books."

"What if they are just having an innocent meeting and your assumptions are getting the better of you?"

"What if they're not?" I countered.

"Okay, I'll play along. If you're right and they're working together to steal the books, is it the best idea to confront them? Thieves can turn violent when threatened, you know."

"I'll make sure I find a good spot to eavesdrop without being seen. And I should probably record them. You know, for evidence."

"This isn't a game of hide and seek. If they catch you, who knows what they'd do?" Bella said with a shiver.

"I'll have to be really good at hiding then," I said.

"This whole thing seems like a terrible idea."

"Or is it great?" I said, waggling my eyebrows.

"Nope, pretty sure it's terrible. And stupid. And possibly dangerous."

I linked my arm through hers. "Only time will tell which one of us is right."

Bella muttered under her breath. "Me. It's me. I'm right."

"We'll see."

Magnets, Feathers, and Peanut Butter

Despite Bella's reservations, I woke up early the next morning even more resolved to catch Mr. Puddleton in the middle of his nefarious plot, retrieve the missing books, and secure my future here in Havenwood. I pulled on my jeans and threw on a cute top that matched my eyes. Deciding it was better to err on the warm side, I also grabbed a cardigan embroidered with tiny daisies. By the time I shoved my feet into my favorite boots, I was full of energy and excitement but desperately low on caffeine and Honey's cooking. I clattered downstairs and into the breakfast area, pulling to an abrupt stop at the sight of a police officer in uniform sipping coffee. My pulse raced as I registered the uniform. Was he here for me? Had Thaddeus caught me breaking into his back room on a video camera or something?

Officer Reggie looked up with a wide grin. "Ah, Miss Sullivan, just the person I was looking for, although I didn't think you'd be up this early."

My heart leaped into my throat. It was bad when the police dropped by for an unexpected visit, wasn't it? I tried to keep my voice level. "Good morning, Officer. Why are you looking for me? Did I do something wrong?" I said, a feeling of unspecified dread bubbling to life in my stomach like I'd been called to the principal's office in the middle of a class.

"Nothing like that," the policeman said, waving the hand not holding his coffee. I let out a silent sigh of relief. "When Antonio said you weren't up yet, I was going to leave a note, but then Honey insisted I try her walnut coffee cake, which meant I needed a cup of coffee, and, well, one thing led to another."

I nodded in understanding. "The DeLucas certainly have a way of welcoming you in, don't they?"

"Tell me about it! Not that I'm complaining, mind you," Officer Reggie said quickly.

"Never crossed my mind," I said. "Let me grab a cup, and I'll join you. Then you can tell me all about what brings you out to the Enchanted Oasis this morning." Tension crept up my spine as I splashed some milk and coffee into my mug. My mind was racing. Had they caught the thief? If so, was it Oswald Puddleton, like I suspected? Or was Reggie here to tell me Thaddeus had worked his own brand of magic last night and the shop was now his? I shook my head. No. That wasn't going to happen. Not if I could help it. There was only one way to find out. I settled across from him, coffee in hand. "So, do you have good news?"

"Yes, and no. Would you like the good news first or the bad news?"

"Let's have the bad, then we can end on a positive."

Reggie nodded sagely. "Just what I was thinking. Well, the bad news is we haven't caught the culprit or recovered the books, but we're making progress."

I hid my disappointment behind my mug. "Oh?"

"Well, our lab tech is faster than most. He tested the blood Sheriff Jackson collected from your gargoyle and ran it through the system. No matches, unfortunately."

"What does that mean?" I asked.

"It just means that whoever it belongs to isn't in the system. It happens," Reggie said with a shrug.

"Oh." I repeated, feeling deflated. A thought occurred, and I asked, "What about the fingerprints?"

Officer Reggie's face fell. "I wouldn't put too much hope in finding the culprit through fingerprints. The shop was a public space, after all. We pulled some clean prints from the door, but there were none on the display case, which is unsurprising as it was smashed to smithereens."

My buoyant mood from mere minutes before sank a little more. "Were you able to match any of the fingerprints?"

"Only for those we have in the system already. Some were your great-granny's while others were either not in the system or expected."

"Wait, you have Granny Bea's fingerprints on file?" I asked in disbelief.

Reggie wriggled in his chair uncomfortably. "Well, yes. There was this thing involving magnets, feathers, and more peanut butter than anyone should rightfully lay hands on. Before my time, really. Sheriff Jackson could give you a clearer picture. He was there. Said it was an awful mess, but I think it secretly impressed him that your granny could pull it off."

"Pull what off?"

Reggie blushed. "Like I said, ask Sheriff Jackson. Please."

I hid a smile behind my cup again. Whatever Granny had done to make Officer Reggie blush must've been a doozy. "What did you mean when you said there were fingerprints that were expected?"

Reggie was visibly relieved to have the conversation diverted in another direction. "You know, town employees, family, that sort of thing. We'll track them all down for alibis, of course, although not everyone has an airtight alibi like you."

"I was a suspect?" I asked in surprise.

"Only briefly. But then Sheriff Jackson told me you just flew in from overseas and I called the airline to confirm. Don't worry, you're in the clear."

I let out a little sigh of relief. I hadn't even realized that the police were looking into me. Something else Reggie said caught my attention. I leaned forward, a frown drawing my brows together. "What do you mean, 'family'? Granny Bea didn't have any family in town, did she?"

"Only you and your cousin. Blackwood, was it?"

"Blackwell," I corrected.

Officer Reggie snapped his fingers and pointed at me. "That's right. Theo Blackwell."

"Thaddeus."

"What? Oh, yeah. Thaddeus. Anyway, he had a brush with the law when he was younger, but apparently has been on the straight and narrow ever since. We found some of his fingerprints as well, but because he was around the shop, has keys and might inherit the shop, I told the sheriff we'd better discount him as a suspect." Officer Reggie slapped his hands on the table. "Right. That's me then. I've got to get on my way. Things to be, places to do and all that."

"Wait," I said, throwing my hand out. "You said you had good news?"

Reggie bumped the heel of his hand against his head. "Right. Of course. It was the whole point of me coming down here. Sheriff Jackson says you can start to clean up the shop now. Get it back to intriguing all those tourists with mystic spells and whatnot." He wiggled his fingers and waggled his eyebrows at me like he was a wicked magician in a street magic show.

"I'll do my best," I said with a smile at his antics.

He headed towards the door, but turned and stuck his head back in. "Are you coming to the town hall meeting this evening?"

"I hadn't planned on it. I wasn't invited and don't want to intrude," I said hesitantly.

Reggie waved a dismissive hand. "It's an open meeting for anyone living in Havenwood. I know you've only been here a few days, but it's not like you're a tourist. You should come. Meet some more folks. Get to know the neighbors. That kind of thing."

"Thanks, I'll think about it," I said.

"It starts at six thirty at the library. You know where to find it?"

I gave him a thumbs up. "I do."

"All righty then. You have yourself a great day," Officer Reggie said, settling his hat on his head and tipping it smartly in my direction.

"And you," I returned with a smile.

After Officer Reggie left, I realized that I probably should call Nathaniel Ravenscroft about the cleanup. Spellbooks wasn't mine after all. Not yet. But there might be some rule in place that I didn't know. I wasn't about to give Thaddeus any ammunition for leveraging me out of town. I grabbed my phone and dialed Ravenscroft's number. He answered on the second ring.

"Hello, Nathaniel Ravenscroft speaking."

"Hi Mr. Ravenscroft, this is Harper Sullivan."

"Ah yes, Beatrice's great-granddaughter. Please, call me Nathaniel. How can I help you?"

"I just received word from the police that they've cleared Spellbooks, and we can start cleaning up the shop. Before I went over, I thought I'd better check in with you first," I said.

"Very kind of you, but if the police have given you clearance, then you are welcome to do what you like in the shop. I'll let Thaddeus know about this recent development. Please don't remove anything from the premises, however. Not until next week when the estate is settled," the lawyer warned.

I frowned, the familiarity at which the lawyer spoke of my long-lost cousin rankling at me. What was going on between the two of them? Mentally, I moved both of them to the top position on my suspect list. "I understand. I just wanted to clean the glass up and maybe replace the broken door at the back. Would that be an issue?"

"Not at all. In fact, it would be a great help. Just keep the receipts and we'll settle any expenditures you incur in repairs from the estate. Does that sound like a plan?" Nathaniel asked.

"Perfect. Thanks very much."

"I'm happy to help. Please call if I can be of further assistance," he said before ending the call.

I sat there, enjoying my coffee and the peace of the empty breakfast room as I re-evaluated my plans. Cleaning the shop just jumped to the top of my to-do list. Maybe I could swing by Wildwood Ink later to see Finnegan, I mean, to talk to him about getting someone in to fix the window in the door. Although, seeing the handsome tattoo artist wasn't a bad plan, either. I smiled into my coffee cup. But before heading over, I needed to grab a jacket in case there was an autumnal chill in the air and make sure my keys to Spellbooks were in my purse.

I sat bolt upright. Keys. I'd only gotten my keys to the shop *after* visiting Granny Bea's lawyer, which was the same time Nathaniel had given Thaddeus his. And when I'd run into him talking to Thistle, hadn't he said this was the first time he had come to the shop because he hadn't had the keys previously? I ran through the timeline quickly in my head. I'd met Officer Reggie that morning and given him the ledger. He'd told me that the police finished dusting for prints, and *then* Thaddeus showed up. So, how could his prints have been among those lifted from the scene?

Unless he'd been there before. Suddenly, my suspicions from the day before shifted from Mr. Puddleton to my cousin. Maybe Thaddeus stole the books and was trying to sell them to the competition.

But why?

More importantly, how could I catch him in the act?

Honey stuck her head into the room. "Oh good," she said, bustling in with a tray of steaming blueberry muffins that smelled heavenly. "Did you see Officer Reggie?"

"Yes, he told me I could clean up the mess the thief left in the shop."

Honey slid the tray onto the sideboard. "That Reggie is such a nice young man. Not always the brightest firefly in the glen, but he's a sweet boy."

"He is nice," I agreed.

"Well, I'm happy for you that things are moving in a positive direction. Is your cousin going to come help with the cleanup?"

I shrugged, not really having considered the notion. "I don't know," I said honestly. "I don't have his number, but I suppose the police or Mr. Ravenscroft will reach out to him to let him know. In the meantime, I think I'm going to head over and at least put the books back on the shelves."

Honey nodded. "Well, you are going to be busy. Let me pack up some muffins to keep you going while you work."

"You really don't have to do that," I protested, but my objections were weak because the muffins smelled incredible.

"Nonsense," Honey said, bustling over to a closet tucked in the corner and pulling out a white pastry box, letting me know this wasn't the first time she'd pressed her baked goods on someone. She set four massive muffins carefully in the box and tucked the lid in place. "You take these to get started. We're going to be busy with turnover after the Renaissance Faire and getting ready for the upcoming Harvest Festival, but we will do what we can to lend a hand."

"Lend a hand with what?" Antonio said, poking his head into the room.

"With Spellbooks," Honey said. "The police cleared Harper to go in, and, apparently, it's an awful mess. We're going to help where we can."

"You really don't have to—" I said.

"Pish posh," Honey said. "You're part of Havenwood now. Here, we remember what it means to be a good neighbor."

"I'm not part of Havenwood. Not officially, anyway," I said.

"Well, you are to us," Honey said, giving me a squeeze. "Now, if you want to, I'd be happy to sit and look over your plans for Spellbooks with you. I bet Bella would offer some suggestions as well. She's got a good head on her shoulders when it comes to running a business."

"I'd really appreciate that. Thank you."

"See, you are part of the town," Honey said with a smile.

Antonio came fully into the room, carrying a beautifully painted bird-house. "Spellbooks might not be officially in the books yet, but you've got the right spirit. Like asking for this to help make your friend's situation a little better."

"Oh Antonio! It's lovely!" I exclaimed. The small house looked like a tiny barn, complete with red painted walls, white trim, and a tiny silo at the back. Antonio had even made a little white picket fence around an area to place a bird feeder.

"By the way, I'd be happy to help with any remodels or design features you want to include at Spellbooks. Once this whole inheritance thing is sorted, then we can work on it together. What do you say?"

"I say you are too good to me!"

"It's what folks here in Havenwood do for each other," Antonio said, handing me his beautiful creation.

I reached for my purse. "That might be, but please let me—"

He held up a finger, cutting me off. "Without payment. I was happy to help."

"Well, then at least let me give you both a hug," I said.

"Now that we'll accept anytime," Antonio said.

A warm, fuzzy feeling washed over me as I stood there, wrapped in the arms of the DeLucas. It felt like home. I was grinning widely as I stepped back and looked at them. "Thank you both. You're just the inspiration I needed this morning," I said sincerely, grabbing my purse from the back of the chair, double checking the keys were inside before slipping on my jacket.

"Anytime," Antonio replied with an easy shrug.

"And make sure you eat something," Honey said, handing me the box of muffins.

Antonio carefully balanced the birdhouse on top. "Take care. Have you got it?"

I nodded, shuffling my grip on my load to a more comfortable position. "I think so."

He pushed the door to the B&B wide for me, and they both waved cheerily as I walked towards Spellbooks. The buttery sweet smell of the muffins wafted up to me through the closed lid, making my mouth water.

I just hoped they would be sustenance enough for cleaning the shop, plotting to catch a thief, and maybe a neighborly 'hello' to the local tattoo artist.

Ninja Bunny

I walked around the back of the shop and set down my load before digging out my keys and opening the door.

"Hiiiiiya!" A flying white figure with a flash of red sailed out from the interior of the shop, landing in the middle of the sunny reading room.

I jumped back in surprise, my heart thundering. Then I squinted down at the compact figure. "Luna? What are you wearing?"

Luna posed in front of the entrance to the shop with her paws up in a semblance of a martial art stance and a red cloth tied around her head. "I'm told martial artists are terrifying and proficient at defense. I assumed it was a plausible deterrence tactic. Warpaint my whiskers and call me Flufflebottom the Fearsome," Luna said, baring her teeth.

"No, you're right. And this," I waved a finger at her appearance, "is absolutely terrifying, Flufflebottom. Nearly scared me straight out of my socks."

"Good. That's what I was going for," Luna said with a pleased nod.

"Just one question. How did you tie the headband with no thumbs?"

Luna sniffed, sending her whiskers twitching. "How rude. A lady never divulges her secrets."

I hid a smile. "My apologies. May I please enter, oh Sensei of Spellbooks?"

Luna narrowed her eyes at me and then shifted to the side. "I like it. You may enter. What's that?" she asked as I scooped up the box and the birdhouse.

"The birdhouse is for Thistle. Antonio made it for her. Isn't it beautiful?"

"I always knew he was a good carrot," Luna said, hopping after me as I walked into the shop.

"Umm, you mean a good egg?"

"Do I look like a chicken to you?"

I didn't bother to hide my grin from the testy bunny this time. "Not at all."

"What's in the box? It smells delicious," Luna asked, her nose quivering.

"Blueberry muffins. Honey sent them along, so I could get to work cleaning the shop. The police have just given me the all-clear to tidy up the mess the thief left."

"Well, pass one down here," Luna commanded. "If anyone deserves a treat, it's me. Do you think it's easy monitoring the shop all by myself?"

Rather than try to answer that loaded question, I opted for a safer route. "Can rabbits eat blueberry muffins?"

"Not usually, but they also can't talk, now, can they? Fortunately for you, I can do both."

Not seeing any plates downstairs, I carefully tore the top of the box off and placed it and a muffin on a clear patch of the counter for her. Books were scattered over most of it and a small chalkboard hung on the wall behind the counter, reminding me of the one in Granny Bea's office. "Why is that fortunate again?"

"I'm saving you from the calories, of course! Really, rather noble of me, don't you think?"

"No, that's not what I meant. How can you eat—"

A knock on the front door interrupted me before I could delve into Luna's peculiar eating habits. I looked up in surprise to see Finn's smiling face peering through the window. I hurried to unlock the door.

"Morning!" Finn said.

"Hello," I answered, butterflies fluttering in my stomach. I couldn't decide if it was because of his charming smile or the fact that I really wanted to interrogate him about the theft. I'd never interrogated anyone before.

How did you go about it? I didn't want to upset the neighbor, just in case I was wrong for suspecting Finn in the first place. Still, he knew the shop was empty and could've easily broken in. And then there was the whole looking after the cat and phoning the police thing.

Unaware of my internal turmoil, Finn said, "I hope you don't mind me stopping by, but I saw you in here on my way to work. If I'd known you were coming in this morning, I would've grabbed you a coffee too," he said, holding up his to-go cup.

"That's very kind of you, but I didn't know I was going to be here until just a few minutes ago," I said, trying to play it cool. Maybe I could get him to reveal something if I could keep him talking.

"Oh?" Finn asked, raising an eyebrow.

"The police stopped by to tell me I could start tidying up. It was bad enough that whoever it was stole Granny Bea's books, but did they also have to trash the place?" I complained, looking at the mess around the shop. It looked like the thief had dumped over an entire shelf of books.

"It was rotten of them on both counts. A horrible way to welcome you to Havenwood," Finn said.

"It wasn't what I expected, that's for sure. Did you hear anything? I imagine breaking the glass would've made quite a ruckus," I said, trying to keep my tone curious instead of accusatory.

Finn shook his head. "Sorry, I wasn't in yet and, unlike Spellbooks, my shop doesn't have an apartment upstairs. I just wish that we could have made a better first impression on you. This type of thing doesn't happen in Havenwood. At least, not usually." He took a step towards the door as if to go.

If he left, there went my chance to question him. Quickly, I held up the box from Honey. "You know what goes great with coffee? Blueberry muffins. It just so happens I have some extra. Interested?"

Finn held up his hands. "I wouldn't want to deprive you."

"Trust me, I have it on good authority that these are too big for me to handle them all on my own. Besides, are you really turning down Honey DeLuca's baking?"

"They're from Honey? Oh, now I've *got* to try them," Finn said.

"Right this way," I said with a little maître de bow and wave towards the counter. "I don't have any plates down here, I'm afraid. I could run upstairs and get one if you like. Then you can sit here and enjoy five minutes of peace before starting your day."

Finn shook his head. "No need. I'm house trained. I'll try not to get too many crumbs on your floor." I opened the box, and his eyes went wide. "Wow! You weren't kidding. I'm pretty sure one of those is bigger than my head."

"It's bigger than Luna's for sure, but that's not giving her any problems," I noted. Luna shot me a dirty look but couldn't really protest, given that her muffin was half-gone and her cheeks were nearly bursting with juicy blueberries.

"Well, now I feel even worse about not bringing you a coffee," Finn said as I handed him a muffin.

"Don't be silly. You've been looking after Mr. Wigglesworth for days. A muffin is the least I can do," I said. "What time did you say you found him, by the way?"

"When I got in that morning. He looked a little frazzled, which was strange enough because he's usually such a calm cat." Finn accepted the muffin with a smile and bit into it. He let out a little moan of pleasure. I grinned and plucked one of my own from the box. It was still warm and crumbled decadently on my tongue.

Finn looked at the muffin and swallowed. "Seriously, whatever that woman pulls out of her oven, I'll eat. No questions asked."

"Likewise," I managed around my mouthful.

For a few minutes, contentment and the scent of blueberry muffins filled the shop as the three of us enjoyed our breakfast treats. Finn licked the crumbs from his fingers with a satisfied air. "That was delicious. Now, where's your broom?"

My eyes shot wide. How did he know I was a witch? Suddenly it occurred to me that I was alone with a guy I'd met only yesterday at the scene of a crime with only a ninja rabbit by my side. Real smart, Harper. "Umm, sorry, what now?" I asked, surreptitiously looking around for something I could use in case he tried something untoward.

His eyes twinkled as he looked at me. "Your broom. Didn't you know? It's an old Havenwood custom. You give someone an unexpected muffin and they have to sweep the floors for you."

I chuckled, relief washing over me. Maybe I was jumping at shadows and Finn was just what he appeared to be: a good neighbor. "I've never heard of such a thing."

He nodded seriously. "It's tradition and bad luck if I don't."

I shook my head at the handsome man standing in the middle of Granny Bea's shop. "I'm not sure it works that way."

"That's because you're new to town. It's understandable, but I'm afraid I'm bound by Havenwood's ancient institution of hospitality. What would people say if they found out?"

"That you have your own shop to run?" I asked in a half-hearted attempt to dissuade him.

"That's the great thing about being the boss. I can turn up a few minutes late without being written up. Now, where's the broom?"

I gave up, mostly to not be rude, of course. Not because I wanted to spend more time with the attractive guy from next door. "Granny always kept it in the closet down the hall," I pointed.

"Great. If you grab those books, I'll get to work repaying my debt," Finn said, moving around the counter and down the hallway.

I laughed and scooped up armfuls of books, carefully stacking them on the counter. I'd have to check them for damage and re-shelve them. Luna gave a sleepy little snort and hop-waddled toward the front window, where she promptly curled up for a nap.

Finn brought the broom around and set to work sweeping up the broken glass from the display case. "Those aren't crumbs," I observed.

"Oh? Aren't they?" he said in feigned surprise. "Could've fooled me. Ah well, I've started now. It would be rude not to finish."

"Another ancient Havenwood tradition?" I asked dryly.

"So, you *have* heard of them!" he exclaimed. We shared a laugh at our combined silliness before Finn got back to work sweeping and I tidied up more of the books. While we worked, he asked, "What are your plans for this place? Do you want to keep it a bookstore?" he asked as we worked.

I was taken aback. "Of course! I mean, I used to come here as a kid. I even spent an entire summer here and loved every second." I sighed wistfully. "It was magical, and not just in the obvious way."

"I understand that. I always thought this place was something special," Finn said, brushing the glass into a pile.

"I can't imagine Spellbooks as anything else, you know? I'd love to see people in here browsing, reading, maybe drinking a cup of coffee or something? A place to enjoy the written word but also a place to just relish the small joys of life, if that makes sense."

"It does," Finn said softly, his eyes flicking up to mine and a warm smile on his face.

I felt a blush rise in my cheeks and turned away to grab some more books from the floor before he could see the effect that he had on me. "What about you? What brought you here?" I asked.

"Oh, you know, the usual," Finn said.

"Nothing about this town is usual," I laughed, putting my armful on the counter.

He joined in. "You're right about that. How much do you know about druids?"

"Other than they have long beards, hang out with trees, and like to run barefoot, not much."

"Well, you're right on all counts except the beard," Finn said, stroking his own carefully groomed stubble. "Those long beards get caught in everything. Can openers. Revolving doors. Ritual fires. In fact, that's how I lost mine."

"Really?" I blurted out.

"No," he chuckled. "But it makes a good icebreaker. No, the real reason I moved here was to find some peace. My master, that's the druid I trained with, he was a good guy, but kept getting pulled into darker and darker situations with more powerful people. When I stopped to take stock of what was going on, I realized I didn't want his life to be my life. I wanted to do some good, leave the world a little better than I found it, you know. So, when I finished up my training, I moved here."

"Are all people in Havenwood as open as you are about their powers?" I asked, wondering what the norm here was. I tended to keep my own magic a secret, but maybe that wasn't the way in Havenwood.

"Only with locals. We don't really talk about it with the tourists, although some like to hint at Havenwood's true nature." My mind flitted back to Aria at the Dragon's Den. Finn shrugged and continued. "Some people are pretty open. Some prefer to keep their gifts to themselves. It's kind of an unwritten thing. Share if you want to, but don't pry. You know?"

"Makes sense," I said, feeling relieved to have the custom spelled out for me. At least no one would ask about my own powers. "So, you graduated from druid school and now you own a tattoo parlor?"

Finn nodded and held out his arm, displaying his own impressive ink collection. "These are mostly part of my training, but I've added to them throughout the years. I found it's a way to express my creativity and help my customers. You see, I put runes into their tattoos where I can. Nothing big or flashy, mind you. Just minor spells to bring them extra luck or help them get over colds faster. Something to make their lives just a little easier, you know?"

"That's really sweet of you," I said, leaning over to get a closer look. "Out of curiosity, how does it work?"

He pointed at a line of knotwork on his arm. "Something like this, for example? I could hide the runes in there for 'luck', 'beautiful', and 'neighbor' and then let fate do its thing. It might work and bring a beautiful new neighbor into my life. To be fair, runes can be difficult, but mine usually operate as expected."

I'd been examining the intricate knotwork when his words sunk in. I blinked in surprise and a curl of pleasure sprang to life in my stomach. "Is that what this says?" I asked, pointing at the knots.

He grinned and shook his head. "No, my magic doesn't work on me. Still, it seems like fate might be turning my way." He winked at me with a charming smile. "Do you have a dustpan?"

"Wha—" My brain stuttered for a moment at the abrupt change of topic.

"For the glass?" Finn prompted.

"Oh, right." I hurried behind the counter and grabbed it for him. Together, we swept up most of the broken glass, dumping it in a nearby trash can. I'd have to go over the space again with a vacuum to make sure no one cut themselves, but for now, it would do.

"There, much better. I'll give my guy a call later today to let him know he can come over and repair your door."

"Really, that's so sweet of you. Are you sure there's nothing I can do to say thank you?"

He brushed aside my offer. "Think nothing of it. Now I've fulfilled my traditional muffin obligation. I thank you deeply, milady," Finn said, bowing to me with the broom held across his palms like he was a knight offering his liege a sword.

I laughed and accepted it from him. "If this is the Havenwood way, I'll have to have muffins here every morning."

Finn patted his stomach as I tucked the broom back into its place. "I love sweets, especially Honey's. But I've always been more of a savory guy. Pizza, burgers, steak. That's where it's at."

"Ooh, I tried a burger over at the Dragon's Den. It was delicious, but if spirit animals came in food form, mine would definitely be pizza."

"You shouldn't eat your spirit animal, but if you like pizza that much, check out the Hobbit Hole. Their pizzas are worthy of avoiding any ring-related quests for all time. Perhaps I could take you there tonight?" he asked.

I bit my lip. Dinner with this handsome druid was certainly appealing, and I really wanted to remove him from my suspect list so I could enjoy an evening with him, guilt-free. But, despite his charming behavior, I wasn't entirely convinced of his innocence. Besides, my evening was filling up fast between the town meeting and trying to catch the book thief.

Finn misinterpreted my look. "I'm sorry, I didn't mean to—" He rubbed the back of his head and scuffed a toe against the newly cleaned floorboards. "That is, if you have a boyfriend..."

"No!" I exclaimed, rather more forcefully than I'd intended. "I mean, no, I don't have a boyfriend. But I can't tonight." Finn looked up and gave a tentative little smile. How could someone this nice be a thief? Best-case scenario, I had a hot date. Worst case, I could ask some more questions that might give me some more answers about the break-in. I rushed ahead before I could talk myself out of it. "However, I'm free tomorrow?"

His face lit up, and he dipped his head. "Tomorrow it is. Can I pick you up here, say, around seven?"

"Seven would be perfect," I said, feeling a smile spread up my cheeks.

"Well then, tomorrow it is," he said, scooping his coffee cup from the counter and giving me a small salute.

"Tomorrow," I agreed, walking him to the door. Finn shot me one more smile that warmed me down to my toes as he walked towards his shop. I sighed and pushed the door closed behind him, the tiny bell above it jangling merrily. Either Finnegan Oakheart was the most perfect next-door neighbor a girl could hope for, or he was a sociopathic thief. Either way, we were going on a date. What did that say about me, I wondered.

"Well, you work quickly," Luna said with a yawn and a stretch from her nap in the sunshine.

I jumped, having forgotten she was there. "What? Why? What do you mean?" I asked.

"The shop. It looks better already." She tipped her head, her ears twitching at me. "Why, what did you think I meant?"

"Nothing," I said hastily. "Oh, look, I'd better take Thistle her new birdhouse." Luna shot me a strange look as I scooped up the birdhouse and headed outside. I needed to escape, though. If I'd stayed in the shop, my smile would've given me away for sure. Even with all that had gone wrong since I'd come here, there were things that made me wish like mad I could permanently make Havenwood my home, and currently at the top of that list was Finnegan Oakheart.

The Giant and the Nymph

How did one announce one's presence to a tree nymph? I stood in the middle of the empty garden, staring at the tree. Did I knock? Was it considered rude? What if I accidentally pounded on her bedroom door? Or she was in the shower? Deciding it might be more decorous to avoid any tree-related faux pas, I called out instead.

"Thistle? Are you home? I have something for you." I stood there, holding out the birdhouse and feeling a little silly for talking to a tree. I was just about to leave when two of the knots on the trunk blinked at me. I jumped and almost dropped the birdhouse in surprise, fumbling to catch it before it hit the ground. When I looked back up, Thistle stood in front of me, dressed in the same leafy green outfit from before.

"A gift? For me?" she asked, her eyes sparkling with delight. She dug her bare toes into the grass and tucked her hands behind her back shyly.

I held out the birdhouse. "You mentioned how much you liked birds visiting, so I thought you might like this," I said, holding out the birdhouse.

Thistle accepted it, examining it from all angles. "Oh! It even has a place for food!" she exclaimed.

"Antonio DeLuca made it. He thought it might attract any birds that had been frightened away by the events of the past few days," I said. A swell of happiness rose within me at the bright joy on her face.

"I want to put it up now! But I don't have any bird food. I know, I'll run down to the pet store and see if they have anything," she said in a rush, darting back and forth in the garden, holding the birdhouse in front of her like she was carrying a priceless treasure. "But what should I do with this?"

I pointed at the bench under the tree. "Why don't you leave it here? You can run your errands, and it'll stay safe until you get back."

Thistle glanced at the bench and blushed. "Yes, yes, of course. Oh, this is just so exciting! I can't wait to see what sort of little feathered friends come to visit." She slid the birdhouse carefully onto the bench and then threw her arms around me. "Thank you, Harper. Thank you, thank you, *thank you*."

I gave her a little squeeze back. "You're welcome, Thistle."

She pulled back. "There's so much to do! First the bird feed. Then I must find the perfect place to mount the house. Maybe I'll add some new flowers to the garden, too. Oh, so much to do!"

I chuckled. "I'll leave you to it then."

Thistle waved at me distractedly as I left her flitting about the garden and making plans to welcome visiting birds to make a more permanent home. The chime of my phone dinged from inside and I went to answer it, leaving Thistle to her plans.

Bella had sent me a message asking what time I'd be back and if we could meet up. I knew she was especially busy with the B&B today, so I suggested getting together later. She sent me a thumbs up in response. I set the phone down and looked around the shop. I had a lot of work of my own to do. I'd better get to it.

A thunderous pounding on the front door of the shop interrupted the rhythm of my cleaning and re-organizing. I blinked in surprise at the long rays of late afternoon light slanting through the windows as I hurried to the front. When did that happen? I must've lost track of time. My stomach growled piteously, despite the fact that I'd wolfed down Honey's muffins. I needed to fill it with something other than sugar, and soon.

Luna hopped up on a book. "I heard that. You're as bad as your granny. At least she was sensible enough to keep snacks under the counter."

"I just got swept away with the cleaning and the memories. I'll grab something as soon as I figure out who's at the door," I said, hurrying past her.

"I know what swept you away. Or should I say, 'who'," Luna called after me.

My brain stuttered over a retort to the smart-aleck rabbit as the looming figure outside the shop blocked out the lazy afternoon sunbeams from shining through the entire front display window.

The man shaded his eyes with a hand the size of a ham large enough to feed eight with leftovers, peering inside the shop. He saw me before I could retreat to the safety of the shelves and waved at me through the window.

"Harper?" he asked, his gravelly voice only faintly muted by the glass.

How did he know my name? Slowly, I moved towards the door, instincts on fire and ready to run at the slightest hint of those ham-like hands crashing through the shop window. "Hello? We're not open now, but perhaps you could come back later?"

The big man held up a toolbox. "Finnegan called me. Said you had some broken panes that need fixing?"

This was Finn's handyman? He looked like he was more inclined to rearrange someone's face than work on restoration with delicate materials like glass, concrete, or small boulders.

"Just a second!" I called, grabbing the keys from the counter despite my initial hesitations about the hulking man. Granny always said judging by the cover was for books, and if we were meant to do that to people, they would've come with their own catchy illustrations and back blurbs. If the guy standing outside the shop had come in book form, there would've been enough room for a small novel on his back cover. Imagining an entire story printed on his back somehow made him less intimidating, and I found the courage to open the door, even though my knees continued to quiver.

The man stayed outside, seeming to wait for me to become accustomed to his massive presence. Biceps bigger than my head bulged, pressing against the neatly ripped edges of a shirt that had failed miserably at confining them. Overalls and work boots completed the man's ensemble, but the shoes looked big enough to stomp on the nearby fire hydrant without giving the guy any problems at all. Shopping must be a nightmare for him. Finally, I dragged my gaze up to the man's face. His skin was a dusky color with an almost gray tint to it. He had curly hair, which was neatly cropped on the sides, prominently displaying his overly large ears with small gold hoops piercing each lobe. His expression wasn't unpleasant, but I read a long-suffering sadness in his deep-set eyes. Granny's admonition about people not being books drifted back to me, and I realized I'd inadvertently been judging him, which was no way to make friends in a new town. Especially in this town, where some residents, through no fault of their own, came from backgrounds that most of the world classified as terrifying. If Finn recommended him, that was good enough for me to give him a chance.

I swung the door wide with a brilliant smile. "Welcome to Spellbooks! I'm glad you're here." As I said the words, it surprised me to find I genuinely meant them. It felt like I had my first real visitor, even though the shop wasn't officially open yet.

The man's heavy eyebrows climbed his forehead like two hairy caterpillars, but he squeezed through the door without comment. As soon as he was in the shop, it seemed like he sucked up all the available space. Unwilling to be deterred, I stuck out my hand. "It is a pleasure to meet you. I'm Harper Sullivan." I chuckled ruefully and raised my shoulder. "But you knew that already."

The man glanced at my hand and then back at me with a surprised expression. I didn't move or let my welcoming smile waver. Slowly, he set down his toolbox and took my hand. He probably could've palmed several basketballs with the callused palm, but gripped mine delicately, as if he were infinitely aware of his size and strength and was doing everything in his power to mitigate the intimidation factor that practically oozed from a man his size.

"Grimgor," he said, softly. His voice still rumbled around the shop, making it impossible to ignore the hesitation in his tone.

"That's an unusual name. Where does it come from?" I asked, genuinely interested.

"My mother's tribe. It means 'small one'."

My jaw almost dropped, but I halted the instinctive reaction before it could be considered blatantly rude. Who would ever consider Grimgor small?

Grimgor sighed, apparently still reading enough of my expression. "My mother's a giantess. Her tribe is known for their intimidating size and impressive physique. They take great pride in it. Size is a mark of honor amongst them, yet my mother fell in love with a human." He paused, the silence communicating a lifetime of pain. I could only imagine what it must've been like for him, growing up and not fitting in with either side of his family. Too small on one hand and too large on the other. No wonder he'd sought refuge in Havenwood.

I nodded and gave him a sad smile. I imagined he probably dealt with a lot of questions about being a half-giant, so I decided to tactfully steer the conversation in another direction. "How long have you known Finn and my granny?"

Grimgor blinked in surprise, obviously having expected to traverse the familiar conversational ground of his past. "I met him when he moved to town. I'd often swing by Spellbooks to check on Beatrice and lend a hand where I could. Elders are to be respected."

A sense of warmth tinged with just a hint of self-recrimination swept up in me that Grimgor stepped in where I hadn't. I straightened my back. This wasn't the time to dwell in the past or my regrets, but to honor Granny Bea's legacy. "Thank you for looking out for her," I said with a heartfelt smile. "I bet she really appreciated having a friend like you. I know I'm not an elder, but you're welcome here anytime you'd like to visit." As the words tumbled out of my mouth, I remembered I didn't officially own the shop, but I didn't want to walk the invitation back.

Grimgor blinked in surprise, not expecting the welcome. He nodded, looking around uncomfortably. His eyes fell on the books I'd collected and stacked on the counter and lit up. "Are you a poetry reader?" The excitement in his voice was almost palpable. He ran a gentle finger over the cover of the top book like he was reacquainting himself with an old friend.

Something in the longing way he looked at the books made me choose my words with care. "I've always found poetry to communicate enormous depths with an extraordinarily few number of words."

Grimgor bobbed his massive head, not taking his eyes off the book. "Poetry is the journal of a sea animal living on land, wanting to fly in the air."

"That's poignant and incredibly apt. Did you write it?" I asked gently.

"Those words belong to Carl Sandburg, not to me," he said, tapping the cover of the book he'd been looking at.

"I see," I said. A poetry-loving giant? Granny must've adored his visits.

Grimgor cleared his throat. "Where is this broken window, then?"

"Right." I gestured at the display case behind me. "Someone shattered the glass here as well as a pane out back. The window is probably the priority, but I'd like to get the display cases fixed too, if you can do that."

Grimgor nodded thoughtfully, pulling a tape measure out of his toolbox and taking some quick measurements. He spoke over his shoulder as he worked. "I have a guy who makes extra tough glass. I tried for ages to get Beatrice to replace the normal stuff she had here, but she could be stubborn."

"That she could," I agreed.

Grimgor glanced over his shoulder at me. "When I say extra tough, I mean enchanted. He's a gnome and works gnomish magic into the glass. It's not cheap, but you also won't have this problem again."

I bit my lip. Until we settled the inheritance, I didn't know how much I could do. Nathaniel Ravenscroft had told me to keep any receipts, but this sounded expensive. Cleaning up and fixing a broken window was one thing. Could I afford buying enchanted gnomish glass, even if I did inherit the shop? "Could you give me a quote?"

Grimgor named an outlandish number.

I swallowed hard. "Can I to get back to you on that? I need to resolve a few things first."

Grimgor nodded and retracted the tape measure with a snap. "Sure. I've got the measurements, anyway. Just call me when you decide." He slid a small white business card onto the counter. "Now, where is this window?"

"This way," I said, leading him to the sunroom at the rear of the shop. "You see, the thieves—"

"Who is *that*?" Grimgor interrupted me, staring in awe at Thistle, who'd obviously returned from her errands. She darted around the garden, deeply absorbed in her plans and completely oblivious to us. A heavy bag of bird seed sat on the bench next to the birdhouse and an array of plants in temporary planters were scattered on the grass around the tree. September seemed late in the year to be planting, but who was I to contradict a tree nymph?

"That's Thistle. She, umm, lives here," I said, not quite knowing how to explain the woman who lived in the tree in the backyard. Thistle scampered back to the bench and carefully lifted the birdhouse. She carried it around the garden, obviously testing it out in various locations.

"A perfect woman, nobly plann'd, To warn, to comfort, and command; And yet a Spirit still, and bright, With something of angelic light," Grimgor recited softly.

"More Sandburg?" I asked.

"Wordsworth," Grimgor said without taking his eyes off the nymph. "Would it...would you be willing to introduce me?"

My eyes widened. "To Thistle? I mean, sure. But she is on the shy side, so don't be offended if she's a little skittish. Or, you know, disappears."

"Nothing that angel does could offend me," Grimgor said reverently.

"Right," I murmured under my breath. Time to introduce the giant to the nymph. At least life in Havenwood was never boring.

Cookies with your Tea

I CLEARED MY THROAT loudly as we exited the shop, hoping the gentle warning was enough not to startle Thistle completely. The nymph still jumped as she turned and then jumped again when she saw Grimgor. Her eyes went wide, and she froze like a doe caught in headlights. Her gaze flickered around the garden, searching for an escape route, but we half-blocked her path to her oak and the only other option was to clamber over the fence and run across an open meadow towards the forest.

I held up my empty hands to placate her. "Thistle, this is Grimgor. He'll be doing some work around the shop, and I didn't want you to be surprised if you saw him around." I spoke slowly and calmly, like I would to a frightened animal.

"Work?" Thistle asked, her breath coming high and fast.

"Work," I confirmed. "Like fixing the broken window. Finn from next door recommended him."

"He knows Finn? You know Finn?" Her voice was thin, almost on the verge of breaking.

"For quite some time now," Grimgor said and slowly sat in the grass, making himself look smaller and less threatening.

His action worked to help calm Thistle slightly. Her breathing slowed, and her eyes stopped darting around, looking for escape. "How do you know Finn?"

"I did some work for him a while back. We hit it off and now we go camping on the weekends sometimes. I'm good with my hands," he said, placing them on his knees, almost like he was meditating. "I could help you with your birdhouse if you'd like."

Thistle started, obviously having forgotten she still held the colorful little house. She looked at it and then back at him. "I don't know where to put it. I want them to come and visit, but if I hang it in my tree, they make such an awful racket. I can't put it on the ground, or the cat might get them. Oh, I don't know where it should go." She spun in a circle, looking distressed as she searched for the perfect place for the house.

Grimgor nodded thoughtfully. "What sort of birds are you looking to attract? Cardinals? Bluebirds? Personally, I like goldfinches. The little pops of yellow always look so happy. Which ones are your favorites?"

"Painted buntings," Thistle said shyly.

Grimgor whistled appreciatively. "They're beautiful, but rare. If you want to invite some to come and visit, your instinct about keeping the house and, is that a feeder?" Thistle nodded. "Well, keeping both away from Beatrice's cat is sensible."

"You knew Beatrice?" Thistle said, kneeling in the grass and placing the birdhouse next to her. I took it as a good sign. She was relaxing.

Grimgor lifted a massive shoulder, not giving any indication of moving from his position. "She was kind to me. She'd often lend me books, and we'd sit out in the sunroom, drinking tea and discussing them."

"I never saw you here," Thistle said.

"And I never saw you until today. But I'd be happy to build you a little tower for your birdhouse. You could put it next to the fence near the pansies."

Thistle glanced over her shoulder. "Do you think that's the best spot? I thought it might be better to put it near the violets, in the shade, by those pine trees."

Grimgor considered thoughtfully and then nodded. "I see your point. That is a better spot. More sheltered."

When the conversation turned from location to food and types of birds indigenous to the area, I slowly backed away. I was out of my depth when it came to discussing birds. Neither Thistle nor Grimgor noticed when I retreated to the shop.

Shadows were stretching across the floor, and it was almost time for Gideon to wake up by the time Grimgor returned. I looked up from the shelf where I'd been alphabetizing the overturned poetry books.

"Did everything go okay with Thistle?" I asked as Grimgor set his toolbox on the ground.

"She blossoms, a garden in her soul. A tapestry of colors, vibrant and bold. With each step, she weaves a path; An angel's essence, I bask in the aftermath," Grimgor said, looking back towards the garden.

"That's beautiful," I said. "More Wordsworth? Or was it Keats? Not Shakespeare. Was it?" I needed to brush up on my poetry.

"Grimgor and it needs work," Grimgor murmured.

"You write poems as well? I'd love to hear more of your work sometime," I said.

Grimgor blushed and pulled at his collar. "I, um, don't really share my poems. Ever." The finality in his voice rang through the shop like a death knell.

I kept my expression interested but neutral, not wanting to pry into the reason for his discomfort. "Well, you should. It's good, even if you say it needs work. But speaking of poetry, I thought you might enjoy this." I grabbed a small tome from the counter and passed it over. "It's a series of collected works about nature from a variety of famous poets."

Grimgor accepted the book on instinct, his eyes lighting up as he gently ran his fingertips across the cover. He carefully opened the book at random, lips moving as he silently read the poem on the page. I watched him enjoying the book I'd selected for him. Is this what Granny Bea had felt each time she matched a person to a book? It felt good. Like sunshine, a warm hug, and hot chocolate on a wintry day all rolled into one swell of emotion.

Grimgor regretfully closed the book and passed it back to me. "I can't accept this," he said.

I folded my arms over my chest. "Why not? You seemed to enjoy it."

He shook his head and placed it on the counter next to me. "Do you know what people would say if they saw someone like me reading something like that? It's already hard enough to fit in, even here in Havenwood."

"Couldn't you just take it home?" I asked.

"Home is...complicated." He tapped the cover, his hand lingering just for a moment. "Thanks for the thought, but I'm going to have to pass."

Inspiration struck, and I blurted out, "What if I keep it here?"

"What?" Grimgor asked.

"What if I keep it here?" I repeated, forming the idea more fully as I talked. "I could put it behind the counter for you, and you could come and read it here whenever you like. People are hardly going to comment on someone reading in a bookshop, are they? Besides, it seems you'll be in here quite a lot with the window and the display case and the birdhouse."

Grimgor glanced toward the sunroom and the garden beyond. "I don't know..." he trailed off.

"I'd love to see you around here more, Grimgor, and I'm going to put *your* book on *your* shelf back here." I picked up the book on the counter and made a show of tucking it away on the floating shelf next to the chalkboard. "It will be here waiting for you whenever you want to visit, which I hope you do, and I don't think I'm the only one around here who feels that way."

Grimgor blushed again as his eyes flicked towards the back of the shop and the garden beyond. "Well, I need to come back with a pane for the window and to help Thistle with her birdhouse."

"Exactly. And don't forget the display cases. They will take some work as well," I said, immediately making a list in my head of other things that might need fixing around the shop. Surely, I could create a project or three for Grimgor to do around here. Just until he felt comfortable enough to come in on his own.

"Maybe I could expand Luna's hutch outside for her," Grimgor mused. "I know she doesn't like it very much, but I could turn it into something special for her."

"You can stay!" Luna shouted from somewhere deep in the shelves of the shop. "For as long as you want. Read all the poetry you want. It's all yours."

Grimgor looked around with a surprised guffaw, and I let out a little laugh. "What was that you said about respecting elders? Well, the elder of this shop has spoken, and I think her demands are clear."

Grimgor dipped his head, an amused expression crinkling the corners of his eyes. "Far be it from me to gainsay such a wise sage."

"By the floppy ears of Harebourg, it's good to see you people finally figuring out the way of things here at Spellbooks," Luna grumbled, hopping out from behind a shelf of historical fiction. "Nice to see you again, Grimgor."

"And you, Luna." Grimgor performed a respectful bow as Luna hopped up a pile of books and onto the counter. He turned to me and dipped his head again, pressing his hand to his chest. "It was a pleasure to meet you, Harper. I look forward to spending time in Spellbooks once more."

I opened my mouth to explain the complexities surrounding the shop and the inheritance but decided at the last minute not to spoil the moment. "I look forward to hearing more of your poetry." He opened his mouth to protest, but I held up a hand, speaking before he could. "When you're ready, of course."

He smiled, a genuine one that lit his entire face with an open, joyful expression. "Sounds like a plan. I'll be back tomorrow to fix the window, but what Thistle wants for the birdhouse might take me a little longer."

I moved towards the door to open it for him as he hefted his toolbox. "Like I said, you're welcome anytime."

"Much appreciated," Grimgor said, squeezing through the door.

I was already adding to my list of enhancements to the shop as I waved goodbye to him. Not just things like birdhouses or rabbit hutches, but poetry readings, open mic nights, or local talent incubators. I'd have to give it more thought to come up with something that the Grimgors of Havenwood could really embrace as their own. Was a games night taking it too far? Did folks here even like things like Settlers of Catan or Dungeons and Dragons? Were those types of games somehow considered insensitive? What would a dungeon master say to a bunch of gamers who were fantasy creatures?

"And in the next room, we have an orc. What do you do?"

"Well, considering my mom's an orc, I'll apologize for not calling her enough and then sit quietly in the corner while she tells me how I'm not making grandbabies fast enough."

"No, that's not how this works. You have to do something to get past the orc. What are you going to do?"

"I'll drink my tea and try not to start any family drama."

"No. That's not how the game...You're supposed to...fine. Roll to see if you get cookies with your tea."

Okay, so that game probably wasn't the best idea, but maybe something else? I ran through a list of games in my head as I shut the door. What else could I do to give Spellbooks the same wonderful feel it had when Granny was alive while still being true to myself? I stood just inside the shop, pondering this question, when a movement on the street caught my eye. The shadows of evening were already spilling across the road, but shadows couldn't move independently, not even in this town. All thoughts of games tumbled out of my head as a shadowy figure wearing a fedora detached itself from a darkening alleyway and hurried down the street, away from the shop.

Ice crept up my spine as I watched him dart down the street and disappear around a corner. I'd seen him before. Several times, in fact. This wasn't a coincidence. I couldn't brush it off as part of living in a small town. I shuddered. What did he want? Should I tell someone? I should definitely tell someone, right? But who? Officer Reggie? Was that too extreme? What about Finn? But what if it turned out the man in the trench coat and Finn were partners or something? I never thought that I'd be frightened in the idyllic Havenwood, but here I was, sending nervous glances out the window, all too aware that I was a woman on my own. Who was the mysterious hat aficionado, and why was he watching *me*?

Ghosts versus the Vicar

Unfortunately, I didn't have time to explore those questions and still make it to the town meeting on time, but they niggled at the back of my head as I rushed to close up the shop.

"Luna!" I called. "I'm heading out to the town meeting."

She hopped around a shelf. "Don't you want to wait and touch base with Gideon before you go?"

I glanced at the time. "I'd like to, but I'm already going to have to hurry to make it to the library on time."

Luna's ears twitched. "Oh, for the love of radish marmalade! Your generation is always in such a rush."

"I didn't set the town meeting time," I said mildly.

"Not the point," she sniffed.

I hid a smile. "Would you mind telling Gideon about Grimgor? He won't be back tonight, but he might be around in the future making additional repairs to the shop. I don't want Gideon to be surprised." I thought about warning Luna about Fedora Man but decided against it. Knowing the rabbit, she'd wage war on any passing person unfortunate enough to have selected a hat to complement their outfit.

Luna huffed out an aggrieved sigh. "Very well, I'll play glorified messaging service before I get my beauty sleep in return for a nice fresh cabbage and some carrots tomorrow."

"Deal," I said, grabbing the keys. "See you tomorrow."

I locked up the shop and hurried down the street. It might have been my imagination working overtime, but after seeing the guy in the hat again, it felt like someone was watching my every move. I swear I could feel eyes on the back of my neck. By the time I rounded the last corner and saw the warm glow of the library's lights, I was nearly running. My breath was coming in sharp and fast gasps. I felt like prey running from a lurking predator, but whenever I looked around, there was nothing.

The flow of foot traffic increased near the library. I slowed my pace so as not to look like a crazy person. I slipped into the meeting room and selected a seat near the back. I glanced around the room, picking out some faces I recognized. Martha Morningstar, the librarian, sat near the front. I also saw the Puddletons, Madame Fontaine with her penchant for strange predictions, and the vegetarian vampire lawyer, Nathaniel Ravenscroft. A small man with a charming smile and a rumpled suit at the front of the room stepped up on a raised platform and lifted his hands in a plea for silence before I could finish my examination of those present. The room quieted as all attention turned to him.

"Ah, thank you ever so much. I see some fresh faces in the crowd tonight, so allow me to introduce myself. I am Mayor Flavian Featherfoot and I have the privilege, nay, the joy of helping guide Havenwood as mayor. For the third consecutive term, I might add."

Whispers rolled around the assembled crowd. But from what I overheard, Mayor Featherfoot seemed to be well-liked, even if he seemed a bit disheveled on stage.

"Right, let's get on to business then, shall we?" the mayor said, patting his coat and eventually finding a bright pink index card. He peered at it intently and then nodded his satisfaction. "Of course, the first order of business is the Renaissance Faire. Very successful, I might add. Best one yet."

"You say that every year," someone interrupted from the audience with a distinctive Scottish burr to the grumble.

The mayor pointed with his index card. "And every year it's true. Which is a credit to all of our hard work as a community, don't you think,

Mason? But a special thanks needs to go to the Silverthornes for all their help in the set-up and maintenance of the Faire. Let's give a big round of applause for Vivienne Silverthorne and her family, shall we?" Mayor Featherfoot led the clapping enthusiastically, directing the attention towards a lady in the front row. She stood, waving with all the grace and elegance of a queen. Vivienne Silverthorne looked like she was in her mid to late fifties, but given that this was Havenwood, I suspected her actual age might differ from her appearance by quite a bit. Silver streaked her dark hair, and she appeared rather severe and stern as she graciously accepted the crowd's polite applause before sitting back down.

The mayor checked his card for the next order of business. "Coming up is the annual Harvest Festival culminating in the Pumpkin Parade. I'm told it's going to be...smashing!" The mayor paused, his eyebrows doing a jovial dance as he waited for applause. A few people humored him, but most just shook their heads. He continued, his enthusiasm undeterred. "The planning committee has been at it for weeks and will present at next week's town meeting, but if you have any strokes of brilliance before then, make sure you talk to Martha Morningstar. In the meantime, dust off those decorations, folks! We want the town looking its very best. We expect everyone to get involved, and, yes, Mason, before you ask, that means you, too."

"Don't see why an auto shop needs decorations," a man near the front, who I presumed to be Mason, grumbled. It had been a while since I'd seen the dwarf who ran the auto repair shop, but Mason seemed to fit my memories of the man.

"For town spirit, Mason!" Mayor Featherfoot cajoled.

"Can't I get the ghosts down at the cemetery to do a couple of fly bys? That should be *spirited* enough, eh?" the mechanic said.

The mayor stomped his foot as chuckles rolled around the room. I don't know if it was because the mayor disagreed, or if he was upset the joke had gotten more of a response than his had.

"No, for so many reasons. One, ghosts hardly count as decoration."

"It's not their fault they're nearly invisible," Mason protested.

"And two, you remember the incident from last year, don't you? We don't want a repeat, do we?" Mayor Featherfoot tried doing his best stern-teacher stare, but it didn't quite sit right on his face, making him look quizzical and ever-so-slightly constipated.

"How was I to know they liked a drink? Besides, we all apologized to the vicar. Eventually."

A man in a dark shirt and a white collar sitting two seats down from me leaned over to his companion and whispered, "I actually thought it was quite funny. You see, the ghosts—"

I was suddenly interested, but, unfortunately, the mayor's voice cut through the vicar's story. "It. Is. Not. Happening. Again. Not on my watch!"

"Then we'll just do it when you're not watching," Mason said. "I enjoyed hanging out with those lads. Who knew that ghosts could be the life of the party?" Another laugh rose from the crowd at his comment. The mayor looked around, seeming unsure of how to regain control of the meeting.

A blonde lady stood from the side of the room. I recognized Martha, the librarian, and she had quite an effective disapproving stare. "Now Mason, this is a library, and we have certain rules about talking out of turn. Besides, if you keep pestering Mayor Featherfoot, we might all still be here at Christmas, which would put the entirety of my lovely planning to waste. Let's not have that, shall we?" The back of Mason's head dipped low as he sunk lower in his chair. Martha turned back to the mayor. "You were saying?" she asked sweetly as she resumed her seat.

"Ah, yes. Thank you, Martha. Onto the next order of business."

The rest of the meeting passed quickly, with little heckling from the gathered citizens, including Mason. It was interesting to see just how much planning and cooperation went into creating Havenwood's idyllic, touristy atmosphere. The meeting sparked a couple of new ideas for how I could encourage both tourists and locals to come to the shop. Not wanting to forget them, I jotted them down on my phone.

As the meeting ended, I was typing the last of my notes down when a familiar voice interrupted me.

"Harper? Is that you?"

I looked up to see Mrs. Jenkins hovering in the middle aisle at the end of the row of folding chairs. I thumbed off the phone and inched down the aisle to say hello. "Mrs. Jenkins, how are you? I didn't expect to see you here."

The secretary clutched a book to her chest and looked around at the milling crowd. "I love all the town events and try to help whenever I can."

She leaned in closer and whispered, "but the Harvest Festival really is my favorite."

"It seems to be a popular event, based on the little I heard tonight," I said.

"It's wonderful. I do hope you'll join in all the fun."

I bit the inside of my cheek, not knowing what to say. If the meeting with my cousin and her boss didn't go well for me, I would be out of a business and a home. I wasn't sure how I'd stay in Havenwood if that happened. Rather than dwell on the unpleasant future, I nodded at the book she held. "Still searching for pirates?" I asked, noticing the replica journal.

Mrs. Jenkins ran a hand down the cover. "That's why I wanted to come over here. To thank you. I've been doing more research into Benedict Starling and Blackfin. I even visited a rare bookseller, although he wasn't very helpful, but now more than ever I'm convinced Starling and Blackfin are the same man. Who knows? He might have hidden his treasure somewhere near Havenwood. Stranger things have happened here."

"Of that, I have no doubt," I said, sincerely. "I hope you find your answers."

Mrs. Jenkins lifted a shoulder shyly. "Even if I don't, I'm very much enjoying discovering more about this part of history."

"Isn't that what life's all about: the journey, not the destination?" I asked.

A fresh voice broke into our conversation. "Sometimes, it's about both." I looked up to see Nathaniel Ravenscroft coming down the aisle between the chairs. "Speaking of, I'm looking forward to seeing your plans for Sullivan's Spellbooks on Friday. I've already spoken to your cousin and his plans are very impressive, even if they are still in their infancy." The lawyer tipped his head across the room. I followed the gesture, picking Thaddeus out the of crowd. He stood at the edge of the room, talking in low tones to Oswald Puddleton. They moved towards the exit together with Hortense trailing behind.

The lawyer cleared his throat. "Harper?"

I jumped. Both the lawyer and his secretary looked at me quizzically. "Yes. Journey. Destination. I completely agree. Will you excuse me? I just saw someone I have to talk with about...the shop! That's right. Big plans. Can't wait to share them!" I felt myself rambling but couldn't stop it as I extracted myself from them and the crowded room. If I was right, Thaddeus and Oswald were about to make a dirty deal for my great-grandmother's stolen books, and when they did, I'd be there to catch them in the act.

Secret Sales and Blood Suckers

It didn't take me long to realize that tailing someone was harder than it looked in the movies. For one, there was no conveniently crowded marketplace in which to hide. In fact, once I'd left the library and the dispersing town meeting, the streets weren't very busy at all. The second thing I learned was the citizens of Havenwood had far too few trash cans. Not because there was litter covering the streets. Far from it, in fact. But the lack of something to duck behind meant I had to either risk discovery or lag incredibly far behind. The only lucky part of the whole tailing experience was that I knew where they were going.

The lights from the Dusty Tome flooded the sidewalk with a warm glow as I peeked around the corner onto Arcadia Avenue. I couldn't see anyone moving on the street. Deciding I could legitimately claim I was on my way to Spellbooks, I headed down the street to investigate. Even though there was no one who could hear me, I tiptoed along the sidewalk, craning my neck to get the best angle to see the inside of the Puddletons' bookshop.

I couldn't see anyone through the front window crowded with garish book displays as I drew level with the shop. That was odd. Had I misheard them? Or had they changed the meeting place? I found both possibilities unlikely. I'd been in the same room when they'd made their plans, and I watched them turn onto Arcadia. There were no other lights that I could see illuminating the road. They had to be here somewhere.

The Dusty Tome seemed to lean on the building to the right, like it was too tired to hold itself upright under the weight of unrealized expectations, but there was an alley on the left side, similar to the setup at Spellbooks. It was dark, but I could see a light glowing near the rear corner of the shop. Maybe they were meeting in the back? I slipped down the side of the building to look.

I moved as quietly as I could along the narrow pathway. When I reached the end, I took a deep breath and then quickly darted my head around the corner. Too fast. I didn't see anything clearly in the dark. I steeled my nerves and took another, slower look. A small patch of withered grass and a rusted table and chairs that someone tried to spruce up with a badly applied coat of paint were the only things in sight. The Puddletons could really use someone like Thistle to brighten up this area.

No, not the point. Focus, Harper!

A set of three concrete steps led up to the back door of the store, and a light from a window illuminated a square out onto the sidewalk next to them. Two shadows passed across the square of light, one much shorter and rounder than the other. It had to be Oswald and Thaddeus. I bet they were negotiating the sale of Granny Bea's books right now.

The very idea of it lit a fire within me. Part of me wanted to march right in there and demand they return the books at this very minute. But, as much as I might want to, I wasn't a police officer, and, even if I was, I didn't have any proof. Not yet, anyway.

Before I could talk myself out of it, I slipped around the corner. I pressed my back to the cool wall as the two shadows stopped in the square of light directly to my right. Muted voices drifted through the glass. My heart thundered so loudly in my chest that I was sure they could hear it. However, the shadows drifted away, and the voices faded. The two men must've moved deeper into the shop. I cautiously stood on tiptoe and poked my head up over the windowsill. Hortense wandered back and forth across the doorway leading to the main shop, talking on her cell phone. Oswald and Thaddeus stood next to a table, engaged in what appeared to be an intense conversation. A stack of books balanced precariously near Oswald's elbow, looking like they were in imminent danger of crashing to the floor as he gesticulated wildly. Thaddeus picked up the top book, flipping through it as Oswald talked at him. Thaddeus turned to acknowledge him, facing toward the window. I squeaked and dropped out of sight. I couldn't very well stand here, peeking in. One of them was bound to notice my head framed against the darkness, but I was sure I'd just witnessed the sale of illegal goods.

How to get closer? I was sure they were trying to sell Granny's books. Both had motive as far as I was concerned, but which was responsible? There was only one way to find out.

I had to get closer.

I cautiously peeked over the window again. Hortense had moved to the front of the shop. I could see the slump of her shoulder and her long hair as she peered out the storefront window onto the street. Oswald and Thaddeus pointed excitedly at the stack of books, shifting them around as they talked. I ignored them, focusing instead on what I could see of the interior. Was there a hallway leading to the side door along the alley? Maybe I could use my magic to pick the lock, slip in, and eavesdrop on their conversation.

Bingo! Behind Thaddeus, a door stood ajar that looked like it might connect to the one in the alley. I dropped back down and tiptoed back into the narrow alleyway. Was this a good idea? Probably not, but if I could catch the thief who stole Granny's books and smashed up the shop, then I had to try, didn't I?

I put my hand on the doorknob, closing my eyes to concentrate on the tumblers. They were sticky and ever so slightly rusty. What had the Puddletons been doing to this lock? Carefully, I used my magic to wiggle the first one into place. A soft click rewarded me. I was just about to start on the second one when I heard voices from inside the shop coming closer and I froze.

"...so much for coming down, Officer Johanna."

"You say you saw someone following you?" A second female voice asked in a brisk, commanding tone.

"Yes, and then I heard something outside, like someone was trying to break in."

"I'd like to look, please."

A key scraped in the lock. I felt the knob jiggle in my grip. I dropped my hand like it had burned me and looked around frantically. Only seconds before they came out and nowhere to hide! I did the only thing I could think of. I ran a couple of steps towards the opening onto Arcadia Avenue, then spun to face the door and dropped to my knees.

Not a moment too soon. The door swung open, light flooding out into the alley. The officer clicked on her flashlight for added illumination and swung it around, catching me in its intensely bright beam.

"Hey! You! Don't move! What are you doing here?" The commands rattled out sharply.

I held my hands up, showing I meant no harm. "Hi, umm, sorry to bother you, but have you seen my cat? Well, not *my* cat precisely. He belonged to my great-grandmother, Beatrice Sullivan. He's missing, and I thought I saw something run down the alley here, so I came to look for him. Here, kitty!" I called.

The officer flicked the harsh beam of the flashlight out of my eyes, but kept it trained on me. "You're Bea Sullivan's granddaughter? Is this your brother or something? Is he looking for the missing cat, too?"

"Brother?" I asked stupidly.

Thaddeus, Oswald, and Hortense crowded through the open door. "I'm her cousin, not her brother, and this is the first time I'm hearing about any cat," he said with a nasty smile.

I stood, careful not to make any threatening gestures. "How could you not know about Mr. Wigglesworth?" Which reminded me, I really needed to take him off Finnegan's hands just as soon as that naughty kitty stopped fictitiously running all over the neighborhood.

Hortense spoke over me. "Really, officer, aren't you going to do anything? That woman is prowling around outside our shop doing who knows what in the dead of night."

"It's eight o'clock," I said.

"What?" Hortense looked taken aback.

"It's eight o'clock. It's hardly the dead of night. And, like I said, I'm looking for my cat. Spellbooks is just down the road. I saw something and thought he might've wandered over here," I said.

Hortense snorted. "Likely story. She's prowling around here trying to..." Mrs. Puddleton trailed off, looking flustered.

Officer Johanna looked over at her curiously. "Trying to what?"

"Trying to scope out the competition, no doubt," Mr. Puddleton broke in. "In case you haven't heard, she and her cousin are engaged in a rather unfortunate dispute over the inheritance of Sullivan's Spellbooks, although I don't really know why there is any dispute at all. Thaddeus here is obviously the better man for the job." He reached up to clap Thaddeus on the shoulder.

Officer Johanna's eyes sharpened. "Not Thaddeus Blackwell?" she asked.

He looked uncomfortable at the officer's obvious recognition of his name, but Oswald didn't notice either reaction, steamrolling ahead. "One and the same, my good woman! He's the man responsible for the impressive little stall of books down at the Renaissance Faire. Why, that's why we were meeting this evening. Finalizing a rather lucrative deal for some rare books." Oswald elbowed Thaddeus good-naturedly, but I noticed my cousin looked a little green and like he wanted to be anywhere but here.

"Rare books, you say?" Officer Johanna asked.

"Quite! Expensive books. *Very* expensive books," Hortense said.

Her husband chimed in. "I don't know what Beatrice was thinking, rest her soul. Thaddeus really is the most qualified candidate to run a bookstore." Oswald put his fists on his hips, attempting to shake his head sorrowfully at both Granny Bea's passing and her unfortunate decision making. The expression made him look like he'd eaten week-old fish and was regretting the choice. Thaddeus, on the other hand, acted like he wanted to be as far away from the Puddletons, the officer, and me as possible.

"There seems to be a lot of interest in rare books this week," the police officer said.

"Well, I am the only true expert in town," Mr. Puddleton said, puffing himself up. "Although that won't be the case when Thaddeus here takes over Spellbooks. A bit of healthy competition never hurt anyone, though," he said with a jovial grin as he jostled Thaddeus.

"Shut up," the bigger man muttered under his breath.

"I'm curious about these books. Just how rare are they?" Officer Johanna said, turning her full attention to the Puddletons, obviously not thinking the girl with the missing cat was much of a threat.

"It's quite a remarkable collection. Quality merchandise only a true connoisseur would recognize," Mr. Puddleton said, glaring at me.

"A rare book deal happening, as your wife put it, in the middle of the night, so soon after there was a theft of rare books just down the road. One marvels at the coincidence." Officer Johanna's tone was light, but I heard the steel behind it.

"What?" Mr. Puddleton spluttered.

"Obviously, not *those* books. We would never traffic in stolen books!" his wife blurted out, looking frantically over her shoulder.

"Quite right, Hortense. Not those books at all!" Mr. Puddleton's bluster faded, and he seemed to fold in on himself.

"Just. Stop. Talking." Thaddeus bit the words out.

"You've piqued my curiosity," Officer Johanna said. "Would you show me these books? I might not be a connoisseur, but I do like to read." She smiled widely, revealing a set of overly long and especially sharp incisors. Suddenly, I remembered the comments I'd overheard earlier about her only working nights. It didn't take much to put two and two together. She was a vampire. A vampire who looked like she just scented blood in the air.

The color drained out of Mr. Puddleton's face. "Oh, well, I'm not so sure this is a good time," Mr. Puddleton backpedaled.

"Come now. You said you'd nearly concluded the deal with Mr. Blackwell here. Surely you have the books on site. It wouldn't be too much of an inconvenience for me to just take a little peek, would it?" Officer Johanna raised an eyebrow.

Mr. Puddleton looked sick to his stomach. I bit my tongue, thankful they'd all forgotten about me for the moment, especially the clever vampire cop. She'd pieced together the situation faster than I would've thought possible.

"Now's really not a good time," Mr. Puddleton said weakly.

"Oh, I won't delay you too long," Officer Johanna said with a predatory gleam in her eyes. She was on the hunt.

"Perhaps another—"

"I really must insist," the vampire said firmly, taking a step back and placing her hand on her hip, close to the baton strapped to her leg. "Please lead the way."

Oswald muttered unhappily but turned back into the shop, followed by Hortense and Thaddeus. Officer Johanna's eyes flicked to me, and she tipped her head towards the shop. "I don't know what your role in all this is, but until I figure it out, you're staying where I can see you."

I kept my hands far away from my body as I moved cautiously towards the open door. "I don't know what you're talking about, officer. I was just looking for Granny Bea's cat."

"Right," she said dryly.

I bit my tongue. After all, I was getting what I wanted: a closer look at Thaddeus and Oswald's rare book deal. I could tolerate a prickly police officer. Having her around might even play in my favor.

"Stand over by the wall," Officer Johanna instructed all of us. Hortense's face was blotchy with rage, whereas her husband's was ghostly white. He was even shaking under the vampire's stony stare. Thaddeus folded his arms across his chest and glared at me like I was responsible for the cop showing up. I tried to ignore all of them, focusing on Officer Johanna instead.

She picked up the top book piled on the table. "Is this one of the rare books?" she asked, turning the book over in her hands.

"Yes. Please be careful," Mr. Puddleton said, reaching out his hands like he thought the book was a baby and she might drop it.

The officer opened the book, looking at the inside. "Hmm, Walt Whitman. First edition?"

"Yes," Mr. Puddleton said softly. I frowned. There wasn't a book by Whitman listed among the ones stolen from Granny's shop.

Officer Johanna shut the book with a snap and placed it on top of the pile. She pulled out her phone and started snapping photos of the stack of books. "You know who loves old books? Sheriff Jackson. He's going to get such a kick out of seeing all these together. Might even come down to have a little look before Mr. Blackwell takes them off your hands." She turned a brilliant smile on the two men, showing more than a little fang.

"I, um, didn't know the sheriff was a fan," Mr. Puddleton said lamely, fiddling with the bandage on his hand.

"Huge fan. The biggest. These must cost quite a pretty penny. You'd better be careful with all that cash," she said, pinning Oswald with a sharp gaze. He looked shaken and his eyes slid to the side, unable to hold her gaze.

Thaddeus spoke up coolly, apparently unaffected by the police officer's tactics. "No cash. Wire transfer. Safer that way."

"Smart," Officer Johanna said, tapping the side of her nose knowingly. She shifted some of the loose papers on the tabletop. "And what do we have here? Building plans?"

Mr. Puddleton blurted out. "Thaddeus is talking of expanding. He asked my...umm...advice...one professional to another, you know."

"Oh, I see. As long as you aren't planning a book heist, it's all good then." Officer Johanna laughed loudly, Hortense and Oswald joining in a beat too late. Thaddeus just glowered at the room in general.

"Heist? Us? Not a chance, Officer," Oswald guffawed, slapping his leg with his bandaged hand. He blinked at it and then swiftly tucked it behind his back.

Officer Johanna tapped her phone against her hand thoughtfully and then her face lit up like a thought had just occurred to her. "You know what? I'd better cross check these books against the list of the ones stolen from Spellbooks. Due diligence and all that," she said with a breezy wave of the phone.

Hortense's face actually turned purple. "Just what are you implying, Johanna? That we're thieves? You're welcome to look around our store any time you like. You'll find no stolen merchandise here!" Oswald flinched as his wife's shrill voice crescendoed. I wondered if it was from the volume or from guilt.

The police officer nodded thoughtfully. "I may have to do just that, purely as part of my official responsibility, you understand. Now, I've taken quite enough of your evening. Miss Sullivan, if you will accompany me, I'd like a word." She gestured towards the door. I was happy to escape the tense room, even if it meant having a conversation with a cop that I'd rather avoid.

I preceded her to the door, where she stopped and turned to look back at Thaddeus and the Puddletons. "Thank you for your time. Oh, and Hortense? It's *Officer* Johanna. Goodnight."

There's Never a Cat

I TRIED NOT TO fidget like a kid caught with her hand in the cookie jar as Johanna marched down the steps of the Dusty Tome. She tucked her phone into her pocket and folded her arms across her chest, staring at me sternly as we stood on the sidewalk in front of the Dusty Tome.

"Now, what were you doing here?" she asked.

"Looking for my cat," I said, sticking to my story.

She licked a fang and considered me thoughtfully. "Let's try this again. What were you *really* doing here?"

I paused, considering my options. Lie to the vampiric police officer or 'fess up to a little casual snooping? It wasn't a hard choice. "I overheard Thaddeus and Mr. Puddleton discussing the sale of rare books and thought..." I trailed off and lifted a shoulder in a self-deprecating shrug.

"And thought they might be your gran's?" Officer Johanna sighed. "I wouldn't put avarice outside of Oswald's capabilities, but breaking and entering? The man couldn't even manage a pickle jar this week. In some freak accident, he managed to smash it and slice his hand open. Needed stitches if you can believe it! Spent most of Friday night in the emergency room and gave a buddy of mine an awful headache with his whining. Somehow, I can't imagine him going straight from the ER to breaking into your gran's place. Especially with all those bandages."

"But he has the most to gain," I protested.

"Does he now?" Officer Johanna cocked her hip to the side and pulled out a notepad and pen. She flipped it open and started scribbling. "Are they looking?"

I frowned. "Pardon?"

Johanna flicked her eyes up to the right without moving her head. "Behind me. Are they looking?"

I glanced up to see Hortense smirking smugly down at me while Oswald fiddled nervously with his bandage. Thaddeus was nowhere to be seen. "Yes," I said, trying not to move my lips.

"Good." She raised her voice and shook her pen in my face. "And don't let me hear of you disturbing anyone else, you hear me?"

I blinked in surprise, my mouth hanging open as she tore a paper from her notebook and shoved it into my hand. She winked at me as she did it, then stuck her notebook back in her pocket and strode off down the street, whistling a merry little tune.

I looked at the note in my hand. A doodle of a simple cartoon cat peered up at me. Above it, Johanna had written, "Come up with a better story. There's never a cat."

I gaped after her and then looked up at the Puddletons. Hortense looked triumphant as she sneered down at me, obviously thinking I'd gotten my comeuppance. On the other hand, Oswald seemed like he was on the verge of a nervous breakdown. Rather than antagonize them further, I spun on my heel and headed towards Spellbooks.

If Officer Johanna had her facts right, and there was no reason to believe she didn't, Oswald couldn't have broken in, or, at least, it was highly unlikely. And if Thaddeus was making deals for rare books, it seemed unlikely he'd have a stash of stolen books just lying around. If I were in his shoes, I'd be keeping my head down and trying to avoid suspicion. I blew out a frustrated breath and mentally crossed off both of my best suspects. If not them, who else stood to profit? Who stood the most to gain from a theft? Was this just about the money? The books were expensive, after all. Or was there something else I was missing?

I replayed the events of the past few days in my head as I walked. What if Bella was right and my assumptions had just gotten me into trouble? That would mean I'd have to go back and examine the rest of my list of suspects. Without Oswald or Thaddeus, I was left with only Finn and Nathaniel Ravenscroft. Despite the opportunity both men had, I didn't really see a motive for either. After all, the bookshop had been empty for a while and both men had ample access. Why wait to steal the rare tomes until now?

The answer hit me like a ton of books. *I'd shown up.* Thaddeus even said in the lawyer's office that he'd found out about me the day before the theft, and I'd only confirmed my flight details with Ravenscroft a day or so before that. Maybe Thaddeus assumed, since I'd flown in from overseas, that Granny Bea cut him out and left Spellbooks solely to me. Maybe he'd given himself the family five-fingered discount before ownership of the shop became official. Or maybe Ravenscroft had acted out of desperation, knowing his time as legal custodian was drawing to a close. Finn could've heard gossip about the heirs' arrival from Ravenscroft or even Mrs. Jenkins. I didn't know how tight-lipped either was, although nothing I'd seen gave me any real reason to doubt their professionalism.

I chewed on my lip. That was a lot of maybes, none of which helped me to narrow down my suspect list. As standoffish and distasteful as I found him, Thaddeus could be completely innocent. Or completely guilty. The same could be said of Ravenscroft or Finn. If only there were some clue, some detail that could point me in the right direction.

"Harper?" a voice rusty with disuse called down to me as I neared Spellbooks.

I looked up. "Hello, Gideon." And then I nearly facepalmed myself. Of course. *Gideon.* Maybe he'd seen something or could remember something about the night of the theft. Some minor detail that he'd left out before.

"Out for an evening stroll?" Gideon asked, fluttering his stony wings.

"Something like that. Honestly, I've been trying to piece together who might be responsible for breaking into the shop. Do you remember anything else? Any minor details? Anything at all might be a clue."

Gideon stretched his wings and coasted on the light fall breeze, landing on the windowsill and dexterously dodging the late blooming flowers in the window box. "Well, Sheriff Jackson seemed particularly fixated on the books on the floor," he said, adjusting his wings and toying with a stone feather.

"What do you mean?" I asked.

"Just that. I don't remember them being there. I landed on the hardwood floor. No books. When I wake up, I'm covered in books. Weird, right?"

I nodded thoughtfully. "That means whoever he is, the thief came back in the shop once you'd shifted back into stone."

"She."

"I'm sorry, what now?"

"She. The thief was a she. Or at least, I'm pretty sure she was a she," Gideon said, shuffling back and forth.

"Why do you say that? I thought you didn't get a look at him. Her."

"A *clear* look. Sheriff Jackson made me do this sensory memory exercise down at the station after he took his samples, and I got cleaned up. The bathrooms down there could really use some work. Not that I use bathrooms regularly, what with being a gargoyle and all, but really! Our police officers deserve better. Or we could all chip in and—"

"Gideon!" I interrupted. He blinked owlishly at me. "Sensory memory? The thief is a woman? Care to elaborate?"

"Oh, right. Well, just before the change took me, I saw a blurry image. It's hard to focus when you're changing into stone, you know. Although I've heard rumors of gargoyles made of limestone being able to last a little longer into the day, but those may just be rumors. Why, just last week—"

I didn't feel bad about interrupting him this time. "Gideon? The thief? What did you see?"

"Of course. The thief. How silly of me. Well, like I said, Sheriff Jackson did this sense memory interrogation, and I remembered that there was a sweep of fabric, long like a skirt or something, which is why I think it was a she. A lovely shade of purple, almost royal, you know, but it clashed so horribly with those bright shoes. Not just red either, but scarlet. Why anyone would pair those together is beyond me. Although I had this friend who knew—"

I didn't want to let him get sidetracked, not when it seemed like I was on the verge of discovering a vital piece of information. "So, a purple dress and red shoes? Was there anything else?"

Gideon shook his head. "Next thing I know, I wake up covered in books. That reminds me of the time—"

Normally, I would've stayed to chat for a while with the long-winded gargoyle, but I had too many thoughts whirling around inside my head. "Thanks so much Gideon. Are you going to be okay here for the rest of the night? I'm beat. Jetlag, you know," I said, yawning for emphasis.

"Look at me talking your ear off when you need to catch up on your sleep. Go on then, and we'll talk another night," he said, making shooing motions with his talons.

"Thanks Gideon. I'll try to get in early enough to see you tomorrow," I said, waving at him.

He fluttered off the sill as I walked down the street towards the Enchanted Oasis, my mind churning. If Gideon was right, and a woman was behind the theft, then neither Thaddeus nor Oswald could be responsible. I couldn't bring myself to believe either of them would dress in a fancy skirt and bright red shoes to commit a crime. Thaddeus seemed to favor jeans and t-shirts outside of the Renaissance Faire and Oswald liked his matching pants and vest. But if neither one was responsible, why were they acting so cagey earlier? What did they have to hide?

No answers came to me by the time I reached the end of Arcadia. Maybe a good night's sleep would shake free some answers, but if I didn't come up with something soon, I was afraid that Nathaniel Ravenscroft would agree with Oswald Puddleton's assessment of who should inherit the shop and I'd be out on my ear. On paper, Thaddeus was better in nearly every category save one: I wanted it more. I knew, deep in my bones, that he couldn't possibly want to make Spellbooks his as much as I wanted to make it mine, but I feared that wouldn't be enough to sway Granny's lawyer.

I sighed and glanced over my shoulder at Spellbooks. Why had Granny made things difficult? A simple "no" would've been easier to handle than building up my hopes just to have them dashed against the shards of broken dreams.

A movement caught my eye. I squinted even as I started retracing my steps. Something was moving near Spellbooks.

"Hey!" I called.

A shadow detached itself from the wall of the shop and started walking briskly away. I picked up my pace. Even at this distance, I could tell the person wore a long coat and a hat. I was willing to bet Oswald Puddleton's Whitman first edition that it was a fedora. It hadn't been my imagination. Someone was following me. And now I was determined to find out who.

Chasing the Hat

The man in the hat looked over his shoulder and saw me coming. He started to run. I wasn't about to let him get away. I pounded past Spellbooks, shouting, "Hey! Stop! Come back here!"

He didn't listen, just turned the corner on Arcadia and disappeared from sight. I forced my legs to go faster, but it didn't matter. When I reached the corner, he was gone. My immediate thought was to go after him, but common sense finally kicked in. Who was I to be chasing strange men down at night? I didn't have any secret martial arts training, just the basic self-defense stuff my dad had drilled into me on base. Okay, given it was my dad, maybe I knew more than just the basics. Nevertheless, he'd berate me for prowling through dark alleys by myself.

Footsteps slapped the pavement behind me, and I spun, thinking my quarry had somehow circled around. I raised my fists and braced, only to drop them again as soon as I recognized the bright red hair belonging to my neighbor, Finn.

"What happened? What's going on?" he demanded as he ran up. "I saw a guy run past, and then you chase after him. Are you okay?"

"Yeah," I said, my heart racing, and it wasn't entirely from the quick sprint. "I keep seeing this guy in a fedora hanging out around the shop. I even think I saw him once at the Renaissance Faire. I think he might be following me, and I want to know why."

Finn frowned and looked around, seeing no one. "So, you chased him down? I'll give you points for gumption but might have to take them away again for lack of common sense." He smiled to soften his words.

"I know, I know, I wasn't thinking," I groaned, rubbing a hand over my face. I peeked through my fingers at him. Come to think of it, had I ever seen him and Fedora Man in the same place at the same time? I didn't think so. Could he have ditched the coat and hat somewhere before circling back?

"We should call the police," Finn said.

"And say what? I saw a suspicious shadowy figure?" If Finn and Fedora Man were the same person, it's not like we'd find him, anyway.

"Why not?" he asked.

"Because they've got enough on their plates. Let's have a quick look around to see if we can find him. He's likely long gone anyway, but it will make me feel better." Which was only partially true. If Fedora Man was still out there, having a look with Finn might uncover a clue to his motives for following me. On the other hand, if Finn was my stalker, then wandering off with him was a terrible idea.

"I'm not sure that's a good idea," Finn said uneasily.

"C'mon," I pleaded, pulling out my phone. I held it up and tapped out a quick message to Bella. "Look, I'm letting Bella know where we are and to call the police if I don't contact her in ten minutes." That should negate any nefarious plots on Finn's part, if he was anything other than a helpful neighbor. I put my phone away. "There's two of us now. Besides, what if he was the one who broke into Spellbooks and is casing another shop?"

Finn scratched at the stubble on his chin. "Well, I don't want a marauder on the streets of Havenwood."

"That's the spirit! But *marauder*? Really? And gumption? Which century are you from?" I started walking down the street, scanning the darkness on both sides. Finn fell in beside me. It was comforting to have him with me, although I wasn't sure I was making the best impression on the cute guy next door.

Finn chuckled. "That's from Beatrice. She used the most interesting vocabulary, and it must've rubbed off. She used to come by now and then with some cookies and tea. We'd have a chat, catch up on the local news, that sort of thing."

"Next you'll be telling me that you gave her a secret tattoo," I joked.

Silence met my words, and I glanced up at Finn. A small smile danced at the corners of his mouth. I grabbed his arm. "Wait a second. *Did* you give her a tattoo? What was it?"

Finn shook his head. "If I did, and that's a big if, I wouldn't say. Client-artist privilege."

"That's not a thing," I protested.

"It is with me. But secret tattoo or not, your granny was a special lady."

I decided to let the tattoo thing go for now. "I miss her. I wish I'd been around more, but Dad's work kept us moving around the world and then there was university..." I trailed off.

Finn's fingers brushed my hand. "She always spoke warmly of you," he said sympathetically.

"Thanks," I said, brushing the back of my hand across my eyes. Talking about Granny Bea with Finn made me feel simultaneously nostalgic and guilty, but mostly, I just missed her. "Speaking of Granny, I need to come by for Mr. Wigglesworth. I'm sure he's becoming a handful," I said, remembering Officer Johanna calling me out on my lame alibi for being in Dusty Tome's alley.

"He's more than a handful," Finn said with a chuckle.

"Oh, no! I'll figure something out and pick him up tomorrow. I hope he hasn't caused too much trouble!"

"What? No. Nothing like that," Finn said, waving a hand in negation. "It's just that...You know what? You'll understand when you see him. But he's really a sweet cat and mostly a lump that loves the sunshine and a good nap. Honestly, no trouble at all."

"Well, alright then. But if that changes, please let me know," I said.

"Promise," Finn replied as we neared the end of the street.

Although I'd been distracted by the handsome tattoo artist and our conversation, I hadn't forgotten my original purpose. But the man in the fedora had disappeared, just like I'd predicted. However, something else strange at the end of the road caught my eye.

"What's that?" I asked, pointing.

Finn looked and shrugged. "The parking lot? There isn't a ton of room on some streets in town, especially for larger vehicles. This is a popular place for people with camper vans or RVs to park, although they usually head out to Pixie Hollow for the night."

"Pixie Hollow?" I asked.

"The campground outside of town," Finn pointed off to the west. "It's nice enough but gets a little crowded in the summer for my tastes."

"Okay, so what's a lone RV doing here when there's a campsite close by?" I asked.

"I'm not sure. Do you think the guy you were chasing is in there?" Finn's voice was hushed.

"Maybe." I noticed some fancy lettering on the side of the RV and squinted as we drew closer, trying to make out the words illuminated only by dim streetlights.

"Blackwell Books!" I exclaimed when I finally worked out the curling lettering. This was Thaddeus' vehicle, but it looked empty for the time being. Perhaps he was still in the Dusty Tome. If he was, there would be a small window of opportunity for me to poke around.

"The book stall from the Renaissance Faire?" Finn asked. "But that wrapped up this afternoon and most non-locals leave right away. Why is this vendor still in town?"

"A better question is, do you think someone might have witnessed a shadowy guy in a hat running by?" I asked.

"And the best question is, do you think the guy in the hat is inside?" Finn said in a low voice as we approached the medium-sized RV.

"Only one way to find out," I said and knocked loudly on the door.

"What are you doing?" Finn hissed. "I meant call the police or something?"

"Well, I picked the 'or something'. In this case, I'm getting some answers," I said, trying to peer through the darkened windows. Nothing moved inside. At least, not that I could tell. Inspiration fueled in equal parts by curiosity and deviltry struck, but I needed a distraction. "What was that?" I whispered.

"What?" Finn said, looking around wildly.

"I thought I heard something on the other side," I whispered. "Maybe someone is coming back?"

"You stay here. Let me check it out," Finn said.

"Okay." The second he disappeared around the bumper, I put my finger on the lock and used my magic. It unlocked under my touch in mere moments, which was simultaneously surprising and gratifying. I eased the door open a crack. Then I crept to the edge of the vehicle to wait for Finn. He came back a moment later, shaking his head.

"I couldn't see anything," he said.

"It must be my nerves getting the best of me. Hey, did you notice the door was open? Why would someone leave their door ajar?"

Finn ran a hand through his hair. "I can't think of a single good reason, but plenty of bad ones. That's it. I'm calling the police." He pulled out his cell phone and flicked on the screen.

"Sounds sensible," I said, even though I didn't want the police showing up before I could explore the RV myself. What if Thaddeus really was behind the theft? I couldn't think of a better place for him to keep the books, especially if the buildings for the Renaissance Faire were going to be changed over for the Harvest Festival. "I'm just going to make sure no one has collapsed or anything," I said.

"Be careful. You never—Oh, hello. Is that Sheriff Jackson? Finn Oakheart here," he said, taking a step away.

I eased the door open and called into the RV. "Hello! Is anybody here? Are you okay?" I spoke loudly, so my voice carried through the enclosed space. When there was no response, I pulled out my phone, switched on the flashlight, and used it to find the light switch. Light flooded the empty living space a moment later. It was definitely Thaddeus'. He'd piled boxes of books on the floor, making it difficult to navigate the already cramped space. They looked familiar, like the ones I'd seen in the back of his stall at the Renaissance Faire. Taking a gamble, I ignored them and headed towards the back of the RV and what I presumed to be the bedroom. A narrow door separated it from the living space. When I eased it open, I saw a rumpled, unmade bed filling most of the space. It faced a wardrobe, small dresser, and TV unit. There was a door to my right, so I opened it and revealed a tiny bathroom completely devoid of books.

I scuttled across the room and opened the door to the narrow wardrobe. Two wrinkled shirts hung in the closet and a pile of laundry mounded on the floor. Thaddeus obviously wasn't the best housekeeper. The door had apparently been holding the pile in place because as soon as I opened it, the whole thing shifted and tumbled across the floor. My mouth hung open. When the pile of clothes shifted, it revealed a small stack of books. I recognized the title of the top one. *The Enigma Codex.* It was one of the missing books from Spellbooks. Quickly, I pulled out more of the clothes to reveal the entire stack of books. I sucked in a breath. I'd been wrong. Thaddeus *had* stolen the books, not Oswald Puddleton. But why?

"Harper?" Finn called.

"Back here," I said over my shoulder. Time for snooping was running out. Hurriedly, I pushed the rest of the clothes aside. I didn't want to touch the books in case I left fingerprints, but I pulled out my phone and snapped as many pictures as I could in rapid fire.

"How did you get through here?" Finn grunted from the living area, obviously having more trouble than I had. I stuffed my phone back into my pocket and then stepped back by the entrance to the bedroom door.

"No one's here," I called.

"Okay, well, we'd better wait for the police anyway and give them our statement. I'd hate for them to think we'd broken in or anything."

"Yeah. Wouldn't want to be accused of trespassing," I agreed and thought to myself, *for the second time tonight.*

"Exactly," said Finn, coming up behind me.

I pointed towards the stack of books in the closet, behind the clothes now strewn all over the floor. "Does that strike you as odd?"

Finn craned to look over my shoulder and I scrunched to the side to allow him an easier view. "What? A book vendor who owns books?" he asked, perplexed.

"No, that he keeps them in the closet under his clothes. I mean, he's got boxes of books in the other room. Why hide these away?"

"Maybe they're part of his private collection," Finn ventured.

"Maybe," I said. "But why not display them? Why hide them under the laundry?" What I really wanted was for Finn to go look for himself. Two of us witnessing the books' presence would be more convincing when the police showed up, which could be any minute now.

Luckily, Finn stepped across the room and crouched down by the pile of books. "*The Enigma Codex,*" he read the title out and then looked at me. "Does that mean anything to you?"

I snapped my fingers like I'd just made a connection and pulled out my phone. "It sounds familiar. Wait a minute." I opened my gallery and found the picture of Granny Bea's ledger. "Here! It's on the list of rare books that were stolen from Spellbooks!" I exclaimed, waving the phone at him.

Finn frowned and came over to look. "How likely is it that these are two different copies of the same book?" he asked.

I shrugged. "I'd say pretty unlikely. If the book matches the description in Granny's ledger, we'd know for sure."

"Or if the rest of these are the other missing books," Finn said, pushing to his feet.

"Aren't you going to look?" I asked.

He gave me a strange, searching stare. "No. What we are going to do is wait for the police. Outside. We're going to tell them everything and then let them sort it out." He ushered me out of the RV. In my hand, my phone buzzed repeatedly. I glanced at the screen. Bella was texting to see if she needed to call the police and was giving me a countdown. I tapped out a quick message, canceling the need for a distress call. We'd just stepped outside when a familiar police officer appeared out of the darkness.

Out of the Shadows

Officer Johanna put her hands on her hips and quirked an eyebrow at me. "Let me guess. You're searching for your cat," she said dryly.

I shook my head. "Nope, not this time. Haven't you heard? There's never a cat."

Officer Johanna smiled wickedly at me while Finn looked between us in confusion. Before he could explain about Mr. Wigglesworth, I jumped in with as much of the truth as I cared to share. "When I left the Spellbooks earlier, I thought I saw a guy wearing a trench coat and a fedora. I've seen a similar man lurking around town recently, and it seemed like he was watching me, so I chased him. Except I lost him when he turned off Arcadia. Finn saw me out of his store window as I ran by and thought I might be in trouble, so he came after me."

"Very chivalrous," Officer Johanna murmured, taking out her notebook and scribbling furiously.

Finn picked up the story. "We thought the guy might live in the RV, and I was going to give him a piece of my mind for stalking young women. However, when we got here, the door was ajar. We thought it was odd and that someone might be hurt. That's when I called it in."

"What happened next?" Officer Johanna asked briskly.

"While Finn called the police, I shouted inside to make sure no one was injured. I didn't get a response, so I went inside to make sure the owner wasn't unconscious or something," I said.

The officer glanced up at me and arched an eyebrow. "It seems awfully convenient that the door was just standing open," she said.

"It wouldn't have been if someone had been hurt," I said, working to keep my face as innocent as possible.

"She's right," Finn chimed in. "As soon as I hung up with the Sheriff, I went inside to see if I could help."

"And was there anybody inside?" Officer Johanna asked.

"No, but we found something interesting," Finn said. I nodded vigorously, thankful he was taking the lead.

"Oh? And what was that?" the vampiric officer asked.

"Books," Finn said.

The officer *tsked* and shook her head. "Doesn't strike me as odd coming from an RV with a bookshop's name emblazoned on the side."

Finn frowned. "Not just any books. There's a pile of rare books in the closet. Harper recognized the title of the top one as a book stolen from Spellbooks, but we didn't want to touch anything and possibly contaminate the scene. We stepped outside to wait for you and here we are."

She sighed. "I can't just ignore the possibility of stolen goods. It's especially handy that the thief left them in plain sight." Officer Johanna glanced at me again. "Are you sure there's no cat?"

"Positive," I said.

"I'd better take a look then. You two wait here," she ordered and then ducked inside the RV.

"What's her obsession with cats?" Finn whispered to me.

"Inside joke," I whispered back.

"Who has inside jokes with the police?" Finn asked.

"Are you saying you don't?" I quipped.

"I can't say that I've ever had a cat-themed inside joke with anyone, let alone a police officer, but now I feel like I'm missing out."

I smirked. "Haven't you heard? A good cat joke can break the ice in any crime scene."

"And just how many crime scenes have *you* been to?" Finn asked.

Officer Johanna stuck her head out of the RV, saving me from having to answer by obviously using some sort of supernatural speed to navigate the maze of books. "Look, I'm going to have to call this in and get someone to check the register of stolen books. I don't think there's anything further I need from you two, but I'm sure Sheriff Jackson will want to talk to you, probably tomorrow."

Finn insisted on walking me back to the Oasis, but it was a quiet journey, each of us lost in our own thoughts. When I got to the door, I paused awkwardly, not knowing if I should wave or give him a hug or a firm handshake. I mean, what was the appropriate goodbye gesture for someone who was going to take you on a date and also helped you uncover a crime, but may be involved in stalking and/or a crime himself? And also unintentionally helped you commit one in the process?

Finn answered the question for me by shoving his hands in the pockets of his jeans and smiling up at me from the bottom of the porch steps when I turned to face him. "So, I'll pick you up around seven for pizza tomorrow?" he asked.

I nodded. "It's a date."

"I'm looking forward to it." Finn winked at me and then turned back up Dragonfly Lane, disappearing into the darkness. Was that the same way he'd disappeared while wearing the fedora and now I was going on a date with the man? Mentally, I threw up my hands. The constant suspicion was making me dizzy, and I was tired from all the excitement on top of the jetlag. Besides, that wink was enough to make me start asking all kinds of other questions. Like, where was this date going to lead and did he like pineapple on his pizza?

I slipped inside the B&B and quietly made my way upstairs to Bella's room. It was empty, for which I was grateful. If Bella had been back, she would've peppered me with questions that I didn't feel up to answering at the moment. The calm lavender pastel of the bedspread on the sofa bed promised a cozy night's sleep. Fairy statues peeked out at me. The one perched on the nightstand caught my eye as she smiled cheekily from under a wide red hat. Something about her reminded me of Madame Charmaine Fontaine. The woman also seemed to love striking fashion choices. The purple and red outfit from the library was unforgettable, that's for sure.

I sucked in a breath, remembering Gideon's claims that the person who broke into Spellbooks had been wearing a long purple skirt and red shoes. Could Madame Fontaine be responsible for the break-in? My gut told me no. She might be as sharp as Sherlock Holmes when it came to solving mysteries, but I couldn't imagine the elderly lady smashing the display case at Spellbooks. Besides, her magical gifts were in predictions, not invisibility spells.

Suddenly, I remembered the strange words she'd said to me in the library. Hadn't it been something about blood's bond and shadows? I wracked my brain, trying to remember the exact wording. Slowly, the strange rhyme floated to the front of my mind.

To the chosen kin, hold true and strong.
For when blood's bond falters, trust goes wrong.
In shadows deep, help shall appear.
As unexpected aid hovers unseen, but near.

A chill ran down my spine. Martha Morningstar had said that Madame Fontaine's predictions were right once out of every twelve, like clockwork. Was the prediction she'd given me a true one? Could Thaddeus' theft be a blood bond faltering? Or was I stretching to make a connection where there wasn't one? But then Finn appeared out of the shadows to help. If it was an accurate prediction, what unexpected aid was hovering nearby, and who was the chosen kin? The questions danced around my head as I got ready for bed and continued to keep me awake long after I turned off the lights.

The Ninth Book

EVEN THOUGH I WAS exhausted, sleep wouldn't come. Something felt off, and it wasn't just the strange rhyme keeping me up. I couldn't figure out what was so unsettling. After tossing and turning for over fifteen minutes, I finally gave up and pulled out my phone. I'd planned on mindlessly losing myself in social media until my eyes grew heavy, but instead, I opened my photo gallery. Absently, I flipped through the pictures I'd taken of Granny's ledger, the list from Thaddeus' shop, and the ones I'd just taken from inside the RV.

I mulled over familiar questions in hopes something I hadn't considered would shake loose. Why would Thaddeus have broken into Spellbooks to steal the books when he had keys? It didn't make any sense. He was in town with the Renaissance Faire long before I arrived. Why wait? The answer popped into my head almost instantly. The theft occurred *before* he'd received the keys from the lawyer. If he wanted the books, he would've *had* to break in. But why break in the night before I arrived when he'd already been in town with the Renaissance Faire? Why the delay? Was it just because he'd heard I was coming or was there something more here that I was missing?

A memory of Gideon's recounting of the theft surfaced. He'd said he heard a smash, immediately flew into an empty shop and then, according to the blood sample taken from his wings, cut someone. How could he cut someone that wasn't there? Unless they were there, and he couldn't see them. But even if that were the case, wouldn't it be difficult for someone to carry eight rare books and a possible scroll out of the shop while avoiding a kamikaze gargoyle? Especially while wearing a skirt? Besides, I'd been in Thaddeus' place and didn't see any evidence of a purple skirt or red shoes, which Gideon claimed he saw as the perpetrator fled. How could someone be invisible and then not? And what about the bizarre clothing choices?

I flicked the next photo on my reel, pulling up the list of books I'd discovered behind the desk in the backroom of Thaddeus' stall. Suddenly, I sat bolt upright in bed. There were only eight books on his list. But there were nine taken from the shop. I thumbed through the pictures to the ones I'd taken of Granny's ledger and counted carefully. Yep, it was right there in her elegant scrawl. Nine books. I flipped back and forth, comparing pictures until I figured out which one was missing from Thaddeus' list. *A Maritime Meteorological Compendium.* That was strange. Of all the books to be missing, I wouldn't have picked that one. What happened to it? Had he sold it already? Decided to keep it?

I considered one idea after another and discarded them all. If I was right, Thaddeus had set up the meeting to sell the books to Oswald Puddleton, but Hortense calling the police on me wrecked their deal. The other books could have just been a cover. The Dusty Tome was a bookshop after all. It would've been easy enough to claim the negotiations were completely innocent. If that was the case, I suppose it was possible Thaddeus had brought one of the stolen books along as a good faith gesture, but he didn't strike me as the type.

Another possibility occurred to me. What if Thaddeus was responsible, but he wasn't the only one? Maybe he had an accomplice? Someone who could do an invisibility spell, perhaps? That would explain away some inconsistencies. The invisible-not-invisible thief in the purple skirt broke in first and stole the books. Thaddeus then gives her a book as payment. It was a convoluted theory, but it explained everything. Or perhaps there were two completely separate thieves. The first one stole one book and then Thaddeus came along later, saw the break-in had already occurred and took the rest. I shook my head. No, that was even more complicated.

The simpler theory was that Thaddeus was solely responsible. From his experience in Granny's shop, he knew once the sun hit Gideon, the little gargoyle would be turned to stone, so he just waited for the magical transformation and finished his theft. Didn't the detective always discover that the simple version ended up being the way the crime actually happened?

Regardless, that didn't answer the most pressing question. Where was the missing book?

Deciding to go out on a limb, I returned to the photo of the ledger entry. "What would someone want with an old weather almanac?" I whispered into the darkness.

Of all the questions plaguing me this evening, that's the one that kept me up late into the night.

matching wits

My phone jangled more happily than any phone had a right to early the next morning. Light poured through the curtains of Bella's empty room. She must've snuck in and then out again without waking me. I groaned. I'd told Gideon I'd try to swing by and catch him before dawn. I'd obviously slept through my early morning alarm. I slapped my pillows until I found the noisy phone. An unknown number with a local area code met my eyes. Groggily, I answered.

"Hello?" I groaned.

"Miss Sullivan? Sheriff Jackson. Is this a bad time?"

My eyes flew open, and the morning fog instantly retreated from my brain. "Not at all."

"Good. There's been a development in the case."

"Did you find the man in the fedora?" I asked.

"No, there's been no sign of him, but I was hoping you wouldn't mind coming down to the station."

My stomach sank. "Am I in trouble, Sheriff?"

"Is there something you should be in trouble for?"

I waited for him to elaborate, thinking guiltily of breaking into the RV. When he didn't, I filled the awkward silence. "Well, I can be there in about thirty minutes. Is that okay?"

"The sooner the better," he said, and then disconnected the line.

I stared at my phone. Getting a phone call to come to the police station before eight in the morning? I had a feeling this was the start of a very bad day. I pulled on a pair of black trousers, my most professional looking blouse, and my sensible black shoes. If I wanted him to take me seriously, I needed to look the part.

Twenty-seven minutes later, I gave my name to the receptionist on duty. She smiled pleasantly at me and asked me to take a seat. I sipped the to-go cup of coffee Honey had pressed into my hands and thought longingly of the breakfast at the Oasis I'd been forced to skip. Less than five minutes later, Sheriff Jackson poked his head out of his office.

He strode over, looking serious and distinctly more caffeinated than I was. "Ah, Miss Sullivan, good. Thanks for coming down. Much appreciated." He extended his hand and pumped mine up and down perfunctorily.

"Sure, anytime. Can you tell me what this is all about?"

"Let's talk in my office," he said, ushering me inside and shutting the door behind me.

I settled awkwardly on the plastic chair in front of his desk while he leaned a hip against the desk and folded his arms. "Officer Johanna told me what happened last night, but I'd like to hear it in your own words, please."

"Did you recover the books?" I asked, excitement getting the better of me. "What about Thaddeus?"

"I'd like to hear your version first." The shuttered expression on his face let me know I wouldn't get anything else out of him until I'd played by his rules.

As quickly as I could, I told him about the events of the previous evening, leaving out the illegal entry to the RV and snooping in Thaddeus' closet. When I finished, Sheriff Jackson sighed and put his hands on the desk, leaning backwards.

"That matches with the reports from Officer Johanna and Finnegan Oakheart. What I'm having trouble reconciling in my mind is that Mr. Blackwell swears up and down that he locked his RV, and the closet door was closed. Yet when my officer arrived on scene, both were open. Puts us in a bit of a tricky situation."

I shrugged, praying my poker face was good enough to hold up under the werewolf's penetrating gaze.

The sheriff flipped open a small notebook. I recognized it as the one he'd written in during our first meeting. "I seem to recall you saying that you had a minor talent for magic. Can you figure out a way that a locked RV door could be opened without any signs of forced entry? Hypothetically, of course."

I tried not to squirm under his direct stare. "Are you thinking magic was at play?" I asked. Was it my imagination or had my voice sounded a little too shrill?

The sheriff shrugged. "Perhaps. But I've never heard of a magic that could open doors without a trace. Do you know of any? Air blowing hard enough to open tumblers or making a bump key out of earth or something like that?"

His tone was neutral, yet curious. However, I could tell what he was doing. I'd told him I had some sort of elemental magic when we'd met but hadn't specified which branch. He was trying to figure out what my magic was and if I could be behind the incongruity of the locked/unlocked door.

I paused, seeming to consider his questions seriously, and then shook my head. "I don't think so, Sheriff. All the major magic elements that might work at unlocking a door would leave a trace, like fire or earth. I don't think water and air would work at all." I looked innocently up at the sheriff, praying he wouldn't try to get me to admit what my particular element was.

He grunted. "I see your point. But how do *you* account for Blackwell swearing he locked the door?"

"Maybe he just thought he did. Or he's trying to muddy the waters. You know, throw you off the scent."

The Sheriff twirled his mustache. "I thought of that." He paused, considering me. I met his gaze, feeling a bead of sweat form between my shoulder blades and slowly roll down my spine.

Finally, he grunted and pushed off the desk. "Come with me. There's something I want you to see."

"Where are we—" I started to ask, but the Sheriff was already out the door and halfway across the public space of the station. I had to jog to catch up with him.

Without a word, Sheriff Jackson led me down a hall and opened a plain gray metal door. As soon as I was inside, I recognized it from the police procedural shows my mom enjoyed. I was in an interrogation room, but the side you'd choose to be on if you had to be in one at all. Through the slightly darkened one-way mirror, Thaddeus Blackwell sat behind a narrow table next to Nathaniel Ravenscroft and across from Officer Reggie. My jaw dropped. How did the vampire get here in broad daylight? Not only that, was he *representing* Thaddeus? I didn't know much about the law, but that seemed like a conflict of interest to me. Was this proof they were in cahoots and conspiring to take Spellbooks from me? I narrowed my eyes, evaluating the pair. My cousin looked haggard and angry, whereas the lawyer was impeccably groomed and displayed only the slightest trace of mere annoyance.

"What's going on, Sheriff?" I asked as I entered the room.

"Like I said, tricky situation. I'm hoping you might help me find a solution."

"I don't see how—" Before I could finish, Sheriff Jackson shut the metal door with a clang. A moment later, he walked into the interrogation room. Officer Reggie jumped to his feet. The sheriff tipped his head towards the glass wall and Reggie left the room, only to appear beside me a moment later.

"What's happening?" I whispered as he entered.

"Sheriff wants you to see what happens next," Reggie said, his typical smile completely absent from his face. The serious expression made him look older and a lot more mature. Before I could ask another question, a tinny version of the sheriff's voice echoed from a small speaker in the corner.

"Let's go over this one more time."

The lawyer sighed. "Really, Sheriff. We've been at this all night."

"Humor me."

Thaddeus looked at the lawyer, who gave him a begrudging gesture to acquiesce to the sheriff's request.

My cousin leaned his forearms on the table and glowered at the sheriff. "After your officer illegally broke into my RV and rummaged through my belongings, you hauled me down here and proceeded to pester me all night. What's there to say except the lawsuit we're going to slap you with is going to be so huge it'll make your head spin."

"Now, now, Thaddeus, there will be plenty of time to discuss how we handle this matter," the lawyer said calmly, but the coldness in his eyes spoke volumes. I shivered even though I was on the other side of the glass.

Sheriff Jackson seemed unmoved by either man. "Let's pretend for just a moment that stolen goods were found in your place of residence. How did they get there?"

Thaddeus groaned loudly and scrubbed his hands through his hair. "I told you; they weren't stolen. I swung by the shop and saw the window was broken. I went inside to check what was going on. When I saw the broken display case, I knew someone else had been there. I grabbed the rest of Granny's expensive books. As I did, I thought I heard a noise. An enormous orange beast appeared out of nowhere. I thought Bea had some sort of weird supernatural security system. I took the books and ran. I even knocked over a shelf of books when I did. That thing was massive!" Thaddeus folded his arms across his chest, a challenging glare pinching his features as he stared across the table.

"Orange beast?" I whispered to Officer Reggie.

"Beatrice's cat," he whispered back.

I opened my mouth to ask just how big this feline was when Sheriff Jackson cut me off, his voice sounding unruffled through the tiny speaker. "And at no point did you think to call the police?"

Ravenscroft cleared his throat in annoyance. "We've been over this, sheriff," he said.

Thaddeus pinched the bridge of his nose, speaking over his lawyer. "I was upset and distracted. I had a business to run and a Faire to wrap up. On top of that, I just found out my great-grandmother did some stupid inheritance experiment. Not only am I not getting my fair share of her money, but she pitted me against a naïve little girl who is supposedly my cousin. Why would she do that when I'm obviously the better choice to run Spellbooks? Should I have called the police sooner? Maybe. But you can't keep me here for protecting what I thought was mine."

Ravenscroft leaned forward, inserting himself into the conversation once more. "Mr. Blackwell has already admitted all of this. Yes, his decisions might have been in error, looking at the situation retrospectively. He admits that. However, he can hardly be accused of theft when he thought the books were his by right of inheritance. I admit, I'm only a lawyer, but even I thought stealing from yourself wasn't included in the Connecticut penal code." His tone was so cutting, it surprised me Sheriff Jackson wasn't bleeding.

The werewolf drummed his fingers on the table and then pointed one at Thaddeus. "And when my officer came to speak with you? You swore you had no knowledge of the theft."

Ravenscroft sighed in exasperation. "He misspoke. Thaddeus admits to being emotionally compromised. Distraught, even. Once he calmed down, he saw the error of his ways and told you the entire story. Repeatedly. For the entire night."

I snorted softly and muttered. "Yeah, after they caught him with the stolen goods in his possession." Officer Reggie grunted in agreement next to me.

Sheriff Jackson didn't sound like he bought the story either. "And the meeting with Oswald Puddleton?"

"Was about a different matter entirely. They were discussing a deal regarding another set of books because, in case you hadn't noticed in the last eleven hours, my client is, in fact, a book dealer." Ravenscroft clipped each word short, the biting tone of sarcasm of his tone speaking volumes beyond the actual words.

The sheriff raised his index finger from the table. "I just have one more question. What happened to the missing book?"

Thaddeus pounded his fist down on the metal tabletop, making me jump, even though I was behind the glass. "As I told you before, it was gone when I got there," he gritted out.

The sheriff seemed to consider and then pushed to his feet. "I'll be right back."

"Really Sheriff, this is too—" Ravenscroft protested, but the heavy thud of the door shutting cut off the sentence.

"What do we do now?" Thaddeus groaned.

"Wait. Silently." Ravenscroft snapped, pointing up at what I assumed to be a camera in the corner and out of my sight line.

Sheriff Jackson reappeared on my side of the glass a moment later and silently led me back to his office. This time he sat across from me, which should've been less intimidating than watching him work in the interrogation room but wasn't.

"What was all that about?" I blurted out as soon as we were both seated.

"I wanted you to hear Blackwell's story firsthand."

"Do you believe him?" I demanded.

Sheriff Jackson pursed his lips and shook his head slowly. "Not for a second. But the whole matter of inheritance throws a wrench into the situation. We can't prove he didn't think the books belonged to him when he took them and the fact of the matter is they might, in fact, belong to him come Friday."

"So, what happens now?" I asked.

"With a lawyer as good as Ravenscroft, I don't think we'll be able to hold Blackwell much longer. They've already laid the groundwork to cast doubt onto his motive and the books have been returned."

"Except the missing book," I said.

The sheriff nodded. "Yes. Except that one. However, we have no evidence of events happening other than the way he described. Unfortunately, we have little else to go on."

"What happens next?" I asked, feeling a little bummed now that the adrenaline of Thaddeus' story was fading, and the repercussions were setting in. Despite the answers, I was basically back at the starting point of the investigation. Looking for suspects. But by removing Thaddeus from the mix, who should I focus my attention on? Ravenscroft? Puddleton? Finn? Or was I being too short sighted? Did I need to broaden my search?

The sheriff cleared his throat, looking at me expectantly, as if waiting for an answer. I must've missed whatever he said.

"Sorry, could you repeat that, please?" I asked.

"As the other heir to Beatrice's estate, you have to decide whether you or the estate will press charges."

I paused, not realizing the decision would come down to me. I thought the discovery of the stolen books would be enough. Apparently not. I wriggled in my chair. "I'm not sure how these things go. What happens if I press charges?"

"We'll build the best case we can, using all the evidence to find the truth. Ravenscroft explained how Beatrice structured the inheritance. It's a sticky situation. If Thaddeus ends up inheriting the shop, then he's essentially just moved his property to a different location. No crime there. But if you do, then he's stolen from you. Either way, if you decide to pursue the matter, both you and Blackwell would need to secure representation. Ravenscroft couldn't represent either of you against the other. Regardless, Blackwell will probably be out on bail in the next few hours. After that,

I'm not sure how this one would play out. Things could get nasty. There might even be a trial."

"Wow. Way to sell it," I muttered.

"Just giving you the truth," the sheriff said with a shrug.

"And if I don't press charges?" I asked.

"We might be able to charge him with a minor misdemeanor, but he'd probably just get a slap on the wrist. Maybe community service."

I weighed my options. "What do you think I should do?" I finally asked.

The sheriff leaned back in his chair and considered me thoughtfully. "It's always more complicated when family is involved," he said noncommittally.

"That's all the advice you have?"

"Yep."

Well, that didn't help at all. I bit my lip, considering the options. What I needed was to talk to a lawyer, but I didn't know anyone except Granny's lawyer, and he'd already sided with my thieving cousin. Anger bubbled in my stomach, rising and clogging my throat. My vision went red at the edges. How could Granny have trusted someone like Nathaniel Ravenscroft? The thought of him conspiring with Thaddeus made me sick to my stomach. What match was I against the two of them? In my mind's eye, I watched my dream of establishing roots, a business, and a home all vanish.

If Thaddeus ended up with Spellbooks, I wouldn't be staying in Havenwood. I knew I didn't want to stay just to fight a legal battle that probably wouldn't go my way. But if I didn't press charges, what would keep him from trying to steal the books all over again? I didn't like the lack of consequences, but unfortunately, I didn't control the outcome, just the next step. Neither option looked appealing. Was there a middle ground I could take?

I stalled to buy myself some time to think. "Sheriff, will you continue looking for the missing book?"

He nodded. "Of course. Naturally, we'll do our best, but there isn't a lot to go on. However, I'm not one to give up on a case. People have often compared me to a dog with a bone." He smiled wryly at the analogy, alluding to his werewolf nature.

An idea formed, and I spoke slowly, "Would you be willing to keep the rest of books here until the matter of the inheritance of Spellbooks is settled?"

Sheriff Jackson's eyes glittered with understanding. I was asking him to remove the proverbial pieces from the playing board by keeping the books. He twirled his mustache thoughtfully and then nodded. "I don't see why not, assuming Mr. Blackwell and his lawyer agree."

"Could it be a condition for me not pressing charges? Along with Thaddeus paying for the restoration for any damage done to the shop? And possible damages done to the books in case he handled them improperly?" I asked, trying to think of everything I could to throw at Thaddeus. I might not win an actual lawsuit, but I'd do my best to make him pay. "Oh! And he should have to turn over his key to you. To ensure he won't help himself to any more inventory until this inheritance matter is settled."

"Those are very reasonable suggestions, so I don't see why they wouldn't agree to it. I'll be right back." The sheriff strode from the office and was only gone for a few minutes. When he returned, he settled back in his chair before speaking. "Mr. Blackwell has agreed to place the books in police custody until the matter of the inheritance of Sullivan's Spellbooks is settled, at which time they will be returned to the rightful heir. He has also agreed to pay all damages, including repairs to the shop and books, along with turning over his keys, but requests that he is able to do some work in the shop under the direct supervision of Mr. Ravenscroft, which the lawyer has agreed to," Sheriff Jackson reported, his tone formal.

I shifted uncomfortably. I didn't like the fact that I still might run into Thaddeus at Spellbooks, but did I have a better option here? Probably not. Besides, the lawyer was supposed to be working for the estate, wasn't he? He wouldn't, *couldn't* let anything happen to Spellbooks before the inheritance was decided, right?

I hesitated a moment longer, weighing my options. However, it wasn't a completely unreasonable request. Finally, I sighed and said, "Then I don't wish to press charges."

The sheriff considered me thoughtfully. "Noted. I'll let Mr. Blackwell and his lawyer know." He paused, giving me the chance to jump in and explain my motives. When I didn't, the sheriff sighed and pushed to his feet, extending a hand over the desk. "Thank you for coming down, Miss Sullivan."

As the sheriff walked me to the door of the station, I caught a glimpse of Thaddeus and Nathaniel Ravenscroft exiting the interrogation room, heads close together as they whispered back and forth. Both appeared inordinately pleased with the turn of events. Thaddeus glanced around the station and caught me staring at him. He smiled triumphantly at me and winked before disappearing around a corner. My stomach dropped. Had I made a mistake? Whose side was Nathaniel Ravenscroft on? Did I just win the temporary battle for the books while simultaneously losing the ultimate war for the bookshop?

On the Hunt

I'D SKIPPED BREAKFAST IN my hurry to get to the police station, but my appetite had deserted me. As I wandered through the streets of Havenwood, I was too distracted by my thoughts to contemplate food. Did I make the wrong decision not to press charges? It seemed like the only sensible path, but after seeing the confident expression on Thaddeus' face? I wasn't so sure.

I felt myself spiral as the horrible consequences of my choices played in the cinema of my mind. I took a deep breath and blew it out. This was not productive. Rather than torture myself with "what if" scenarios, it would be better to focus on the next steps rather than the ones I could've, would've, should've taken.

I dug the brainstorming list of ideas for the shop out of my purse as I wandered down the street. Somehow, they all seemed so small. Poetry reading, open mic nights, and book clubs were all sweet ideas a naïve little girl might entertain, but were they enough to win me Spellbooks? For that matter, did anything I put forward really matter, or had Thaddeus already convinced the lawyer to pick him? But didn't they have to abide by Granny's wishes? Maybe if things went against me, I could demand to see the letter and then fight his decision.

No! That was a defeatist attitude! I couldn't think that way. It wasn't helpful. Instead, I should hold the course, develop my ideas, and put forth the best presentation for developing Spellbooks as an active part of the community. Thaddeus might know the book business, but I felt I knew Havenwood better. I knew how to fit in with the community here. I definitely knew how to get along with people better. He had his strengths; I had mine.

"All right," I said to myself. "Game on. And he should know, I'm playing for keeps."

I headed down to the library and to talk with Martha Morningstar. She might be able to help me refine some ideas on my list or possibly even contribute some new ones. Another thought occurred to me. My original plan had been to find the stolen books to prove myself worthy of the shop. I'd partially achieved my aim. Most of the books had been recovered, except for the compendium. Maybe I could do some digging at the library and uncover something I couldn't find in an online search for the missing book. Armed with my dual goals, I felt marginally better or, at least, better distracted from the events of the morning.

Martha looked up with a smile as I entered the library. "Harper, how nice to see you again! I'm afraid there aren't any book clubs meeting today, but I could give you the entire schedule if you like."

"Thanks, but I was actually looking for you. I need some advice," I said.

Martha interlaced her fingers and put her chin in the resulting cradle, giving me her undivided attention. "Sounds interesting. Tell me more."

"Are you sure you don't mind?" I asked, glancing around the empty foyer area of the library.

She lifted her shoulder. "We rarely get visitors this early on a Monday. Most people are at work, and those with young children are likely in the midst of wrangling breakfast. We probably have a good half hour before anyone shows up today. Tell me what's on your mind."

Deciding I should stop equivocating and just get to it, I outlined the inheritance situation and my plan to expand Spellbooks' offerings by getting involved in the community and hosting more bookish events. I passed over my brainstorming list and shared how I was inspired by people around town. Writing and publishing workshops for people like Mrs. Jenkins, poetry slams for the Grimgors of Havenwood, book clubs, kids' book readings, and so on.

Martha nodded. "Some of these are fantastic ideas, but you need more than scribbles on a piece of paper. How are you going to draw in locals *and* tourists? We already run some things on your list at the library. How are yours going to be different? Ultimately, if you are trying to impress Nathaniel Ravenscroft, you need a solid plan for how you are going to develop the business side of Spellbooks. This is a start to get people in the door, but how are you going to turn readers and browsers into customers? You also might want to create something a little more aesthetically pleasing than this lovely scribble," Martha said with a disarming smile as she handed my list back to me.

"I'm planning on making a presentation for him by the end of the week," I said, tucking the list back in my bag. "The DeLucas have offered to help, and I have a ton of my own ideas for Spellbooks."

"I might suggest that you use the library's printers. Nathaniel, like many people in this town, is a touch old-fashioned. A hard copy approach may serve you better," she said with a knowing smile.

"He sounds like Granny Bea. Speaking of, she kept all of her records in a handwritten ledger, including the ones of the books that were stolen. I've been trying to find more information on one book, but an internet search turned up absolutely nothing. Do you think you might be able to help me with some research?"

"I'm happy to help. Give me the information and let's see what we can turn up." Martha cracked her knuckles and then hovered her fingertips over the keyboard attached to the computer on her desk.

I pulled out my phone, double checking the photo of Granny Bea's ledger. "Okay, the title is *Maritime Meteorological Compendium.*"

Her fingers flew across the keyboard. She hit the last key dramatically and then sighed. "There's nothing in the library with that title. Let's try an author search instead. Can you give me the name?"

I zoomed in on the screen. "It looks like B. Storking? Maybe? I don't know. Granny's handwriting isn't the neatest."

"Okay, we'll try that first. Bea the name or B the initial?"

"Initial."

Martha typed in a few more commands and then hit enter. She shook her head. "Nothing's coming up, but that could be because we haven't entered the information correctly. Could I look, please?"

I passed over my phone, zoomed in on the compendium entry. Martha pursed her lips. "I see what you mean about the handwriting. Well, maybe this 'o' is really an 'a'. I'll try Starking instead." She edited the entry and then shook her head again, passing the phone back over to me. "Sorry, nothing here with that information."

"Could we do a broader search? Maybe keywords about maritime weather?"

Martha clacked away on her keyboard, obviously adding to the keyword search. "Can you give me the year of publication?" she asked without looking up.

I checked the photo and my mouth nearly dropped open. "It says 'circa 1700', but that can't be right, can it?"

Martha froze, her eyes moving to mine in slow motion. "Are you serious?" she asked. When I nodded, she slowly typed in the date and hit enter.

"Did anything turn up?" I asked.

"Apparently, we have several logbooks from a captain from the 1700s, but they're all on microfiche still and haven't been updated in the electronic system yet. However, the captain's name is Starling, not Storking."

"Starling? As in Benedict Starling?" I asked excitedly.

"One and the same." Martha gave me a strange look. "How do you know a sea captain from the eighteenth century by name?"

"I think I know why someone broke into Spellbooks!" I exclaimed.

"Why?" Martha asked.

"If I'm right, someone is hunting for lost pirate treasure!"

Whiskers and Runes

I TRIED TO GET a hold of Mrs. Jenkins immediately upon leaving the library, but a temp answered the phone. It took a little bit of wheedling, but the young man eventually told me she was visiting a sick friend up north and wouldn't be back until Saturday. He wouldn't give me any more details. Frustrated at the delay in my plans and not knowing what else to do, I headed to the shop. Maybe I could find some inspiration for a brilliant plan that would absolutely decimate Thaddeus' attempt to claim the inheritance. If not, at least I'd have one more day in Granny's shop before it was bequeathed to my loathsome cousin.

By the time dinner rolled around, I'd had a busy day with nothing more satisfying than a couple of granola bars. I'd made a point of swinging by the B&B to change into something date-worthy yet casual before my dinner plans with Finn. After numerous outfits, I finally settled on a cream-colored sweater and dark wash jeans with my brown boots and some simple gold jewelry. I added the green scarf for a pop of color under my coat before heading out the door. The resulting look was classy yet functional, which was good because I wanted to do a few more things around Spellbooks before dinner.

Grimgor stuck his head into the shop a little after five with the replacement windowpane. The quick repair job should've taken less than twenty minutes, but an hour later, he still hadn't left. I took a peek to see how he was doing. When I poked my head into the sunroom, I could see Grimgor and Thistle sitting on the bench under the oak tree engaged in conversation through the sparkling glass of the new window. I smiled to myself and left them in peace. Grimgor wandered back into the shop about fifteen minutes after that as I was doodling plans for the addition of a coffee bar or tea station on the back of an old receipt.

"Did you find everything you needed?" I asked.

Grimgor nodded. "It's all fixed."

"Thanks for getting it taken care of on such short notice. What do I owe you?"

Grimgor named his price, and I was glad I'd put the stipulation of Thaddeus paying for the repairs in the deal I struck with the sheriff. I didn't have that much cash on me. "There's been a slight change in payment," I said, a blush rising in my cheeks. I didn't want Grimgor to think I was taking advantage of him. "Nathaniel Ravenscroft is the estate's lawyer. He'll be able to settle up with you as soon as possible, but I don't want you to think I'm trying to pull one over on you."

Grimgor waved away my words. "Not a worry. I know Nathaniel is good for it. I'll swing by his office tomorrow with the bill. He's a good man and has always dealt fairly with me in the past." I frowned, Grimgor's description of the lawyer at complete odds with my own recent experience. Grimgor didn't seem to notice my hesitation. He tipped his head at the broken display case. "You just let me know when you want me to come fix that, too."

"Honestly, I'd love for it to be done as soon as possible, but the payment's going to be the same," I said.

"I'll mention it to Ravenscroft when I see him then and we'll sort it out," Grimgor replied, not looking the least bit upset, which made me feel better about the whole situation.

"I appreciate you coming to help me out. Don't be a stranger, okay?" I stuck out my hand and waited.

He narrowed his eyes, looking between my outstretched hand and me like he was waiting for me to snatch it back. When I didn't move, he eventually shook my hand gently, a genuine smile blooming across his craggy face. It seemed like he was slowly warming up to me. "You know, I may just take you up on that."

"I hope you do," I said, walking him to the door.

After Grimgor left, I lost myself in plans for making a small coffee alcove for the shop. I thought it could be a nice way to encourage customers to browse. Five minutes before seven, I heard a soft knock on the front door of the shop. I looked out the window to see a fuzzy cloud of orange fur hovering outside.

"Fiddlesticks and lettuce leaves, it's back," Luna muttered.

"What's back?"

"The living muppet masquerading as a cat," Luna groaned.

Finn must be hiding somewhere beneath the mound of fur. I hurried to open the door for him.

"Thanks," he said, turning sideways and sliding into the shop with his armful. "Meet Mr. Wigglesworth," he said with a grunt of effort.

"*That's* Mr. Wigglesworth?" I asked, my jaw dropping open as Finn set the cat carefully on the ground. The orange tabby wound his way sinuously through Finn's legs, almost knocking him off-balance. A purr rumbled out of the cat like a small engine. He sat on Finn's foot and blinked amber eyes up at me.

"Yes, this is the official cat of Sullivan's Spellbooks," Finn said.

"Nope, that's not a cat, it's a mini tank!" I exclaimed.

Finn chuckled. "He's a Maine Coon. They can get pretty big. Even bigger than this magnificent beast, if you can believe that, but he's such a sweet guy. All he wants is a cozy place to nap in the sunshine, lots of food, and someone to tickle his tummy occasionally."

"And to cause havoc whenever he can," Luna said with a sniff from her place on top of the counter. Her ears twitched in agitation as the cat's luminous eyes swung to her. He blinked, and then his pink tongue poked out of his mouth, running around his lips. Luna squeaked and scrambled back while Finn and I suppressed matching grins.

Mr. Wigglesworth swung his head to consider me as I crouched, cautiously extending a hand towards him, hoping to make a connection. His amber eyes met mine, filled with a mixture of curiosity and a touch of aloofness. Tufted ears poked into the air, reminding me of those of a lynx. His thick, luxurious fur had intricate tabby markings, a tapestry of dark lines and swirls that added to his allure.

I ran my fingers through his soft, dense coat. With each stroke, he leaned into my touch and emitted a low, rumbling purr. Despite Luna's grumbling, I knew we'd get on just fine.

Mr. Wigglesworth jumped onto the windowsill and curled up around the books on display. Luna muttered darkly. I didn't catch all of it, but there was something about carrot spears and shoving them up the cat's nose, I think. Deciding it was probably better overall not to know any more details, I grabbed my bag and smiled brightly at Finn. "I don't know about you, but I'm starving."

Finn grinned and held up a canvas bag that had been hidden under all the cat fur. "I packed up his extra food so he wouldn't ransack the place when he got hungry. Don't worry, Luna, I grabbed some things I think you might like as well," he said.

Luna sniffed, her whiskers twitching. "You're a good boy, Finnegan Oakheart." I noticed her eyes never wavered from the front window where the dozing cat lounged, his flicking tail the only sign he was still awake.

Finn winked at me and swiftly set out his offerings. Two metal bowls went on the floor. Finn tipped a small mountain of food in one and I filled the other with water. Next, Finn spread a fine array of vegetables in front of Luna. She started munching on a piece of lettuce absently, her eyes never leaving the cat.

Finally ready to go, Finn offered me his arm. "There. That should keep them both satisfied for a while. Now, I believe I promised you a pizza. Still interested?" His eyes sparkled warmly.

I linked my arm through his and nodded. "Lead the way!"

He grinned and held the door wide for me, letting in a cool blast of wind from the autumn evening. Based on the chill in the air, winter was fast on the way. I locked the door behind us and called up to the gargoyle crouching above the door. "We're heading out. Will you keep an eye on the two of them and make sure they play nice?" I asked.

"You got it!" The gargoyle's gravelly voice floated down to us. He waved his wing. "Enjoy your evening."

I waved back. "Thanks, Gideon!"

As we started walking down the street, Finn said, "I hope you're hungry. Even though it's a hobbit-themed restaurant, the portions are huge."

"Sounds perfect," I said with a smile.

We chatted as we walked, keeping the pace brisk to combat the chilly breeze that had kicked up. Luckily, it didn't take us long to reach the Hobbit Hole. The building was on a well-landscaped corner plot, leading out to an adorable little park with a small duck pond, some walking paths, and even a cute play area for kids. The restaurant itself exuded a warm, inviting atmosphere, which reminded me of everything I'd ever imagined about a hobbit dwelling. Laughter and light poured from the packed establishment onto the street as the round wooden door swung wide and a couple bundled up against the chilly weather, carefully balanced to-go boxes as they left the cozy warmth of the restaurant.

Finn held the round green door open, allowing me to be swept away by the rustic charm of the place. The interior was adorned with earthy tones, warm lighting, and cozy nooks that offered a sense of intimacy even in the crowded space. Wooden tables with intricate carvings and mismatched chairs made me feel like I just walked into someone's home during a party rather than a public dining establishment. The aroma of freshly baked bread permeated the entire restaurant as servers in themed costumes bustled around tables carrying baskets of steaming rolls, replacing empty ones where diners had already enjoyed their offerings. My mouth watered. If everything here tasted as good as the bread smelled, I was in for a treat.

A young woman in a long skirt and a floral blouse hurried over. "Well, hello there! I'm Rose. Can I get you a table for two?" she asked.

"Yes please. I made a reservation," Finn said, giving his name.

The woman checked her list and then favored us both with a cheery smile that lifted her rosy cheeks and made her eyes sparkle. "I've got you right here. Now, are we celebrating anything special? An anniversary perhaps?" she asked with a wink.

"Nothing like that," Finn said.

I spoke at the same time. "We're just friends." Did my voice come out a little too loudly, or was that just me?

The hostess shot me a confused look that obviously said, *Are you crazy? Have you* seen *this man?* However, she put on a professional smile. "Alrighty then. Follow me, please." She settled us at a small table and handed over thick menus. "Sammy will be right over to take care of you folks. Enjoy!"

A blush crept up my cheeks as she left. I felt like I had to explain myself. "I'm sorry. I didn't mean—"

"I get it," Finn said. "You're new in town. I don't know your past and you don't know mine. This is a getting to know you date."

"Exactly," I said with a sigh of relief. But why did I suddenly want it to be more than that? I shouldn't. He was still a suspect, after all. Wasn't he?

Confused at my own emotions, I hid behind my menu, trying to regain my equilibrium. We browsed the selections in silence, which was good because it gave me a chance to compose myself while appreciating not only the creativity in naming the dishes, but the chef's attention to detail. By the time I'd read the second option, I knew I needed to come back here another time because everything on the menu looked incredible.

"What are you thinking?" Finn asked, glancing up at me.

"I can't decide between the Elven Delight pizza with the goat's cheese and sun-dried tomatoes or the Dwarven Feast with the BBQ braised beef, caramelized onions, and bacon," I said with a groan. "What are you getting?"

"The Shire Supreme," Finn said. "It's my favorite."

I glanced back at my menu for the description. "Savory roasted veggies topped with artisanal cheese and a drizzle of herb-infused olive oil? How do they expect anyone to make a choice here when it all sounds so good?"

Finn grinned. "Well, I'll be happy to let you have a slice of mine if that helps to make up your mind."

"It doesn't but thank you. I'm definitely going to take you up on your offer."

Our server, Sammy, came over with a wide smile, curly hair, and wearing a plaid waistcoat over a billowing cream shirt. I glanced down, half-expecting to see large, bare feet, but the man wore normal loafers. He caught me staring and winked. "They say it's a health hazard to not wear shoes. I've tried telling them that hobbit feet can take it, but they won't believe me," he said with a chuckle. "Now, what can I get started for you folks?" Finn ordered his supreme pizza, and I decided on the Dwarven Feast. We both asked for water. Sammy nodded, not needing to write down the order. "I'll get those in for you right away. Would you like some of our fresh bread and infused butter while you wait?"

"Yes please, it smells amazing," I said as another waiter with a tray full of steaming bread baskets strolled by. Sammy grabbed one from the tray, along with an oval dish decorated with small pats of butter.

He set them on the table between us and pointed out the different flavors. "This one is garlic and parmesan butter, which is my favorite. I can never get enough of the stuff. In the middle is a sea salt and herb version, and, if you have a sweet tooth, try the cinnamon and brown sugar there on the end. Enjoy!"

"Thanks, Sammy," I said, snagging a roll without hesitation. I couldn't wait to try all three options.

Finn selected a roll of his own. "It seems like you're really settling in here," he observed as he spread some of the garlic butter on his bread.

"Well, it's only been a few days, but I've really enjoyed my time here so far, apart from the whole mess with the shop," I said. I considered telling him about everything that had happened at the police station, but quickly decided against it. I was here to get information from him, not the other way around. Besides, I had to remind myself, he might be the responsible for the missing book.

I spread a generous dab of the herb and sea salt butter on my bite of bread and popped it in my mouth before I could second guess my decision and tell the handsome druid everything. It turned out to be an excellent choice because that morsel was delicious with a capital Yum.

"And the guy in the hat stalking you? I never imagined something like that happening here in Havenwood," Finn said, a dark look crossing his face.

I swallowed my tasty morsel. "Well, it is a small town. Maybe it was just a wrong-time-wrong-place thing, and I scared him as much as he scared me," I said, but even as I spoke the words, I didn't believe them. He'd been following me, and I still didn't know why.

"I don't think so. Not if you've seen him hanging around before. Once or twice might be a coincidence, but anything more than that? I'm not convinced."

"You may be right," I admitted.

"And speaking of coincidences, don't you think it was a little convenient that the RV was just standing open last night, and the books were just sitting out in plain sight?" Finn asked, raising a brow.

My mouth went dry, and I had to force myself to swallow the suddenly tasteless lump of bread I'd just popped in my mouth. "What do you mean?" I asked, stalling for time. I really didn't want to explain about my magical abilities in the middle of a crowded restaurant. One of the things I'd learned early on as a witch was not to share the extent of my gifts with just anyone. As a teen, careless bragging caused me more problems than I'd ever expected. I wasn't about to relive that mistake if I could help it.

Finn shrugged and slathered more butter on his bread. "It just seems negligent, you know? Blackwell went to all the trouble of stealing the books just to leave them out in plain sight for the police to find? I'm not buying it. Frankly, I'm surprised the police did."

I squirmed in my chair and lowered my voice. "Well, once I saw no one was hurt, I might have taken a quick look around. I overheard Thaddeus and Oswald Puddleton talking about a book sale, and I assumed it was to do with Granny Bea's stolen books. I wanted to know, so I did a little snooping."

Finn rubbed a hand through his hair. "This is serious, Harper. Something like that could get you in trouble with the police if they find out."

I chewed on my lip, wondering how much to tell him. How much could I really trust him? Did I really think he'd robbed the shop? In my heart of hearts, the answer was no, but after putting him on my suspect list, it took conscious effort to give him the benefit of the doubt. Finally, I decided on most of the truth, at least, the truth from this morning's encounter at the police station. As quickly as I could, I filled him in on what had happened, including the as yet missing book. I paused my narration only when Sammy delivered our massive pizzas to the table.

The conversation lapsed for a few minutes as we enjoyed the incredible balance of flavors. Finn offered me a slice of his, so we swapped. The supreme was good, but mine was better. The BBQ beef melted in my mouth with just the right combination of salt, spice, and sweetness. Combined with the sauce and cheese, it made for an excellent pizza, and the caramelized onions really took it to the next level. As nice as it was to share with Finn, I was secretly glad I only had to give up one slice. Conversation drifted as we chatted about the food and life in Havenwood.

Sammy cleared our plates away and brought coffee. Finn ordered an espresso, but I had to try a Misty Mountains macchiato made from their own unique blend of coffee. I inhaled the fragrant steam as I lifted the small cup to my nose, smelling the earthiness of dark chocolate, a subtle sweetness of caramel, and a hint of spices and cocoa from the dusting, creating a mountain decoration on top of the foam.

Finn sighed in appreciation as he sipped from his own tiny cup. "So, what now?" he asked.

My mind had drifted back to the shop. "Well, I asked the police to hold on to the books until the matter of the inheritance can be settled. After that, along with a few other stipulations, I decided not to press charges. Until then, I guess my best course of action is to focus on developing a plan that will blow Granny's lawyer away and hope the police can find this missing book."

Finn's eyes twinkled. "I meant dessert," he said.

I blushed. "I'm sorry. Here you are, taking me out, and all I can do it talk about the break-in and my own problems."

His expression softened. "You've got a lot on your plate, and I don't just mean the pizza. Talking about problems helps, and I've been told I'm an excellent listener," he said with a smile.

"You know what's been bugging me since this morning?" I blurted out. "Magic."

"It is a vexing topic from time to time," Finn said mildly, settling back in his chair. He really did have a charming smile. I felt a soft smile tug my lips upwards as I contemplated how nice it would be to —

No. Focus, Harper.

"Whether you believe Thaddeus' story about someone breaking into Spellbooks before him or not, what happened to the purple skirt?" I asked.

"Is this some kind of riddle? What skirt?" Finn looked perplexed.

I shook my head, realizing I hadn't told Finn or anyone about Gideon's revelation. "Gideon, the gargoyle who watches the shop at night, said he didn't see anyone break in, but he heard it. The sound of breaking glass caused him to fly into the shop, but there was no one there. No one he could see, at least."

"Okay, so you think someone cast some sort of camouflage spell?" Finn asked.

"Maybe. But as Gideon flew around, trying to find the source of the break-in, he crashed into someone, cutting them. The last thing he remembered before turning to stone was seeing a purple skirt and red shoes as the thief ran out of the shop."

"And you're wondering if Thaddeus has questionable color-matching skills? Or maybe likes to cross-dress while robbing local bookshops?"

I chuckled. "The more I think about it, the less sure I am that it was him in the skirt. I didn't find anything remotely like that in his RV, and the place was small."

"He could have borrowed a costume. He works at a Renaissance Faire, after all," Finn pointed out.

"So, we're going with the theory that he borrowed a skirt and an invisibility cloak?" I asked.

Finn laughed. "You never know. This town is full of surprises. But seriously, if it's bothering you, we can keep an eye out for any peculiar oc-currences. Maybe invest in some medieval-themed surveillance equipment to catch any Renaissance Faire thieves."

I rolled my eyes playfully. "Medieval-themed surveillance? You're pushing it, now."

He winked. "Hey, we're dealing with an invisible skirt-wearing suspect here. Anything's possible in our line of 'detective' work."

"Our work?" I asked, feeling a slight uplift of my spirits. I was sure he disapproved of the whole RV thing and wouldn't want to be entangled in any sort of investigation with me.

"Sure. I could hardly let you go after a skirt wearing thief on your own. It's one of the more obscure of the ancient Havenwood traditions of hospitality, but I promise you, it's there," he said, his eyes twinkling.

I laughed. "I'll have to take your word on that. But if we're going to be amateur sleuths, you've got to admit a skirt is an odd choice of clothing when you are planning a burglary, isn't it? However, putting the skirt aside for a moment, what could cause someone to go from invisible to visible in a matter of moments? An invisibility cloak wouldn't do that, even if such an item existed outside of Harry Potter."

"You think it was magic fizzling out?" Finn asked.

I lifted my shoulder and let it drop. "This is Havenwood, after all. Besides, once you rule out everything else, whatever is left must be the truth, however improbable."

Finn rubbed the stubble on his cheek. "Well, assuming you are correct, there are several possibilities. Maybe Gideon crashing into the thief caused them to lose focus. Or perhaps it was a timed spell. Whoever cast it only had enough power to last a few minutes, and the appearance of your gargoyle delayed them enough to interrupt a clean getaway."

"Is that possible?" I asked.

Finn shrugged. "It's magic. Pretty much anything is *possible*, but whether or not it is *probably* really depends on the person and their unique brand of magic."

"Okay, put yourself in the thief's shoes. How would you have done it?" I asked.

Finn drummed his fingers on the table, considering my question. "I don't have the magical juice to power an invisibility spell, even for a few minutes. My talents are in rune-crafting or creating what my master called bindings. Linking two objects or ideas to each other and borrowing enough power from the natural world to 'make it so'," he said the last words in a deep, wizardly voice, but broke the illusion almost immediately with a rueful smile.

"Could you create an invisibility rune?" I asked, sensing a fresh path for investigation.

"Technically, it's possible," Finn allowed. "But there isn't one invisibility rune. Several runes need to be carefully linked using the correct order and placement to create the complex rune, which grants invisibility. Besides that, the runes are complicated and drawing them correctly is difficult to master. I know some of them, such as the rune for 'sight', but I don't know enough to create true invisibility. Even if I knew the runes, if I drew one wrong line or if someone smudged the drawing just like that," he said, snapping his fingers, "I'm back in the visible spectrum."

"I don't know much about creating runes. Could anyone draw them if they spent the time to learn or do they need some kind of innate magical talent?" I asked.

Finn toyed with the tiny espresso cup in front of him. "Sure. I guess anyone *could* draw it with enough time. Technically, even humans without an ounce of magical ability could draw the runes, but you'd still need magic to activate them."

I was curious. I didn't know anything about runes or Finn's abilities, and I found the conversation fascinating. "How much magic?" I asked.

Finn wavered a hand back and forth. "Less than it would take to power a spell, but more than most people have. At least, more than most people in this town possess. Off the top of my head, the Silverthorne family could manage it, but that's probably about it," he said.

"From what everyone says, it's highly unlikely a Silverthorne would be responsible," I said.

Finn nodded. "Next to impossible. Vivienne Silverthorne is very strict on rules and her children aren't the kind who rebel, at least not at this level."

I bit my lip, trying to put the pieces together. "Why would it take less magical energy to power a rune than a spell?" I finally asked.

"Because of the nature of runes. Think of them as simple machines. A lever or, better yet, a pulley. Let's say you want to move something heavy from the first to the second floor of your shop. Sure, you could carry it, but it would take a lot of energy and strength. That's spell-craft. Or you could rig a pulley to do the heavy lifting for you, which is more like rune-craft."

"So, you still need a little strength, in this case, magical ability, and the technical know-how to create and activate the magical pulley, aka the runes?" I asked.

Finn snapped his fingers and pointed at me. "You've got it. But I don't know who else in town might know the proper runes and have the power to activate them. A powerful mage might be able do both. Maybe a handful of others in town? I'm not sure."

"So, it's a possibility that the thief used runes to cover their entrance?"

Finn lifted his hands, palms up. "Maybe? But that's just how I'd do it, given my abilities and the limitations that come with my magic. However, this is Havenwood. I'm sure that there are as many possibilities as there are magic users. But creating the runes necessary to rob a place would take considerable time and at least a moderate level of magic. I'd rather spend my time and energy helping people instead of plotting to steal from them, you know?"

I considered his words as the conversation drifted away from the break-in and to the residents of Havenwood. Despite the charming man sitting across from me, my thoughts kept returning to the shop and the missing book.

Could Thaddeus be telling the truth? Was there a second thief, or rather, a first thief who had stolen the old weather book before Thaddeus had even arrived? If I couldn't find the missing compendium, maybe figuring out the kind of magic that the thief had used to cover their entrance would help me identify them. But how?

The questions swirled through my head, keeping me awake long after Finn walked me back to the Enchanted Oasis, and I tucked myself into bed.

Distractions and Discoveries

THE NEXT THREE DAYS passed in a blur. I spent as much time as I could in the shop trying to hone my plans. I shared my ideas with the DeLucas, and they were all incredibly helpful in helping me craft the best presentation possible. Surprisingly, Bella had a keener business acumen for someone her age than I'd ever imagined. We spent hours poring over ideas in between her work at the B&B.

When I wasn't at the shop, I spent most of my time in the library trying to find everything I could about Benedict Starling, his logbooks, Blackfin, and pirate treasure. My search turned up depressingly little more than what Mrs. Jenkins had already told me. Many people suspected Starling and Blackfin were the same man, but several prominent scholars disagreed, pointing to the dates in his travel logs and improbably fast travel. Starling couldn't have been robbing ships outside of Boston if he'd been in New York just a few days before. Which all made sense if your view of the world was strictly mundane. Mine, however, was not. To my mind, Starling might have easily made the journey much faster than his competition if he was gifted with water magic. Even wind magic might do the trick, but I doubted the scholars accounted for that in their calculations. Other than my suppositions, I found frustratingly little evidence to support this possibility. The library had a few copies of Starling's legitimate journals on microfiche that hadn't yet been digitized, but without the missing compendium, I didn't have much to go on.

When my eyes went fuzzy and the tension in my shoulders from hunching over the reading tables gave me a headache, I knew it was time to take a break. If Thaddeus was still in Spellbooks under the supervision of Mr. Ravenscroft, I'd walk on by and explore the town. I visited Stella's flower shop and bought a bouquet of bright blooms for Honey. I wandered past Mason's auto repair shop but didn't see any ghosts. However, it was during the day, and they might not come out until later. I discovered Pixie Pastries over on Enchanted Lane and bought myself a salted caramel pumpkin bar that was delicious. Whenever I was out of the bookshop, I made it a point to wander around the town, learning as much as I could about Havenwood and its inhabitants.

On my rambling around town, I tried to talk to as many people as possible. I drew up sketches for creating a coffee bar in Spellbooks and ran my plan by Grimgor. He offered some insightful points that I incorporated into my proposal before showing it to Antonio, who suggested some decorative flourishes. Honey added to her husband's ideas, sketching out a place to serve some light snacks or cakes in addition to the coffee. Mostly, I spent time with Bella, turning my plans into a tangible presentation that any business would be proud of. When Bella was at work, I chatted with Madame Fontaine who thankfully spouted no more predictions, but she did offer some advice about engaging with the readers in the community through book clubs and other book-related meetups. With Halloween just around the corner, she wanted me to host a murder mystery dinner at the shop where everyone came in costume and played different roles. I used the opportunity to ask her about a purple skirt and scarlet shoes, but she looked at me like I was crazy, claiming she owned nothing so dramatic. I secretly disagreed, looking at the enormous hat pinned atop her head, but wasn't about to gainsay her. Instead, I admitted her idea sounded like fun but that I needed to focus on one thing at a time. Secure the shop first, plan dinner parties later.

Finn found a reason to swing by at least once a day. It was nice to have the handsome neighbor so interested in me, but I found it hard to fully commit to the daily flirting as the deadline with the lawyer loomed ever closer. If I didn't win the shop and I had to leave, I doubted a couple of days flirting with a cute guy would transition into anything more than that, anyway.

In between all the activities, I still found plenty of time to wonder about the missing book. I even compiled another list of suspects, putting everyone I knew on it and then crossing them off one by one. Thistle? No, too naïve. Finn? Opportunity, but no motive. And wouldn't he want to avoid the place if he was the thief? Oswald Puddleton? A possibility. He definitely had the motive, but his injury placed him in the hospital at the time of the break in. His wife, Hortense perhaps? Another possibility, although I couldn't imagine anyone who called the police as swiftly as she had done to be a criminal. So, who else was there? That question plagued the quiet moments of my days, almost driving me crazy as I tried to figure out who was behind the missing compendium.

The hours felt long, but the days flew by, and before I knew it, Friday rolled around again. I sat bolt upright in my bed at the Oasis. Friday. Which meant it was time for Nathaniel to make his decision. I was simultaneously confident in my plan and nervous it wasn't enough. I'd done my best on my plan for the shop, and I knew it was solid. Maybe not the flashiest or fastest way to make money, but it was something I was proud of. I just hoped it would be enough to compete with Thaddeus. Our plans were going head-to-head today, not only because Granny Bea designed it that way but also because I hadn't found out anything more about the missing compendium.

I headed downstairs for breakfast. Honey, Antonio, and Bella were all gathered around a table in the center of the otherwise empty breakfast nook.

"What's going on?" I asked.

"We know today's the day, and we wanted to wish you luck," Antonio said with a wide smile.

"And make sure you have the energy you need," Honey added, handing me a plate with a giant pecan sticky bun generously smothered in a luscious caramel glaze and studded with crunchy roasted pecans.

"To finally claim what's rightfully yours," Bella finished, pouring coffee into a white porcelain mug with a flourish and handing it over to me.

I settled down at the table with the DeLucas, happy and feeling bolstered by their loving support. Everyone should start every morning with pastry, coffee, good friends, and a cheerful outlook. I was lucky to have the first three and was working my way towards the last one.

"I'm not sure it's going to happen; despite all I've done. After all, Thaddeus—"

"Has nothing on you," Antonio said sternly, wagging a finger at me. "And don't you forget it." He couldn't hold the serious expression longer than a few heartbeats, and his typical sunny smile broke through a moment later.

"Maybe. But I still think he and Nathanial Ravenscroft might be in cahoots," I admitted.

"Well, you'll only know when you know. Until then, do you have everything ready to go?" Honey asked.

"I think so. I've done all I can, at least."

Bella slid a small envelope across the table to me. "Speaking of your meeting with the lawyer, a courier dropped this off for you earlier."

I tore the envelope open to reveal a single sheet of expensive card stock. The invitation was concise.

Please join me at Sullivan's Spellbooks at seven o'clock this evening. This meeting is exclusively for designated heirs. The matter of the estate's rightful heir will be finalized after hearing the future plans for Spellbooks from both parties.

- Nathaniel Ravenscroft

"This is it," I said, passing the note around. A tendril of dread wove its way past the nervous butterflies in my stomach. How could I possibly compare to my book-selling cousin who'd been in the business for years? At least the lawyer was going through the motions to make it seem like I had a chance, but did I really? With each passing moment, I felt less sure of myself.

Honey must've read a fraction of my feelings on my face because she reached out and patted my hand. "Don't worry, Harper. It will all turn out just fine, you'll see. Eat your breakfast. No one should ever confront their problems on an empty stomach." Dutifully, I took a bite of the sticky bun. She'd baked it to perfection, not that I expected anything less from Honey.

Every bite of the soft, pillowy dough dripping with rich, buttery caramel was a tribute to her magical skills in the kitchen.

Antonio chimed in. "Then I think you should go out on the town this morning. Take your mind off things. Maybe do a little shopping."

The idea was a good one. I swallowed my bite of sticky bun. "I should really get my mom and dad something. They're both so busy on base that they can't get the time off to come and visit. Who knows? Maybe this is kismet, and I'll be ready with their souvenirs when I have to catch a flight back to Germany."

"Don't think like that!" Bella exclaimed. "You're just getting prepared for when they come to visit you and your new bookshop."

I smiled at her gratefully. "You really are a good friend."

"Friend?" Antonio demanded indignantly. "Why, you are like a second daughter! You're family to us, and that's just how it is!"

Bella smiled fondly at her father. "You'll have to forgive Papa. His Italian blood sometimes gets the better of him and he brings the drama."

Antonio pretended to frown at his daughter. "Is it dramatic if it's true?"

"Yes," chorused Honey and Bella with matching smiles. Honey reached across the table and squeezed her husband's hand. "But that's part of your charm, my love. Never, ever change." His fake frown cracked, and he grinned back at his wife.

A line from Madame Fontaine's strange prediction drifted back to me.

> *To the chosen kin, hold true and strong.*
> *For when blood's bond falters, trust goes wrong.*

In this moment, it certainly felt like the DeLucas were my chosen kin. I'd assumed the blood bond faltering referred to Thaddeus' betrayal and theft of the books, but what if it had to do with Granny Bea herself? What if things didn't work out in my favor today? Would that be a bond faltering and my trust going wrong? I shook my head. This was the problem with predictions. They could be interpreted in enough ways to drive a person mad. Besides, who knew if it was even one of Madame Fontaine's true ones? Instead of worrying about that, I focused back on my breakfast and the cheerful conversation floating around the table.

Twenty minutes later, I was caffeinated, sugared up, and in a much happier frame of mind, thanks to the DeLucas' infectious, cheerful attitudes. Antonio, with his charismatic charm, offered insights into the historical significance of the Spellbooks, weaving tales that elevated my narrative for the shop into a captivating saga. Honey's culinary artistry with apple cinnamon tarts not only enchanted our taste buds, but served as a metaphor for the irresistible allure my plans would hold. The tarts, like my proposal, had to be a perfect blend of sweetness and substance. She nailed it. I just hoped I would as well. Bella, with her keen intellect, delved into last minute logistical intricacies, suggesting ways to intertwine modern conveniences with the shop's timeless charm. As we shared laughter and ideas, the room echoed with the harmonious blend of preparation and familial support, which became the pillars of a practice session that transcended mere planning.

I turned to Bella. "I don't suppose you have some time to hang out? I'd like to run a couple more things by you?" I asked hopefully, as Antonio cleared away the dishes.

Bella shook her head regretfully. "Maybe later? We're expecting to be full for the entire weekend, so I need to help Mama and Papa make sure the rooms get flipped over and everything is perfect for our new guests. Perhaps you could indulge in a little retail therapy to get your mind off things? If you do, check out the Curiosity Corner over on Unicorn Avenue. It's an interesting place and they have the cutest gifts."

Antonio appeared from the kitchen just in time to catch the tail end of our conversation. "Don't listen to a word she says. The best souvenirs are at Timeless Treasures."

Honey wove her arm through her husband's. "Both are fine, but if you are looking for something a little more unique, check out Zephyrus's Antique Emporium."

"Zephyr? Like the Greek god of wind?" I asked.

Honey tipped her head to the side. "Similar, but no connection apart from the name. In fact, the man who runs it is a distant relation to Vivienne Silverthorne."

"Her great uncle once removed, isn't he?" Antonio chimed in.

"Something like that. His name is Henry Silverthorne, but no one calls him that these days. He had a magic show years ago and went by the stage name 'Zephyrus the Mad Mage'." She swept her hand through the air like she was displaying a marquee sign at a theater.

"The only problem was, he wasn't very good either at real magic or stage magic," Antonio explained.

"A bit of a black sheep in the Silverthorne family, but a nice older gentleman. He prefers going by his stage name, so that's what he called his business when he retired. I saw him spending quite a bit of time with your great-grandmama in her final few months," Honey said with a fond smile.

"I'd like to meet him, and a little shopping sounds like the perfect distraction this morning," I said.

Honey pulled out a map from the tourist brochures near the door and marked the locations of the souvenir shops for me. She also handed me a reusable bag folded over on itself in a neat little bundle. "For anything special you might find," she said with a knowing wink. "It's always better to be prepared."

I thanked her, grabbed my coat and scarf, and headed out the door. They were right. I'd already done what I could for the time being. I needed to get my mind off Spellbooks for a little while, or I'd drive myself crazy before the meeting this evening. Besides, exploring the town was fun, and I always seemed to discover something new. I set off at a brisk pace, partially driven by excitement but mostly trying to outrun my nerves about the upcoming meeting that would decide my fate here in Havenwood.

The Mad Mage

THE FIRST TWO SHOPS were cute but full of standard touristy souvenirs. T-shirts printed with silly sayings like "My other car's a dragon", snow globes full of glitter and sparkling fairies, coffee cups, hats, and every sort of fantasy-related figurine you could imagine. I browsed for a while, but nothing caught my eye. I couldn't imagine Master Sergeant Sullivan wearing a hat with horns coming out the sides that read, "Keep Calm and Steer Clear of the Labyrinth."

I wandered into a coffee shop and bought myself a hot apple cider. The warm, comforting spices made walking through town on the cool fall day feel more like an event and less like a typical Friday. I strolled, sipped on my drink, window shopped, and indulged in the town's ambiance. I waved at the locals I recognized and smiled knowingly as a handful of tourists exclaimed over how this town was so into cosplay. Little did they know they were commenting on a pair of real-life witches going about their everyday lives. The two women just did so in black capes, pointed hats, and carrying broomsticks.

I consulted Honey's map and eventually found the antique emporium on a quiet little side street with almost no traffic. The front window was crowded, items tossed together with little rhyme and absolutely no reason. A cute little glass globe balanced precariously on a chessboard caught my attention. I leaned closer, cupping my hand around my eyes to block out the glare. A tiny landscape of moss, delicate flowers, and painted miniature houses were encased in a glass sphere. Light sparkled and danced as glitter seemed to float through the globe, moving as if on its own secret air current. I shook my head. That was impossible inside a sealed glass dome. Wasn't it?

Deciding to get a closer look, I pushed through the door. A bell tinkled merrily as I entered the otherwise empty shop. I looked around, searching for the owner. The place was crowded with trinkets, some stacked higher than my head, and smelled musty, like it desperately needed a window cracked and some air freshener. When no one stuck their head out of a back room, I called out. "Hello? I'm interested in the globe in the window. Is it okay to take a look?"

Silence greeted my call. I waited awkwardly for another moment, not knowing if I should leave or not. I'd just decided to come back later when the shop seemed to darken, and a booming voice echoed through the piles of antiques.

"Welcome! I am Zephyrus! Mad mage, keeper of ancient secrets, and weaver of mystical charms! How may I make your wishes come true today?"

I spun around in a circle, searching for the creature attached to such an imposing voice. Was he a really the mad mage or just a theatrical employee? When no one appeared, I spoke to the shop in general. "Hello, umm, mighty Zephyrus? I'm interested in the globe in the window. Could you tell me how much it is, please?"

"The fairy dust globe? Real fairy dust in there, you know. That's why it shimmers in the sunshine. How often can you say you've bottled magic? But that's what I've done here. Bottled magic. Don't let it out, though. No, no, no. That won't do at all." The man's voice started in the basso boom from before, but, as he continued, it sounded nearer and had more of a quaver to it. Finally, I saw a wild white head of hair bob between stacks of antiques until the owner finally extricated himself from his merchandise. I nearly gasped when I realized I recognized the elderly face peering at me from behind the wild white mop of hair and a long white beard.

"Hank?" I asked, surprised.

He held up his hands, looking around the empty shop like the statue of the griffin in the corner might overhear us. "Zephyrus, please. I'm on duty," he whispered. Then he threw his arms wide and said in a booming voice. "What can I do for you today?" It spoiled the effect when his voice cracked and went spiraling up into the stratosphere on the last word. He shook his hands angrily and glowered at them. "Fiddlesticks! Still haven't mastered that spell!"

"Han—I mean, Zephyrus?"

He looked at me and blinked in surprise. "When did you get here?"

I bit my lip, not sure if he was playing a trick on me. "I've been standing here. I asked about the globe in the window. The one with the fairy dust?"

"Oh. Right. Fifty-nine, ninety-nine and I'll throw in the dust for free," he said, shooting finger guns my way along with a cheery smile.

I bit my lip. That was a lot of money for something so small, even if there was genuine fairy dust inside. Besides, I probably wouldn't be able to get it through customs if the plants were real, and I had to fly back to the base. A display of books on a low table caught my eye, and I realized I recognized one. I picked up the book with the purposely distressed leather cover and flipped through the empty pages.

"Good eye." Hank, I mean, *Zephyrus* said, appearing at my elbow. "That is an authentic replica of a merchant captain's journal. He's a bit of a local legend around here. If you believe the stories, he turned pirate and buried his treasure somewhere in the area. Bit of a local hero of mine, he is." The old man nodded and stroked his beard. "Captain Benedict Starling, or as I like to call him—"

"Blackfin," I whispered, turning the journal over in my hands. It was an exact copy of the one Mrs. Jenkins owned. I wondered if this was where she bought hers.

The old man turned to face me, his eyes shining with interest. "Precisely! How did you know that?"

I frowned at him, wondering if he'd truly forgotten me from the book club or if this was all part of his act. If he was as mad as his moniker suggested, I didn't want to hurt his feelings. "I know Mrs. Jenkins from the book club. She has a similar journal."

"Ah, Maggie. Fascinated by pirates, she is. Bit of a flighty girl if you ask me, but I've no doubt she'll put her best foot forward when she grows up a bit. I heard she's going to start working for that Ravenscroft lawyer. He'll straighten her out if anyone will. You mark my words."

I pretended to be deeply absorbed in the empty book in my hands as I considered what he said. He sounded confused, and it definitely seemed like he'd lost track of a year or two or maybe even ten. "Umm, I think I'll just take this, thanks," I said, holding up the journal. Mom would get a kick out of the story while Dad would immediately start researching everything he could find about Benedict Starling. Actually, he and Mrs. Jenkins would probably make a great team of amateur treasure hunters.

"Do you want some booty?"

I blinked in surprise. "I'm sorry, what?"

"Booty. Pirate trinkets. You, know...treasure." The old man waved his arms in bigger and bigger circles.

"Oh. No, thank you, I'm okay with just the journal, thanks," I said.

"Really, I've got some right here," he replied, dashing around the untidy piles of antiques with more speed than I would've expected from someone with his advanced...beard. He thumped a fist on a heavy wooden chest held shut with a heavy, old iron lock. Rusting iron accents and faded carvings of sea creatures and nautical motifs adorned the weathered exterior. "Wait. No. No, treasure here. I forgot. The lock is jammed. Such a shame. Can't get it open. But I have some nice bottles in ships. I mean, ships in bottles."

"I think just the journal is enough," I said, moving towards the counter.

"Are you sure? I've got them in all shapes and sizes. Big ones, small ones. Any color you like. Why, I even have a replica of old Captain Starling's ship if you're into the pirate lore."

"I'm good, thanks," I said with a forced smile.

Hank scampered around the counter and rang me up. As he did so, I pulled out the bag Honey had given me. It was fortuitous she had because the journal was too large to fit into my purse. He held out the credit card machine for me, and I tapped my card to pay for the journal. When he passed the book to me, a framed picture behind the counter caught my eye. I paused, almost fumbling with the book. Finally, I stuffed the journal inside the tote bag and nodded at the photo.

"Is that you?" I asked in what I hoped was a nonchalant manner.

Hank looked over his shoulder and smiled. Carefully, he lifted it off the nail and put it on the counter between us. "This was my very first performance. Back then, I was only little Henry. Hank to my friends. But this was the day I became Zephyrus, the Mad Mage!" He waved his arms dramatically around his head, a fearsome expression darkening his visage.

A moment later, he dropped his arms and smiled fondly at the picture. "Those were the good old days."

"You look so handsome and very impressive in that robe. It looks custom made. Is it?"

"Oh yes. The grandmother of the man who owns the best tailor shop in town made it especially for me. She even did the embroidery all by hand. I wanted the robes to be black with silver designs, but she insisted purple was more my color. Less sinister and more magical, those were her words."

I leaned over to get a closer look at the heavily embroidered robe he wore in the photo. The high neck brushed his jaw line and swept down the arms to a dramatic flare at the wrists. The cascade of purple draped from his shoulders nearly to the floor. "I can see why you liked them. You look very dashing in this photo," I said.

"It was my lucky robe. I never performed without it. Not even once." He shook his head solemnly.

"What happened to it?" I asked, keeping my tone innocent and inquiring.

"It got damaged. In...a trick. I used to do magic shows, you know. One day, a trick went wrong, and I lit the whole sleeve on fire," he said, forcing out a nervous laugh.

I felt like I'd just discovered a loose thread and decided to tug on it. "That's such a shame. A magician's robe like that should be in a museum! Oh, and look at those shoes!" I exclaimed, pointing at the picture. "Please tell me you still have those!"

Hank lifted his leg and tugged up his trousers to reveal a scarlet shoe that seemed to sparkle with glitter. Or maybe it was fairy dust. "These are my favorites. If red shoes were good enough for Dorothy, they're good enough for me."

"There's no place like home," I agreed enthusiastically. "I've never seen ruby slippers like that before, but on you, they just work."

Hank did a happy little wiggle-jig at the compliment. "Thank you. Although, in the original story, her slippers were silver. I like the red though. Brings a bit more drama, don't you think?" He struck a pose, like he was waiting for applause.

I gave him a polite round and then raised a finger like a thought had just occurred to me. "You know what? I think I would like to look at one of those ships in a bottle. I bet my dad would get a kick out of getting one of those as a souvenir."

"No doubt," Hank said, rubbing his hands together. "What size are you thinking?"

"How big do they go?" I asked, my tone awestruck.

Hank held his hands about two feet apart. "My largest one is a beauty. I bet your father would love something like this. Just let me run in the back and grab it for you."

"If you don't mind, I'd appreciate it. I bet Dad would love to have it on his bookshelf at home."

"Not at all, not at all. I'll be back in two shakes." Hank hurried off, winding through the cluttered shop carefully so as not to knock anything off a shelf.

As soon as he disappeared, I bent over the photo, tracing my finger over the glass as I examined the long purple robe and red shoes. It couldn't be, could it? Was Zephyrus aka Henry "Hank" Silverthorne the thief who'd stolen the compendium from Spellbooks? As quickly as I could, I ran through what I knew about Hank. He'd known Granny Bea, so it stood to reason he might have seen the compendium in her shop. Perhaps they'd even discussed it. He seemed to know quite a bit about the legend of Blackfin. Maybe he'd discussed the matter with Mrs. Jenkins at their book club. She could've told him her suspicions that Benedict Starling was Blackfin, and his missing journals might be the key to recovering lost pirate treasure. Who knows, she might have even mentioned when Thaddeus and I were coming into town. She would've known, being Nathaniel's secretary. And Hank was not only a stage magician, but also a Silverthorne which meant he probably had both the knowledge and the power for an invisibility spell.

I tried out my theory. Hank thinks he knows where one of these so-called missing journals is, and it's right here in town, but has been mislabeled as a weather compendium. But then Granny passes away, and Spellbooks looks like it's going to be passed down to one of her heirs, including the book with the possible treasure map. So, Hank, aka Zephyrus, employs a little of his stage magic to steal the book before an heir claims Granny's estate. However, something goes wrong, and Gideon gets a peek at Hank's stage costume before he turns to stone.

I bit my lip. It was all just a theory, of course. I couldn't exactly get Sheriff Jackson to come in and search the antique store just on my say so.

Besides, Hank might not be keeping the compendium here, if he even had it at all. No, I needed proof.

"Here we are," Hank grunted, lugging a large bottle towards the front of the shop. He had to move slowly because the glass container was bulky. Even with my limited knowledge, I had to admit that the ship nestled inside was beautifully constructed. I knew it had been painstakingly crafted outside of the bottle with the utmost diligence and then carefully arranged within, but there was still a magical element of seeing such a large model inside a bottle with such a tiny neck. The elegant vessel seemed to float effortlessly upon a glassy sea, frozen in a moment of maritime glory.

I made the appropriate awed noises and then stood back, considering the monstrosity on the counter between us.

"What? What is it? Is it not big enough?" Hank demanded.

I shook my head. "No, it's beautiful. But I don't think I can fit it in my suitcase. Do you have anything a little more travel sized?"

Hank perked up. "I have just the one!" he exclaimed and hurried toward the back of the shop once more.

I felt bad for about a nanosecond, but if I was right, he'd broken in and stolen from Granny. Now, if I were a mad mage, where would I hide a book about pirate treasure? I looked around the shop desperately, feeling despair mount. Where would I even begin to search in this mess? My eyes fell on the heavy wooden trunk on the floor. It couldn't be. Could it? Surely, he wouldn't have hidden the book in an actual treasure chest. Would he?

In a moment, I was kneeling next to the box. The heavy iron lock did its job admirably, protecting the secrets within with a tenacity most people would've found intimidating. But I was not like most people. I placed my hand on the rusting lock, closing my eyes. The image of the lock's interior mechanisms sprang into my mind's eye. A series of interlocking levers and tumblers greeted me, showcasing the skilled handiwork of a bygone era. It was a fabulous piece of craftsmanship, but not what I needed now, when the time was so short. I took a deep breath and got to work.

A bead of sweat trickled down my temple and onto my cheek as I used my magic to shove the last tumbler into place. It took more effort than I'd expected, but given the age and complexity of the mechanisms, perhaps I shouldn't have been surprised.

"Here we are," Hank called merrily from behind the nearest pile of antiques. "A travel sized ship in a bottle."

I took two quick steps backwards, leaning an elbow on the counter and surreptitiously wiping the bead of sweat away with the back of my hand as he came into view, holding his prize. This bottle fit in the palm of his hand. The ship inside was delicate and beautifully hand painted. Slender masts adorned with billowing sails made me think I could almost hear seagulls and smell the salty brine of the ocean air. The artist meticulously replicated each intricate feature from the anchor to the crow's nest in miniature. The small vessel was almost more stunning than its larger compatriot, simply because of the diminutive size and exquisite attention to detail.

"It's beautiful," I said, and meant it. The tiny ship was truly a work of art. I had to remind myself that I wasn't actually in the market for miniature boats, or I might have bought that one immediately. I tipped my head back and forth, crouching down to make a show of examining the bottle and its treasure trapped inside. "It's just that..." I trailed off.

"It's just that, what?" Hank demanded.

"Don't you think it's a little *too* small?" I asked, pushing upright once more and putting my hands on my hips. The bag with the journal thumped against my thigh.

"What are you talking about? It's a masterpiece!" he protested.

I held up my hands in a silent plea for understanding and told a white lie. "I agree with you, but it's not for me. It's for my dad. Between you and me, he's getting on in years and his sight is starting to go." I cringed at the lie, knowing what my dad would say if he could hear me now. Luckily Hank didn't seem to catch my reaction, so I bulled ahead. "I'd hate to see him squinting at such a tiny ship all day and not able to really appreciate it. Perhaps you have something in the back that's not too big, not too small. Just right." I said, hoping to buy myself a few more minutes to snoop.

Hank narrowed his eyes at me thoughtfully. "What? Like Goldilocks?" he asked.

"Exactly like Goldilocks. Minus the porridge, of course."

Hank stroked his beard. "I think I have just the one. Be back in a jiffy." And he was gone again.

I waited for three breaths before I sprang towards the trunk. I took a deep breath and heaved with all my might. The latch caught for a moment, but then the lid swung open a few inches with a loud squeak from the hinges. I paused, waiting to see if Hank would come running back into the main room of the shop. When he didn't, I carefully opened the lid the rest of the way. Someone wrapped a thin cream fabric covered in black lettering around a rectangular object at the bottom of the chest. I pulled back the cloth wrapping to reveal the author's initials burned into the leather cover and dyed black.

B. S.

My jaw dropped. Benedict Starling? Was this the book that Mrs. Jenkins claimed led to buried treasure?

The Greatest Reward

"You'll like this one, I just know it," the old man called cheerfully from the back of the shop. I only had a moment or two before he'd make his way through the haphazard piles and see me. Without a second thought, I lifted the book from the chest and shoved it into my bag with the journal, wrappings and all. Thank goodness the tote Honey lent me was so large! I eased the lid of the chest shut, wincing as the hinges let out a squeal of protest. I didn't have time to lock it. I hoped Hank didn't decide to open the treasure chest before I had time to make a hasty escape. I dashed to the counter, crouching to examine the ships once more as he came into sight.

"Here you go," Hank said, carefully placing the bottle he carried in front of the other two on the counter. "I bet your father will love this one. He must be a man of impeccable taste, especially to have raised such a thoughtful and caring daughter." He smiled charmingly at me.

I pulled out my phone and pretended to be surprised by the time. "Oh, would you look at that? I must go meet a friend. Yeah, a friend for lunch. So sorry to have made you carry all these out here, but you know what? I'm going to take a picture of these boats, sorry, ships. Then I can show my dad and let him pick his favorite," I said in a rush.

"Very thoughtful of you," Hank said, stepping back to allow me to snap a few pictures. I dutifully took the photos and then beat a hasty retreat.

"Thanks so much for everything. I appreciate all your help." I waved as I hurried out the door, leaving Hank staring open-mouthed at me as the bell above the door announced my abrupt departure.

As soon as I was on the street, I started walking back towards the Enchanted Oasis as quickly as I could. I'd done it! I'd found the missing book! Now, I finally felt like I had a real chance at earning Spellbooks. This was indisputable empirical evidence that I have the best interests of the shop at heart. Maybe if I could present it publicly, there would be no way Nathaniel Ravenscroft could pick Thaddeus over me, even if they were in cahoots. Now, I just had to make sure there were other witnesses present.

I glanced at my phone. This time it was really for the time. I had a few hours before my meeting at the shop with the lawyer. My mouth went dry. Lawyer. Law. Police. I'd just stolen the book. Walked right out of the antique shop with it, in fact. Did that make me a thief? Surely not. I was more like a bounty hunter, right? Recovering missing property and all that jazz. I suppose I could claim the book was potentially mine, just like Thaddeus had with the other books. Using his argument made my skin crawl, though. Maybe I should take the book to the sheriff and tell him the whole story. But would I get in trouble for taking it in the first place? Perhaps it was a better option to go see Nathaniel. I could employ him as my lawyer and ask him to give me advice. After all, Granny had trusted him, hadn't she? And he had helped Thaddeus. My mind flashed back to the glimpse of Thaddeus and Nathaniel drinking in his office and then to the lawyer defending my cousin at the police station. Maybe going to the lawyer wasn't the best option after all.

The bag thumped heavily against my leg as I briskly turned onto Dragonfly Lane. It felt like the clapper of a bell, knocking against me with each step and announcing my crime to the world. By the time I reached the B&B, I was half-jogging and constantly looking over my shoulder. When I entered, I saw Bella behind the reception desk. She was checking in a middle-aged couple and shot me a smile before turning back to her guests. I let out a brief sigh of relief. With her occupied down here, I would have the room to myself for at least thirty minutes. I hurried past her and up the stairs. As soon as I got to her room, I shut the door firmly behind me. I collapsed on the sofa bed, breathing hard.

I'd done it. I solved the robbery. Sure, I may have accidentally committed a theft of my own while doing it, but I recovered Granny's stolen book.

Or rather, *books*. No matter what Thaddeus claimed, I knew in my heart he'd been planning on stealing those books in his RV. Maybe he hadn't originally intended to, but he had plenty of opportunity to come and turn the books over. His lack of action spoke volumes. I pulled the journal and what I believed to be the stolen compendium out of my bag. If I didn't hand this over to the police, was I no better than Thaddeus? I tried to convince myself the situations were completely different. I hadn't stolen the book, at least not originally. But what I did next mattered. The problem was, I didn't know what the right course of action was. The only thing I knew was I didn't want to be anything like Thaddeus.

I set the journal to the side and carefully unwrapped the stolen compendium. The cream cloth was soft, lightweight, and oblong, almost like a fashionable summer scarf. Except the design was unlike any scarf I'd ever seen. Someone had drawn symbols all over the creamy fabric in what looked like permanent marker. As I studied the drawings, there seemed to be an order to the precise arrangement of cryptic sigils. Maybe they were runes, like Finn had described. He might be able to shed some light on what they meant. When I reached the end of the scarf, my fingers brushed something hard and crusty embedded in the soft fabric.

Curious, I set the book to the side for a moment and looked at the cut in the fabric. Something sharp had sliced through the scarf, cutting through the drawn design like a knife. I sat up straighter. Or like a gargoyle's wing. Dried blood edged the cut. Rusty brown splashes further marred the sigils and the fabric of the scarf. I traced a finger over the perfect symbols, pausing when I reached the ones destroyed by blood and the cut. Was this how Hank had snuck in without Gideon seeing him? He had the magical capability and, after a lifetime studying the arcane arts, I wouldn't be surprised if he was familiar with the runes needed to block sight. But he hadn't accounted for the gargoyle crashing into him. When Gideon's wing sliced through the scarf, it must have disrupted the rune work. Either that or the blood had. That accounted for Gideon's last memory before turning to stone. A purple skirt and red shoes. Just like Zephyrus, the Mad Mage's stage outfit. I clutched the strip of cloth tightly, the scarf solidifying my theory about the compendium.

Feeling invigorated, I carefully folded the scarf and set it to the side. I wanted to examine the book in more detail. The dark leather cover, once supple and rich, was now weathered with the passage of years and exposure to the elements. It might have been my imagination, but I thought I could detect the faint scent of saltwater lingering on its surface, hinting at its past. I ran my fingers over the raised bands on the spine, worn and scuffed by the long journey the logbook had taken to reach my hands. The initials burned into the cover hinted at long hidden mysteries and I couldn't stand the suspense any longer.

Carefully, I flipped open the cover and read the title page. Instead of the weather compendium I'd been expecting, it was something entirely unexpected. I stared at the words. This was a logbook belonging to Benedict Starling. What was going on? Had Hank swapped out the books? Perhaps all my assumptions were wrong. A new thought popped into my head. Maybe it wasn't Hank at all, but Granny. She could've mislabeled the book on purpose. But to what end?

There was only one way to find out. Read the book.

I don't know what I was expecting, but what I saw wasn't it. Instead of revealing the deep mysteries of an illicit life at sea, the supposed pirate logbook read more like a dry recitation where even the author had gotten bored and started doodling in the margins. Mrs. Jenkins had been right, Benedict Starling recorded meteorological information along with tides, weather patterns, and animal sightings in a scrawl that was difficult to read, let alone interpret. Somehow, it looked familiar. I wondered if they had forced everyone to write in the same cramped yet fluid penmanship back in the day. Between the old-fashioned spellings and the nautical terms, the reading was slow. By the tenth page, I was scanning the words, and by the time I was halfway through, I just flipped through the pages. Something caught my eye. I turned back a few pages. There it was again. A small bee. Why would a sea captain doodle a bee into the margins of his logbook? Dolphins, crabs, clouds, even the occasional mermaid I could understand. But a bee? When was the last time a bee took itself to sea? There were no flowers for nectar. Nowhere to build a hive.

I flipped through the book, ignoring the words completely and focusing my attention on scanning the margins. There it was again! And again. And again! There were bees doodled on nearly every page of the captain's logbook. I grabbed my phone and turned on the flashlight, examining the bees in greater detail. The author positioned them differently on every page. Wings outspread, wings tucked in, two bees together, one landing on a flower. The detail on the body was also incredible. I'd thought the author-slash-artist had just been doodling, adding a bit of shading to pass the time, but the drawings were actually quite intricate.

I froze, peering closer at the bee on the page in front of me. There, on its wing. Was that a tiny letter "B"? I snapped a photo on my phone and then flicked my fingers across the screen to zoom in. It was! And next to it, was that an "S"? I flipped to another page. Sure enough, the bee on this page had a hidden "B" and "S" on its leg. I turned the page again, searching. The letters appeared again, but in the bee's stripes this time. What were they? Initials? Did they stand for Benedict Starling? But why would the captain take time to hide his initials in his own logbook? Was it just an act of self-indulgence when bored at sea?

I flipped the page again, trying to search for more letters in the drawings, but I was too intent on the incongruities on the page and knocked my phone out of my hand. It clattered off the sofa bed and fell. I hissed out a breath, jumping off the bed as I tried to catch it before it hit the floor. I'd broken too many screens in my life and didn't want to pay to repair another if I could help it. My fingers brushed the smooth screen, but it tumbled through them before I could grip the device, crashing onto the carpet. In my effort to fumble for the phone, I knocked the strange book onto the thick carpet as well. It landed on the spine with a dull thud. I ignored it for a moment, snatching up my phone. I breathed out a sigh of relief and pressed it to my chest. No cracks indicating a broken screen. I'd been lucky. I glanced back at the screen as something niggled at my subconscious. In my efforts to save the device, I'd inadvertently opened my gallery of photos. A collage of my latest pictures filled the screen. One caught my eye. I flicked it open and sucked in a breath of surprise.

"No way," I breathed to myself. I fell to my knees next to the open logbook and held up the photo of Granny Bea's ledger. I knew the scrawl in the logbook had been familiar! Looking between the image on my phone and the logbook on the floor, there was no doubt in my mind. The same person had written them.

Granny Bea.

The realization clicked into place. Bees. BS. Beatrice Sullivan. Granny hadn't just written the book; she'd hidden clues about her identity in the margins. But why? For just a moment, I considered the possibility that Granny Bea was in fact Benedict 'Blackfin' Starling but discarded the notion almost immediately. Witches lived longer than the average human, but I'd never heard of a witch living for three hundred years. So why had Granny created a fake logbook and tried to pass it off as the real thing?

I scooped up the logbook to get another look at the bees when something shifted under my fingers. Confused, I flipped the book over. One of the raised bands on the spine was askew. I frowned. That shouldn't be possible. I knew from Granny that raised bands were an old book binding technique before modern practices became the default. The leather cover wrapped around cords binding the leaves of the book together, creating the ridged effect. But the band shouldn't be able to move independently from the book's cover or leaves. I brought the phone's flashlight closer. A tiny ridge of dried glue marked the original place of the displaced band. This was an intentional addition. But why?

I was too caught up to even consider the consequences of what I was about to do. Carefully, I wiggled the loose band. It popped off the book with little effort, leaving a small rectangle of aged and yellowed glue behind. I turned it over in the palm of my hand and was surprised to see a tiny roll of paper within the hidden compartment. Minuscule lines of text covered the page. My heart beat faster. What sort of secrets had Granny hidden here?

I set the book on my bed and dashed to the bathroom for my tweezers. Carefully, I wiggled the scrap of paper from its hiding place and unrolled it, pinning it open with two fingertips. Granny had typed the message on both sides of the paper, using an incredibly tiny font to fit. I guessed she couldn't do it small enough by hand and had to resort to using a computer even if she hated technology. I squinted, trying to decipher the meaning, but it was almost as difficult to read as her elegant scrawl. Slowly, her message became clear.

Dear Treasure Hunter,

Congratulations on successfully tracking Blackfin across the annals of history! As you have already surmised, Benedict Starling was, in fact, the infamous pirate captain, Blackfin, and he hid clues to his amassed treasure in his real logbook. What he and you, dear reader, did not realize was that his treasure was cursed. I have taken great pains to hide the real logbook to keep the treasure from falling into unsuspecting hands. There are no further clues, and I'm afraid your journey ends here. However, I didn't wish you to leave empty-handed, so I left you the greatest reward a student of history could ever dream of: answers. I hope it is enough.

Wishing you luck on your next grand adventure,
Beatrice Sullivan

Dreams Made and Broken

I THOUGHT RECOVERING THE stolen book would wrap up the theft. Instead, it left me with more unanswered questions. I was reeling and my mind was whirling through the possible scenarios. Had Granny Bea discovered the treasure or just the logbook? If she had discovered the treasure, where would she have hidden it? Where was the real logbook? I assumed she'd swapped her forgery for the real compendium or mislabeled the logbook as a maritime book to throw others off the treasure's trail. Or was she so concerned about this supposed curse she destroyed the real logbook to keep the treasure hidden and used the fake to cover her tracks?

Feeling like I was getting pulled apart by the questions and the simultaneous lack of answers, I decided to head to Spellbooks. Maybe being closer to Granny would help me center myself and find some peace, which I desperately needed before my meeting with the lawyer to decide the fate of the shop.

I tucked the scrap of paper inside the front cover of Granny's replica logbook and placed it back in the tote, along with my presentation. I contemplated the stained scarf on my bed, but decided I didn't want to haul that crusty old thing around. Not today. I needed to focus on the upcoming presentation and tune in to Granny Bea and what she would've wanted for her shop.

Although it was much too early, I headed over to Spellbooks anyway, hoping that either the walk or the time in Granny's space would help to settle me. Luckily, when I got there, the shop was empty and dark. Not even Luna answered my call as I pushed through the front door, locking it behind me as I flipped on the lights. Mr. Wigglesworth blinked sleepily at me from the front window and stretched in the lazy way that cats do before padding over and leaning into my leg, knocking me slightly off balance. I chuckled, hefted my bag onto the counter, and crouched down to pet him.

"Okay, I hear you, big guy. Back scratches first. Everything else can wait." He purred approvingly as I stroked the swirling patterns in his soft fur.

When I'd completed my obeisance to the cat, I headed upstairs. I don't know if I expected to find a clue or if I just wanted to feel closer to Granny Bea, but it felt like the right thing. The cat padded alongside me, like we were old friends rather than new acquaintances.

I found myself talking to him. "So, Mr. W, would you be happy if I shared your space here? I'd really like to. I've never really had roots, not in the way some people do. I can't imagine what it would feel like to stay in one place that was truly mine. To have my space, my people, my community around me all the time?" I sighed. "It's like a dream. My dream."

This time, I ignored the office and opened the door to Granny's living area. It still smelled like her. A mixture of roses, sunshine, and happiness. I continued talking to the cat as I let a wave of sadness, and memories wash over me. "This was always her place to be her. I remember reading in that big armchair over there with her or baking cookies and then eating way too many. I think going through her apartment might be the most difficult thing to do if I actually inherit the shop. Even if it would be the most sensible place to live, I'd feel uncomfortable disturbing her things, you know? To me, this is still her space. It even smells like her still."

Mr. Wigglesworth wound himself around my ankles, almost unbalancing me again. I laughed and crouched to pet him, answering the question I imagined he asked. "What would I do? Well, if time and money weren't issues, I'd love to have more windows up here to let in the natural light. Oh, and I've always dreamed of curling up on a window bench full of cushions right over there to watch the people go by." I pointed at the far wall with the windows that overlooked the street. "I'd definitely clean the office as well. I don't know how she worked in such a cramped, dark space. I like light, natural wood colors, and simple clean lines."

I traced the patterns on the cat's fur and trailed off. My thoughts ran in all directions, flowing from my grief at Granny's passing to my dearest hopes that I still, by some miracle, might put down roots here in Havenwood. A loud knock on the front door downstairs jarred me back to reality. I glanced at the clock on the wall. It wasn't even six yet. It couldn't be Ravenscroft, not yet. Whoever it was, couldn't they read the closed sign on the door?

With a sigh, I shoved to my feet. The cat mewled in protest. "I know," I said to him, "but duty calls."

Sheriff Jackson's serious countenance peered through the front window and behind him, I saw an irate Hank fluttering his hands and talking at a rapid pace behind him. The elderly man didn't look like a former or current mage pacing outside my shop. He looked angry and slightly unhinged. As soon as the sheriff saw me, he waved me over. My stomach dropped and a cold sweat broke out on my brow. That old feeling of being summoned for punishment was resurfacing, except this time, I really had done something wrong. Well, perhaps not wrong exactly, but definitely questionable.

As soon as I opened the door, Hank blew in like an angry gust of wind. "She stole it! I know she did! It was there before she came into my shop and was gone after she left. She's responsible!"

My mouth dropped open. Not at the accusation because, in all fairness, he was entirely correct, but at the stupidity. If he accused me of stealing the stolen book from him, the self-incrimination was obvious, wasn't it? Apparently not to the irate former stage magician.

Sheriff Jackson folded his arms across his chest and glared at the smaller man. "I said I would handle this, Hank. Calm down and let me do my job." The magician stopped shouting, but glowered at me from behind the sheriff, continuing to mutter angrily under his breath.

The sheriff nodded his approval. I barely had time to school my features into something I hoped resembled innocence before Sheriff Jackson turned his attention back to me. "Now then, Miss Sullivan, Hank here claims that you stole a book from him. From a locked box. This is the second time a lock has been conveniently left open when you were around when the owner swears it was locked. Care to explain what you were doing at his shop today?"

I swallowed hard, deciding right then I never, *ever* wanted to get on this werewolf's bad side. I needed a good cover story and, more importantly, I needed to sell it. Holding my hands out in front of me to show my innocence, I said, "I don't know what to tell you about the lock situation, but I was shopping, looking for souvenirs for my parents. Nothing to do with locks at all. I looked at some ships in bottles and then bought a journal, but I didn't steal it. I paid for it, fair and square." Which was the truth, but not the whole truth. I pulled out my phone and showed him the credit card notification, complete with the name of the shop.

Hank stomped his foot from behind the sheriff. "Not the journal! The *compendium*! The *Maritime Meteorological Compendium*! She took it! I know it!"

Sheriff Jackson froze and slowly turned his head to look at the elderly man. "What did you say?" I knew what the sheriff was thinking, but Hank couldn't see the trap of his own words closing around him.

"The book! She stole it, right out of a locked box in my shop. I can see it, right there in her bag!" He pointed a quavering finger at the open tote on the counter.

I fished the logbook out. "Is this what you're talking about? This isn't the compendium. It's a replica of a sea captain's journal my Granny made. I found it in the shop recently. I compared the handwriting, and it's definitely a match for hers. It even has a note from Granny Bea. See? Look at this." I opened the front cover and passed the scrap of paper over to the sheriff, who examined it carefully and the photo of Granny's ledger I pulled up on my phone to match the handwriting. "I found that tiny note in a hidden compartment in the book. I still don't know what happened to the missing compendium, but I find it strange Mr. Silverthorne here knows anything about it. I thought that was all privileged information. But what I do know is this journal is not a compendium from the 1700s, not if it was written by Granny Bea, which I can assure you, it was." I kept my voice innocent, with just the faintest tinge of confusion.

"Indeed," Sheriff Jackson said, turning a steely gaze on the smaller man. Hank seemed to wither under the lawman's stare. "I think you and I need to have a talk, Hank. Let's head down to my office. Now." He gestured towards the door, and Hank preceded him out of the shop, shooting me dark, yet puzzled looks. The sheriff nodded at me. "Apologies for the disturbance, Miss Sullivan."

"Not at all," I murmured, moving to lock the door once more. Sweat trickled down my spine and my heartbeat thundered in the sudden silence. I leaned my back against the door and blew out a breath, my pulse slowly returning to normal.

Mr. Wigglesworth sat on his haunches, staring curiously up at me. "I know," I said to the cat. "I'd be an awful thief. But in all fairness, I'm a decent book-recovery person. Perhaps, if the shop goes to Thaddeus, that can be my new job. Do you think there's much of a market for finding old books?"

The cat tipped his head to the side and blinked once.

I sighed. "I agree. Not a wonderful career opportunity. I don't know what I'll do if Mr. Ravenscroft gives the shop to my cousin. Back to Germany, I guess." I ran a hand over the wooden door frame and whispered. "I just really wanted to stay here."

As if the cat could sense my melancholy mood, he padded over and sat on my foot, staring up at me imperiously. I laughed and tickled his ears. "You're right. At least I have a little more time before the lawyer decides. Better make the most of it."

Resolutions and Revelations

Precisely at seven o'clock, Nathaniel Ravenscroft rapped crisply on the front door. I'd been going over my presentation one more time to prepare for his arrival, but I still jumped at the knock.

"Good evening," the lawyer said as I opened the door. He strode in, Thaddeus on his heels. My cousin smiled nastily at me as he looked around the shop in a proprietary manner. I shivered and shut the door.

Ravenscroft also glanced around the bookshop, a fond smile on his face. "This place still reminds me of Beatrice, but she was never big on sitting. Always on the move. However, I think it would be best to be comfortable for this talk, don't you?"

"I think there are a few chairs out in the sunroom," I offered.

"Thaddeus, do you mind grabbing four please?" the lawyer asked. Thaddeus moved off towards the back of the shop without a word.

I raised both eyebrows. "Four?"

"I'm expecting someone and perfect timing. Here he is!" The lawyer opened the door, allowing the newcomer to enter the shop.

The big man shivered despite his long trench coat. "It's getting cold out there. Fall is going to be a cold one this year, you can mark my words," he said as he swept the fedora from his head, revealing neatly groomed sandy hair, a thick beard, and piercing hazel eyes that seemed to take in every detail at once.

"You're the one who's been following me!" I blurted out, staring at him in surprise.

The man jerked a thumb towards the lawyer. "You can blame him for that. Hired me to monitor both you and your cousin." He extended his hand. "Reed Flynn, private investigator. Nice to formally make your acquaintance, Miss Sullivan."

I shook his hand on reflex, not really knowing what to say. Nathaniel Ravenscroft spoke up. "Mr. Flynn is an excellent member of my team. Fantastic observational skills, a keen mind, and a good heart, once you get to know him."

I wasn't sure I wanted to get to know him. Not after he'd been spying on me for the last week. Thaddeus thumped back into the room carrying four metal folding chairs he must've dug out of the closet in the sunroom. I hadn't even known they were there.

He glared at the new arrival. "Who's this?" he demanded.

Swiftly, Ravenscroft filled him in as the private investigator silently arranged a small circle in the open space in front of the counter. Thaddeus' scowl deepened with each word, his eyes narrowing into slits of barely contained fury. He clenched his fists, knuckles turning white, as the realization dawned upon him that he had been followed. However, both of us were in a precarious position, and neither wanted to upset the lawyer by protesting too much before he made the all-important decision of who would inherit Spellbooks.

"Please, sit down," Ravenscroft said when he finished, taking a chair for himself. Once we were all settled, the lawyer turned to his private eye. "Now, if you don't mind, please share your observations of the past week."

It was strange to hear my actions recited back to me. It made me feel like a bug under a microscope, especially when Reed got to the part about the RV. He didn't mention anything about my magic, probably because he couldn't have known I was using any, but I blushed and wriggled in my chair uncomfortably, anyway. Finally, Reed turned his attention to Thaddeus, obviously having divided his time between watching both of us. It instantly made me feel a little better that I hadn't been the sole subject of his spying. Thaddeus had apparently split his time between the Renaissance Faire, Spellbooks, and the Dusty Tome, where I assumed he'd been colluding with the Puddletons, no doubt making nefarious plans for what he'd do with the bookshop once he inherited it. Thaddeus didn't look uncomfortable. He just looked angrier and more brooding with every passing minute.

When the investigator finished, Ravenscroft said, "Thank you very much, Mr. Flynn. Your services are no longer required." Reed picked up his hat and left without another word.

"What was the point of that?" Thaddeus asked as the door shut behind the investigator, leaving the three of us alone in the shop.

"I have my reasons," Nathaniel said cryptically. "Now, let's get down to business. Thaddeus, please tell me your plans for Sullivan's Spellbooks if you were to end up inheriting it."

Thaddeus handed three binders to the lawyer, each clearly labeled. One said "Renovation/Expansion", the second was "Revenue streams" and the third was "Projected Growth." Seeing the business-like efficiency in Thaddeus' manner made me feel like the naïve little girl he'd once called me. I clutched the slim folder containing my plans tighter to my chest, seeing my hopes of inheriting Spellbooks fade with every page Ravenscroft turned.

Thaddeus leaned his forearms on his knees, focusing his intense gaze on the lawyer and completely ignoring me. "Spellbooks needs to be brought into the twenty-first century. I don't know how my great-grandmother turned a profit running it the way she did. The first thing on my list is to knock down the back wall and expand the shop as far as the property line. That garden out back is a waste of space and should be used to increase floor space. Then, we need to update the shop. Bring in more shelves, get rid of all this kitschy junk that's just cluttering up the space. Also, I have no intention of living here, so I'll convert the upstairs apartment into more shelving space for books. I'd use the space to put the foreign language books or a kiddie section, that kind of thing."

I bit the inside of my cheek to keep from screaming. How could he so casually dismiss the garden or Granny's apartment? Didn't he see the work and love that had gone into both? And what about poor Thistle?

But Thaddeus wasn't done. Not by a long shot. "I've already contacted the bookshop down the road, the Dusty Gnome?"

"Tome," Nathaniel corrected.

Thaddeus waved a hand. "Whatever. Anyway, the Piggletons have expressed interest in a partnership."

"Puddletons," Nathaniel said.

"Right. Them. Anyway, they've agreed to a preliminary deal where they move over here and run the shop once it's expanded. With them here, I'll take the brand on the road. Buy a bigger RV, maybe make it a traveling bookshop, hit all the fairs, and then come back here to restock."

"Ambitious," Nathaniel observed, his expression the same mask of calm interest that he'd worn since Thaddeus began his recitation.

"Yeah, well, I'm an ambitious guy. Figure you can't do much better than that. Expand and improve the building, increase the amount of space for stock, eliminate the competition by teaming up, and increase brand recognition by traveling all over the state. Maybe even the region." He sat back in his chair with a self-satisfied smirk and folded his arms over his chest like he'd just laid down the winning poker hand. "That's my plan, and I doubt you'll find a better one for this little place."

The lawyer's expression did not change one iota as he nodded and set the binders aside. The lawyer turned to me with an expectant look on his face. "Harper? Your turn."

Nervous butterflies started a cyclone in my stomach. Thaddeus had taken such a different direction from my own plans. What if Ravenscroft thought my ideas were childish? I took a deep breath, trying to quiet my nerves. There was nothing to be done now but to go forth boldly and hope my vision aligned with Granny Bea's.

I handed over my carefully organized and printed plans to Nathaniel in their slim folder. I'd spent a great deal of time choosing the fonts, colors, and decorations, but, as I passed it over, I felt like I was back in grade school, handing in an assignment to my teacher.

He took one look at it and then placed the folder in his lap. He folded his hands on top, not even bothering to page through my proposals like he had done with Thaddeus'. My heart sank. I was done for. I just knew it. Ravenscroft had already made his decision, and it wasn't me.

"Thank you for the preparation. Please, would you be so kind as to walk me through it?" the lawyer asked courteously.

I licked my lips and glanced at Thaddeus nervously. He glowered back at me. Somehow, the brooding anger directed at me from the man who'd stolen from my Granny's shop was enough to galvanize me into action. I took a deep breath and started to speak.

"When I was a child visiting Spellbooks, it always stuck with me how much being a part of the community here in Havenwood meant to Granny Bea. She was forever helping someone. Friends were constantly dropping by. That's what I want Spellbooks to be, an integral part of the community. I've been talking to people all week and have so many ideas." I paused, thinking back on all the people I met this week. Madame Fontaine and her book club, Grimgor, Thistle, Mrs. Jenkins, Martha, Finn, and, of course, reconnecting with the DeLucas.

When the silence stretched, Nathaniel cleared his throat. "Can you give me some examples of these ideas?" he asked gently. Thaddeus snorted out a derisive laugh.

I blushed and spoke in a rush. "Well, for starters, I'd like to supplement the book club offered by the library with a twist by hosting themed book events here. Like having a murder mystery dinner party that links to the mystery book of the month or a chocolate and wine tasting to go with a romance book. I want to host events for indie authors to debut their books and help them connect with the local book clubs to read their works. I'd like to create monthly poetry slams for people to share a favorite piece of poetry. Or their own original works, for that matter. I want to run classes to help kids get excited about reading and to help new authors take the first steps of their writing and publishing journeys. Then I could help them—"

"Are you running a store or a community center?" Thaddeus said derisively, interrupting me.

I frowned at him, feeling unsettled and thrown off my game by both Ravenscroft's seeming lack of interest and now Thaddeus' belligerence. Irritation rose inside me, and I spat out, "I believe building relationships with the community is the way forward. For me and for Spellbooks. That might be hosting events for those who feel ostracized." I remembered what Bella had told me about the people like her who were half-supernatural and half-human. "Or it could be wholeheartedly joining in events like the town's Harvest Festival. I'm sure, with time, I can find even more ways to connect with the community."

"Playing pat-a-cake with the neighbors isn't the way to build a business," Thaddeus pointed out.

"Perhaps not, but I believe building a community is like writing a good book; it takes all sorts of characters to make a beautiful story," I shot back.

"Which is still not a business plan," Thaddeus muttered.

"It might not be *your* business plan, but it is mine, and I believe it's the perfect plan for Havenwood, for Spellbooks, and for me." My words had a theatrical ring of finality to them, and I settled back in my chair, channeling as much confidence through my stare at the lawyer as I could muster. Had I followed in Honey's footsteps and included just the right balance of substance and sweetness? I was worried I'd thrown too much salt in the mix, and it was going to wreck the balance I was striving for.

The lawyer nodded thoughtfully, steepling his long fingers and drumming the tips together. "What about the animals?" he finally asked.

Thaddeus coughed into his fist and shook his head. "They're cute, but this is a bookshop, not a pet store. I'll find suitable arrangements for them, of course," he said.

Ravenscroft turned to look at me. I maintained my air of confidence even though the unexpected question rattled me slightly. "Luna will always have a place at Spellbooks with me if she wants it. The same goes for Mr. Wigglesworth. Oh, and Thistle," I added, not wanting to leave out the tree nymph.

"Is that the cat or the rabbit?" Thaddeus asked. I shot him a withering look.

Nathaniel nodded thoughtfully, the same carefully neutral expression never wavering on his face. He then turned over his shoulder and spoke to the empty space behind the counter. "You've heard it all. What do you think?"

I looked around at the otherwise empty shop in bewilderment. Who was he talking to?

Thaddeus leaned over and whispered, "Is Granny Bea a ghost? Has she been here the whole time?" I froze, my eyes darting everywhere at once. Was Granny really here?

Nathaniel frowned, cracking his composure for the first time. "Don't be ridiculous. Beatrice had no unfinished business and was very much ready to embrace whatever adventures follow this existence. I doubt we will ever see her shade."

I raised a hand, immediately feeling like a school child as I did so, but unable to stop myself. "If you weren't talking to Granny's ghost, who were you talking to?"

Nathaniel lifted a single eyebrow, looking back and forth between us. "Why Spellbooks, of course. Don't tell me that Beatrice didn't tell you?"

"Tell us what?" Thaddeus demanded.

"What Beatrice meant when she said I knew her wishes regarding the inheritance of the shop. She didn't own it so much as it was a symbiotic partnership," Nathaniel said, his tone indicating that everything should now be abundantly clear. It wasn't. At least, not to me.

"I don't get it," Thaddeus said, making me feel better that whatever Nathaniel was talking about went over his head as well.

"Me neither," I chimed in.

Nathaniel looked back and forth at us in surprise. "I can't believe Beatrice never told you. I knew it was a secret, but I thought for sure she'd told her family."

"Told us what?" Thaddeus and I said in tandem.

"It's a closely guarded secret that only I and a handful of others in town know. I assumed Beatrice had shared it with you both, but, well...I guess that duty now falls to me."

"Spit it out already," Thaddeus exclaimed in exasperation.

Ravenscroft shot him an annoyed look, but his next words shocked me to the core. "Spellbooks is sentient. It is, for all intents and purposes, a living spirit confined within these walls. It was Beatrice's last wish that Spellbooks pick whoever will become its new partner. In case you haven't read the fine print in the documentation, the person not selected will need to sign an ironclad NDA or will forfeit all of his or her inheritance." He paused, pinning each of us with a look.

"Understood," I whispered, even though I wasn't entirely confident I did. Spellbooks was sentient? What did that mean? Had I impressed the...building? Spirit? Thing? What did one call a living building? Moreover, how did one live inside a sentient shop?

Out of the corner of my eye, I caught Thaddeus nodding in silent agreement. My only consolation was that he looked as shell-shocked as I felt.

The lawyer twisted around to look behind him. "Ah. It seems Spellbooks has already reached a decision. Look." He pointed over his shoulder to where a message was being written by what seemed to be an invisible hand on the chalkboard behind the counter.

I caught my breath, unable to believe it as the meaning of the message from Spellbooks sunk in. It read:

CONGRATULATIONS, HARPER!

New Beginnings

Although I was ready to move into Spellbooks right away, it took a couple of days to work out the legal details with Nathaniel. I felt guilty about doubting his intentions, but after working with him on settling Granny Bea's estate, I could tell he was about as by-the-book as one could ever hope for in a lawyer.

The day I got the okay to move in, Spellbooks had a surprise waiting for me. A note on the chalkboard said, "Look upstairs."

I glanced over at Luna. "Any idea what this is about?" I asked, pointing at the note.

She wiggled her paws at me. "No thumbs, remember? Besides, I know better than to upset Spellbooks, even if it has terrible taste in pets." Mr. Wigglesworth opened one eye and glared half-heartedly at the rabbit from his favorite napping spot in the front window.

"I guess I'd better look upstairs then," I said, suppressing a smile. I had a feeling the ongoing battle for the bookshop mascot between Luna and the cat would be a source of constant amusement for me.

As I lugged my suitcase upstairs, I noticed something different. Instead of roses and sunshine, the scent of warm vanilla and spice drifted to me. Had someone lit a candle? I looked around and caught my breath. Granny's apartment was no longer Granny's. A large, mostly empty space flooded with natural light from windows that hadn't been there a few days ago met my eyes. The hardwood floors shone like they'd been freshly polished, and a brand-new window seat nestled in the large bay window overlooking the street, practically crying out to be filled with as many pillows as I could find.

"You did this for me?" I whispered in awe.

Luna hopped up behind me and sniffed. "What good is it living in a magical bookshop if there aren't some perks along the way?"

"I just never imagined this." I waved a hand at the beautiful space. "It's everything I ever wanted and more."

"I think Spellbooks is trying to make a good first impression," Luna said, hopping around the empty apartment. She jumped up on the window seat and pressed her nose against the glass. "For a store, Spellbooks has done a truly marvelous job with this place. Except this seat could really use some pillows."

"I was thinking the same thing," I said, sitting next to her.

"While you're at it, you'd better get some sheets for the bed. Spellbooks does what it can, but you can really only expect so much, even from a magical building," she said, twitching a paw across her whiskers.

"Speaking of beds and furniture, where are all of Granny's things?" I asked.

A door at the end of the hall swung open in a silent response, revealing a narrow set of stairs leading upwards.

"I think Spellbooks put it all up in the attic for you until you are ready," Luna observed.

"That was...kind. Thanks, Spellbooks," I said, awkwardly speaking to the empty air of the apartment. I felt a little ripple in the seat under me, as if Spellbooks were purring at the appreciation. I glanced at Luna. "Is that normal?" I asked.

"What? Living inside a sentient building? Or having the building communicate with you? Or perhaps you're asking about the talking rabbit? Or maybe—"

"Okay, okay. I take your point. I need to redefine my concept of normal," I said, holding up my hands in surrender with a laugh. I pointed at the open door. "I never knew that door was there. Or that there was an attic."

Luna eyed me skeptically. "Even *I* don't know all the secrets Spellbooks keeps. You've been here five minutes, and you're surprised about a door?

Please. You have no idea." She hopped down from the bench and out the door.

"I have no idea about what? Luna? Luna!"

Two weeks later, I opened the doors of Spellbooks to a select number of close friends in what I grandly called a soft reopening. Really, it was just an excuse to have a party with the people who had been so generous with their time and talents. I tugged my new blue sweater into place, liking the way it set off my eyes and fiddled with a single pearl on a gold chain I'd found next to my bed this morning. I assumed it was a gift from Spellbooks, but it still felt strange speaking my thanks to empty air.

Luna called from downstairs. "Stop fussing and hurry up! They're here!"

I dashed out of my apartment, which was feeling more like a home with each passing day, and hurried downstairs to welcome my guests. When I reached the bottom of the staircase, I took one last look around, making sure everything was in order. Spellbooks had helped me restructure the interior of the building based on the sketches I'd made with Grimgor and the DeLucas. Shelves were built into all the walls now and I'd used the preexisting standing shelves to create little reading nooks and crannies all over the shop, which I thought made it an intriguing place to get lost in new worlds. Spellbooks had created a little cat apartment for Mr. Wigglesworth in the old front window on one side of the shop and created an entirely new window with a small hutch for Luna on the other. Both animals seemed happy with the arrangement.

Spellbooks also created an open space at the side of the shop for a coffee bar and a couple of tables and chairs. Grimgor and Antonio both helped me with the construction of the bar and Bella went thrifting with me to find some tables and chairs to up-cycle. They were mismatched in style, but somehow seemed the perfect fit for a quaint bookshop being brought into the modern age by a new owner. We had so much fun working on the project that we purchased a few extra. I planned to put our finished projects outside when the weather warmed up for readers to enjoy Thistle's garden. Grimgor promised to help me build a patio off the sunroom in the spring, but I thought his motive might be more to see a certain tree nymph than it was to work on a new project.

Finn came to visit a few times to help Grimgor build the display case holding Granny's faux-pirate logbook. Together, they'd placed in a prominent spot right behind the counter and encased it with enchanted gnomish glass. Finn was also trying to learn the runes necessary to allow Gideon to stay awake during the day, which I thought was awfully kind of him. The project required him to come over frequently in the evenings to study the stone and chat with the gargoyle. Not that I minded in the least. Now that he wasn't a suspect, a seed of hope had sprouted in my heart. Maybe I could get to know my handsome neighbor better without the pressure of the mystery and the inheritance. And then, who knows what might happen?

Another knock sounded at the door, and a group of smiling faces peered in. It was at that moment that I realized the truth behind the prediction Madame Fontaine had uttered weeks ago. By holding true to my friends, my chosen family, I'd earned the chance to live my dreams. Okay, I'd had more than a little help, especially from Spellbooks, but who could've expected aid to come from an actual bookshop? Not me, that's for sure.

I smiled and waved back at the group outside the window as I hurried to open the door. Honey blew me a kiss as she carried a massive box towards the counter that would one day hold my coffee machine. Antonio followed, balancing two more boxes and shouting good-naturedly over his shoulder at Finn, who carried two bottles of sparkling grape juice. Mrs. Jenkins followed, raising two more bottles towards me with a grin.

"If it's good enough to bless the maiden voyage of a ship, it must be good enough to bless a shop."

I grinned at her. "Are you sure you aren't part pirate, Mrs. Jenkins?"

Nathaniel frowned as he entered, carrying a package of paper cups. "I hope not. If she is, we might find ourselves at opposite ends of a court-room."

Grimgor, Thistle, Bella, Martha, and Officer Reggie filled out the party. I'd invited the sheriff, but he'd politely turned me down. When I spoke to Officer Johanna, she'd also declined, citing the vampiric allergy to the sun. Someday, I'd have to ask Nathaniel why he seemed to tolerate it when others couldn't. Maybe it was a vegetarian vampire perk, or maybe it was something else entirely. Either way, it was a conversation for another day.

An unexpected knock sounded at the door. I turned to see some members of the book club. Madame Fontaine, Stella, and Jeremy all waved cheerfully as they entered. It didn't surprise me that neither the Puddletons nor Hank had shown up, even though I'd sent a collective invitation to all the members of the book club through Martha. Following close on their heels was an unexpected, but all together welcome face.

"Aunty Agatha!" I cried as she pulled me in for a tight hug.

"I love what you've done with the place. Beatrice would be so proud," Agatha whispered in my ear. Tears of happiness welled up in my eyes to hear those words from Granny's best friend. She gave me another little squeeze and then pushed me back to arm's length. "We'll have a proper chat soon, I promise, but for now, let's celebrate!" Cheers of approval met her words.

I circulated around the shop, chatting with my guests. That's how I found out, through Officer Reggie, that Hank's niece, Vivienne Silverthorne, stepped in on his behalf. Only the sheriff and the Silverthornes knew exactly what sort of deal they struck, but Vivienne took Hank away. Two days later, his shop was closed, and no one had heard from him since. I was curious what had happened to the mad mage, but that was a mystery for another day.

As for Thaddeus, he'd left town shortly after our encounter. I hoped the ironclad NDA would be enough to keep him from revealing the truth behind Spellbooks, but a sliver of uncertainty lingered. He didn't seem the type to easily let things go, and I couldn't help but wonder if we'd truly heard the last of him.

I shook my head, focusing on the friends in front of me rather than absent foes. Greetings were exchanged, and we indulged in the treats Honey provided. I looked around the shop, happy that there were finally people back in Spellbooks, even if it was just a soft opening. There were still things to be done. I wanted to attach a retractable sunshade for the sunny summer days and get Thistle to help me with the flower boxes out front in the spring. Not to mention working with Honey to develop a small menu for the coffee shop. Maybe I could even negotiate a deal with her for morning pastries. But all of that would come with time. For now, I wanted to focus on the moment. A roll of laughter rose from my friends. I glanced over as Bella called my name.

"Harper, come and join us! It's time for the toast," Antonio called, pressing a paper cup filled with sparkling juice into my hands.

Everyone turned their attention to me. I looked around the room at the smiling faces, savoring the moment. I cleared my throat. "This whole thing feels like a dream to me. The first time I visited Granny Bea, I thought this place was magical. I just didn't know how right I was." Chuckles rolled around my friends, and I felt a subtle shift in the floorboards as they shuddered with Spellbooks' silent mirth. "I couldn't imagine then what sort of twists and turns my life would take to lead me to be here with each of you, but I feel like I'm living my own personal fairy tale. Getting to run a bookshop in a magical town and putting down roots with so many wonderful people living close by. I am the luckiest girl alive." Tears threatened to blur my vision, and I knew I had to wrap this up or risk becoming a blubbering mess. I raised my cup, and everyone followed suit. "So, here's to good friends, to Granny Bea, and most of all, to Spellbooks!"

"To Spellbooks!" Everyone echoed enthusiastically.

I felt a faint tremor under my feet that I interpreted as a purr of pleasure. I wondered if this was how the shop would communicate with me from here on out. Well, that and the chalkboards. Maybe I should keep one in the apartment as well as in the office and the shop. A babble of excited chatter sprang up as my guests started to mingle. I felt a hand at the small of my back and turned to see Finn.

"To the future," Finn said softly, tapping his cup against mine. Butterflies sprang to life in my stomach at the warm smile on his face and the sparkle in his eyes.

"To the future," I returned, sipping from my drink to hide the blush creeping up my cheeks. Spellbooks seemed to rumble in a silent laugh, sending little vibrations of mirth and approval tickling under my feet.

I wondered what sort of secrets were yet to be uncovered in my magical bookshop, and I was already looking forward to seeing what the next chapter with my handsome new neighbor held, but all of that could wait for the time being. This was a moment for celebration, for new friends and for old as well as for new beginnings. I planned to take Granny Bea's advice and savor the start of my next grand adventure.

Thank you

Dear Wonderful Reader,

Thank you for making it this far. I hope you enjoyed the story. Now, I'd like to share another, albeit much shorter one with you, along with a piece of my heart.

Once upon a time, I was a kid with mountains of notebooks, each one bursting with stories and dreams. Writing was my sanctuary, my escape from the world. But as I grew older, reality knocked on my door and whispered, "Writing won't pay the bills." So, I did the "sensible" thing and focused on the real world. For a while, at least.

Then came 2020, a year that turned many of our lives upside down. As an athlete and musician, I suddenly found myself unable to do the things I loved most. In a desperate bid to fight against depression, I turned back to writing. It was like finding a long-lost friend. The stories poured out of me, and I started to feel alive again.

Not that it has been without struggle. Trying to fit writing in around work, kids, and life is like juggling flaming torches while riding a unicycle. But I've kept at it. Since then, I've written and published over 20 books, each one a labor of love and infused with a piece of my heart. I'm not an overnight sensation or a best-selling author, nor do I have a stack of rejection letters from traditional publishers. Instead, I've taken a different path, connecting with incredible readers like you who cherish a good story and a touch of magic.

This is where you come in. Your review is more than just words on a screen—it's a lifeline, a beacon that helps me reach new readers and continue this incredible journey. If you could take just a few minutes to share your thoughts, I would be deeply, deeply grateful. I read every single review, and they touch my heart in ways you can't imagine.

So, if my stories have made you smile, laugh, or brought a little magic into your life, please let me know. Your support and feedback mean everything to me, and they help keep the dream alive.

Thank you for being a part of my story, for believing in my characters, and for sharing this journey with me.

With all my gratitude and a heart full of hope,

L.L. Gray

Grab your FREE novella now!

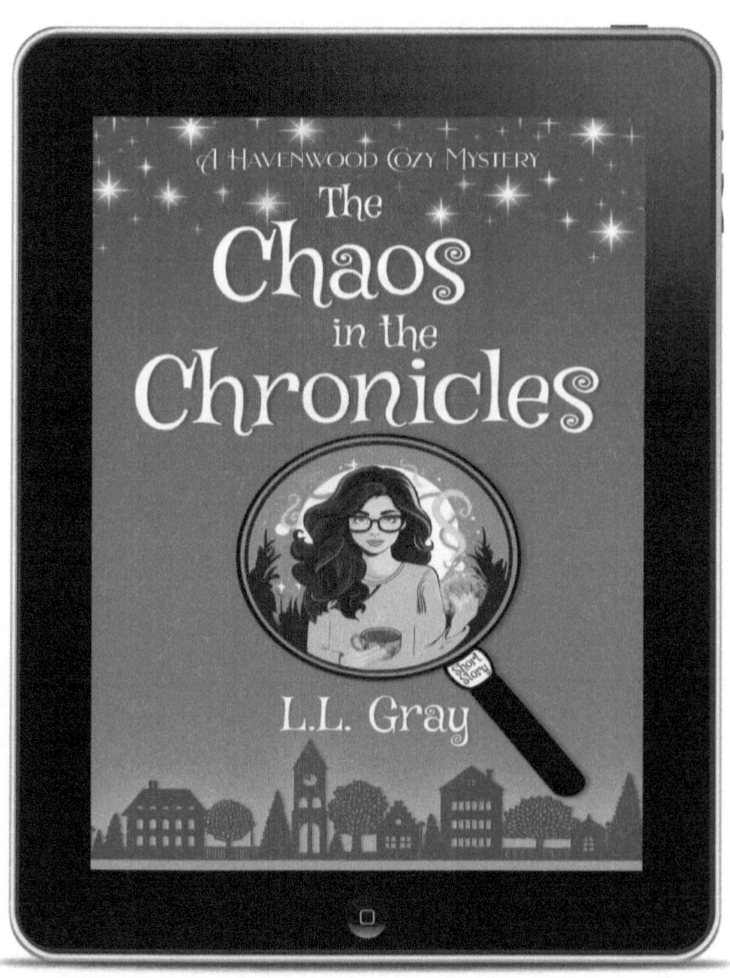

Want a free book?

Of course you do, what madness could possess someone to **not** want free books?
There's no catch - you do sign-up for my mailing list but you can unsubscribe at any time. □
There's also no spam. □
Ever.
Sign up here to get your free book!
https://www.subscribepage.io/havenwood

Also By

Havenwood Paranormal Cozy Mysteries

The Mystery in the Margins

The Chaos in the Chronicles (exclusive novella)

The Puzzle in the Pumpkin Patch

The Secret of the Silver Serpent

The Riddle at the Revelry
The Heist of the Hidden Heart
The Mayhem in the Masquerade
The Legend of the Leaf

Smoke and Shadows Series

Shadows and Relics

Pixie Pranks (exclusive novella)

Felons and Fangs

Bones and Blades

Tempest and Treason

Daggers and Deception

Sleuths and Scoundrels

Legacy and Lies

Crossroads and Curses

Children's Books

The Secret About Mistakes

Corner of the Sky

To Mom. Love, Me

To Dad. Love, Me

To Grandma. Love, Me

To Grandpa. Love, Me

About the Author

L.L. Gray writes funny, fast-paced fantasy with captivating characters. When she isn't writing, she embarks on magical adventures with her children by having make-believe battles with invading elves or righting ridiculous pranks by those mischievous gnomes who live next door.

As a long time lover of fantasy and myths, she hopes you enjoy her contributions to the world of magic.

**Psst, it's me. L.L. Gray. Nice to meet you! Connecting with fellow lovers of the written word and crazy adventure stories is important to me. If that sounds like your cup of tea (or coffee, or other beverage) please hop over to my website (www.llgray.com) and join my newsletter where you can grab a FREE, exclusive goodies or hang out with us on my Facebook readers group.

However, if email is more your speed, then please feel free to drop me a line at info@llgray.com should the mood strike.

I hope you stay in touch!

Acknowledgments

First, I need to thank my fabulous team. They have become like a second family to me. I couldn't do it without die-hard supporters like them.

I'd also like to thank you, the reader. I hope you enjoyed reading this story as much as I've enjoyed writing it. If you'd like to stay in touch or be kept up to date with upcoming releases, please head over to my website. If you'd like to hang out with some like-minded readers on Facebook , come and join our wonderful community.

And last, but definitely not least, I'd like to thank my wonderful husband. Without your support, none of this would have been possible.